New York Times and *USA* ███████████████
B.J. Daniels lives in Mo██████████ ███ ███ ███████,
Parker, and three springer spaniels. When not writing,
she quilts, boats and plays tennis. Contact her at
bjdaniels.com on Facebook or on X @bjdanielsauthor

Nicole Helm grew up with her nose in a book and the
dream of one day becoming a writer. Luckily, after a
few failed career choices, she gets to follow that
dream—writing down-to-earth contemporary romance
and romantic suspense. From farmers to cowboys,
Midwest to *the* West, Nicole writes stories about people
finding themselves and finding love in the process. She
lives in Missouri with her husband and two sons, and
dreams of someday owning a barn.

Discover more at millsandboon.co.uk

MISSING: BABY DOE

B.J. DANIELS

COLD CASE MURDER MYSTERY

NICOLE HELM

MILLS & BOON

First Published in Great Britain 2025
by Mills & Boon, an imprint of HarperCollins*Publishers* Ltd
1 London Bridge Street, London, SE1 9GF

www.harpercollins.co.uk

HarperCollins*Publishers*
Macken House, 39/40 Mayor Street Upper,
Dublin 1, D01 C9W8, Ireland

Missing: Baby Doe © 2025 Barbara Heinlein
Cold Case Murder Mystery © 2025 Nicole Helm

ISBN: 978-0-263-39698-0

0225

This book contains FSC™ certified paper and other controlled sources to ensure responsible forest management.

For more information visit: www.harpercollins.co.uk/green

Printed and Bound in the UK using 100% Renewable Electricity at CPI Group (UK) Ltd, Croydon, CR0 4YY

MISSING: BABY DOE

B.J. DANIELS

This book is dedicated to my granddaughter Alayna, who always has a notebook and pen with her. May she write her own books one day.

Chapter One

The front door of the Fortune Creek, Montana, Sheriff's Department swung open with a swoosh. A gust of cold mountain air blew in along with a frantic and very pregnant brunette.

Acting Sheriff Catherine "Cat" Jameson looked up in surprise. Since she'd taken over the job here while the sheriff was on his honeymoon, she'd come to believe that nothing happened in this tiny town in the northwest corner of the state. Certainly nothing that required a sheriff—or even an acting one.

"You have to help me!" the woman cried.

Cat's first thought was that the woman was in labor and about to have her baby right here in this office. Her own hand went to her much smaller baby bump. By the time she gave birth a couple of months from now, her job here as acting sheriff would be over. That was as far into the future as she let herself plan.

As the pregnant woman rushed toward the acting sheriff's minuscule office, Cat wished she'd done more reading on the delivery part of pregnancy. Dispatcher Helen Graves, a gray-haired sixty-something tank of a woman, could and would stop a freight train from getting past her and into Sheriff Brandt Parker's office. But as the brunette lumbered past, Helen simply shrugged.

So that's how it's going to be, Cat thought, getting to her feet. Apparently, the dispatcher-receptionist was only protective of *Sheriff* Parker, who had recently *extended* his honeymoon.

"Please," the brunette cried, cupping her protruding baby bump protectively.

Cat's mind whirled. The nearest hospital was miles away. Calling an ambulance would only waste time. Helen, she doubted, would be of any help. Cat would have to take the woman to Eureka in her patrol SUV and hope they got there in time.

It was the next words out of the pregnant woman's mouth that sidelined those thoughts. "He's going to kill me and my baby."

"Wait." Cat thought she'd heard wrong. "You aren't in labor?" Head shake. "You believe someone is trying to kill you and your baby?" Hurried nod. Delivering a baby was out of Cat's wheelhouse, but attempted murder? She told herself that the woman had come to the right place. This is what she'd been trained for. Also, she definitely needed a case she could sink her teeth into before she died of boredom at this isolated outpost only a stone's throw from the Canadian border.

Then again, wasn't that why she'd gotten the job? Because she was pregnant, no one would hire her except for a desk position. Fortune Creek was the definition of a sleepy wilderness.

"No one is going to kill you or the baby in here," Cat assured her. "Please have a seat," she said as she reached for her box of tissues.

As the brunette awkwardly lowered herself into a chair,

Cat slid the box across the desk to her. "Why don't we start with your name?"

"Lindsey," the woman said and blew her nose into a tissue. "Lindsey Martin."

As she watched Lindsey pull herself together, Cat took the measure of the woman. Late twenties, early thirties, about her own age. Manicured and polished from her nails to her hair. No apparent shortage of funds, given the SUV parked out front and her clothing and footwear—not to mention her watch and other jewelry.

Lindsey Martin still looked terrified, glancing over her shoulder toward the empty street every few moments, but she'd quit crying.

"Lindsey, can you tell me why you think you and your baby are at risk?"

"It's the father of my baby." A domestic situation. So far Cat had only had to break up a bar fight while in charge in Fortune Creek. "He's denying that it's even his baby."

"I see. How long have the two of you been together?"

The woman looked confused. "We aren't together."

"Okay, maybe you need to start at the beginning."

Lindsey took a few breaths. She was pretty, her long hair tucked up in a twist on the left side of her head with an obvious expertise that Cat had never mastered. The woman's eyes were a rich chocolate brown, her olive skin well-tended. She either didn't wear makeup or her tears had washed it away. "I met him nine months ago in Washington, DC."

"Love at first sight?"

"*Hardly.* It was supposed to be a one-night stand. We'd both been drinking. He said he had protection. I think he put something in my drink because I don't remember anything after that until I woke up…pregnant." She glanced down at her extended belly.

This was definitely not the romantic story gone wrong that Cat had been expecting. "Are you saying you were assaulted?"

She hesitated. "It was consensual—but…" She glanced down at her extended abdomen. "This wasn't part of the deal."

Cat sat back. "I'm confused. If you thought you'd been drugged, did you go to the police and report it?" She already knew the answer even before the woman shook her head. Otherwise, Lindsey Martin wouldn't be here now. "What brought you to Fortune Creek?"

"My baby's father bought a ranch and moved out here. When I couldn't reach him by phone, I drove out here to confront him."

"From Washington, DC?" Cat asked in surprise.

"No, I've been living in Denver. He wouldn't even talk to me, let alone allow me on his property."

"You said he threatened to harm you and the baby?"

"I left him a note in his mailbox with my phone number and where I was staying in Eureka. This morning, I got this." She reached into her shoulder bag, dug around and came up with a sheet of folded paper. Slapping it down on Cat's desk, she said, "It was pushed under my motel room door at the address I'd left him."

Cat drew out latex gloves before picking up the sheet of paper and unfolding it. *Stop causing trouble or I'll get rid of both you and your baby permanently.* It wasn't signed. She looked from the words to Lindsey and back. "You're sure this is from the father of the baby?"

"Who else?"

Exactly. "And you say this is the first time you've contacted him?" A nod. "Is there anyone else who might wish you harm?"

"In Montana?" She let out a laugh that was close to a sob. "Even if there was, he's the only person who even knows I'm in Montana."

"Okay. Do you mind if I keep this?" Lindsey shook her head. Cat bagged the note and asked, "You're sure you've never tried contacting him before this? Because the note makes it sound like you have." Adamant head shake. "Okay, then I have to ask. Why now? You're about to have this baby. What is it you want from him?"

The question seemed to surprise her. "I never asked for any of this. I thought I could do it, have this baby." She shook her head. "He did this to me. He owes me. At the very least he shouldn't threaten me. He needs to admit what he did and take responsibility for it." Tears filled her eyes. "I don't think I can do this alone."

"Do you know the sex of the baby?" Cat asked, thinking of the baby girl she would be giving birth to soon and raising alone.

Another head shake. "I don't want to know."

"Are you thinking about giving the baby up?" More tears and no answer.

Cat could see how conflicted the woman was—and with good reason if what she'd told her was true. The father of the baby had threatened her. If he was the man who'd drugged her and impregnated her, then he could be dangerous and there might be real malice behind the threat.

She pulled out her notebook and picked up her pen. "What's the man's name?"

Chapter Two

When Cat had been offered the job, she hadn't quibbled or even asked a lot of questions. That her first law enforcement job was in the middle of nowhere was perfect. It was wild country, only a few camps along the only highway that followed the Yaak River. Otherwise, it was just mountains and pines, lots of pines.

She hadn't cared that the closest real town was Eureka, miles away, across the narrow Lake Koocanusa that crossed the border into Canada. She was exactly where she'd wanted to be.

She wondered if Dylan Walker felt the same way as she headed south of town toward the ranch Dylan had purchased almost a year ago, but apparently had only moved full time to the ranch three months ago. He'd paid a small fortune for the large, remote, exclusive ranch a dozen miles from Fortune Creek.

From what Cat had learned about the man, he was a thirty-seven-year-old retired construction consultant who had worked abroad much of his career. His former address was in the DC area. He had no social media presence, had apparently never been arrested, and other than a short marriage, had left little to no paper trail. She could find no photograph of the man other than the poor quality mugshot on his Montana driver's license.

What was interesting was that nine months ago he'd lost his wife in a car bombing in DC following a charity event that they had attended. The same event where Lindsey Martin swore he'd impregnated her. Nine months. There seemed to be a pattern here, Cat told herself.

After getting the pertinent information about the night in question from Ms. Martin, Cat suggested the woman get a room at the Fortune Creek Hotel across the street from the sheriff's office. "You'll be safe there. I'll let you know what I find out," she promised.

Now, as Cat drove the narrow, winding, seldom-used road south through thick pines toward the posted and gated entrance into the isolated ranch, she wondered about the man she'd come to see.

If what Lindsey had told her was true, Dylan Walker probably wasn't going to talk to her either—not without a warrant. This trip was a fact-finding mission. She had to make at least an attempt to talk to the man before she could go to a judge. But with only a threatening note, she doubted she could get a warrant.

As Cat drove up to the unmanned gate, a camera lens followed her every movement as she approached what appeared to be an intercom system. She pulled out her badge and held it out the patrol SUV window, not sure if the camera would pick it up before pressing the intercom button. "Acting Sheriff Cat… Catherine Jameson to see Dylan Walker."

For a moment, she thought she wouldn't get an answer. Then a deep male voice demanded, "What's this about?"

"I need to speak to Dylan Walker about a law enforcement matter," she said.

"You have a warrant?"

"I just need to ask a few questions, but if you insist, I'll get a warrant." She waited, expecting she was going to get the same reception Lindsey Martin had, when she heard the gate clank and begin to slide open.

Relieved and yet wary, she drove in before the gate swung closed behind her. Why all the security? It seemed overkill. Maybe the man had more to hide than even Lindsey Martin knew. Then she reminded herself that his wife had died in a car bombing. Maybe he had reason to fear for his own life.

Before driving out here, she'd read as much as she could find on the car bombing in DC. Lindsey Martin claimed she'd been at the same fundraiser gala as Dylan Walker— the same night as the car bombing. While Cat doubted one had anything to do with the other…it was an interesting coincidence.

Also, it brought up all kinds of questions. If Dylan and his wife, Ginny Cooper Walker, had been together at the event, how did he find time to slip away with Lindsey Martin? Also, how was it that his wife had died and not him? Had they taken separate cars? Or was he busy possibly drugging and then taking advantage of Ms. Martin? Had the bomb been intended for both husband and wife? If so, why would anyone want to kill them? And where did Lindsey Martin fit in all this—if she did.

Cat drove along a narrow road through the thick pines until the trees finally opened up and she caught glimpses of the ranch house. The first word that came to mind was opulent and massive. Stone, giant timbers and walls of glass rose to three stories and stretched across the landscape directly ahead.

Off to one side was a five-car garage constructed of the

same materials. She noted a small cottage some distance away. The sprawling three-story mansion made it look like a dollhouse. There was no sign of anyone around except for a large black SUV parked in front of the smaller dwelling.

As Cat drove closer, a man came out of the cottage and stood, hands on his hips, watching her from the front deck. He wore a flannel shirt, jeans and boots, no hat. Her first thought was that he must be the caretaker. He was tall, broad-shouldered, imposing, his stance impatient as he raked a hand through hair that gleamed in the sunlight and curled at his collar.

She felt suddenly uneasy, her reaction to the man a surprise. There was no way this was the man of the manor, was there? *Dylan Walker?*

DYLAN MOVED SWIFTLY to the patrol SUV, planning to make this as painless and quick as possible. He regretted letting in the local law. But he had to know what this was about and nip it in the bud. He'd moved here to disappear. He didn't want attention called to him—especially by some *acting* sheriff. Better to get this out of the way and be done with it. Whatever this was.

Before he could reach the patrol SUV, a small, slim woman climbed out. It wasn't until she turned that he realized she was pregnant. She wore jeans, a tan short-sleeved shirt with a silver star on it and a Stetson over fire-engine red long curly hair that seemed to be fighting to free itself from the elastic around her low ponytail.

He hadn't gotten a good look at her on the gate surveillance camera, so it wasn't until she turned to him that he saw her face beneath the shaded brim of her hat. He'd never seen so many freckles. Nor had she made any attempt to cover them with makeup.

Struck by how young she looked, fresh-faced with a no-nonsense nose and a generous mouth, he found himself fighting a smile. He couldn't imagine anyone wearing a silver star looking more harmless—until he met her eyes. They were an intense blue like the sky overhead. But it was the way those eyes bore into him that sent his pulse racing. There was intelligence there, a sharp mind, and a whole lot of determination mixed with suspicion. Whatever this woman was doing here, she meant business.

"Acting Sheriff Cat... Catherine Jameson," she said again, holding out her hand to shake his. He was looking at her left hand and the plain gold band on it.

Her grip was firm. As they shook hands, she studied him as if looking for something. It felt like she could see into his soul, and he didn't like that feeling. "I need to ask you a few questions. Maybe we should step inside your house." She glanced toward the larger of the structures.

"That's not my house."

She raised a fine pale brow, those deep blue eyes narrowing a little.

"It's my house, but it isn't where I live." He definitely didn't like the way she was looking at him. "What's this about?"

CAT COULD SEE that she wasn't going to be invited inside even the small cottage. Okay, if he wanted to do this out here, she was fine with it. She'd get right to it. "I'm here about a woman named Lindsey Martin."

He frowned, furrowing his brows, making his light blue eyes narrow under brows as dark as his espresso brown hair. "I don't know anyone by that name."

She noticed that he definitely needed a haircut and had for a while now. A lock had fallen over his forehead. He brushed it back with obvious irritation as if he normally wore it much shorter. He also needed a shave, his strong jaw bristled and dark.

"Ms. Martin claims that the two of you met in Washington, DC, about nine months ago."

The nine months seemed to make his eyes darken even further. "If we met, I have no memory of it."

"She claims you had a one-night stand at a gala after drugging her and not using protection, which left her pregnant." He started to interrupt, but she continued. "After she recently contacted you, she also has what appears to be evidence that you threatened her and the baby."

Dylan Walker's face clouded over. She could see him fighting to rein in his anger. He lifted a large, suntanned hand, took a couple of deep breaths and said calmly, "I can assure you that I didn't impregnate anyone—let alone drug and assault a woman I've never heard of. She is mistaken."

"She claims she came out here to the ranch yesterday morning, but that you wouldn't let her in, denied everything, and after that she received a death threat for both her and her baby if she kept causing you trouble. Are you telling me that a woman didn't contact you at your gate yesterday?" she asked. "And you refused to let her in?"

He frowned. "When was this?"

"About 8:00 a.m."

"I take a long ride every morning—just as I did yesterday. There is no way she talked to me."

"Who would she have spoken with then, if not you?"

Letting out a sigh, he said, "I had a guest here. She must have spoken with the woman, though she didn't mention it to me."

"That's odd since Ms. Martin indicated it was a man's

voice on the intercom, a man she assumed was you," Cat said.

He shook his head. "I don't know what I can tell you. Like I said, I wasn't here and the only other person on the ranch was Rowena."

"Rowena? I'm going to need her full name and a number where I can reach her." She pulled out her notebook and pen and waited.

"Rowena Keeling." He spelled both names and she wrote them down. "I don't know her cell number. I'll have her call you."

Cat raised a brow. "She's still staying with you?"

He didn't look sure. "I believe she went into Eureka. I'll ask her for her number when she gets back." Apparently, he and his guest weren't very close if he really didn't have her number.

"Ms. Martin left her information about where she was staying in Eureka on a note in your mailbox. Do you still have it?"

He raked a hand through his hair irritably. "I never had it. Maybe Rowena does. I can ask."

Cat studied him, wondering why his guest would take something from his mailbox. Also wondering if he really was the wrong man. He was smooth, controlled and came off as if blindsided by the accusation. She tried to decide if she believed him or the terrified pregnant woman who'd come to her for help.

What would motivate Lindsey Martin to lie? The obvious reason was money. Walker appeared to have a lot of it. Was it possible Lindsey had cooked this up to try to cash in?

But there was one surefire way to prove that Dylan Walker was the father of her baby—a DNA test.

"You do understand that once the baby is born and a DNA sample is taken, the truth will come out," Cat said.

"I certainly hope so because whoever this woman is, she isn't having my baby."

"You're certain?"

"Positive."

Cat wasn't sure what to think. Dylan Walker sounded convinced that a DNA test would prove he wasn't the father of Lindsey Martin's baby. But the fact that they were both in the same place at the same time at a fundraiser gala for an art center nearly nine months ago made even the rookie cop in her suspicious. One of them was lying.

She thought about Lindsey's answers to her questions. Why hadn't she called the police if she really thought she'd been drugged? Because she couldn't be sure. She'd had a lot to drink and the sex had been consensual, she'd said.

All of that could be true. How the pieces fit together— if they did—was beyond Cat at this point. Was it possible Lindsey was mistaken about the man who she claimed had impregnated her?

"Ms. Martin claims she met you the night of an art gala," Cat said.

He shook his head. "Like I said, I don't know anyone by that name. I met a lot of people at the galas. I didn't sleep with any of them."

"The accusations against you are serious, if true."

"I'm aware of that." Dropping his gaze, he shoved aside that errant lock of dark hair. As he did, his fingers absently traced the half-moon scar at his temple as if it was something he often did. Had he been injured that night in the bombing? A muscle tensed in his jaw as he ground out, "I was at an art gala at the same time as your victim, but she's mistaken about me being with her. I was with my wife."

But not all night, Cat thought but hesitated to bring up the bombing or his deceased wife. Clearly, they hadn't been together at the time of the bombing. "You'd be willing to take a DNA test if it comes to that?"

His look confirmed that he was losing his patience. "If it comes to that. But it's a waste of your time, I can assure you. I wasn't the man."

Cat heard pain in his words. She could tell he was regretting opening his gate and letting her in. So why had he talked to her without his lawyer present? Because he really had nothing to hide? Maybe he thought he could convince her of his innocence.

The thing was he kind of had, she realized. She believed him. Or maybe just wanted to believe him. Dylan Walker appeared to be a grieving man in a great deal of emotional pain. He'd bought this ranch before the bombing. Had he planned to live here with his wife at some point? Cat got the impression that he wanted to be alone, and from what she could tell, he was. Except for a woman named Rowena Keeling.

"I'd like to speak to Ms. Keeling." She glanced at the large house where he said he didn't live. Is that where she was staying or in this cottage with him? "When do you expect her back?"

He shook his head. "I have no idea. I'll tell her to call you if I see her. I'm sorry. I don't have her cell phone number. She was a friend of my wife's."

"If you see her, you might want to also ask her for the note Ms. Martin left in your mailbox." When he didn't respond, she added truthfully, "I hope I won't have to come back," as she put away her notebook and pen.

"So do I, Acting Sheriff *Cat* Jameson." His gaze met hers and she felt a shiver run the length of her spine at both his look and the intimacy of calling her by her nickname after her slip-up. Dylan Walker was a very attractive man—in a dark kind of way, but when his gray-eyed gaze softened and he looked at her like that… She had a feeling that he was used to getting what he wanted, she thought with another chill. Right now, he just wanted her gone.

Climbing back into her patrol SUV, she drove around the loop past the big house. It appeared to be empty. No car out front. No sign of anyone else on the property, but with a ranch this size, it would be impossible to know for sure.

She glanced back. Dylan Walker no longer stood outside. If her visit had upset him, he hadn't shown it. Because he wasn't afraid of some acting sheriff out of Fortune Creek, Montana?

She headed for the road out, the gate opening as she approached. She glanced toward the security camera that followed her departure, wondering if he was watching or if he'd already put all of this out of his mind. She made a mental note to see about getting footage from the surveillance camera that would prove Lindsey Martin had come out here and tried to see him. It could also prove that he was lying about not having spoken with her.

But for now, there was nothing more that she could do until she had enough proof to get a warrant. Cat was more anxious than ever to talk to Lindsey Martin again.

Chapter Three

Dylan stepped into the cottage, closing the door behind him as he swore. What had Rowena been thinking answering his intercom, let alone turning someone away and not even mentioning it to him? Add to that she'd apparently taken a note from his mailbox?

It made him even more suspicious as to why she was here. He couldn't shake the feeling she was waiting for something. Or was it *someone*? He hated being this distrustful, but then again, his deceased wife's former friend had always made him feel like that. Too bad he hadn't been more distrustful of his wife. Maybe then he wouldn't have looked like such a fool when the truth came out.

He went into his small study, swung a shelf of books aside to reveal the safe and opened it. Inside, he took out the phone, unable to shake the foreboding feeling he'd had the moment the acting sheriff had shown up. He saw that he had a message.

Instantly, he knew there was trouble. Only two people had this number and one of them was dead.

Hurriedly, he listened to the message. *Disturbing news. Allen Zimmerman. Cops have ruled it an apparent suicide. Watch your back.*

His pulse jumped, heart dropping. Dylan swore and hurriedly put the phone back before quickly closing the safe and replacing the shelf of books. There was no way Allen had killed himself. No possible way. This had to be because of the rumored leak he'd been warned about.

Feeling shaken, he walked back out to the living room to find Rowena pouring herself a drink. He glanced back at his open study door. Had she heard the voicemail? He felt anger race through his veins like hot lava.

"I didn't hear you buzz to get in the gate," he said, drawing on training he'd been trying hard to forget. "Nor did I hear you drive up." Never show anger or any other emotion when confronting a suspected enemy. Never show your hand—until you're ready.

She turned toward him and smiled. "I didn't buzz in. I got your passcode from your groundskeeper. I didn't want to bother you."

"You've certainly made yourself at home," he commented, keeping both his concern and his irritation at bay—at least for the moment. "I need your cell phone number."

She beamed at that as if she thought he might call her for a date and told him her number, which he wrote down. "Make you a drink?" she asked still smiling as she finished making one for yourself.

"Thanks, but I'm fine."

"Suit yourself," she said as she sighed and made her way to one of his deep leather chairs. She dropped into it and kicked off her heels.

Dylan Walker hadn't wanted company. He'd certainly not invited anyone to his ranch—especially the woman who'd shown up.

"I have to ask, what are you still doing here, Rowena?"

He'd been caught off guard when she'd showed up at his gate and he'd foolishly let her in.

"How can you even ask that?" she said with a laugh as she flipped her blond bob. "I'm worried about you. Ginny would have wanted me to make sure you were all right."

Ginny. He hated to even hear his deceased wife's name on this woman's lips—even if Rowena still called herself Ginny's best friend. He couldn't imagine what Ginny had seen in her, but as it turned out he didn't know either woman—his bride or her alleged best friend—very well.

During his short marriage, Ginny had a lot of friends from different walks of life. She'd never had trouble keeping them at arm's length if she didn't care for them. That's why Rowena had been such a surprise, especially when she kept turning up at their house, at parties at other friends, at fundraisers. He'd wondered what Ginny saw in Rowena, who wore her wealth like a lot of people Ginny had known—and disliked.

"I'm fine, so you need not have worried—let alone come all this way," Dylan assured her.

Rowena raised a finely shaped brow, her lips tilting up in a smile that didn't seem to reach her green eyes. "I thought you'd be glad to see me." She glanced around. "I would think you'd get lonely out here all by yourself." She took a sip of her drink, looking relaxed, too relaxed.

She was beautiful, rich and privileged. Like him, she'd apparently grown up in the rarified air of a Manhattan high-rise penthouse, summered abroad or jetted with friends to exclusive locations. Surprisingly, his path had never intersected with Rowena until Rowena and Ginny had become friends.

He studied her for a moment, remembering the day she'd been the one at the gate wanting to be let in. That had been four days ago. He'd been more than surprised to see her. She'd said she was passing through Montana. People didn't pass through Montana, not unless they were coming from Chicago or Seattle or on a backroad to Canada.

Dylan had called her on it, and she'd admitted that she'd come to see his ranch. Another lame excuse. "You know how close Ginny and I were. She would have wanted me to check up on you."

He wasn't sure about either of those answers. Rowena was the only one who said she and Ginny were best friends. He'd often thought the friendship was one-sided, so why had Ginny let Rowena cling to her like she had?

Shaking his head, he realized he'd let her do the same thing. When he'd let her in the gate, he'd thought she'd be gone by morning. Just passing through, like she said. So why was she still here, and why was he letting her stay?

"What are you *really* doing here?" he asked as he sat down on the edge of the chair across from her and leaned forward to rest his elbows on his knees.

"I beg your pardon?"

"It's a valid question."

Rowena gave him an irritated look. "I told you. I wanted to see your ranch I heard you'd bought." She sighed. "I also wanted to see how you were doing. It hasn't even been a year since Ginny died."

"Do you really think you need to remind me how long ago it was that my wife was murdered?" he demanded as he pushed to his feet. "And no, I don't want to talk about it."

"Maybe you should," she said. "Have you talked to any-one about it?" He mugged a face in answer. "Don't you think you need to deal with all of it?"

"I just told you I don't want to talk about it. Let's talk

about your life. What happened to your last relationship, which number was he?"

She rose as well. "You're just being spiteful now."

Dylan didn't want to take out his frustration on this woman. But what was she doing here? Surely she didn't have romantic designs on him. She wasn't that clueless.

"The sheriff was here wanting to talk to you," he said, watching her. "I just texted her office your number."

"I saw her. Wasn't she just cute as a button?" The use of the phrase made her sarcasm irritate him even more. "And pregnant!" She laughed.

"How do you know she was pregnant unless..." He stared at her. "You were parked close by watching her?" *Watching me*, he thought.

"I waited until she left," she said. "Why would she want to talk to me?"

"She wanted to know about a visitor I apparently had at my gate while I was out horseback riding yesterday morning," he said.

"A visitor?" She took a sip of her drink.

He glared at her. "Apparently you failed to mention it."

"Oh, that deluded woman? I wasn't about to let her in. I really couldn't understand anything she was saying."

"Probably made it easier to find out what was going on when you read the note you saw her leave in my mailbox."

Rowena froze for a moment, then sighed. "It was all nonsense, I couldn't make heads nor tails out of—"

"I want to see the note."

She blinked then finished her drink. She stood and walked to the bar to make herself another one. "I threw it away."

"Did she mention on the note that she was pregnant?"

"Do you think that was her problem?" Rowena asked,

turning to look at him wide-eyed. "Must be something that's catching up here in these parts."

"I'm serious."

She waved a hand through the air as if swatting away a pesky fly. "What does it matter?"

"Maybe it's nothing," he admitted. "The sheriff just had a few questions. But you've only made things more difficult for me."

"If it makes you happy, I'll talk to the sheriff when she calls." She looked at him, brow raised, as she walked to her chair with her fresh drink. "Is this all that has you so upset? I thought it was because you'd heard the news out of DC."

He looked at her in surprise, almost expecting her to tell him about Allen Zimmerman, his old boss, except she shouldn't know anything or anyone from that world. She'd been the rich divorcee who moved in next door and became friends with his wife. The party girl who he'd often found finishing off a second or third bottle of wine in the afternoon with Ginny while he'd been at work.

"I was afraid it would upset you when you heard that they were reopening the car bombing investigation that killed our Ginny," she said, making a sad face.

Our Ginny? At least she was smart enough not to mention his brother, Beau, who just happened to be in the car with her when it exploded. "Where did you hear they were reopening the case?"

"A friend who works in the prosecutor's office. Maybe they'll finally find the person who did it and you'll get closure. That is why you moved way out here, wasn't it? To forget?"

"Did your friend say why they were reopening the case?" he asked.

"No, they're being really hush-hush about it," she said and shrugged. "I do wonder why."

So did he. He realized he did want that drink. At the bar, he found he was anything but calm now. "Does the name Lindsey Martin mean anything to you?" he asked as he poured some bourbon into a glass.

"No, should it? Who is she?"

"The woman who'd tried to get in yesterday, the one you turned away, the one whose note you destroyed," he said and took a gulp of his drink. "But you wouldn't know anything about that, right?"

"Really, Dylan," she said as she rose to join him at the bar. She stood so close that he could feel the heat coming off her well-toned body. She dropped her voice and asked seductively, "Whatever are you accusing me of?"

He'd felt uneasy before Rowena had shown up at his door and then the acting sheriff. He couldn't believe Zimmerman was dead and now this news about the bombing case being reopened? Trouble often seemed to hitch a ride on an ill wind, as his brother Beau used to say. Rowena, he suspected, like his dead brother, was that ill wind.

He'd thought he'd left that life behind him when he'd moved to Montana. Clearly, he'd been wrong. His past was coming for him and anyone who got in the way—like the acting sheriff, he thought with a curse—could be in the line of fire.

"Are you in some kind of trouble, Dylan?"

Turning toward Rowena, he smiled and dropped his voice just as she had done. "Seriously, I think you've accomplished whatever it is you've come here for."

"You're wrong about that," she said, almost sounding sad. "Would you mind terribly if I stayed just a few more days? I've come all this way. There are some things I want to see while I'm out here. I promise to stay out of your way, if you don't mind me remaining in the main house that long."

He wasn't sure why he did it. Because it wasn't that much to ask? Or because it would give him time to try to find out what Rowena was really doing out here. "A few days, but no more. I'm sorry, but I need this time alone. That's why I bought this place."

"I understand," she said. "I know how much you loved Ginny and she loved you." He nodded, even though it was hard to do so. Not everyone knew about Ginny's betrayal—or his brother's. "I'll be gone by the weekend," she promised and moved to kiss his cheek. "Thank you," she whispered next to his ear.

With that, she left, leaving behind the scent of her perfume. He watched her walk over to the main house and disappear inside as he locked the cottage door behind her and went into the study. He reminded himself to change the passcode on the gate as soon as she was gone.

But right now, he desperately needed to find out what was going on. Why would there be something new in the almost year-old bombing case now?

BACK IN FORTUNE CREEK, Cat went straight to the hotel across the street from the sheriff's department. The entire town was only a few blocks long, with an old hotel, a general store with a gas station, a bar and a sheriff's office. The main drag dead-ended at the creek. She'd been shocked that there was even a sheriff's department here at all. But it was the only law in this part of northwestern Montana, only miles from the Canadian border.

The hotel was a four-story narrow building that was being restored after years of remaining empty. Former high school and NFL football star Ash Hammond had returned to town to buy the hotel after a career-changing injury. He was behind the counter when she walked in. Young and good-looking with dark-hair and a ready smile, Ash greeted her cheerfully.

He'd been one of the few people who had welcomed her with open arms. Most of the locals preferred Sheriff Brandt Parker and made no bones about it, even when she pointed out that she was only acting sheriff until he returned.

"Beautiful day, isn't it?" Ash said smiling. "I was just about to head up the street to get some lunch." His options were limited for lunch—the café or the convenience mart. "Want to join me?"

"Thanks, but I need to speak with one of your guests, Lindsey Martin. What room did you put her in?" she asked as she started for the stairs. The old elevator had been refurbished, but she needed to get her steps in.

"In 307, except she isn't there," Ash said. "Checked her in, took her bags up and the next thing I knew the elevator opened and there she was with her bags saying she couldn't stay."

"She checked out?" Cat couldn't keep the incredulity out of her tone. She'd told the woman that she'd be safe here in Fortune Creek—especially staying right across the street from the sheriff's department. "Did she say why she was leaving?" Ash shook his head. "Did she at least say where she was going?" Another shake of his head. "Surely she left me a message." He'd already started to shake his head before she said, "Any chance she went across the street to my office?"

"Sorry. I carried her bags out to her vehicle, she got behind the wheel and left."

Was it possible she'd gotten another threat? Cat wondered. One that had scared her away? "What was her general demeanor?"

Ash shrugged. "Maybe a little anxious to be on her way, but she wasn't acting scared, if that's what you're thinking. She just seemed to have changed her mind."

About the hotel room or about her allegations against Dylan Walker? Cat wondered as she headed back across the street to her office. As she did, she saw a vehicle drive in and park in front of the hotel. She stopped to watch two men dressed in business attire climb out of an SUV.

She watched the larger of the two look around, his gaze lighting on her and the small sheriff's department building before he turned and the two disappeared inside the hotel. The men couldn't have looked more out of place, which made her wonder what had brought them to Fortune Creek.

Definitely not tourists, not this time of the year, she thought, as she made her way to her office and put the two men out of her mind—at least temporarily as she hoped Lindsey Martin and her baby were okay. As pregnant as Lindsey had been, maybe she'd decided she needed to be closer to a hospital.

The entire Fortune Creek, Montana, sheriff's office was matchbox size, with only Cat and Helen holding down the fort, so to speak. As uneventful as things had been in town since she'd taken over, Cat wondered how Helen spent her days—let alone how the sheriff did. Given the amount of knitted throws the elderly woman had produced in the short time Cat had been there, she had a pretty good idea at least how Helen filled her time in the office.

As Cat walked in, still worried and confused about Lindsey Martin's quick exit, she found Helen knitting—of course. The older woman barely looked up as the acting sheriff approached her desk. "By any chance did the pregnant woman from earlier call and leave me a message?"

Helen didn't look up from her knitting. "Called. In your office on your desk."

"Thank you." Trying not to sigh, she went to her desk. The message was written in Helen's neat cursive. *Lindsey Martin: I changed my mind.* The time and date were written after it. Lindsey had called the office with the message shortly after Cat had left town to talk to Dylan Walker.

Sticking her head out her door, she asked, "Did you get a phone number from her?"

"Called from the hotel right after you left."

Back in her office, she glared at Helen through the office window, saying to herself, "Would have been nice to know on my way out to see Dylan Walker." Helen didn't look up, which was probably just as well. Cat wondered how she could ever get the woman to quit treating her like an outsider. For that matter, it was the same with a lot of the residents of the town. It wasn't just that they liked Brandt Parker better, even though they did. They seemed to question how a woman had gotten the acting sheriff job—especially a pregnant one who, while wearing a wedding ring, clearly didn't have a husband living with her.

Cat figured it was none of their business and definitely *not* something she wanted to talk about. She reminded herself that she only had a few months here. She was determined to make the best of it, as boring and uneventful as the job had turned out to be.

Sitting down at her desk, she did question what she was doing here especially when she didn't seem to be wanted. It wasn't as if she was interested in a popularity contest with the handsome cowboy sheriff Brandt Parker, because she would lose hands down. He was loved and admired and apparently so handsome that some New Yorker named Molly had turned his head, tricked him into marriage and taken him off on some long honeymoon—at least that was the local story. Cat almost felt sorry for the woman she'd never met. This was a rough town to win over. She wondered how Helen had taken it. She guessed not well.

As for the locals wanting to know her story, she saw no reason to share it. She told herself that she wouldn't be here that long. *Let them speculate all they wanted*, she thought as she laid her palm on her stomach. As she felt her baby move, that wonderful flutter she loved, she smiled to herself. This was her story and no one else's.

Turning back to business, she studied the message Lindsey had left. Had the woman gotten cold feet after her get-rich plan hadn't worked? Or had she been threatened again and scared off?

Cat balled up the message and chucked it into the trash. She reached for the notes she'd started with the complaint against Dylan Walker. She'd asked Lindsey if she wanted to get a restraining order against Walker. She hadn't.

Seeing how scared the woman had been, Cat had figured she'd speak to him first. After that Ms. Martin could decide how she wanted to proceed.

Now that she had talked to Dylan Walker, she wasn't sure who she believed. Lindsey had appeared frightened for herself and her baby. Dylan had seemed straightforward in his responses with nothing to hide. Which one was telling the truth?

A thought struck her. Could Lindsey have been faking the pregnancy with a cushion under her clothes hoping to shake down the apparently wealthy Walker?

But if she was truly having his baby, why change her mind? Cold feet?

Cat thought about calling him to let him know that the woman had changed her mind. But he'd said he didn't know a woman by that name, and he hadn't seemed worried that it would go any further than it had. Also, he'd been willing to prove that he wasn't the father of the baby—if it came to that.

She jotted a couple of notes down, retrieved Lindsey's note from the trash, flattened it out and put it in a file folder in case the woman returned. At least it had been a break in the monotony that was Fortune Creek law enforcement, she told herself.

Maybe she should ask Helen to teach her to knit, she thought, watching the blur of needles in the woman's hands. Might be a way to bond—and not go mad for the rest of the time she had left as acting sheriff.

Then again, could she trust that Helen wouldn't "accidently" jab her with a knitting needle?

Chapter Four

The call came in the middle of the night—two days after Cat met Lindsey Martin and Dylan Walker.

She'd been in the middle of a dream where she was drowning and couldn't seem to kick to the surface. Fighting her way out of the twisted sheets, she sat up gasping for breath to find the phone ringing. Her heart still pumping hard, she struggled to breathe. As she put her hand on her stomach, she looked around the small upstairs apartment over the Fortune Creek Sheriff's Office, trying to assure herself that she was safe—and so was her baby.

It had just been a bad dream. Except that it had felt so real. Snatching up her phone, the dream slipped back into her unconscious ether-land. "Acting Sheriff Catherine Jameson," she said, her voice sounding as shaky as she felt. Maybe the nightmare hadn't gone completely away.

"There's a body on the side of the road a mile out of town," a male voice told her. "Looks like a young woman. Thought you'd want to know."

She took down the rancher's name, the mile marker on the road where he'd pulled over, told him she'd be right there and called the coroner.

Twenty minutes later, dressed and armed, Cat stood on

the side of the road. Coroner JP Brown was already down in the ditch hunkered over the body. He'd beaten her to the scene after her urgent call since he lived closer and probably dressed faster, Cat thought. He was already taking photos when she arrived.

Since he seemed to know what he was doing, she let him continue. She'd been trying not to step on anyone's toes after taking the temporary job. She'd been warned about JP Brown. Helen wasn't the only one who wanted Sheriff Brandt Parker back and Cat long gone. It was as if she wore a sign around her neck: Just Out of the Academy. Add Pregnant and it was no wonder some just assumed she wasn't up to the job.

The worst part? It was true. She was green, and this was her first baby and her first law enforcement job at the ripe old age of thirty-two. Wasn't that why she'd gotten this gig? Nothing ever happened in Fortune Creek, Montana, right? Even she should be able to handle filling in for the sheriff for a few months before she was to give birth.

The bite of the wind warned that the weather had changed. In this part of Montana that could mean anything, even snow any month of the year. But it was late fall so all bets were off when the first snow would hit. Often once flakes did hit the ground, they remained until April, and sometimes May.

From where she stood, Cat could tell the body in the ditch was slim and female. "Think she was hit by a vehicle?" Cat asked, hugging herself against the cold. The woman was curled up almost protectively, her back to the road, most of her head covered by the hoodie she wore.

Coroner JP Brown looked up from where he was crouched down by the body and shook his head. "Shot. Looks like a .38 to the heart. Three times at close range."

He yelled up to his van, telling a young assistant huddled in the passenger seat to get the body bag and cart ready.

"Mind if I take a look first?" Cat said. JP Brown was a large older man who'd grown up in Montana, collected guns and spent his free time killing things. He fished year around, hunted during the seasons and did taxidermy in between being called out as coroner. He'd been married a couple of times and then had stayed single saying he hadn't found a woman who could put up with him.

That he had little patience with most people, law enforcement even less, was well known around the state. That he especially had no patience with green acting sheriffs was the first thing Cat had been warned about.

Flashlight in hand, she stepped off the side of the road and dropped down into the steep ditch, sliding partway down to where the body had come to rest. From the lack of blood in the grass as she slid, Cat guessed the woman hadn't been killed here. "Dumped?"

JP didn't bother to answer.

She moved carefully around the body. "Why three shots to the heart?" she asked and got only a grunt from the coroner. Seemed like overkill to Cat, but apparently, he wasn't interested in discussing it.

From what she could see in the beam of her flashlight, the woman was slim, wearing sweats, a hooded sweatshirt, no shoes. The bottoms of her bare feet were clean. She'd definitely been killed somewhere else and dropped here.

"Find an ID?" she asked.

"Nope."

"Why dump her so close to town and right beside the road?" This was Montana. There were miles and miles of places to hide a body where it might never be found. "It almost seems as if the killer wanted her to be found. Or wasn't able to carry her far."

No response. Cat hunkered down to move the hoodie back. A lock of long brunette hair fell across the woman's cheek. Cat felt a jolt of recognition. "*I know her.* She came into my office two days ago." She moved the flashlight down the woman's body and felt suddenly sick to her stomach as she let out a gasp. "Where's her baby? She was very pregnant, looked as if she might give birth at any moment." Cat looked up at the coroner. *"Where's the baby?"*

"You're sure there was a baby?" he asked.

Cat had already questioned that herself, especially since the woman hadn't stuck around after making her accusation. What if the whole thing had been a scam? "I'm not sure," she admitted. "She certainly looked pregnant. But she did claim that someone wanted to kill her and her baby and now she's dead—and the baby's missing."

"*If* there *was* a baby," JP said. "Better get her to the morgue and find out."

HAD IT ALL been a ruse? But to what end? She almost hoped it was true because she couldn't bear the thought that there was a baby out there missing or maybe dead. The woman had definitely acted pregnant. Cat had bought it—until the woman took off saying she'd changed her mind. She couldn't believe that she'd fallen for Lindsey Martin's story—if that was even really her name—and that she'd made it all up. Now Cat doubted everything the woman had told her.

Back in her office after a preliminary search of the highway near where the body was found, Cat opened the temporary file she'd started on the woman. She put everything she'd learned into a computer file. There wasn't much to add so far. She was waiting for a call from JP, needing to know whether or not the woman had been pregnant.

In the meantime, Cat went online to find there were dozens of Lindsey Martins, but none of them were the woman who'd come crying into the Fortune Creek Sheriff's Office.

No social media. Also, no record of a Lindsey Martin her age living in the Denver area. Either that or she'd lived off the grid, no television, no internet, no electricity, no water, no sewage, no taxes, no driver's license, no purchase of anything that left a paper trail.

How was that even possible? Because that Lindsey Martin had never existed. The woman had lied about everything except, she reminded herself, someone wanting to kill her. Once they had her prints, maybe they would find out who she was—let alone if she'd been pregnant. And if true, who might have killed her. She kept thinking about how frightened the woman had been that Dylan Walker was going to kill her and her baby. So why hadn't she stayed at the hotel so Cat could have tried to keep her safe? Where had she gone after she left Fortune Creek? Out to Walker's ranch again?

Her phone rang. "Acting Sheriff Catherine Jameson," she said quickly.

"She'd recently given birth," JP said without preamble. So, there was a baby! "It was a live birth."

Cat had been warned not to ask JP a lot of questions. Not that it stopped her. "How can you tell that?"

"She breastfed the baby before she was killed."

"You can tell that?" Cat felt physically ill at the thought of the missing baby. She'd been hoping that the woman had been a scam artist, that there hadn't been a baby. Now she had a dead woman and a missing baby. Had the killer taken it? Dumped the infant along the road miles before dumping the mother's body? Was the baby even still alive?

Her hand went to her own baby bump as she rose quickly from her desk, phone still in hand. "We need to organize a search party along the road and—"

"Already did it at first light," JP said. "Covered all the miles from Eureka to Fortune Creek. No baby."

"Thank you," Cat said, even though she wished he'd let her know about the search. Clearly, he didn't think she was capable of helping.

Admittedly, she felt she hadn't handled things well so far. The woman was dead, her baby missing. But short of locking Lindsey Martin in a cell, she didn't know how she could have protected her. She'd thought she would be safe at the hotel across the street, but the woman had bolted on her.

"You're sure her name was Lindsey Martin?" JP asked.

"That's what she told me," Cat said, hating that the woman's purse was missing. There would have been a driver's license in it.

"Wait," the coroner said. "She showed you her identification when she came in to file a complaint, right?"

"No." *Novice.* She could hear the coroner echoing her sentiments. "She hesitated about filing a written complaint so I told her we could do it after I verified her story. I talked to the man in question, planning to talk to her again but she'd taken off."

He grunted.

She couldn't argue that. Why hadn't she asked for identification? Because she tended to take people at face value. "I do have the threatening note she said she received. Her fingerprints will be on it. I'm waiting to hear back from DCI's crime lab. They'll be trying to get prints off the note."

"I'll take her prints and send them to you," JP said.

After she disconnected, she thought that maybe Ash over at the hotel had asked for the woman's ID. She quickly called.

"Sorry, she paid cash. When I told her I'd need a credit card for incidentals, she told me she had one in her other purse in her suitcase and would bring it down later. Maybe that's why she split because there wasn't another purse— let alone a credit card in the name she'd given you."

Yep, that was pretty much what Cat was thinking. She thanked him and got off the call so she could start contacting hospitals, motels and hotels to see if a baby had been born there last night. The hospital would have required more information from her than Cat had gotten. She had no idea where Lindsey Martin had gone, let alone where she might have given birth. Maybe she knew someone in the area and felt safer staying with them, although that hadn't seemed the case. Or she gave birth in the motel in Eureka where she'd been staying. That was the problem, Cat had no idea. But she had to do something to find that baby.

"I'm going to alert the newspapers and radio stations in the two closest towns, Eureka and Libby, as well as the radio and TV stations around the state about the missing baby," Cat told JP when he called.

"Every crackpot in the state will be calling you, but if that's what you think is best." His tone made it clear he didn't think it was best, but Cat was determined.

"The sooner we find the baby, the better."

JP cleared his voice. "If you're going to do it, maybe you should let them know that the missing baby was a boy."

"A boy?" She didn't ask how he knew, just assumed he

did. "Glad you agree with my plan," she said. She waited, expecting him to tell her she'd better turn the whole case over to DCI. "I guess I don't have to tell you that this is my first murder."

"Nope. What *was* the story she told you, anyway?"

"Said the father of her baby threatened her and the baby. I spoke with the alleged bio-father. He swore he'd never heard of her and that he hadn't gotten her pregnant—and could prove it if he had to."

"Well, he has to now. Get a warrant now. Call Judge Nicholas Grand."

"Thanks." She really was grateful, feeling that she probably was in over her head and suspecting Helen and JP knew it. And yet neither had said she should call in help. Yet.

"What about the car she was driving?" JP asked. "Did you happen to get the license plate number?"

"No." *Another rookie mistake.* The car was missing. What if the baby was inside? "She told me she drove up from Denver."

"Probably did drive. Flying would be risky so far into her pregnancy," JP said.

"I'll see if there's a car registered to her." Cat said. "If her name really was Lindsey Martin. Otherwise, I'll check flights and car rental agencies."

"Get some of the deputies out of Eureka and Libby to help," he said.

"Also, might want to know that she was about three weeks overdue. It's a wonder she didn't give birth in your office the day she came in to see you. Maybe that's why she left the Fortune Creek Hotel."

"To get help from someone?" He grunted in reply.

"Which means she didn't get pregnant at the gala…" she said more to herself than the coroner.

"Hopefully her prints will confirm who she is," JP said. "Sending them to you now."

Cat knew it wouldn't help unless the woman's prints were in the system. She had her fingers crossed as she made the calls to the police chiefs in the two closest cities and got the word out about the missing baby. She just hoped that one of her inquiries would give her the information she needed before she went to the judge for a warrant to search Dylan Walker's ranch for any sign of the crime or the baby. She wasn't looking forward to questioning him again—if he was still on the ranch.

To her surprise, the prints she sent to the IFAIS database got a match at once. They belonged to a woman named Athena Grant, an import-export manager who had worked for several large companies abroad. After a quick check, Cat found that she was nowhere on social media—just like Dylan Walker. She also had no home address or phone number listed in the Denver area.

When Cat dug a little deeper, she found that Athena had only returned to the states three months ago—about the time Dylan Walker moved to his ranch. She called JP back with the news, asked him to send a photograph of Athena, then contacted the judge for a warrant.

Before walking out the door, she made copies of Athena Grant's passport photo and those from JP of the deceased woman lying on his morgue table. Then she called her friend Traver Lee, who she'd known since he roomed with her cousin in college. He now worked for the tabloid. She couldn't shake the feeling that Athena's death tied in somehow to the DC bombing and Dylan Walker and his dead wife.

Chapter Five

On the way to Dylan Walker's ranch, Traver Lee called her back. She picked up immediately, anxious to hear what he'd dug up on the background information she'd given him about on Dylan Walker and the car bombing that killed his wife.

Cat couldn't help being curious about the bombing that had killed Dylan's wife. But after meeting Dylan Walker, she'd been curious about the woman he'd married. Earlier she'd found photos of Ginny Cooper Walker from the bombing story. Dylan's wife had been beautiful, super-model stunning with long dark hair, huge blue eyes and a body that would stop traffic with those long legs that seemed to go on forever.

"So what do you have for me?" she asked Traver, knowing how he loved digging up dirt. He was apparently exceptionally good at it.

"How much do you know?" he asked, sounding downright gleeful.

"Just what I've been able to find online, which isn't much. I wanted to ask if the husband, Dylan Walker, had been injured in the bombing."

"According to his statement to the cops, he was almost

to the town car when it had pulled away from the curb, gone up the street and exploded. He apparently had gone out into the street as if he planned to chase it down when it blew up. The explosion was contained so he received only minor injuries, was taken to the hospital for observation, and released later that night. Everyone in the car was killed instantly, but bystanders were relatively unharmed."

"So, the idea was to kill whoever was in the car," she said. "Wait, you said *everyone* in the car? I thought it was just the wife and driver?"

"Beau Walker was driving the car. Ginny Walker was in the front. Both were killed," he said.

She frowned. "*Beau* Walker?"

"Dylan Walker's younger brother. There were rumors about Beau being with Dylan's wife, Ginny. I never could get verification, but Ginny and Beau had been seen together more than once before that night."

Cat had tried to picture it. Dylan hurrying after the car as it was pulling away. Which meant that he and his wife hadn't been together all night. So much for his alibi. "So, the car bomb wasn't designed to detonate when the car was started?"

"No, it was on a delayed electronic trigger," he said. "The killer was probably either watching from somewhere or had someone else telling them when to detonate the bomb."

"Do the cops know who the actual target was?"

"Nope, the case has never been solved," he said.

"I'm curious about the wife and brother."

He made a sound of agreement. "Beau Walker worked abroad as an independent contractor on construction projects." Apparently, like his older brother Dylan. "At the time of his death, he was in between jobs. He and his brother both came from old family wealth, I'm talking loaded, and the surviving brother inherited it all." That could definitely have given Dylan motive for murder—not to mention if he suspected his wife and brother were having an affair.

"What do you know about the wife?" she asked, trying to hide just how curious she was.

"Ginny Cooper Walker was playing above her league. Middle-class family and upbringing. BFA after majoring in art. Taught children how to finger paint through a program Dylan's family had started. They met at one of the events. Love at first sight, according to friends."

"The marriage?" she asked.

"True love according to her sister, Patty. Dylan idolized Ginny. But they hadn't been married long. Patty Cooper Harper teaches middle school in Denver."

Denver? Where Lindsey Martin said she was from. Coincidence?

"So why the car bomb?" Cat asked as she made the turn toward the Walker ranch.

"Could have been a case of mistaken identity," he said. "There were a half dozen black town cars hired at the event that night."

Cat thought of Lindsey Martin aka Athena Grant again. "Did the brothers look anything alike?"

Traver laughed. "Odd you should ask, but no more than most brothers. You know something I don't?"

She wasn't about to tell him about the murder case she was working on. He was a reporter and there was no way he could sit on this story. Maybe when she solved the murder, she could give it to him. "You think the bomb was meant for Dylan?"

"I think it had something to do with the brother and Dylan's wife."

"An affair then?" she asked.

"Why not? Makes you wonder why Dylan didn't leave the event with his wife. The rumor is that Dylan didn't even know his brother was in town."

"Were they close?" she asked.

"Wouldn't be very close once Dylan found out that his wife was sleeping with his brother."

"You know that for a fact?" Cat asked.

"Honey, let's not even pretend I work on fact," he said with a laugh. "I just try to answer the questions everyone is asking."

Cat could see the gate ahead and two rigs with the deputies she'd called from Eureka and Libby waiting to help with the search. "I'm going to have to let you go."

"I hope you can tell me soon why you're asking about this now."

"You're the best, Traver," she said with a chuckle and disconnected as she reached the gate.

Cat tried to make sense of what she knew. Athena Grant was more than nine months pregnant and in trouble. She'd come to Montana thinking she could get Dylan Walker to help her. But she had to know that was a longshot. Was that why she hadn't used her real name? Because once he knew it was her, there was no way he would see her? Or worse, what if she planned to kill him if she'd gotten in through the gate that day?

She shook her head, reminding herself that law enforcement operated on facts and evidence, not conjecture and rumor. But right now, conjecture and rumor was about all she had. She did wonder though if Athena had had a backup plan. If so, something went wrong.

IT WAS LATE afternoon on Saturday when Dylan looked out to see Rowena headed his way. She'd said she'd be gone by the weekend, but here she was. He hadn't seen much of her over the past few days. She had come and gone. From what little he'd seen of her, she seemed to be sightseeing around the area, leaving early in the morning and returning late.

The first words out of her mouth were, "I know what you're going to say. What am I still doing here." She gave him a smile. "Make me a drink and I'll tell you."

"Rowena—"

"Seriously, Dylan, you'll want to hear what I have to tell you. I talked to my friend in the prosecutor's office. Make it a gin and tonic with lime," she said as she stepped past him.

Tamping down his growing irritation, he closed the door and followed her into the living room, where she'd already taken a seat on the couch. He'd done his best to find out what she was doing here, but none of his contacts knew anything. That was the problem with Rowena, he couldn't remember how she'd come into Ginny's life—and now his own.

Maybe she was just this pushy woman who latched onto people and hung on for dear life because she didn't have other friends. Is this what Ginny had had to contend with? Or was Rowena really her best friend, the one she told all her secrets to? He might never know. The one thing he did know was that he couldn't get Rowena to tell him the truth.

Dylan made her a drink and one for himself while he was at it. He figured he was going to need it. He handed her a glass, she gave a nod and made herself at home. "Well? Let's have it." He did his best not to sound as angry as he felt as he perched on the arm of the chair across from her. Or as worried. Whatever she was doing here, it was more than to visit him.

His stomach roiled as he watched her take a sip of her drink, lick her lips and carefully put down the glass on the coffee table before she answered. She was making him wait, maybe gauging just how anxious he was to hear what she'd found out. More than likely torturing him for the fun of it. Still, he waited, sipping his drink, trying his best to look calm and casual.

"They've reopened the case because there's some question about who died in the car," she said.

"*What?* After this long there's a question?"

"Something to do with identifying the remains, a possible mix-up."

Dylan shook his head. "I saw Ginny get into the car and head up the street right before it blew up. I provided a sample of my DNA. It was my brother in that car."

Rowena picked up her drink, took a sip before she said, "I don't know what to tell you, but it sounds as if there might have been a major screwup if the people in the car weren't your brother and wife."

"That's impossible."

"Just telling you what I heard. Why else would they reopen the case?" she asked.

He had no idea, but he had a feeling she might be making this all up since he hadn't been able to confirm the case was being reopened. This could be Rowena playing him. But for what end? So she could hang around longer? But why? Not that it mattered, he was done.

"It's time for you to leave, Rowena."

She raised a brow and let out a little laugh. "It's not even close to bedtime and I'm lonely in that big house of yours. I really don't understand why you don't live in it. You could come stay with me and then it wouldn't be so—"

"Not leave to go back to my house. Leave the ranch. Leave Montana. You said you'd leave by the weekend. Time's up."

Rowena cocked her head at him. He could see sparks coming from her blue eyes as she downed the rest of her drink. "Ginny said I was wrong, but you never liked me, did you, Dylan?"

"No. I never understood what Ginny saw in you."

"Ouch, the gloves are off, huh. I'll tell you what Ginny saw in me. I was fun, something she found in short supply with you." She rose, taking her empty glass to the bar and pouring herself another drink. After downing it in one gulp, she slammed her glass on the bar before turning to him. "I really did come here to help you get over your...loss," she said meeting his gaze with a fiery one of her own.

"I highly doubt that. Did you ever contact the sheriff like I told her you would?"

"*Acting* sheriff," she said, with a shake of her head.

"You should give her a call on your way out of town."

"What makes you think I'm leaving town," she said with a bitter laugh.

"Montana's a big state. There is no reason you and I should cross paths again."

She let out a huff and started for the door but stopped at the sound of the gate buzzer. Turning, they exchanged a look as a familiar female voice came over the intercom.

Dylan swore under his breath. He had feared Acting Sheriff Cat Jameson would be back. Just a gut feeling he hadn't been able to explain. He touched the intercom flat-screen display and her face appeared. "Unless you've brought a warrant, Sheriff—"

"Got it right here, along with some deputies to help with the search."

"Search? Search for what?"

"It's all spelled out in the warrant," she said, holding it up.

He felt his pulse begin to pound. "Come on in then." He opened the gate, dreading what he feared was coming as she drove in followed by two different cars of deputies apparently from nearby cities. What the devil was this about?

Turning back to Rowena, he said, "I need to handle this. I'm serious about you leaving."

"But didn't you tell me the cute little acting sheriff wanted to talk to me?"

He growled under his breath. "That's right. Unfortunately, you involved yourself in this."

She smiled and raised a brow. "Nor would I want to miss this for anything. They're really going to search the place? Seems you're in some kind of trouble, Dylan. Now I'm really intrigued. Whatever have you been up to?"

Chapter Six

Dylan ground his teeth as he waited for the sheriff to reach the house. Worse, he waited with Rowena, wondering how much she already knew since she seemed to be enjoying herself. She'd been the only one around when a woman named Lindsey Martin had tried to get in to see him. She'd not just read the woman's note to him—she'd destroyed it. Why would she do that unless she knew more about what was going on than he did?

He told himself that it didn't matter. It wasn't true and he was about to resolve this once and for all. Although he did wonder how the sheriff had gotten a warrant. Based on what? None of this boded well, he told himself as he heard the vehicles coming up the road.

"Stay here," he told Rowena, who immediately began to pour herself another drink. "Try not to get too drunk."

Going out onto the small bungalow deck, he waited as the sheriff drove up, parked, and two other law enforcement vehicles pulled in next to her.

From her demeanor the moment she set foot on his property, Acting Sheriff Cat Jameson was all business and so were the four deputies she'd brought with her.

"I have a warrant to search your house and property,"

she said as she marched up to him and handed him the folded paper.

He quickly glanced at it, then at her as the deputies scaled the steps to the porch. "You're looking for a *baby*?" Dylan said unable to keep the shock out of his voice.

"While the deputies search your house and property, I need to ask you a few questions on the record," she said. "We can do it here or I can take you to the sheriff's office in Fortune Creek. Your choice."

"Here is fine," he said wondering how this situation had gone this far this fast.

"Shall we step inside then," she said and, hefting the bag she carried, started for the door.

All he could do was nod as the deputies entered the house, the acting sheriff right behind them. Dylan brought up the rear. The warrant had caught him off guard. He'd thought he would be safe out here in Montana on a ranch as big as some towns. He hadn't expected a warrant because he couldn't imagine what judge would give her one without sufficient evidence.

Which meant she'd found evidence that incriminated him—or…the woman who'd implicated him had given birth to her baby—and someone had taken it? Why else would they be searching for a baby?

"Let me save you some time," he said once he and the acting sheriff had stepped into the bungalow's bright, sunny kitchen. He could hear the deputies searching the cottage. He knew it wouldn't take them long since the place was small. Then they would want to search the big house. "There's no baby here."

She pulled out a chair, indicating he should do the same. With a sigh, he said, "Also my…houseguest, Rowena Keeling, is here. She's the one who must have spoken to the woman who stopped by the ranch. She also was the one who took the note from the mailbox."

As if on cue, Rowena stepped into the doorway. "Before you ask, I don't have the note. The woman sounded irrational and unhinged. I didn't open the gate to let her in and while I did check the mailbox to see if maybe she left a bomb or something, I did find the note and throw it away."

"Excuse me, what is your name?"

"Rowena Keeling."

"Did you read the note?" Cat asked her. Dylan saw her react to the waves of alcohol coming off his so-called houseguest.

"It was chicken scrawl. I couldn't make heads nor tails of it. I just figured she had the wrong house and tossed it." Rowena shrugged. "If that's all, I've had a long day." She turned and, when the acting sheriff didn't stop her, walked toward the front door.

"Ms. Keeling, I'd appreciate it if you wouldn't leave the area for a few days. I'd like to talk to you again."

Rowena shot Dylan a smile, then walked out. The acting sheriff didn't try to stop her, but she did watch her go for a few moments. Then she reached into the bag she'd brought, pulled out phone and a stack of what looked like photographs. She turned on the record, gave the date and time and his name and her own and looked up at him.

He was struck again by the intelligence she saw in her eyes. He wondered how many people had underestimated this woman because she was petite and cute as a button, as Rowena had said.

"I already told you that I don't know anyone named Lindsey Martin," he said. "Nor did I get her or anyone else pregnant."

"How about a woman named Athena Grant?" she asked.

He blinked. "Another woman says I've knocked her up?" he demanded.

CAT SLID THE top photograph over to him. It was a copy of the headshot from Athena's passport. As Dylan picked it up, she saw the moment of recognition. "You do know her, don't you, Mr. Walker."

He looked up. His eyes had widened, his jaw had gone slack and some of the color had bled from his face. "I only met her once."

Cat felt her pulse jump. "At the gala you and your wife attended nine months ago?" She knew they had met before that and waited for him to deny it.

He frowned over at her. "No. It was at the wedding."

"Whose wedding?"

"Mine and my wife Ginny's a few weeks earlier. The woman was my sister-in-law Patty's plus one. I'd never met her before."

"You didn't remember her name?"

He shook his head and glanced at the other photographs she'd brought. His eyes widened and shifted from the next photo taken on the morgue table. "She's *dead*?" He sounded shocked. "And the baby?"

"Missing," she said as she watched him put the pieces together.

Dylan leaned back in the chair as if trying to distance himself from all of this.

"It turns out that Athena Grant was more than three weeks overdue," Cat said, recalling what JP had told her. "Which means she didn't get pregnant the night of the gala. Mr. Walker, did you have sex with Athena Grant during your wedding party?"

"No! Are you serious?" he demanded. "I've never heard of anything more…ridiculous. This woman swore to you that I was the father of the baby?" She nodded. "Well, it's not medically possible. Not long after Ginny and I were married, we discovered that I was sterile, something to do with chemicals I came in contact with in my line of work."

"I'm sure that can be proved. Why would Athena Grant tell me her name was Lindsey Martin?"

He shook his head. "I have no idea. I don't recognize either name, and it's not my baby."

She withdrew a form and slid it over to him. "I need you to sign that, authorizing me to take a DNA swab." He was still shaking his head. "I thought you said you weren't the father?"

"I'm not."

"Then there is no reason not to prove it, right?"

He hesitated, but only a moment before he signed the paper and slid it back to her. "Let's get this over with."

Cat met his gaze. Did he think it would be that simple? The deputies returned to say they hadn't found anything in the cottage and were going to the other house and grounds. The moment they were gone, she took the swab and restarted the video recorder. "Tell me about the night of the gala."

His frown formed a deep-set line between his eyes. "I don't understand your interest in the gala, especially if you now think this woman conceived weeks earlier at my wedding."

"Please, Mr. Walker. You were there with your wife. Did you see Athena Grant at the gala?"

"No, I told you. I met her at the wedding. I don't remember seeing her again after that. I was with my wife all night."

"Except she left the gala without you. Where were you then?"

He sighed. "It was only for a few minutes when Ginny and I got separated. A friend detained me. Other than to get us a drink or go to the men's room, we were together all night. I certainly wasn't away from her long enough to impregnate anyone then or at my wedding."

"Apparently it was a pretty quick seduction."

"Definitely not me then," Dylan said and held her gaze. "I never rush something so important."

Cat felt heat rise to her cheeks. "Why would Athena Grant lie?"

He shook his head. "I have no idea."

"Where were you yesterday evening and night?"

"Here at the ranch. I didn't leave."

"Can anyone corroborate your alibi?" she asked.

He sighed and shook his head. "I was alone. Rowena had left. I don't know what time she got in. Sheriff, the sooner you get that swab to the lab, the sooner you can find out not only who impregnated the woman—but also who killed her and who might have taken the baby. Again, it wasn't me."

"Let's say the baby isn't yours," Cat said. "That doesn't mean you didn't kill her."

Dylan pushed back his chair. "I didn't want to do this, but I'm not going to answer any more of your questions until my lawyer is present. By then, you should have the DNA results and hopefully have found the missing baby and realized I had nothing to do with any of this."

Chapter Seven

Dylan just wanted everyone to go away. He needed to be alone to think. It felt as if everything was closing in. As he watched the acting sheriff walking up to the big house, he swore. Rowena. What was she still doing here? Certainly, she wasn't here for any reason she'd offered him so far.

In his business, everything had been about careful preparation and timing. Especially timing. That's why it was too much of a coincidence that she happened to be here when Athena Grant had come by the ranch. He didn't believe for a minute that she'd destroyed the note because she couldn't read it and thought the woman was unhinged.

After Ginny's death and what he'd learned about his wife, he'd begun to question everything. Picking up his phone, he searched for Ginny's sister's phone number. Disappointed, but not too surprised, there wasn't a listing. Everyone had gone to cell phones. Still, he searched to see if he could find an address in Denver for Patty Cooper.

When he struck out, he called his friend who'd worked with him on government projects. "I need to know everything you can find out about Ginny Cooper Walker, my late wife, and Patty Cooper, her sister. Last known address,

Denver. And Athena Grant and Lindsey Martin, also supposedly out of Denver."

"What specifically are you looking for?"

"I wish I knew. Also…" He wondered why he hadn't thought about this before. "Could you see what you can find on Rowena Keeling. She should still have a DC address."

"Want to tell me what's going on?"

"I would if I knew. Maybe I'm just being paranoid. Or not. Thanks, I appreciate this."

"I'll get back to you as soon as I can. You know if you're in trouble…"

"Not yet. At least not that I know," he said as he watched Acting Sheriff Cat Jameson disappear into his big house, the one Rowena had made herself at home in.

When Rowena Keeling answered the door, Cat could see just how much the woman had made herself at home. She got the feeling that the woman had checked everything out. There were marks on the rug where something had been dragged and some of the high wood cabinet doors had been left slightly ajar.

Not that she blamed Rowena for wanting to explore the beautiful house. Cat wondered if Dylan's wife, Ginny, had decorated it. If so, she had good taste.

As for Rowena, that she might have designs on Dylan Walker seemed obvious. Even he had had trouble explaining their relationship. Cat had a feeling Rowena wouldn't have that problem.

"I have a few questions," the sheriff said as the woman waved her inside.

"You're really the sheriff?" There was humor in her voice, her expression saying what everyone else was too polite to say. Cat didn't look like she could handle the job—especially pregnant. But she'd been underestimated her entire life. Cat thought in this instance it might actually work in her favor.

"*Acting* sheriff. Why don't we have a seat," Cat suggested since the woman hadn't. "I'll try not to take up too much of your time."

Rowena raised a brow but motioned toward a seating area by the window.

"I'm investigating a murder," Cat said once she'd sat down. Rowena had moved to take a chair closer to the window. She saw at once what the woman had done. The bright sunlight coming through the large windows behind Rowena cast a shadow so Cat wouldn't be able to see her face well—let alone read her expression. It made her wonder if the woman had been interviewed by the law before.

"If you don't mind…" Cat said, motioning to the seat adjacent to her. Rowena pretended not to understand what the problem was but moved nonetheless. "That's much better. I just need you to write down your full name and address and phone number for me." She handed over the notebook and pen and watched the woman scribble it all down before thrusting it back at her.

Flipping to a clean page, she said, "Mr. Walker tells me you're his…?"

A little laugh as she tucked a lock of her blond bob behind her ear and lifted a brow. "Are you asking me what my relationship is with Dylan?"

"Sure, why not? How do you two know each other?"

"I was his wife's best friend. I lived next door. Ginny and I were practically inseparable."

"Oh, so you were at the gala the night she was killed."

Rowena's smile fell. "No, fortunately, otherwise I would have probably been in that car with her."

"With her and Dylan's brother? That's right, you were Ginny's best friend, so she would have confided in you if she was having an affair with Beau Walker."

Rowena waved the question away, pretty much answering it. "I thought you wanted to ask me about that unhinged woman who'd come to the gate."

"Oh, I do, I just need some background. Why weren't you at the gala nine months ago?"

"Shouldn't you be asking me questions about the local murder?" Rowena sighed, then said, "There was a mix-up or something. Ginny felt terrible because she'd paid for my ticket." She glared at the sheriff, fury making her blue eyes bright and brittle.

"When did you arrive here at the ranch?"

"About a week ago."

"Before the woman calling herself Lindsey Martin stopped by the ranch?"

"If you say so."

"Were you at Dylan and Ginny's wedding?" When Cat waited, pen posed over her notebook, Rowena finally said, "No." She hesitated for a moment as if about to lie before she said, "I hadn't met Ginny yet."

"Do you know a woman by the name of Athena Grant?" She saw something in the woman's gaze before Rowena looked away.

"I don't recognize the name. Ginny had a lot of friends."

"This wasn't Ginny's friend. It was her sister Patty's friend that she brought to the wedding."

"What does any of this have to do with the local murder?" the woman demanded impatiently.

"Apparently something since Lindsey Martin lied about

her name." Cat pulled out the photos and passed them to her. She saw Rowena's reaction and knew that she was on the right track.

"Her real name was Athena Grant, and she was pregnant with allegedly Dylan Walker's baby and that's why she left the note telling him where she was staying. But Dylan never got that note because you did. And that is why you went to the motel where she was staying and left her the threatening note." Rowena started to protest, but Cat talked over her. "Fortunately, Athena gave me the note and it is now evidence. I suspect your fingerprints are on it, but if not, we can have a handwriting expert compare it with your handwriting."

Rowena seemed to realize that she'd just given the sheriff a sample of her handwriting. Her cheeks flushed, eyes snapping with fury and seemed about ready to argue Cat was wrong.

"You might as well admit it. You are the only one who knew where she was staying. It explains your real reason for not letting Athena in the gate, as well as why you destroyed the note. I'm assuming it has something to do with why you're here on Dylan Walker's ranch as his... houseguest?"

Rowena shot to her feet. "I'm not saying another word without a lawyer."

"I can understand that, but keep in mind, Athena is dead, and the baby is missing. The sooner I find the baby, the better for you since right now you are a suspect in my murder-kidnapping investigation. I could arrest you for threatening the woman only days before she was murdered."

Cat closed her notebook and rose. "What I don't know is if you did it out of jealousy or some other reason you wanted Athena Grant dead and her baby to disappear."

Rowena looked as if she could chew nails—or strangle one pregnant acting sheriff. "I'd appreciate it if you hung around the area for a while. But I can always have you picked up if I need to."

DYLAN HAD BEEN watching from the cottage. Not long after the acting sheriff left, Rowena came out of the house, got into her white SUV and took off. Dylan waited until she disappeared into the trees headed for the gate before he grabbed his Stetson and hurried out to his pickup.

He was determined to find out what Rowena was up to. She hadn't just come here to check up on him. Nor was he buying that she had romantic intentions when it came to him. No, something else had brought her to Montana, and he was going to find out what.

When he reached the road, he saw her car in the distance. He'd expected her to go north toward Fortune Creek and Eureka—the same way the sheriff would have gone.

But instead, she was headed south toward the town of Libby. He waited until her car disappeared over a rise in the narrow hilly road before he went after her. He was definitely curious as to where she went every day. How many massages could a woman get? If she was Rowena Keeling, as many as she wanted.

He drove, keeping a good distance between them, which meant that a lot of the time, he couldn't see her ahead of him. It was another beautiful spring day in Montana, not a cloud in the clear robin's-egg blue sky. Snow capped the mountains, glittering in the sunlight. He thought about the mess he was in, but especially the acting sheriff. Did she really suspect him of murder and kidnapping?

As they neared the town of Libby, he turned his thoughts back to Rowena. The town was sprawled next to the Kootenai River, the major river of the Northwest Plateau and one of the uppermost major tributaries of the Columbia River, the largest North American river to empty into the Pacific Ocean.

Not that any of that was why Rowena Keeling had come to town. He'd seen her turn south toward what he guessed was the center of town. Letting a car or two go in front of him, he continued to follow her, all the time hoping this wasn't a wild goose chase.

When she finally pulled over, he did the same a block behind her. He watched her get out of her car and look around before she headed down the sidewalk away from him. Hurrying, he got out and started in her direction. He hadn't done surveillance in years. Had he had time to plan this, he would have at least changed his clothing.

But Rowena didn't look back before turning into a doorway along the main drag. He waited a couple of doors down. If she'd spotted the tail, she might have just stepped into the store to see if he hurried to catch up to her. After a few minutes, he decided that she hadn't spotted him and walked closer to the business where she'd gone inside.

Swearing, he saw that it was a massage studio and hair salon. Turning back to his pickup, he debated how long to hang out. His impulsive decision to follow her felt foolish and a complete waste of time. But time was something he had a lot of these days. He climbed behind the wheel to wait. Massages could take an hour or more. Or at least Ginny's had taken that long. Then again, for all he knew, she'd used them as an excuse to meet someone. His brother?

He shoved that thought away and realized he was thirsty. He should have at least brought something to eat and drink if this was going to take—

Rowena came out of the studio, looked both ways, then

walked quickly back to her car. He started his pickup. She hadn't had time for a haircut or a massage. So why drive all the way down here when whatever she'd done probably could have been handled with a phone call?

He hadn't gone far when Rowena turned off the main drag, went a block and turned again. She was making it harder to follow her, but he wasn't about to lose her. She turned left again, taking her back to the main highway.

By the time he saw her again, she was turning north toward the ranch. He followed for a little way, seeing her car in the distance, then turned off and went back to Libby. He had no idea what he was going to do at the studio salon, just that he couldn't leave yet.

After parking, he walked down the block and pushed open the door. He was instantly hit with the sweet scent of pampered women. Moving to the reception desk, he said, "I'd like to get a package for my wife's birthday. The whole ballgame. What would you suggest?"

The just-out-of-high-school-looking girl behind the counter smiled and pulled out a brochure. "What of these do you think she would like?"

He glanced down the list, thinking of Cat. "She's seven months pregnant."

"We have someone who does pregnancy massages. Also, she might like this." She pointed to a body moisturizer wrap.

"This is more difficult than I thought it would be," he said glancing at the hair salon along one side of the building. Several women were getting haircuts, chatting with the stylists. "My wife's friend was just in here. Rowena Keeling? If you can tell me what she gets done."

The young woman hesitated for a moment. "Let me check."

He spelled the name. She leafed through the reservations book but found that Rowena Keeling had never had a massage or hair appointment. "That's odd," he said frowning. "I just saw her coming out of here." He described her.

"Oh, her," the receptionist said. "I believe she just went back to talk to one of the massage therapists."

"Oh, which one was that?" he asked, trying to be as nonchalant as possible.

"Sharese." He waited for a last name but saw one wasn't coming.

"Thank you. Clearly, I need to give this more thought." He took the brochure and walked out. Back in his pickup, he looked on the brochure. Just as he expected, Sharese's last name was listed. Sharese Harmon.

Dylan smiled to himself. It hadn't been a wasted trip after all.

Chapter Eight

Cat had a lot of time to think on her way back to her office in Fortune Creek. Her thoughts kept circling back to Dylan Walker. Did she just want to believe him because he seemed so sincere? Or was she being taken in by his extremely good innocent act? She'd never let a handsome man unnerve her, yet the pain she saw in him did make her feel compassion for him. It hadn't been all that long ago that he'd lost his wife and now this. Whatever this was.

All Cat knew was that she had a dead woman and missing baby mystery to solve. She didn't feel like she was getting anywhere with this case. Yesterday, she'd made dozens of calls to hospitals, motels, hotels, bed and breakfasts. No woman matching Athena's description had checked in. As pregnant as Athena was, she would have stood out.

Cat found Helen knitting. "Any messages?"

The older woman shook her head without looking up from whatever she was making. It wasn't until Cat was sitting in her office that she noticed how small the knitting project appeared to be. What startled her most was that the yarn was blue.

She opened her door and approached the receptionist-dispatcher-knitter. "Are you making this by any chance for the missing baby?"

"What if I am?" Helen said without missing a stitch.

"I think that's nice, but what makes you think the infant is a boy?" Cat had only recently learned that the baby was male.

"I saw the way she was carrying. Low. Knew it was going to be a boy."

"Huh," Cat said.

"Just like you're carrying high. Girl."

She didn't comment on that, but she hadn't told anyone that she was having a girl. Nor did she feel any compulsion to admit that Helen was right. She was more interested in where Helen got her information. "What else do you know about the woman?"

"She was lying."

"Based on what?"

"Years of experience in this office," the older woman said with authority.

So maybe she hadn't been listening in on phone calls from the coroner. "All right, then who's the father of the baby?"

"That's the million-dollar question, isn't it." She reached over as a call came in, picked up her old-fashioned headset and answered, "Fortune Creek Sheriff's Department. Yep, she's right here. It's for you," she said as she put the call through to Cat's desk and went back to knitting.

Helen was making baby clothing for the missing infant. Maybe it was the pregnancy hormones, but she liked this side of Helen.

In her office, she took the call. It was the coroner asking if she'd gotten his report. She'd just dropped off Dylan

Walker's DNA sample, too early to have results. She tapped her computer to life and saw that JP had sent her the autopsy results. The weapon used to kill her had been a .38 caliber. Three shots to the heart at close range. Why would Athena Grant have let the man who threatened her get that close? Unless he forced his way in to wherever she'd been staying.

Nothing made sense. Why hadn't the woman stayed at the hotel across the street? She might still be alive and her baby… Where was her baby? Was he still alive?

She turned her attention to what JP was saying. "Wait, what?"

"She had help delivering the baby."

"But the hospitals and emergency rooms—"

"Not at the hospital. That alarm you put out about the missing baby got a response. I know the woman who owns the motel. She called me."

"The baby's been found?"

"No, but a motel maid called to say she thought a woman had given birth in one of her rooms she cleaned. Bloody bedsheets and the placenta in the trash. The man in the next unit hearing a baby cry in the middle of the night." He gave her the name of the motel, The Siesta Vista, and told her to talk to the owner.

The moment she disconnected, she found what photos she could of anyone who might have helped Athena that could have been connected. The list was short: Ginny Cooper Walker (dead), Patty Cooper Harper, Ginny's sister, and Rowena Keeling, a complete stranger according to her. She got mugshots from drivers' licenses or in the case of Patty Cooper Harper, her school ID.

If it hadn't been either Patty or Rowena having helped Athena have her baby, then Cat was out of suspects.

BACK AT THE RANCH, Dylan noted Rowena's car was in front of the house. As soon as he'd returned to where he had internet service, he'd made the call to a contact he could trust. The conversation though now had him feeling as if he'd fallen in a rabbit hole.

"Are you aware that all of the women you asked me about were adopted?"

"Why is that important?" Dylan had asked.

"Russia formalized its international adoption program in the middle of 1991," his government contact had told him. "That year only twelve children were adopted by American families. That number topped a thousand by 1994."

"Wait, you're telling me that Ginny, her sister Patty and Athena Grant were all born in Russia and adopted by American families?" Dylan had said.

"All adopted the same year by families in the Denver area," his friend had told him. "Ginny and Patty to the same family, the Coopers. Athena Grant to Lindsey and Lloyd Martin."

He let out a curse. Now at least he knew where Athena had gotten the name she'd used the day she'd come out to the ranch. Because she thought he would recognize it? He frowned and felt a start. Had Rowena recognized it?

"What about Rowena Keeling and Sharese Harmon?" he asked, waiting for confirmation as he looked toward the big house and saw Rowena headed his way. He wasn't surprised that she would come down to see him. She'd be curious to know what he'd told the sheriff and deputies earlier.

"Keeling and Harmon were in a later batch of Russian babies adopted to American families that same year, along with Harmon's brother Luca. You had no idea your wife was adopted?"

"Not a clue. But there was a lot about Ginny I didn't know, as it turns out. Wait, Sharese has a brother named Luca who was also adopted. By the same family? Where?"

"By Bob and Lynette Harmon of Missoula, Montana."

"Whoa, that close by," Dylan had said, unsure what to make of the information, but knowing that it had to be the connection he'd been looking for.

"I'm curious why you would be asking about these people."

He hesitated to even voice it. "Is it possible they are part of a sleeper cell?" He knew from his career that there had been instances of real-life "sleeper agents" who'd dealt in spying, espionage, sedition, treason and even...assassinations on behalf of their mother country leaders.

"It's possible, I suppose. All from the same area. If they all knew they were adopted from Russia, became friends, were approached by someone, I suppose that's what they might have become."

"I'm worried that's exactly what happened," he admitted.

"What do you plan to do with this information?"

"Don't worry, I won't tell anyone where I got it."

"But maybe you should tell someone about what you've discovered," his friend said. "Someone who can stop whatever this group might be up to."

"At this point, I have no evidence. Once I do... Thanks for this information. I owe you." He disconnected, unable to shake off the feeling that he was on to something. He remembered some of the questions his wife had asked him about his job. He'd assumed she only knew about the real one—not the undercover one. But now he wondered if it was why she'd married him.

She'd definitely been the one to pursue him, he thought looking back. It had been more than flattering. She'd literally swept him off his feet with her enthusiasm for all things, especially him. What a fool he'd been, he thought with a curse.

What scared him was where his brother might have come into all of this—if he had. Beau had always colored outside the lines. His job, like Dylan's, had put him in places and situations that were dangerous in so many ways. Had Beau gotten involved with the wrong people? The wrong people being Ginny Cooper Walker? Is that why the two of them were targeted?

He thought about the acquaintance who'd detained him the night of the gala. The man had saved his life. Was that what he'd intended to do? Now he was suspicious of everyone and everything that had happened.

Raking a hand through his hair, Dylan felt his mind spinning. What if nothing was as it seemed? And more to the point, what if Rowena Keeling had been in on all of it? That would certainly explain how she'd gotten into their lives and why Ginny had let her.

But right now, he didn't have the time to consider what to even do about it. Groaning, he saw Rowena climb his deck steps.

The acting sheriff—he couldn't help thinking of her as Cat from the first time she'd introduced herself—had asked his houseguest not to leave the area. Which gave Rowena the perfect excuse for hanging around longer. Not that he couldn't kick her out. But wasn't he smarter to keep her close?

Athena Grant was dead. The acting sheriff seemed to

think not only had he fathered the woman's child, but also that he'd killed her and done what with the baby? He felt sick at the thought of the infant. He had wanted a child so badly with Ginny.

As Rowena reached the deck, he walked out to her. As he did, he tried to gauge how her interview had gone with the sheriff earlier. He really doubted Cat would have been intimidated by Rowena in the least. "Have a nice talk with the sheriff? You left pretty quickly afterward."

She mugged a face. "I had an appointment. Do you even have to ask how it went with the *acting* sheriff?" She sounded cocky, but when she moved to the edge of the deck and took hold of the railing, he thought she looked...nervous? Or was it scared?

Until that moment, he hadn't even suspected that she might have done something to Athena Grant and her baby. But it had been Rowena who'd turned the woman away at the gate, who had gone down to the mailbox to take the note. He swore under his breath as he moved to her, touching her arm, forcing her to look at him.

"Tell me you had nothing to do with that woman's death or her missing baby."

She stared at him as if shocked that he would ask such a thing. "You can't be serious. Who do you think I am?" she demanded indignantly, but she didn't quite pull it off.

"That's just it, I have no idea."

Her expression changed quickly to coy, which he assumed was her default. "Because you haven't wanted to get to know me, your loss." She cocked her head at him, her blue eyes alight with mischief. "What did you tell your cute acting sheriff about me?" she asked coquettishly. "I'm curious how you described our...relationship."

"We don't have one, and quite frankly, I'm not even sure

how to describe you, let alone explain what you're doing here," he said.

"You shouldn't have to explain yourself to some small-town sheriff. *Really.*" Rowena could get more meaning into a single word. "Who does she think she is to question you—let alone me, your houseguest?"

His houseguest. It hadn't slipped his mind that Rowena had arrived shortly before all this had begun. He couldn't imagine how she might have orchestrated it, though. But then again, there was a good chance that she'd lied about having never met Athena Grant. He had no proof that the women had all known each other, but he'd bet his life on it. The thought unsettled him as he realized he just might be doing exactly that.

He frowned, trying to remember if Rowena had been at the wedding. No, Ginny allegedly hadn't met her yet because Rowena hadn't moved in next door. But that didn't mean the two of them didn't know each other *before* Rowena moved into their building. How could he forget that everything Ginny had told him probably was a lie? But did that include her relationship with Rowena—and Athena Grant? He now knew that all four of them were connected by birth in Russia. All four adopted by American families in Denver. And now there were two more, Sharese and Luca Harmon, adopted in Missoula—not all that far away.

He shook his aching head, afraid it was starting to make sense. Rowena had paid a visit to Sharese, he had to assume she too was in on whatever they were up to. His wife's supposed best friend being here now wasn't a coincidence.

Still he wasn't sure how all the pieces fit together. Athena Grant had been pregnant, that much was true. For some reason she'd tried to contact him with this bogus claim that he was the father of her baby. She even went to the sheriff to get him to talk to her. Why go to all that trouble? Because she was trying to warn him?

Dylan hated to think she'd done it so she could get to him without the others suspecting her true reason. Maybe she'd wanted to tell him about Ginny and his brother. Or warn him that they were coming for him next? If he hadn't gotten stopped on the way out of the gala, he and his brother and wife would have been killed. But if Ginny and Beau were working for Russia, why kill them? His head whirled with too many possibilities.

"Are you all right?" Rowena asked, frowning at him. He realized he'd been rubbing his temples, his head aching. "I could use a drink. Why don't I make one for you too?"

Earlier he'd wanted Rowena to leave. Now though he realized that nothing was quite like he'd thought. No way was he going to let this woman make him a drink. He'd never mistrusted her more than he did right now.

But he also needed to now what was going on. "Maybe it's time you tell me who Rowena Keeling really is."

Chapter Nine

The motel was a former motor inn on the edge of Eureka, U-shaped with scalloped gingerbread trim over the windows and a general look of neglect. Cat entered the office, a bell dinging overhead as she did. The smell of cooked cabbage was almost enough to bring back her morning sickness.

An older woman appeared looking harried as she wiped her hands on her apron. The sign on the registration desk said Karla Brooks, owner. "Only have one double left. Seventy-five dollars. Just one night?" She looked up for the first time and noticed the uniform. Disappointment made her face seem to sag.

"I'm Acting Sheriff Cat Jameson from Fortune Creek. I'd like to ask you a few questions about the woman who gave birth in one of your units."

Sighing, she said, "Could we make this quick. I'm in the middle of making dinner."

"No problem. Did you check her in?" A nod. "Did you get her name?" The woman opened her book and turned it so Cat could see the name Lindsey Martin. "She pay cash?" Another nod. "Was the woman alone?"

"Far as I know."

"Did she seem to be in distress? In pain?" A shrug. "Did she make any request other than a room?"

"Wanted the one at the end."

"Is that the one you gave her?" A nod. "Did you see anyone else with her before she left?"

"Nope."

"I'm asking because the baby she gave birth to is missing and the woman was murdered."

The motel manager swallowed, her eyes misting over. "She was the one?"

"It would appear so. If you saw something, anything at all, it might help us find her killer and—"

"That's the missing baby boy?" Her voice broke. "I have a son." She looked away for a moment before she turned back to Cat. "The next morning, the man in the adjacent room did come by to complain about not being able to get any sleep. Said there were people coming and going. He heard a car pull up, door slam and someone enter that room in the middle of the night. He couldn't get back to sleep because of the moaning." She lifted a brow as if it was obvious what he thought that was about. "Then he said he heard a baby cry. Sometime later he was relieved to hear the person leave and drive away so he could get some sleep."

"He didn't hear the baby cry again?" A head shake. "I'm going to need his name," Cat said. "But this has been really helpful." She thought about asking to see the room but knew there would be nothing to see after all this time.

Outside in the parking lot, she made the call from her patrol SUV. She couldn't help thinking about Athena in labor, giving birth in a motel room instead of a hospital, someone helping her. The same someone who took the baby?

The man who'd been in the adjacent motel room told

her pretty much the same thing the motel owner had. "Do you remember anything else that could help? The sound of the car engine? Perhaps you heard a voice."

"Two females," he said. "Not sure how I know that, just that I do. Also on the car… Sorry, they all sound alike now. There is one thing. The one who left, she opened the car door, but took a few minutes before I heard the engine start up. I think she put the baby in some kind of car seat."

"You didn't look out the window?" She heard him hesitate.

"I did look." He sighed. "I didn't get a good look at the woman, but she definitely had the baby."

Cat pried a description of the woman out of him. He'd gotten a better look than he'd thought. He described Patty Cooper Harper.

She hurriedly called the DCI, Montana Division of Criminal Investigations, and asked for their help in locating Ginny's sister, Patty Cooper Harper.

According to the description the man in the motel room next to Athena's had given Cat, Patty had helped deliver the baby. That meant she had to have known the baby was coming and had been prepared with whatever she needed, including a car seat. That gave Cat hope that the infant was safe and being cared for.

It was dark by the time she headed back to Fortune Creek. She drove along the narrow road, trees etched dark against the fading light of day. The cool spring night, as pretty as it was, made her melancholy. She hadn't let herself think about the future—or the past, determined to live day by day and think only of her daughter growing inside her. Tonight, though, the past came creeping in, bringing tears of pain and sorrow.

Her cell phone rang as she neared Fortune Creek. She hurriedly wiped her tears and picked up.

"This case just keeps getting more interesting," JP said the moment she answered. "Did you know that male cells have been found in maternal blood even decades after a pregnancy?"

"I did not," Cat said, darkness dropping like a cloak over the road ahead. Her headlights cut a swatch of light through the trees standing like sentinels on both sides. "But if you're trying to tell me that you obtained the father of the baby's DNA from the deceased woman's blood—"

"I am."

That stopped her. "I thought we'd have to wait until we found the baby," she said. "You know who fathered Athena Grant's baby?"

"The crime lab just called to tell me that they found a match. Are you sitting down?"

"I am." She braced herself, thinking of how absolutely sure Dylan Walker was that he hadn't fathered Athena Grant's baby. "Is the baby Dylan's?"

"Looked that way at first. Definitely a relative. Does he happen to have a brother?"

"He did. Beau Walker. But he died nine months ago."

"Like I said, interesting case. It appears that Beau is the father of the missing baby, unless there is another brother."

"Nope. Looks like I'm going back out to the ranch to-morrow," she said as she saw the lights of Fortune Creek ahead and felt a strange sense of relief. Something about the night was getting to her, making her feel anxious, making her feel afraid. She was tired from being on her feet all day and hungry. Once in her apartment, she planned to make herself some canned tomato soup and a grilled cheese for dinner.

As she pulled into the tiny, isolated Montana town, she saw Rowena's vehicle was parked up the street. Movement caught her attention. A woman and man arguing in the shadows on the side of the Fortune Creek Hotel across from the sheriff's office. She probably wouldn't have noticed them except that a car went past, its headlights bathed the two in light for a moment. They'd both looked in her direction as if surprised to see a car going by.

She recognized the woman first. Rowena Keeling. The man was one of the two she'd seen going into the hotel whatever day that had been. She was losing track, each day slipping away so fast, and the baby still not found.

Parking behind the sheriff's department building, she made the hike to the second floor over her office. As she did, she speculated on what the two had been arguing about. Clearly, they knew each other. She'd gotten the impression that the only reason Rowena had come to Montana was to see Dylan Walker.

Once in her apartment, she didn't turn on the lights. Instead, she moved to the front window to look out, curious if the two were still out there in the dark. But the spot where they had been was now empty, just like the main street of town. Nor was the vehicle she recognized as Rowena Keeling's still parked down the street in front of the café any longer.

As Cat turned on a lamp and closed the curtains, she made a mental note to ask a few more questions when she saw the woman at Dylan's ranch in the morning.

Unfortunately, things didn't go as she had planned, though. The next morning, she was awakened by the two men she'd seen going into the hotel. They'd flashed their FBI IDs, demanding the file on Athena Grant.

"I'M GOING TO be honest with you, Dylan," his lawyer said. "I don't like them reopening the bombing case. It was never really closed, but all I can think is that they have new evidence. I have to warn you, I have been contacted by the prosecutor's office. They wanted your address in Montana and a phone number. Said they were updating their contact sheet."

He swore under his breath. "Right. You have no idea what might really be going on?"

"No, since they haven't filed any charges against anyone. But if they suspect that your wife and brother were having an affair…they might get the idea that you had something to do with the bombing. Your experience in the service, as well as with your job, puts you in the category of explosives expert."

Dylan didn't need his lawyer to tell him that. "You think someone is trying to frame me?"

"You liquidating everything you owned and moving to Montana does look suspicious."

"Anything I do right now makes me look suspicious," he said, thinking of the trouble that had followed him out here to Montana. Ginny's sister's friend was dead, her baby missing. Did it matter that it wasn't his baby? It would still raise suspicion. The timing couldn't be worse, but maybe that too wasn't a coincidence.

He ended the call and tossed down his phone. No one seemed to know exactly why the investigation into his wife's and brother's deaths was being reopened. But Rowena had been right at least about that. Was she also right about there being some discrepancy with identifying the remains? Or was his lawyer closer to the truth and they were coming after the jealous husband.

Rowena had stopped by early this morning. She'd mentioned a massage appointment in Eureka and had left. He thought this time she might be telling the truth and didn't follow her. Instead, he called an old friend for surveillance equipment, saying he needed to do some tracking. He planned to put it on her car if he got the chance.

Now, standing out on his deck, he ran a hand through his long hair, wondering idly when he'd last gotten it cut. Not that it mattered—at least to him. He had more important things to worry about. The last thing he wanted to think about was Ginny and her death. He could still see her in his mind's eye quickly getting into the town car that pulled up to the curb and it quickly driving away—only to stop up the street. As he'd stepped into the street, planning to try to catch her, it had blown up. He had tried to recall his mindset at that moment. He'd known something was going on with his wife that night. She hadn't been herself. That she would get into a car and take off like that—

At the time he hadn't known who was driving. That came later. He hadn't even known his brother was back in the states. Why had Beau been picking up Ginny? He didn't know, probably never would. Or why she'd seemed to be in such a hurry. At the gala, she'd been by his side on her phone when he'd been stopped on the way out. When he looked again, Ginny was heading for the door. He had excused himself and tried to catch up to her. Hadn't he known then that something was up? That she'd been acting oddly all night? He'd gotten the feeling that there was something she wanted to tell him.

He thought about how upset she'd been when they'd discovered he couldn't father a baby. They'd actually talked about adopting. What a fool he'd been, since after her death, he'd found the birth control pills she'd been faithfully taking in her side of the bathroom cabinet. Ginny had never wanted to have a child with him—or anyone else apparently.

What he would never understand is what his brother had to do with any of it. He assumed Beau and Ginny had been having an affair. He'd found evidence of the two of them meeting at hotels and bars before the day they died. If he had been able to find that evidence, he didn't doubt the investigators looking into the bombing could find it as well.

But what if it hadn't been an affair? What if Beau had gotten involved in something even more dangerous and now the feds had discovered it? Dylan just hoped that the two of them hadn't made it appear that he was part of it.

The gate intercom buzzed, making him start. He moved to it and his heart fell. The acting sheriff was back.

"Need to see you," she said.

He didn't even ask, he just buzzed her in.

Chapter Ten

Dylan was standing on his deck as Cat drove up—in the same spot where she'd first seen him. Only then, she'd thought he might be the ranch caretaker. Today he was dressed much as he had been that day. Jeans, boots, a flannel shirt. Except today, he wore a Stetson over his dark hair.

Under the brim of his hat, he looked just as grim as he had the first day she'd met him. Maybe even grimmer as if now expecting bad news. She glanced toward the cottage and then up to the big house. She didn't see Rowena's car and, while relieved that she wasn't here since she wanted to talk to Dylan alone, Cat hoped she hadn't taken off. She now knew the woman was up to more than just trying to lasso herself a rich rancher.

"Rowena's not here," Dylan said as if reading her mind. "But she hasn't left for good." He didn't sound happy about that. "Come on in. Can I offer you some coffee? Decaf if you'd like. I have tea too."

The FBI agents had grilled her all morning and part of the afternoon about the case. She figured they were going to tell her to step aside and let them take over. To her surprise, they didn't. Apparently, they needed her since they were after who had given the order for Athena to be killed—not the killer.

Were they willing to tell her what all this was about? No. "But you're willing for me to risk my life and my baby's not knowing who I can trust?" she'd demanded.

"Isn't that your job?" one of the agents asked.

She'd smiled. "Yes. What about Dylan Walker?"

"We're not interested in him," one of the agents said.

She'd been relieved to hear them say that. Her instincts about him had been right. She needed to keep trusting herself. But that also meant trusting Dylan Walker. So, it was late afternoon by the time she'd driven out to the ranch.

"Decaf would be fine," she said, smiling her thanks and following him into the kitchen. She noticed that his hair was still damp from a shower. She caught the fresh scent of him and couldn't blame Rowena for having designs on the man—if that's what at least some of this was.

Dylan poured them both a mug of coffee, then offered her a seat at the table. She sat, cupping the mug in her hands. Her daughter had been kicking up a storm all morning.

"I know you didn't come here to tell me that my DNA matches," he said. "I can also tell that the baby hasn't been found so there's still hope."

She smiled in surprise. "I didn't know you were psychic."

"I'm usually not good at reading people, terrible at it, but you…" He shrugged. "You've got news though, but it's not horrible news. Am I right?"

"We have a DNA match. Athena Grant was pregnant with your brother's child."

Dylan put down his mug, sloshing the coffee onto the table—not that he noticed. "What?"

"Unless you have another brother with similar DNA…"

He shook his head. *"Beau?"* He scrubbed his hands over his face. He looked up. "I don't understand."

"From what the coroner said, she probably conceived at your wedding. I'm assuming your brother—"

"Was my best man."

She could see how hard this was on him. "Were you and your brother close?"

"I thought so. But then he died with my wife the night of the gala." He met her gaze. "I'm sure you know all about that. I didn't even know he was back in the states. Usually, he called. I have no idea why he picked up Ginny that night. I saw her on her phone and then she left…" He sighed. "After they both died, I just assumed he was having an affair with her. Everyone assumed that." Dylan looked at her hopefully. "Did Athena say she and Beau were together?"

"She said it happened only once, but that doesn't mean it was true. She lied about everything else. Was Athena maid of honor or maybe a bridesmaid?"

"No, Ginny's sister Patty was her matron of honor. It was a small wedding, just friends and family. A short engagement." He seemed to realize she would wonder why the rush. "We jumped into marriage after knowing each other for just a few months. Ginny…" Shaking his head, he continued, "I thought I knew her. I didn't. I wasn't thinking clearly. It all happened too fast and for the wrong reasons." He let out a bitter laugh. "I wanted what she was offering me, settling down, having a home, kids, that whole happy ever after. Turns out I couldn't have made her pregnant even if she wasn't lying and taking birth control pills."

He stopped speaking as if wishing he hadn't said so much and put his head in his hands for a few moments. "This missing baby…"

"Your nephew."

Dylan looked up and swore. "I'm sorry, it hasn't sunk in yet. This is such a shock. It makes me question everything. You still don't know what she did with the infant?" Cat shook her head. "But why would this woman tell you her name was Lindsey Martin, and I was the father of her baby?"

"Maybe she thought that was the only way she could get to see you."

He stared at her for a moment before raking his hand through his hair. "I think you might be right. Otherwise, it makes no sense. You think there was something she wanted to tell me, and she was using the baby as a way to force me to see her? But wouldn't she just leave it in a note?"

"Maybe she did," Cat said, making him curse.

"And my houseguest destroyed it."

"Yes—after Rowena went to Athena's motel room and left a threatening note that was allegedly from you."

"*What?* Rowena admitted that to you?" he demanded, shooting to his feet to pace the room.

"Apparently she has designs on you," Cat said. "And saw Athena as a threat to her plan."

He stopped pacing to look at her, putting her instincts on alert. He knew something and he was debating telling her. After a moment, he said, "This isn't about Rowena having romantic designs on me. I'm afraid it's more cunning and dangerous."

DYLAN SIGHED AS he considered what he was about to do. "I need to be honest with you." He sat back down near her. He'd survived at his job by trusting his gut. He was going to do the same right now. "Rowena isn't here to seduce me."

"No?"

"No. It's complicated." He rubbed the back of his neck.

"I know you're trying to decide if you can trust me. I would have felt the same way."

"But you don't now?"

"Two agents from the FBI stopped by to see me this morning." Her gaze was intent on him. "They were very interested in Athena Grant, but not you. Tell me about your job overseas."

Dylan looked into her eyes, unable to look away even if he'd wanted to. "You know I can't, but still you're wondering if you can trust me. Yet the FBI doesn't suspect me, right? You wouldn't be here unless they already answered your question. Unfortunately, the bombing and now whatever is going on threatens to expose me and others I worked with."

"Does it involve Athena Grant? If you know something about her death, I need you to tell me. I know you want to trust me. You can. Just be honest with me."

He smiled and nodded. "I didn't know anything, until this morning," he said and proceeded to repeat what his friend had found out about Ginny, Athena, Patty and Rowena. "Lindsey Martin was the name of the mother who adopted Athena."

"That would explain why she used that name. Did she think you would recognize it?"

"Maybe. She could have thought that Ginny had told me her mother's name. She hadn't. But all I can think is what are the chances they all four didn't know they were adopted from Russia?"

She hugged herself as if feeling the same chill he had at the news. He wondered for a moment if he'd made a mistake by telling her. He told himself he didn't know this woman. Trusting her could be a mistake. Yet, he didn't believe that. Still, it was risky. But the acting sheriff was already in danger the moment she got the Athena Grant case.

Cat seemed to digest what he'd told her before she said, "You think the four are part of a sleeper cell?"

"I do," he admitted, glad he could say it out loud. "I followed Rowena to Libby where she met with someone named Sharese Harmon. Turns out that Sharese and her brother Luca were also both born in Russia and adopted by a family in Missoula."

Cat was shaking her head. "You think they are all involved?" He nodded. "But why kill Athena?"

"Why kill Ginny and my brother?" he asked with a shake of his head.

"I probably shouldn't be sharing this with you, but the two FBI agents who came by my office this morning demanded everything I had on Athena Grant's death."

"I knew it." He swore, looking relieved. "So, we are on to something. It could be why I've heard that they are looking into the bombing again. What a damned fool I was for marrying a woman with this kind of secret."

"She never told you she was adopted?" He shook his head. "You think it's all tied together, the bombing, what's happening now?"

"I bought this ranch before the wedding, but after the bombing and what I learned about my wife and brother, I moved out here because I wanted to be alone. I was convinced my cover was blown. But then nothing happened." He shook his head. "But I should have known the moment Rowena showed up here. I was certainly suspicious about her motives, but then when all the rest of this began to happen…"

"As I said earlier, I think Athena was trying to tell you something," Cat said. "Which could explain why Rowena destroyed her note telling you where she would be—and then went to the motel to threaten her, leaving her a note when she didn't find her. She was warning her to stay away from you and not tell you whatever it was she really wanted you to know. Obviously, Rowena knew Athena wasn't pregnant with your child, but maybe she wanted you to know about your brother's baby, don't you think? By the time she came to me, she must have known they would kill her. I'm sure she was worried about what would happen to her infant."

He nodded. "I think you're right. She wanted me to know what was going on, but also about my nephew and maybe how my brother was involved." Getting to his feet, he said, "I could use a drink. Can I get you a sparkling water?"

She nodded and followed him into the living room. As he poured Bourbon into a rocks glass, he spoke as if running it all through his mind. "I never could understand what Ginny saw in Rowena. Once she moved next door to us, she was at our house all the time. It felt...off. I got the feeling that Ginny didn't like her, and I certainly didn't. But it wasn't like Ginny not to get her out of her life if that was the case. She'd dropped others who'd tried to hang on to her in a heartbeat."

He brought his drink and her sparkling water over and motioned that they should sit in the living room where it was more comfortable.

"Where do you think your brother fits in?"

"I have no idea. Knowing my brother, he could have been working with them. Maybe he only slept with Athena one time. Or maybe they were lovers and they were working together. But why kill him?" He took a sip of his drink.

Cat thought for a moment. "If Ginny wanted out, is there a reason she would have asked your brother for help?"

He felt his flesh rise in goose bumps. "Instead of me?" He shook his head. "Athena and Ginny must have dragged him into something. I can't imagine what help Beau would have been. Then again, I'd lost track of what he'd been doing while abroad. Who knows what he might have gotten into. Knowing my brother, he might have thought he could handle it and that got him killed."

CAT HAD A moment to wonder what she was doing. Dylan had opened up to her. She'd told him about the FBI. They'd both revealed probably more than they should have since she was the law and not long ago he'd been a suspect. But he was also a man with a past, one apparently he needed to keep hidden.

We all have our secrets, she thought as she looked at him. The question was, did she trust him? *With your life?* She'd better because she was gambling on it by opening up to him.

"This changes things," she said, realizing it was true.

"Look, I understand, Cat—sorry, I meant to say Sheriff. I've been worried that I involved you and your baby in my mess and it's dangerous."

She shook her head. "It's my job. But please, I think after this we could call each other by our first names—at least when we're alone."

"That would be nice. We've wandered into questionable territory. My fault. I just thought you should know what I found out, what we might be dealing with."

What *we* might be dealing with. He was right. They were both involved in this. It made sense to help each other since she couldn't shake the feeling that if this was what they suspected, they were both at risk. Also, she would bet that Dylan might have more expertise in this area than she did.

The two FBI agents had said they would be in touch and had driven away, so she couldn't count on them. All she knew was that at least one of them had met with Rowena. Maybe Dylan had some thoughts about that after what he'd discovered today.

Taking a breath, she said, "I saw one of the FBI agents in the alleyway by the hotel in town the other night with Rowena. They appeared to be arguing."

"You think Rowena is working with them? Or at least pretending to?"

Cat shrugged. "Yesterday I found out that someone helped birth the baby. We know that Athena nursed the infant, then it appears whoever helped her left, possibly with the infant since the man in the next room didn't hear the baby cry again. What might have happened after that, we don't know. In the wee hours of the morning, Athena was shot, killed and dumped along the road near Fortune Creek—just miles from the sheriff's department."

"You're thinking Rowena?" He shook his head. "I can't imagine her delivering a baby in my wildest dreams. But there is one person my friend hasn't been able to locate. Patty Cooper, Ginny's sister."

"I thought of that, too. I'm hoping if true, she has the baby and won't let anything happen to him." She told Dylan what the man at the motel had told her about the person's description fitting Patty and that the person possibly had a car seat for the baby.

Dylan swore. "If only I'd been here the morning Athena stopped by to see me," he said.

"I doubt it would have saved her since Rowena would have found out either way." He nodded and took another drink. She opened her water. "If she is working with the feds, then why not let Athena talk to you?"

"Like I said, she could be a double agent. I wouldn't put anything past that woman," Dylan said.

"What are you going to do about her?" Cat asked.

"My first instinct is to throw her out. But if I want answers, then I need to let her think I'm not on to her."

DYLAN REALIZED THAT she hadn't seemed to have heard him. "Cat?" He liked the sound of her name on his lips. He liked her, and that scared him. He'd liked her from the first time he met her—when she'd come out to accuse him of all kinds of things. He thought about the last woman he fell for quickly and told himself to slow down.

Cat seemed to understand what they might be digging into, but he couldn't stand the thought of anything happening to her or her baby. They already had one mother dead, her baby missing.

"I thought you'd bought the ranch after your wife was killed," she said, looking lost in thought.

"No, months before the wedding."

"Your wife knew about the ranch?"

"I'm not sure what you're getting at, but yes, it was kind of a wedding present to us both, a new beginning." He could see where it could be misconstrued, though, that he had been planning to kill his wife and her lover, but he didn't think that was what Cat was getting at.

"The two of you came out here to see it?" she asked.

He started to say yes but remembered. "Ginny came out earlier to furnish the big house. I came out later." He frowned. "What are you thinking?"

"Have you been over to the house since you've been

back this time? Especially since Rowena has been staying there?"

"No, why?"

"When I went over there to ask her a few questions, I noticed something that at the time didn't seem odd but does now. It looked as if an object had been dragged out from the wall in the living room. It left a mark on the carpet. Also the doors on several of the high cabinets in the hallway had been left slightly ajar." She met his gaze. "Now I'm wondering if Rowena had gone through the place maybe—"

"Looking for something?"

"Had you ever planned to live in the big house?" she asked.

"With Ginny…" he said, "since I thought we both wanted a lot of children." He felt his eyes widen. "You think Ginny left something over there knowing I wouldn't look for it—let alone find it if anything happened to her."

Cat touched the end of her nose and grinned at him. "Think there's time to check it out before Rowena returns?"

"Let's go."

Chapter Eleven

Cat had no idea what they were looking for. But maybe Rowena hadn't either. The house was enormous. She could see why Dylan hadn't wanted to stay here—even with his wife—until they had children to fill it. She wondered how Ginny had felt about that.

Once inside, he said, "Shall we start on the upper level and work our way down?" He pointed to a wooden panel that magically opened as he touched it, exposing a small elevator. "Ladies first."

She smiled and stepped into the confined space, which normally wouldn't have bothered her. But when Dylan entered, it suddenly felt even smaller. He was average height and weight, but in the elevator, he seemed a whole lot larger. She found herself very aware of him and his enticing male scent.

Keep this professional, she thought and almost laughed. *Call me Cat*. They were way past professional. She'd told him things she had no business telling him—but he'd done the same. He however wasn't the law, she was. Yet, they wouldn't be here in this house looking for clues if they both hadn't shared what they knew. Didn't that make her a good investigator?

She didn't kid herself as the elevator door opened and she quickly escaped. The scent of him followed her, as did the memory of his flat stomach, the muscles of his arms, the way his jeans fit in the back. She felt herself flush.

"It was hot in there, huh?" he said, looking a little flushed himself. "Shall we start in the master?"

"The rooms are all furnished?" she asked, diverting her lurid thoughts reminding her how long ago she'd had sex, let alone had a man hold her, make love to her. Was it any wonder Dylan Walker had brought out a need in her for human warmth and support? She was having a baby by herself. Not to mention the hormones coursing through her that made her more vulnerable to even a little attention from a man who was kind like Dylan.

"Ginny ordered it all and saw to the delivery. She wanted it ready when we got here."

"Even though you told her you wanted to live in the cottage for a while?"

"I'm sure she thought she could change my mind," he said under his breath.

It didn't take long to search the room—and realize that Rowena had already looked here.

"If we had some idea of what she might have been looking for," Dylan said. "Drugs? Money? Evidence?"

"Insurance maybe," Cat said, making him stop to look at her and nod.

"Insurance to keep them from ratting each other out. Maybe you're right. Maybe Ginny was trying to get out. Maybe she did go to my brother for help. I'd like to think that rather than the alternative."

They went from room to room, but Cat quickly realized the place was just too big and there were too many places to hide things. "Do you happen to have the blueprints for this place?"

"Hoping for a secret room, stairway, compartment? Sorry, there isn't one."

"What about a safe?"

"Not that I know of. But Ginny could have had one installed, I guess. Even if she did, I wouldn't know the combination." She heard his stomach growl as they reached the bottom floor. "There's also the chance that Rowena already found it—if there was anything to find."

He shook his head. "Now that you've mentioned it, I would say she was definitely looking for something. I can see where she's been in every room of the house. I doubt she found it or I suspect she'd be gone by now. I keep thinking about you seeing her arguing with one of the FBI agents. They want something from her, apparently. Something maybe she hasn't been able to produce."

They went through the bottom floor and found nothing suspicious but did find a mess in the large bedroom that Rowena was obviously using. Dylan looked at her as if to ask, "Shall we take a look through her things?"

Cat shook her head. "It wouldn't be in her things. I think we should quit. It's getting late, and I think you need to get something to eat."

He chuckled at that as they left the house and walked back toward the cottage. She'd wondered originally why he seemed to avoid the big house. Now that she knew he had planned to live there with his wife at some point and fill the place with children, it made perfect sense.

The beautiful spring evening felt as if the air was rarified. The breeze breathed the scent of pine. Twilight cast a silver glow over them. It felt as if they were the last two people alive. Was that why she wasn't any more anxious to leave than he was for her to go as they walked toward the cottage.

"You're a good listener. But you know everything about me," he said as they neared the cottage. "I don't know anything about you. Your baby…" He glanced at her baby bump. "If I'm intruding just—"

"I'm having a girl."

"Congratulations. You and your husband must be excited."

She looked down at the gold band on the finger of her left hand and then up at him before she said, "My husband was killed in a car accident six months ago. We were living in Libby because of his job with the forest service. He'd been on a fishing trip on Lake Koocanusa and heading back when he was hit by a drunk driver. He died in the Eureka hospital. I didn't find out I was pregnant until after he was gone. I never got the chance to tell him."

"I'm so sorry. I should never have asked."

"It's all right. We're fine," she said smiling as she put her hand on her stomach. "I'd just completed my law enforcement training. I was lucky there was an opening in Fortune Creek for a pregnant newbie where there was hardly ever any crime."

"Right." He laughed, surprised at how good it felt. "Well, I couldn't tell you were new at this, if that helps."

"I shouldn't have admitted it."

"It's our secret. A murder though?"

She chuckled. "The truth is I was so bored I wished for something, anything, to investigate. As they say, be careful what you wish for."

"I have complete confidence in you solving this case,"

he said as they reached the cottage, and he led the way into the bright kitchen.

She took a chair, realizing that she was tired.

"Stay and have dinner with me."

Was it that late? She glanced at her phone. "I completely lost track of time."

Looking up at him, she smiled. "It's just so pleasant sitting here in your kitchen. I've been on my feet all day. But I really should go."

"I swear this is why I bought this place, because of this cottage. It was love at first sight. Please stay, I really would love the company. I have steaks for the grill, vegetables for a salad, if you'll stay."

She glanced toward the front of the cottage. "What about your houseguest?"

"Seriously, you'd be doing me a huge favor. She left earlier, and I have no idea when she's coming back, but she's not invited to dinner. She was allegedly a friend of my wife's. Not mine."

"Does she know anyone in the area?" Cat asked.

"Other than Sharese and Luca, if he is in the area, I have no idea. When she leaves the ranch, I just assume she's sightseeing or gone to get a massage—at least that's what she's led me to believe. But maybe there are even more adoptees here in Montana."

"You don't trust her."

"Not any further than I can pick her up and throw her. My stomach is growling. I'm going to get dinner going if that's all right with you."

Cat told herself it was unprofessional to stay for dinner even as she said, "I'd love it, if you're sure you don't mind the company."

He left the room, returning with a small upholstered stool. "Put your feet up. I happen to love to cook and I'm sick of cooking for myself."

"I think I know why your houseguest doesn't want to leave."

"Believe me, she doesn't get this treatment. Anyway, her only interest seems to be my bar. Or whatever Ginny might have hidden in the house."

She realized she was way beyond professional ethics at this point. She'd told this man about the investigation. She'd also told him about Taylor's death, practically pouring out her entire life's history. So why didn't she feel even a twinge of guilt about that?

Because she trusted him. Because the FBI trusted him. Because she liked him, and it felt good being here with him. Even that should have made her feel guilty, but it didn't.

Not just that, it was nice out here, the pine-scented breeze blowing in through the open windows—so different from her efficient apartment over the sheriff's department. Anyway, there was little she could do back at the office. Helen would have left her post long ago. All after-hours calls to the sheriff's department were routed to Eureka's PD. They would call if she was needed.

Cat knew she was making excuses to stay because she wanted to. It felt so good sitting here with this man who was about to cook for her. He'd gone through so much. She felt a kinship with him.

She also liked watching him cook, the efficiency with the way he worked, getting the vegetables out of the re-frigerator, choosing the right size bowl and spoon before washing the produce and carefully chopping it up.

As she sat watching him make dressing for the salad,

she told him about her small efficiency apartment over the sheriff's department. "I do some cooking, mostly for the baby. She's not really picky."

"When are you due, if I may ask?"

"In two months—about the time Sheriff Brandt Parker returns to take over the job again. He keeps extending his honeymoon. I'm beginning to wonder if he's ever coming back."

"How'd you meet your husband?" he asked, slicing a cucumber with a precision that awed her.

"Boy next door, same babysitter when we were little, same teachers at school." She shrugged. "We'd just always been together. It was…comfortable."

He stopped making the salad to look at her. "It sounds nice."

"It was. I miss him."

"I'm sure you do," Dylan said. "Especially now."

She put a hand over her baby bump and felt her daughter practicing her soccer moves. "We'd been married since college. We always thought we'd have kids someday. Our lives were so busy, we weren't worried when I didn't get pregnant. We thought we had time."

He looked away as if he didn't know what to say. "I'm going to get the grill going."

"I'm sorry, I didn't mean to make you uncomfortable," she said quickly.

"No, it's just that I wanted what you had with your husband, and I thought that's what I was getting with Ginny." He shook his head. "After her death, I found out she'd been lying to me about probably everything."

"I'm sorry," Cat said. "That has to have left you with a lot of mixed emotions."

He laughed. "That's what these feelings are? On top of

that, the prosecutor is reopening the car bombing investigation. Not that I think it was ever really closed since they never found out who did it. Finding out that my brother had a baby boy who's missing… It's a lot. I'm not sure how I feel about anything right now. Except steaks," he said brightening. "How do you like yours?"

"Rare."

"A woman after my own heart."

He headed out the back door. Cat leaned back and shut her eyes. She felt herself relax to the point that she could have fallen asleep if the front door hadn't banged open and Rowena stormed into the kitchen.

"Well, isn't this cozy," she said, frowning at Cat. "So where is he?"

"Outside lighting the grill."

Rowena glanced at the salad bowl and the plates Dylan had placed on the counter. "What is this?" she demanded.

"Dinner." Cat caught the smell of alcohol wafting off the woman. "It got late. Dylan was worried about me and the baby not getting dinner." Why was she explaining herself? Because it had felt a little too intimate? Because she liked Dylan and shouldn't, since officially he could still be considered a suspect? Or because she'd let herself enjoy being around another man after Taylor had only been gone six months?

"You and the baby," Rowena said with what sounded like disgust. "Dylan has always wanted one of those. Too bad you're married and unavailable. I can tell he likes you."

The back door slammed as he returned. "What are you doing here, Rowena?" he said, barely giving her a glance.

"I live here," she snapped.

"You're a guest of mine in the other house," he said and gave her a get-a-clue face. "You're lucky the acting sheriff doesn't arrest you for driving under the influence. I suggest you walk to the house, so she doesn't have to."

Rowena stood there for a moment glaring daggers at the two of them before storming out.

"Whatever her reason for still being here, I don't like it, but at least here, I can keep an eye on her. There has to be a reason she's in Montana other than what she's told me." he said, taking down a platter, then pulling the steaks from the refrigerator to season them.

Cat felt the same way. "I wish we knew what she'd been looking for over at the house, but I wouldn't ignore her interest in you."

He turned to look at her, then out the window. "That's just a front for what she's really after." With that he headed out back, promising to return with a beautifully cooked steak for her.

Cat considered that. She thought it was jealousy that had made Rowena threaten Athena. Now she suspected differently. Just because Cat had seen her with one of the FBI agents also didn't mean Rowena wasn't capable of murder.

Five women and one man with at least one thing in common—their Russian births and adoptions. Two were now dead, Ginny Cooper Walker and Athena Grant. Patty Cooper was missing and so was Athena's infant son. What were the chances that Rowena knew where they could find both Patty and the baby? And now Sharese Harmon and her brother Luca might be involved? Was it possible one of them had the baby?

Cat closed her eyes, her head aching as she tried to make sense of it all. Tomorrow she would tell the DCI team about Sharese and her brother. She almost hoped they would find Patty and, fingers crossed, the baby. She kept thinking about that little infant boy, worrying about him.

What seemed like only seconds later, Dylan touched her shoulder waking her up. She felt electricity arc through her at his touch. She sat up to the stomach-growling scent of grilled steak.

"Hungry?" he asked. When he smiled like that, he was even more handsome. She felt a hard tug on her heart-strings as heat raced to her center. She'd loved her husband. But he'd never made her feel the way she was feeling right now.

"Starved," she said, realizing how true it was—and not just for dinner.

Chapter Twelve

It was late by the time Cat drove home. Dylan had tried to get her to stay. He had no idea how badly she wanted to, but not in one of his many guest bedrooms.

She felt as if she'd already stepped over a boundary she shouldn't have as acting sheriff. Worse was where she'd let her thoughts—let alone her desires—go during dinner.

She felt like a schoolgirl with her first crush and was embarrassed by it. She had to remind herself that she was seven months pregnant, a recent widow and acting sheriff. She had no business feeling these emotions, let alone these desires.

Yet, she did feel them. Worse, she fantasized about fulfilling them—if she wasn't seven months pregnant, a recent widow and acting sheriff.

Dylan had proven to be a wonderful host—and a very good cook. Her steak was perfect. She'd had him write down his salad dressing recipe for her since she'd wanted to lick her bowl it was so good.

Once in her small apartment, she checked her messages, then showered and was about to get in bed when Taylor's sister called. She and Lilly had always been like sisters. Cat told her about tonight. "I feel so guilty."

"No," her friend said. "Taylor wouldn't want you to. Anyway, I know he wasn't the love of your life. You're young. You haven't found him yet, and when you do, you go for it, Cat. You deserve to find that kind of love, passionate, crazy, no-holds-barred love."

"Wait a minute," she said laughing. "Lilly? Are we still talking about me? Or about you now? Have you found yours?"

"Well, if I did, what would you say?"

"I'd say go for it." They both laughed. "Okay, now tell me all about it."

An hour later, Cat finally crawled into bed smiling to herself because her sister-in-law had fallen head over heels in love and she couldn't be happier for her.

She must have fallen right to sleep because the next thing she knew she was jolted from a very erotic, wonderful dream to the ringing of the phone.

Picking up, she barely got out, "Acting Sheriff Cat Jameson," before JP interrupted her.

"We got another one."

She tried to clear her head. "Another one what?"

"Dead body."

Her heart in her throat, Cat said, "Not the—"

"Baby? No, sorry," JP said quickly. "An adult male, no identification on him or the female, murdered with him. What is it about you?" he asked. "Three murders in a matter of days? It's a regular crime spree."

Cat disconnected, fully awake, her mind racing. She felt goose bumps ripple over her skin. What was going on?

She got out of bed and moved to the front window to look out across the street at the hotel. The alley where she'd seen Rowena arguing with one of the agents was empty.

The SUV the two feds had been driving was gone. Would they be back when they heard about two more murders?

She feared that she was on her own as she dressed and headed for the murder scene—this one along the Yaak River, not far from the Canadian border. Her daughter was kicking up a storm by the time she pulled over alongside the other law enforcement vehicles and got out.

The bodies had been dumped much like Athena Grant's and not far from the road. With all these places to bury remains, she could only assume whoever killed them had either wanted them to be found or didn't care that they would be.

"Any ID on them?" she asked when she saw JP.

He shook his head. "Want to take a look?" He glanced at her baby bump as if worried she wasn't up to this.

"Yes," she said emphatically. Both bodies had been re-trieved from the ditch and now lay in body bags on two stretchers. JP unzipped first the female's. Cat braced her-self, afraid she was going to recognize the woman. If was a relief when she didn't.

"Shot the same way?" she asked, and JP grunted as he re-zipped the bag and reached for the male's bag. As the zipper came down, she felt a shock. "I know this one. He's FBI." She could feel JP staring at her in surprise. "I saw him across the street from the sheriff's department argu-ing with a woman—not this one, someone else."

"You're sure he's FBI?" JP asked.

"I saw them when they checked into the hotel in For-tune Creek. They paid me a visit the other morning, and I saw their credentials."

"Well, it should make identifying him easier," the coro-ner said. "Let's get them both back to the morgue. I'll send prints right away and let you know."

On the way back to Fortune Creek, she finally admitted to herself that she was in over her head. She put in the call to the DCI and got crime team leader Hank Ferguson on the phone. She quickly updated him on the situation. He promised to send a couple of investigators, but also to keep her in the loop. Cat thanked him and barely got disconnected when Dylan called.

"I've had my people looking for Patty Cooper Harper. I have a lead down in Kalispell. Thought you might want to go with me to check it out. If she has my nephew— Well, I might need an officer of the law with me," he said.

She chuckled. "I suspect you can handle yourself in most situations."

"I hear hesitation in your voice."

"It's not that. I just turned the case and the new one over to DCI. They are sending investigators."

"Great, so you're free to follow a lead," he said. "I promise I won't step on your toes, Sheriff. Except maybe when we're slow dancing. Thought we should take my pickup— your patrol SUV kind of stands out in a crowd. Pick you up at your office?"

She thought of Helen and her eagle eyes and sharp tongue. "Better if I come to you out at the ranch since it's on the way. See you soon." She didn't mention that she was already on the road. Or that there had been two more murders. That they were killed in the same way Athena was told her the cases were connected.

But what that had to do with Dylan's nephew, she had no idea. She suspected the baby hadn't been part of the plan and was now a problem. She just hoped he wasn't disposable.

DYLAN WAS SURPRISED how much he had been looking forward to the trip to Kalispell with Cat. He had a good feeling they were getting closer to finding his nephew. Yesterday had been the best day he'd spent at the ranch. While he loved his horseback rides, he realized now that he'd been lonely, which surprised him. He'd thought he wanted and needed to be alone so he could deal with everything.

He'd spent months dwelling in the past, blaming himself for everything that had happened and trying to understand why he hadn't seen it coming. How could he not blame himself for marrying Ginny so quickly? He had to take some responsibility for the tragedies that had followed.

Learning what he had about Ginny and the others, gave him hope that he could find out the truth and finally put the past behind him. But nothing had made him feel more hopeful than Cat. Look what she'd been through, was still going through, and how she was dealing with it.

He admired her courage and conviction. Hell, he thought with a laugh as he waited for her to buzz in at the gate, he was half in love with her, as ridiculous as it sounded even to him. But he hadn't been able to even think about the future before she'd come into his miserable existence.

Minutes later, he buzzed her in and went out on the deck to wait for her. He had a good feeling about today. With luck they would be at least one step closer to finding his nephew and making sure he was safe. He couldn't imagine going through this without Cat.

CAT SETTLED INTO the seat of Dylan's pickup as he drove off the ranch. It was one of those breathtaking Montana days in the spring when the sky was so blue it almost hurt to look at it. Not a cloud scudded across that big sky. The air smelled so good, Cat wanted to bottle it. She smiled, aware that this was the first day in a long time that she'd felt this good.

"What are you smiling about?" Dylan asked, a laugh in his voice.

"This day, being here...with you and following this lead to Patty Cooper," she said, glancing at him. "I just have a good feeling that she has the baby, that he's safe and that we're getting closer to finding him. I also feel like we're running away. It's a nice feeling. Playing hooky. I should feel guilty, but I turned the investigation over to the state crime investigators. I know when I'm out of my league."

"You do seem freer," he said, "but I can't imagine you walking away completely. You're good at your job. Don't sell yourself short."

She chuckled at that. "And you just met me a matter of days ago. But you're right. I'm still working the case, but it's good to admit when you're in over your head and let the seasoned professionals take over. There were two more murders last night. One of those murdered was an FBI agent. I'm sure they'll get involved now, as well as DCI."

"Two more murders?" He raised a brow. "Are the cases connected?"

"They were killed the same way Athena was, so I'd say yes."

"I just hope we can find Patty and my nephew. After that, let the FBI at it," he said, and she agreed.

"Tell me about this lead you have," she said as they passed Whitefish.

"I called around to motels, giving them a description of Patty and saying she might have had an infant with her. I also had a few friends involved doing the same thing."

"And you got a hit," Cat said, surprised. She and the deputies from other departments hadn't had any luck. But then again, they hadn't had a good description of Patty, while Dylan had met her at his wedding.

"Actually, the woman I spoke to said she was glad I called. She was wondering who to contact about the car. It seems Patty left the car with the license plate number she'd put down on her motel registration form in their parking lot."

Cat shook her head in awe. "Nice work." He would have made a good cop. While she didn't know exactly what work he'd done outside his career, he'd made it sound as if it had been for the government So, she shouldn't have been surprised, but he kept exceeding her expectations.

Once at the hotel, Cat introduced herself to the manager who led them out to the car parked at the far side of the parking lot. It was a nondescript sedan with Montana plates, probably a rental that hadn't been picked up yet. Patty had either been picked up by someone else or had the rental agency bring her another car. Maybe they had planned to come back for this one.

Dylan pulled a device from behind the seats of his pickup that looked like a metal ruler only thinner. It took him only a few seconds to unlock the car. By then Cat had pulled on a pair of latex gloves. She'd learned to always carry several pairs in her business.

The first thing she saw was the blood on the passenger side seat. For a moment, she was taken aback, especially when she saw what looked like a wadded-up bloody baby blanket on the floor. The interior had a smell that threatened to turn her stomach. She made the call to DCI team leader Hank Ferguson so they could get a forensics team to go over the car. Then she finished searching the inside.

When she got ready to check the trunk, she hesitated. Dylan met her gaze. "You want me to do it?" he asked.

She shook her head and braced herself, afraid of what she would find. As the trunk lid yawned open, she saw with relief that it was empty. "Athena wasn't killed in the car," Cat said as she slammed the trunk lid. "But I suspect she was transported in it before she was killed and dumped along the road. It would explain the blood on the passenger seat and floorboard. Have to wait until forensics finishes with it to know for sure."

She looked toward the hotel, thinking of Patty and the baby. Where were they now? Patty could have taken him out of Montana, maybe even out of the country. Unless there was a reason she had to stay around here.

"Why didn't she leave the area right away?" Cat asked herself out loud. "She had to know that everyone would be looking for the baby once Athena's body was found. Why stay?"

Dylan shook his head. "Is she waiting for Rowena to go with them?"

"Maybe," she said as she walked to his pickup and climbed in. "I'll make sure the FBI gets photos of Patty and Rowena in case they decide to skip the country with the baby."

Her cell rang. Checking, she saw it was JP. She picked up.

"He wasn't FBI," the coroner said without preamble.

She knew at once he was talking about the man who'd been murdered the night before. "Then who is he?"

"A Russian geologist over here on a student visa," JP said. "At least that's how he got the visa. The real FBI have been notified."

"And the woman?"

"Nothing yet. I heard you turned the cases over to the DCI."

"It was time," Cat said. "I'm still working the case, though. I needed help."

"Smart decision," he said. She thought she heard pride in his voice. "You've done good." With that he was gone.

She disconnected, feeling a little better. She admired and respected JP, so a compliment from him was worth gold.

"You're not giving up," Dylan said, then looked over at her having obviously heard enough of the conversation to read between the lines. "Calling in reinforcements is just good business."

Cat had to smile even as she fought tears. She wasn't as upset about messing up with the counterfeit FBI agents as she was in what it meant. The men who'd posed as FBI agents said they had no interest in Dylan, and she'd taken their word for him no longer being a suspect in the case.

"But no one should count you out."

She nodded, but she wasn't all that sure that her judgment wasn't flawed—especially when it came to Dylan Walker. She'd taken the word of a man posing as an FBI agent that Dylan Walker could be trusted. Had she jumped at it because she'd wanted to believe it? Because she liked him. More than liked him.

"I should probably get back," she said, hand going to her stomach to feel her daughter moving around. To remind her what was at stake. She couldn't make this about herself. She'd never been able to. She took a couple of deep breaths.

"Anything you want to talk about?" Dylan asked as they climbed into his pickup.

She thought about just brushing it off as "work stuff" but stopped herself as he began to drive through town toward the road that would take them back to his ranch. "Those two FBI agents I told you about? They weren't agents. The one who's dead was a Russian here on a student visa."

Dylan said nothing for a moment. "Now you're thinking of me again as a suspect." He met her gaze. "What do you want to know?"

"Did you leave the ranch last night?"

"No. Can anyone substantiate that? No. I didn't see Rowena's car when I went to bed. I have no idea what time she came in, but she was back this morning when I left. I haven't talked to her."

"What about your gate intercom system? Does it keep track of visitors?"

He chuckled at that. "Before you and Rowena showed up, I hadn't had any visitors for three months so no reason to install a video camera that recorded every wild animal that walked past."

"I don't mean to sound—"

"Suspicious? But you are and that's okay. I don't mind."

She didn't believe that. He looked hurt. She thought about how happy he'd looked when he'd picked her up. She hated that she'd taken that away from him. While she wanted to tell him that she trusted him, she wasn't sure she could right now.

Cat looked out her side window, thinking what a long ride it would be on the way back to Fortune Creek. She was wishing there was something she could say when she spotted Rowena on a side street.

"Stop!" she ordered Dylan. He hit his brakes and pulled over, no doubt hearing the alarm in her voice. She was already getting out as she said, "It's Rowena coming out of what appears to be a baby shop."

DYLAN SWORE. Cat was out of the pickup almost before he got it fully stopped, but he wasn't far behind her. Ahead he could see Rowena carrying a shopping bag with a children's shop logo on it. She slowed, then stopped to take a phone call as they approached her from behind.

All Dylan heard her say into the phone was, "I'm doing the best I can. You yelling at me isn't helping." Rowena looked alarmed and instantly disconnected when she saw the two of them. "What are you doing here?"

"I want to ask you the same thing," the sheriff said. "Been doing some baby shopping?"

Rowena pulled the bag closer to herself. "My niece just had a baby. I was getting her a present."

"Girl or boy?" Cat said, grabbing the top of the bag and pulling it open enough to see what the woman had bought. "A boy, huh? Where is Athena Grant's baby?"

"Who?"

"Don't play dumb," Dylan snapped. "Where is my nephew?"

Rowena looked around nervously as if afraid someone was watching them. "I don't know what you're talking about."

"Murder is what we're talking about and kidnapping," Cat said. "I'm worried about that baby's safety. I think it's time you told me what's going on."

Rowena shook her head and tried to walk around them, but Dylan grabbed her arm. "Enough games. I want my nephew."

"You have no idea what you've gotten involved in," the woman said through gritted teeth as she again looked around, even more nervous now as she pulled free.

"Where were you taking these baby clothes?" Cat demanded. "You need to take us to the baby."

"I told you, they're for my niece's new baby."

"You're lying," Dylan said. "If anything happens to my nephew—"

"The FBI is now involved," Cat said. "The *real* FBI. I saw you talking to a man a couple of nights ago who was pretending to be an agent, but he's now dead, along with an older woman who was with him." She saw surprise on Rowena's face followed quickly by fear.

"Don't threaten me," Rowena snapped looking cornered. "Either of you. You have no idea." She took a step backward, then another.

"Rowena—"

"Arrest me or leave me alone." With that she turned and hurried down the street.

"She knows I don't have enough evidence to arrest her," Cat said. "But let's try to follow her."

Unfortunately, by the time they got back to his pickup, Rowena was gone.

"At least she's buying clothes for the baby," Cat said, her voice breaking.

Dylan pulled over in a residential area under a large weeping willow tree. He cut the engine and turned to look at her. "I hate that you don't trust me now."

The large tree formed a canopy over them, cocooning them in dark shade away from the rest of the world. "I didn't say—"

"You don't have to. I can see it in your eyes. Cat…" He seemed at a loss for words for a few moments. "Right or wrong, I started caring about you. If this case is as dangerous as it appears—and Rowena claims, maybe you should distance yourself from it—and from me. Otherwise…" He reached over, his fingers trailing down her bare arm from the elbow to the wrist before pulling back.

"I can't do that, not from the case…not from you," she said as she met his gaze and held it. "I've never felt…"

"Like this?" He nodded. "I've never wanted anyone the way I do you."

WAS THIS REAL? Cat couldn't believe it. She let out a laugh that was close to a sob. She'd wanted to feel like this her whole life, this kind of all-consuming passion, this desire that made her feel more alive than she'd ever felt. Now that she did meet someone who stoked those fires of desire, she was *pregnant*.

"A woman seven months pregnant?" she cried.

"You couldn't be more desirable than you are right now." He leaned toward her, gently cupping the back of her head with his hand as he kissed her at first gently, then with growing passion. Her mouth opened to his in a wordless surrender as she dug her fingers into his strong shoulders.

She felt her nipples pebble, pressing hard against her bra. Her pulse thundered in her ears, an ache of longing in her chest that shot all the way to her center. She told herself this wasn't her, yet she knew this had been the missing part of her for years, the passionate unfulfilled part of her she'd unconsciously dreamed of.

"We can't go back to my place or yours," he said as he pulled back, sounding breathless. His gaze held hers. "I know somewhere we can go."

Was she really doing this? She nodded.

Dylan kept his hand on her leg as he drove. Cat spent the short drive trying to talk some sense into herself. She didn't have to go through with this. He would understand. Stopping this before it got started was the sensible thing to do.

She'd spent her life being sensible. Isn't that why she'd married Taylor? Because it was the sensible, safe thing to do. She'd known that he loved her, she'd known him practically her whole life. There would be no surprises. Even the first time they made love had been comfortable—expected. They'd been inseparable as friends for years. Of course, there hadn't been fireworks or passion. There had been companionship, safety, a predictable life.

Except a drunk driver had taken that away and now here she was, pregnant with Taylor's baby about to do what?

She looked over at Dylan. The way her heart was pounding she felt as if she was about to leap off a cliff. She was definitely about to leave her comfort zone and careen into the unknown. Her pulse pounded at the thought as Dylan pulled up in front of a beautiful house overlooking Flathead Lake.

"It's my brother Beau's," he said and cut the engine. "He's the reason I bought the ranch out here."

Chapter Thirteen

Her legs felt weak, her heart a hammer against her ribs, as Dylan opened her door and helped her out of his truck as if they were on a date. That sensible side of her kept yelling *Stop! You don't know this man. This isn't you.*

No, it wasn't her and there was something liberating about that. But why now? Why under these circumstances, seven months pregnant in the middle of a triple murder investigation?

Because life threw curves. It had taken Taylor. It had brought Dylan Walker into her life. All he had to do was look at her and she went weak with desire. She wanted desperately to see where he could take her. Her instincts told her she was in for a wild ride, one that her old self had secretly longed for.

He found the key where it was hidden and opened the door. She barely noticed the spectacular view of the lake with the sunlight on the clear water or the array of colored rocks shimmering beneath. The scent of pine and water followed her inside the cool darkness of the house.

She turned as Dylan came in the door behind her. She hadn't known what she was going to say until the words came off her lips. "I trust you."

He looked at her, his gaze on hers as if searching for the truth before he smiled and took her in his arms. The kiss was a promise even before he said the words, as if he could tell that she was scared on so many levels. "We won't do anything you don't want to do. Nor will we do anything that might harm the baby, I promise." Then he swung her up into his arms and, kissing her, carried her deeper into the house.

Dylan broke the kiss to lay her down on a huge bed that seemed to float in front of the window overlooking the lake. She pulled him down next to her.

"I love looking into those eyes of yours," he whispered as his hand cupped her cheek. "I saw your intelligence the first day I met you. I was a little intimidated by it. I still am."

She chuckled and shook her head. "Did you know we were going to end up here today?"

"No. If you're asking if I planned this, definitely not. I had no ulterior motives asking you to come with me today. Except that I wanted you with me."

"When did you know you wanted this?" she asked, her gaze holding his.

"When I saw how hard it was for you to ask the state crime team for help, when I saw how it hurt you. I wanted to make you feel better. I love your smile and wanted the ability to put it back where it belonged."

"And now you think you have that ability?"

He blinked. *"You're challenging me?"* He laughed, smiling down at her. "You want me to prove it." She nodded and kissed him seductively, feeling nothing like her old self. She didn't know this woman, but she wanted to get to.

Dylan took that challenge as he deepened the kiss, burying his fingers in her hair, pulling it free to fall around her shoulders. Shivers of desire rippled over her skin. His skill reminded her of how long it had been since a man had made love to her.

Just the thought of her husband brought with it a deep sorrow. She'd told herself and Dylan that she and Taylor hadn't had children because they'd been too busy. Now she could admit that they had been growing apart from the years together. They hardly ever made love, both involved more in other things than each other.

Dylan pushed her over onto her back. He met her gaze, holding it. She nodded and smiled, even as he noticed what she hadn't. He wiped a tear from her cheek with his thumb. "Is it too soon?"

She shook her head and pulled him down for another kiss. This time when he pulled back, he seemed to see the desire in her eyes, the need, and the pain that came with that naked need.

He kissed her behind her ear, then trailed kisses down her throat. As he did, he unbuttoned her shirt. Goose bumps rippled over her flesh as he met her gaze and drew out her right breast. Bending over it he sucked the taut nipple into his mouth, making her moan as desire shot through her.

She wanted this. Wanted it desperately. She arched against him as he withdrew her left breast, and pressing them together, sucked her nipples into hard, aching points. She moaned, her hands cupping his head and he worked his way further south. His tongue trailed down over her stomach to the V.

Again, he looked at her as if waiting for permission. She spread her legs, making him smile as he slid further down the bed and lifted her. His tongue tentatively touched the aching part of her. Cat could hear herself as she writhed to the movement of his tongue, her moans growing louder and louder until she cried out as the intense release came in waves of pleasure. Gasping for breath, she drew him back up to her and started to unbutton his shirt, when his hands stopped her.

She looked up into his face. Her heart was still pounding, her body weak and still vibrating with the intensity of her climax. She met his gaze in a questioning one of her own.

Dylan shook his head. "Maybe next time, if there is one. This time was about you." He pulled her into his arms and held her close. She pressed her face into his warm shoulder, torn between laughing and crying.

"That was…" She couldn't even formulate words.

"That was just foreplay, Cat," he said with a laugh, then pulled back a little to look at her. "Was there anyone other than your husband?"

She shook her head and waited for him to ask if Taylor had ever… "Not like that," she said, burying her face again. She felt him chuckle.

"Glad I could be the first. Do you mind?" he asked as he put his hand on her belly. His eyes lit up as her daughter gave him her version of a high five. "She all right?"

"We are both more than all right. I can have sex, you know. We just have to be careful."

Dylan nodded. "Like I said, maybe next time." He drew her close again.

Cat felt as if she could stay right there forever. The sunlight on the lake threw shadows on the coffered ceiling of the bedroom. "This is your brother's place? I guess I'm surprised you still have it." She felt his hesitation before he finally spoke.

"I haven't been able to sell it."

Her cell rang. She pulled away just far enough to reach her phone where it had fallen out of her jeans. It was JP.

"I'm sorry," she said to Dylan. "I need to—"

"Do your job," he said smiling as he swung his legs over the side of the bed. "I would expect nothing less of you. I'll give you some privacy." He left the room. Cat answered the call.

"If you tell me that there's been another murder," she said as she reached to pick up her discarded clothing, not even remembering when it had come off.

"Thought you'd want to know. We have an ID on the dead woman found with the bogus fed. Her name is Lindsey Martin. Isn't that the name the pregnant woman gave you?"

"It is. It's her mother's maiden name."

He let out a low whistle. "No doubt the cases are connected, is there."

"No," she said. "But we still don't know what's going on or who else is involved. At least now DCI is on it." She'd told them what she'd found out about the adoptions and the women involved. They knew as much as she did now.

"So, you're still working the case?" JP asked. "I got a call about you finding a car connected with a woman named Patty Cooper. The lab did a preliminary test on the blood found on the passenger seat. It's Athena Grant's."

"I suspected it would be." She'd managed to get dressed as she talked.

"The FBI is involved as well, but I probably don't have to tell you that."

"Guess they all have it covered." She'd never quit anything in her life. Wasn't that why she was having a hard time with this? Just like she would have never thought of leaving Taylor. But life's curve had her husband gone, her pregnant and now passing off her first job and falling for one of her former suspects. "I have to go, JP. Thanks for letting me know."

She hung up and turned to see Dylan standing in the doorway. From just the expression on his face, she knew something was wrong. Then she saw a man she recognized behind him. The second fake FBI man was holding a gun to Dylan's head.

Cat could see her own weapon out of the corner of her eye. It lay on the bedside table almost within reach. But Dylan saw her look in its direction and gave a slight shake of his head.

DYLAN HAD BEEN trained in hand-to-hand combat. But the moment he'd seen the man holding the gun and realized he wasn't alone, Dylan wasn't going to take a chance with Cat's life and that of her baby's. He hoped that wasn't a mistake.

Now he just had to keep Cat from doing anything dangerous until they found out what was going on. Clearly, they'd been followed. If he hadn't been so anxious to get to his brother's lake house and make love with the acting sheriff, he would have been more careful. Then again, it had been a while since he'd had to worry about being followed—let alone killed. He was out of practice. He'd thought when he moved out here that he'd never have to worry about watching for a tail again.

"Someone wants to talk to us," he said carefully to Cat. "It appears we have little choice, so let's hear what he has to say."

"Without your weapon, please, Sheriff," the man said. He motioned her into the living room where she and Dylan were ordered to sit on the loveseat and not move. Dylan reached over and took her hand, squeezing it gently, hoping to reassure her.

The man who'd been standing by the door stepped forward. He was tall, slim and dressed in a suit that spoke of authority. He introduced himself as Brian Fuller, an officer with the regional intelligence agency as he took a seat on a chair across from them.

"Intelligence? I'd like to see some identification," Cat said. "No offense, but your associate presented himself as FBI and isn't, and now he's holding a gun on us, making it hard to believe that either of you are who you say you are."

Fuller smiled. "Jason is homeland security. If it makes you more comfortable, I'll have him put his weapon away." He pulled out his credentials and tossed it to Dylan. "I believe Mr. Walker is familiar with my type of identification." Dylan felt Cat watching him as he studied the ID, then tossed it back.

"You followed us here, your associate broke in and held a gun to my head," Dylan said. "Is that the way your office operates?"

Fuller sighed. "I shouldn't have to tell you that we use any means available to us when necessary. Sorry for the unpleasant tactics, but I need to ask you both a few questions, especially you, Mr. Walker, about your…friend, Rowena Keeling, and I wanted to do it in private."

Dylan didn't hesitate. "She's not my friend. She's an unwelcome houseguest who's been detained in the area because of the recent murders."

"I have a few questions myself," Cat said, speaking up. "You wouldn't be here unless you knew more about what was going on than we do. Who killed Athena Grant and her adoptive mother?"

"I'm sorry, Sheriff Jameson, but I'm asking the questions," Fuller said. "How long have you and Mr. Walker known each other?"

"In other words, you want to know how much we already know," Dylan said. "Ms. Jameson and I met after Athena tried to contact me, and failing, she went to the sheriff for help." Fuller nodded. "Since then, we discovered four women who were born in Russia, adopted to parents living in Denver, who we believe became friends—or at least seem to be in league together—including possibly my deceased wife. We also only recently found two more Russian-born adoptions out of Missoula. We believe they might be spying for Russia."

Fuller sat back in his chair, his expression giving nothing away.

"We are right, aren't we," Cat said. "Is your agency responsible for killing them?"

"We don't operate that way, Sheriff Jameson."

"Do you know where Athena's baby is?" Cat asked him.

"I'm sorry, I do not at this point," Fuller said.

"Are you telling us we're right and that they are Russian spies?" she asked. "Part of a sleeper cell?"

"He's obviously trying really hard not to tell us anything," Dylan said.

Fuller smiled at that. "It's true, the Russian traditional counterintelligence threat continues to loom large in our country. Spies live among us. We estimate there are one hundred thousand foreign agents from not just Russia, but other countries as well, spying on us. Washington, DC, has more spies than any other world city. Often the way we catch them is a tip from a friend or spouse."

Dylan felt Cat's gaze shift to him as he asked, "Are you saying my wife came to you?"

Fuller sighed. "I can't reveal my source."

"Wait, you're saying you were aware of what was going on?" Cat asked.

"That's our job," the officer said. "We've been trying to find the people responsible for the car bombing that killed your brother and wife, but also find out why."

"Was Ginny double-crossing her friends?" Dylan asked.

Fuller looked tight-lipped. "We focus on specific priorities. State agencies, the military and companies working on sensitive technologies as prime targets for foreign espionage." His gaze met Dylan's. "And protecting our asset."

"I'm no longer one of your assets," he said.

"No, but we believe you were caught up in a honey-trap operation," Fuller said and turned to Cat. "Honey-trap operations use sexpionage by a foreign female agent known as a sparrow to compromise an opponent sexually to elicit information."

Dylan swore. "If you think that is what Rowena Keeling is doing—" Cooper Walker, the man said.

"What are you talking about?" he demanded.

"We have it on good authority that Ginny Cooper obtained the names of those we have working in the same capacity you did during your years of service. She was threatening to expose them—and you—when she was killed."

Chapter Fourteen

Cat saw Dylan's flushed face as he shot to his feet. "You can't believe I gave her any such list."

Jason brandished his weapon again but Fuller waved him back.

"Calm down, Mr. Walker. We believe your wife got her hands on the list for her native-born country from someone close to you," he said.

For a moment he looked confused, then he swore. "My brother, Beau," Dylan said, his voice rough with anger.

"We don't know that for a fact, Mr. Walker."

"Then what do you know?" Dylan demanded angrily. "Was it my brother?"

Fuller turned to Cat. "Have you ever heard of the Moscow Rules of spying, Sheriff Jameson? *Assume nothing. Never go against your gut. Everyone is potentially under opposition control. Do not look back: you are never completely alone. Go with the flow, blend in. Vary your pattern and stay within your cover.* Those rules are posted in the International Spy Museum in Washington, DC."

"I don't understand," she said, more than a little confused.

"We are dealing with a different breed of Russian spies.

Spies usually have contact with no one else, never learning the names of any other spies or officials. But these Russian-born females adopted by American families either found each other—or their controller found them and activated them.

"Originally, we believe that Mr. Walker here was the mark," Fuller continued. "But your wife must have realized that you would never give up your associates. So, she found someone who would."

"How was it possible that my brother had such a list?" Dylan demanded.

"We aren't sure that he did have it, but he was apparently involved somehow because he became a target."

Dylan shook his head. "If true and the list is out there, then why hasn't the Soviet Union acted on it? Or have they?"

Fuller shook his head. "We don't believe Ginny Cooper Walker ever delivered the document to the Soviets or anyone else."

"Wasn't it possible she had it with her, and it was destroyed in the bombing?" Dylan asked.

The director shook his head. "It appears to be missing." He looked directly at Cat. "That is why people are dying. There seems to be two factions involved, one trying to get the document, the other killing people to either stop it from falling into the wrong hands or fighting for it because they've already made a deal with another country that wants it."

"And you don't know who is who," Cat finished for him.

Fuller shifted in the chair. "I understand this is your first position in law enforcement. I hope it's not your last."

"Is that a threat?" Dylan demanded.

"Not at all. I admire Sheriff Jameson. I already knew

your abilities, Mr. Walker. I find the two of you an interesting but very capable team."

"Then what is it you want?" he demanded.

"I don't want that document to fall into the wrong hands, and I suspect you don't either since your name will be on that list," Fuller said. "I also don't want the two of you to get killed since right now you are both deep in the middle of this."

"But there is something else you want," Cat said.

The director nodded and turned to Dylan. "Your wife had that document. That means it must still be in your possession, whether you're aware of it or not. Find it."

"If I do, I'll destroy it," Dylan said.

"That would be a mistake. The only way this is going to stop is if both sides know it's destroyed."

"I'll make sure they do," he promised.

Fuller sighed and got to his feet. "I would prefer that when you find it, you turn it over to me. But I understand your lack of trust in anyone other than…" His gaze swung to Cat for a moment, then back to Dylan. "I wanted to alert you both to what a dangerous position you're in."

"Which one of the women is working for you?" Cat asked. "Rowena?"

Clearly ignoring the question, the man said, "There is no shame in walking completely away from this, Sheriff Jameson, especially given your condition. I highly recommend it." With that he pulled out two business cards, handed one to Cat and another to Dylan. "You find the document, you call." He motioned to his companion and the two walked out, leaving Cat and Dylan alone.

For a moment, neither spoke. The house grew uncomfortably quiet, making Cat aware of the growing darkness outside. The sun had long ago dropped behind the mountains, leaving the lake plated in silver light. The mountains beyond the water were etched black against the pale sky. The quiet was deafening.

"You were right, Cat," Dylan said after a moment. "Rowena was looking for the document."

"But is she still looking or is she waiting for us to find it? And if so, who is she working for?"

He shook his head. "Mind if we swing by my ranch on the way home? After our run-in with Rowena, I want to see if she came back to the house."

"She has the code to get back in?"

"I haven't changed it yet. That could have been a mistake."

"You really think she went back to the ranch after we confronted her?" Cat asked.

"Yes. Unless she took all her belongings with her when she left the ranch, she has to come back for them. I don't think she'd finished. Not yet. Unless she found the document. It sure didn't sound that way with whomever she was talking to on the phone when we approached her."

After locking up the lake house, Dylan drove them to the ranch. They didn't speak on the drive. Cat assumed that like her, Dylan was going over everything they'd learned. As they pulled in through the gate and drove up the road, she spotted Rowena's SUV parked in front of the cottage. "Looks like she's changed residences."

Dylan swore and sped up. "Like hell."

As he swung into a spot next to the woman's SUV, Rowena came out of his cottage. "You really should lock your doors," she said, standing her ground as the two of them exited his pickup.

"What were you doing in there?" he demanded.

"Just left you a note," she said. "I'm leaving in the morning." Her gaze swung to Cat. "Unless you're going to arrest me. But I didn't think so."

"Get that package mailed off to your niece?" Cat said.

"As a matter of fact, I did." She eyed Cat. "They say pregnancy makes a woman glow, but I don't think that's what put that color in your cheeks, Sheriff." A big grin spread across her face before she laughed and turned to Dylan. "I saw the way you looked at her. But I have to hand it to you. Didn't take you any time at all to seduce her."

"Rowena—"

"Don't even bother, Dylan." Her gaze whipped back to Cat. "Be careful. My best friend was married to him. He is a man of many secrets. You have no idea what he's capable of. Ginny didn't either. I kept telling her to get out while she could. Too bad she didn't listen. Now she's dead." Rowena lifted a brow. "Think about that, Acting Sheriff."

"That's enough, Rowena," Dylan snapped. "Why wait until morning? Why don't you leave now?"

She smiled at him. "You're right. Why not say goodbye now." She turned to Cat. "Good luck. Too bad about your husband, Taylor Jameson, right? What a terrible accident." Cat saw something unsettling in the woman's expression. "Turns out you aren't as smart as you think you are." She turned to glare at Dylan before walking away. "Enjoy your evening. Too bad it will be your last."

"What was that about?" Cat asked, shaken by her mentioning Taylor and the wreck that killed him as she watched Rowena walk away.

"I have no idea," Dylan said. "But I'm worried that she wasn't in the cottage just to leave me a note." He headed for the door. "You might want to wait here."

What had the woman left? The baby? That thought propelled her toward the cottage door until she realized she hadn't heard a sound from inside. What if—

"Wait here," Dylan said as if thinking the same thing.

Cat couldn't bear to wait. She rushed in behind him. They didn't find the baby, alive or dead, but Rowena had left a note on his kitchen table. Dylan didn't touch it. Instead, he left to search the rest of the cottage, coming back to say he hadn't found anything out of place that he could tell.

They both looked down at the note lying on the table.

Sorry things didn't work out.

Chapter Fifteen

"What *things*?" Cat asked, turning to look at him.

"The document?" he said with a shrug.

"That's only one thing. Maybe she planned to use… what was it Fuller called it? Sexpionage. Maybe she really thought you'd fall for her."

He shook his head.

"I got the feeling that she was jealous of your wife," Cat said.

"Rowena? She had nothing to be jealous of, she was born rich and spoiled. As far as I could tell, she could have any man she wanted and she wanted a lot of them."

"Every man but you," Cat said.

"If she wanted me, it was to rub it in Ginny's face, but Ginny's gone and hopefully Rowena will be gone from here soon. Her note makes it sound as if she's giving up."

Cat shook her head. "I don't believe it. I'm wondering what her next move is. Rowena must realize that you don't have the document and since she has no idea where Ginny might have hidden it—"

"Just my luck." Dylan was shaking his head. "I agree. She's not giving up. I doubt she could if she wanted to. But maybe she wants us to believe she is." His gaze settled on her, warm and inviting. "You sure you have to go home?"

She nodded. "Are you going to be all right here with Rowena still on the property?"

"I plan to sleep with one eye open and my .45 nearby, and as soon as she's gone, I'll reset the gate so she can't get back in."

Cat couldn't tell if he was joking or not about the .45. "Seriously, be careful."

"You too. Maybe I should follow you back to Fortune Creek."

She shook her head. "I'll be fine."

He stepped toward her, hugged her and then kissed her, holding her in the warmth and strength of his arms. She didn't want to leave, but she also couldn't stay. So much had happened today. She needed time and space to try to make sense of it. She figured Dylan did too since Fuller had made it sound as if Ginny had only married him for the list.

Cat was sure that he'd already suspected that had been the case. But it was one more deception, one more lie, one more betrayal.

"When this is over..." he whispered next to her ear.

The words rushed straight to her heart. A promise of what could be. If they survived it. Cat pulled back to kiss him, then stepped from his arms to walk to her patrol SUV before she changed her mind about leaving.

It was later than she thought as she headed for Fortune Creek. She put down her window to drive slowly, letting the cold night air rush in as if it could clear her mind. She could still taste Dylan on her lips and all she could think about was being back in his arms.

She pushed the thought away, a little shocked at herself. Would Taylor be shocked as well, or would he be happy for her? She thought he would be happy but maybe a little worried that she would get her heart broken. He might also worry about their daughter. Who fell in love seven months pregnant?

At least now she knew what Rowena and the others had been looking for. But if the document wasn't hidden on the ranch, then where? She reminded herself that the ranch was over a thousand acres. Ginny could have hidden it anywhere.

Cat hadn't gone far when she spotted headlights behind her. Dylan? After she left had he gotten worried and decided to follow her home? The thought made her smile—until she noticed how quickly the vehicle was gaining on her, its headlights on high beam.

Chapter Sixteen

Dylan found himself more anxious than he'd been in months. He'd watched Cat disappear into the darkness, and he was unable to shake the gut-deep feeling that she wasn't safe. That road to Fortune Creek was narrow and winding and seldom had any traffic on it. If she broke down or had a flat, she might be stranded in the dark and cold until morning.

He grabbed his keys and headed for his pickup. No matter what she said, he was going to follow her home. He wouldn't be able to sleep if he didn't. Once past the gate, he drove as fast as the road would allow, all his instincts pushing him to catch sight of her.

As he came over a rise, he saw taillights and tried to relax. But the closer he got, the more confused he became. The lights were wrong. He wasn't following Cat's patrol SUV. Instead, it was an older farm truck with a wooden stock rack on the back. He frowned, realizing he'd seen the truck before—parked in one of the old barns on his ranch.

He felt a shock rocket through him. What the hell? Who was driving his truck? He punched the gas and tried to pull up beside the large farm vehicle, determined to find out who was driving it and if he was right about it being his.

But as he came along the driver's side almost close enough to see the driver, the truck swerved into his lane crashing into the side of his pickup and sending him flying off the road.

CAT THOUGHT FOR a moment that she saw a second set of headlights behind her, but as she dropped over a rise, both disappeared. Hurriedly she looked for a spot to pull over, but the road was narrow and hilly. There wasn't a wide spot that she could see ahead and the vehicle behind her had topped the rise and was now gaining on her quickly.

She thought about the alleged drunk driver who had killed her husband on this very road, although miles from here, closer to the Canadian border. She touched her brakes, thinking the driver just hadn't seen her, and got over to the edge of the road as far as she could to let him pass.

Except the driver didn't pass. She sped up seeing that the truck wasn't going to pass her. Blinded by the headlights, she couldn't see the driver, but she knew then what he intended to do. She thought of Fuller's warning. She'd become a problem. Dylan too.

The large truck chased after her, barreling down on her. He was gaining. Any moment he was going to crash into the back of her SUV. She gripped the wheel hard, her fingers aching as she fought to stay on the road. All she could think about was her baby. If she went off the road and into the trees—

She felt a hard jolt as the truck rammed the back of her SUV, the back window exploding as the truck made contact. She could feel the cold night air whistling through the gaping hole. Her SUV began to fishtail. She hung onto the wheel, fighting to right the vehicle without going off the rough edge of the shoulderless road. She'd only just gained control when she looked in her rearview mirror.

The truck seemed to back off. What was the driver doing? Then she saw it. He'd only backed off to make another run at her, to increase his speed. This time he planned to hit her harder in an attempt to drive her off the road.

She had the gas pedal to the floor. She couldn't go any faster. Nor was there any place to get off this road before she was forced from it.

In her rearview mirror, she could see nothing but headlights bearing down on her. The truck was coming at her again. Her baby, she thought. She couldn't wreck. She couldn't lose her baby, her life. Not now, not when she'd glimpsed a possible bright future she'd only dreamed possible.

The truck was almost on her again, coming faster this time.

DYLAN'S PICKUP LEFT the road, soared over the shallow barrow pit before touching down hard in a field. He fought the wheel to keep control as he was still going fast. Ahead he could see a stand of pines looming in his headlights. He turned the wheel back in the direction of the road he'd just left. The ground was soft. He could feel the tires digging into the dirt as he roared back onto the road, losing control for a moment as he did.

He hadn't known this kind of fear in a very long time, if ever. He'd never had this much on the line even with his government job. This was personal. He felt responsible for Cat and her baby, for Beau's baby as well. He had to catch that truck and stop it—no matter what he had to do.

In the distance, he could see the taillights of the truck. He didn't kid himself that the driver of the truck had accidently forced him off the road. Where was Cat? If it had been an accident or he'd been the intended target, the truck driver would have stopped. Which meant the intended target was up the road. *Cat.*

The thought sent his pulse racing as he sped after the truck. At the top of the hill, he saw two sets of taillights ahead. The truck was right behind Cat's SUV, barreling down on it. Dylan had no doubt what the driver planned to do. He floored his pickup. The right front tire scraped loudly on the dented panel where the truck had slammed into him. But otherwise, the pickup was still running fine.

Gaining on the truck, Dylan pulled out his gun. His hand shook for a moment. While he could shoot with either his left or his right hand with accuracy, he hadn't been to a firing range in months.

He calmed those thoughts, telling himself that he had to get close enough to make a decent shot. He put down his window, letting the cold spring night air rush in to clear his head and strengthen his focus.

Dylan took aim. He couldn't let the truck drive Cat's SUV off the road, not in this hilly area filled with trees and a creek at the bottom of the steepest of the hills to his right. But if he didn't stop the driver of the truck—

CAT GRIPPED THE wheel as the inside of the SUV filled again with the lights from the big truck. She braced herself for the impact, terrified what would happen if she crashed, especially at this speed. Just the thought of the airbag exploding and harming her daughter—

She shoved her seat as far back as she could and still reach the pedals. She would have disabled the airbag if she could have—concerned only for her baby.

The truck was so close now, she could hear the roar of

its engine. The headlights filled her vehicle, the sound through the broken window at the back deafening. Gripping the wheel, she looked back, but could only see the front end of the huge old truck about to take away everything from her.

Braced for impact, she hadn't realized that she'd been holding her breath when suddenly the truck behind her began to swerve wildly. The sound of the truck's big engine seemed to die as she heard the squeal of brakes. The truck was rocking precariously, the headlights wavering. An instant later, the headlights veered to the right as the truck went crashing off the road and disappeared down a hillside.

That's when she saw the lights of the other vehicle behind her. That driver had hit his brakes. As she slowed her SUV to a stop, she could no longer hold back the flood of emotions. Hugging her belly, she began to sob. She'd told herself that she knew the dangers that went with being an officer of the law. But it had never hit home like it did at that moment. She could have lost her baby tonight. She could have lost everything.

WEAK WITH RELIEF, Dylan jumped out of his pickup and rushed to Cat's SUV. He saw her hugging herself. As he approached, his flashlight in one hand, his weapon in the other, he saw her tears and knew that they weren't for herself, but for her baby. She unlocked her door and stumbled out and into his arms. "Thank you for whatever you did," she said, her voice breaking. She didn't have to tell him how frightened she'd been. He could feel it in her hug, see it in her red tear-streaked face, hear it in her voice.

"Shot out the rear left tire." She nodded, still leaning into him. "You're all right," he whispered as he held her.

"I need to go down the hill and check the truck. Stay here. The driver might come back up the hill to the road. Don't take a chance. Shoot the SOB."

She nodded, wiping at her tears. "I'm okay." Her hand went to her belly. "We're all right."

"You certainly are. I'll be back." He saw her reach for her service revolver and knew that she was indeed okay again, the scare over. At least for now.

With that he dropped over the hill, shining the flashlight beam into the darkness. The hill was steep, ending in a stand of pines next to a creek. He could see the truck's taillights glowing deep in the grove and smelled the scent of burned oil and leaking radiator fluid on the night air.

As he drew closer, he saw that the driver's side door was standing open. He slowed, pocketing the flashlight to ready the gun. Darkness hunkered in the trees along the creek. He could hear and smell the water, mixing with the smells of the wrecked truck. What he didn't hear was anyone moving inside the vehicle.

Working along the side of the large truck, he made his way to the open driver's side door. Taking a breath, he waited then peered around the edge of the open door to look inside.

Just as he'd expected, in the ambient light of the headlights, he could see that the cab was empty. The blood he saw on the shattered windshield and on the steering wheel told him the driver had been injured. He realized that the truck engine had still been idling as it gave a last gasp and quit, the headlights dying with it.

Darkness fell over him with a bone-chilling silence. He listened for any sound, hearing nothing but his heartbeat. He pulled out his flashlight and shone it around the interior of the truck's cab.

He had no clue who'd been driving it or how badly they might have been injured. Not enough to knock them out even with all the blood present. The person had managed to get away. He told himself they had probably run off into the trees.

He walked around the front of the truck and found fresh footprints heading down toward the creek. He saw blood on one of the large stones above the water. Turning the flashlight farther down toward the creek, he saw no one.

Convinced the driver was gone, Dylan quickly made his way back up to the road and Cat. That he'd come so close to losing her tonight still had him shaken. She wasn't his, he told himself. But damned if she didn't feel like his. Was that because from the first time he saw her, he'd been intrigued by her?

Now it had gone far beyond simply being intrigued. He wanted her like he'd never wanted anything in his life. The worst part was that he wasn't sure he could have her. He wasn't sure she wasn't still grieving her husband the way everyone thought he was grieving his wife.

He topped the hill to the road and was relieved when he saw her assessing the damage to her patrol SUV and taking photos. She was again back in acting sheriff mode, trained for the job and leaning on that training for strength. He knew the feeling well. But he didn't doubt that she'd been shaken to her roots tonight. Nearly dying had to have brought the reality of what she might be involved in home.

He thought of the large truck at the bottom of the hillside smashed into the trees. That could have easily been Cat and her unborn baby in that crash. He shuddered to think of how tragically this night could have ended.

As it was, he'd done the one thing he'd tried so hard

not to do. Get involved and put himself and his story back into the news. Once his name was picked up by the media, there would be a rehash of Ginny's death and of his brother's. There would be more speculation—especially if word got out that the prosecutor was reopening the case.

"I've already called DCI," she said. "They're sending a team now."

He nodded. "We need to pull off the road in case there is any more traffic tonight," he said as the reality of the situation settled over him.

"You saved my life and my daughter's," Cat said, meeting his gaze in the light of the vehicle's headlights. "Thank you, but what made you follow me?"

"Just a feeling," he said, realizing how deep he was in with this woman. "I had a feeling you needed me."

She smiled and he felt his heart lift even as he dreaded what was to come. All the media attention again. Only this time worse, because this time Cat would be in the middle of it as well. No one realized how bad it could get until they were the focus of the media for weeks on end. Cat would soon know. But that might not even be the worst of it. Clearly she was now a target.

"I recognized the truck that forced me off the road and went after you," Dylan said. "It's one of mine from the ranch." He shook his head at her quizzical expression. "I have no idea who was driving it."

"Rowena?"

"If so, she put her head into the windshield and could be bleeding pretty badly right now."

"Why would she do this?" Cat said, voicing his own thoughts.

"She must think you're getting too close to the truth.

Or maybe it's to show whoever she works for that she's doing something to keep us from finding the document before she can."

Chapter Seventeen

Dylan hadn't been able to sleep last night. He'd changed the passcode on the gate the moment he got back to find Rowena's car gone. He told himself it couldn't have been her driving his truck last night—unless she had help.

And that was what worried him.

According to Cat, the only time she saw Rowena away from the ranch was when she'd been talking to the man staying at the hotel. The man Cat thought was FBI. That man was now dead.

Who did that leave? Rowena, Patty Cooper Harper, Sharese and her brother Luca. Any of them could have been driving the truck. He knew Cat wanted to believe, as he did, that Patty had helped with his nephew's delivery and taken the infant to protect him. But then who had killed Athena? He hated to think that the woman who'd saved the baby would kill the mother. There was something so cold blooded about that... So even Patty could have been driving the truck since Rowena had access to it thanks to him letting her stay at the ranch.

He reminded himself that his own wife had been in on this and had gotten killed in a car bombing along with his brother. That was stone cold as well. These were apparently the kind of people he and Cat were dealing with. They could have both been killed last night. Whoever had been driving the old truck had certainly tried.

His fear was that the group couldn't find the document and without it, they were desperate because their lives were on the line. Desperate people made desperate decisions.

Dylan thought of Cat, his concern for her growing. She'd been taken off the case, put on desk duty. But that didn't mean she would be safe—even if she did her best to stay out of it. Knowing her, he doubted she would be able *not* to follow a lead if one presented itself.

That's why he had to keep her busy, he thought after hanging up from talking to the manager at the wrecking yard in Eureka. They had the truck. Forensics had finished with it. Dylan didn't hold much hope that they found any prints from last night's driver. But they could find his prints in the truck, possibly along with blood.

He'd really thought he had walked away from all of this. This morning he'd searched the cottage looking for the document. He'd assumed it would be on a thumb drive or something like it. But it could be old school and printed out on plain old paper. Either way, he had no luck finding it.

If Cat was right and Ginny had hidden it somewhere here on the ranch…why would she have done that? Once she had her hands on it, why not give it to her handlers? Unless she was trying to make a better deal. Is that where his brother came in? Beau had contacts around the world. He knew people. Had they been trying to sell it?

A thought struck him. What if she never had the list? What if Beau had contacted her with the list? Dylan didn't want to believe his brother had gone that bad, but right now he had more questions than answers. He feared he might never know the truth. That and worrying about Cat had kept him from sleeping last night. That he'd gotten this involved with her scared him. It had been so fast, so intense, more real than anything he'd ever experienced.

He picked up the phone, needing to see her. He didn't know if they could survive this as a couple, but somehow, he had to get the two of them out of it.

CAT KEPT THINKING about Athena Grant. Pregnant and running scared, the woman knew she was going to die, but Cat knew in her heart that she would have done whatever it took to save her baby—even call someone she knew she couldn't trust, someone who would kill her.

That was a love that Cat could understand better right now.

She'd gotten the call she'd been expecting first thing this morning. She was on desk duty for the rest of her time in Fortune Creek. She still had six weeks as acting sheriff and, while she had turned it over to DCI and the FBI, she didn't want to just walk away. She wanted to stop the people who had tried to kill both her and Dylan last night.

For her safety and that of her baby she'd needed to step back. Which meant she would stay to take calls at the office, sit in her chair and watch Helen knit and try to stay awake.

Her daughter kicked her, reminding her that she'd wished for something to happen to keep her awake and look how that had almost turned out. Well, she'd gotten more than she wished for. What had almost happened last night had shaken her to her core. It made her question if she could do this job even after she delivered her little girl. Could she risk her life knowing there was no one to take care of her daughter without her?

She saw Helen take a call, then look in her direction a

moment before her phone rang. She picked up glad to hear Dylan's voice.

"I'm at the wrecking yard in Eureka. My pickup still runs. How about your patrol SUV?" It did. "Can I buy you lunch?"

"That sounds wonderful. Why don't I meet you there. I want to see the truck." Earlier she'd called the local hospitals to see if anyone had come in with a head injury. No one. If it had been Rowena, it was possible they would find her dead somewhere down in the trees along the creek. Unless her injuries weren't life threatening.

Dylan had called her last night to tell her that when he'd returned to the ranch after the two of them had given all their information to the DCI team and FBI, he'd found Rowena gone—just like his truck from one of the old barns. Everyone was anxious to talk to her.

Last night Cat had gotten only a glimpse of the truck just before it had gone off the road and disappeared. She was anxious to see it as she drove into town to the wrecking yard. Dylan was standing over by the truck when she got there. She parked, got out, and immediately felt off-balance at the sight of the big green truck with the wooden stock rack.

Even from a distance, she could see how the front was caved in from hitting a tree and putting the driver's head into the windshield. She had no idea what year it was, what make or model, just that it was made before seatbelts.

The closer she got to the truck, the more she felt the tiny hairs on her neck stand on end. Cat couldn't believe what she was looking at. It was an old farm truck, exactly as her husband described it to her and the cops in the hospital before he died. The rusted door panel on the driver's side. The faded green body but with a yellow hood that had apparently been replaced but never painted to match. The metal-reinforced wooden stock rack right down to the almost unreadable sticker on the back of the large side mirror from a local café that was no longer in business.

The truck was the one that had killed her husband. Her heart threatened to burst from her chest. She looked over at Dylan, the weight of it pressing on her chest.

"You're sure this is your truck?" Her voice sounded odd even to her. She could feel Dylan next to her.

"It's mine. I found it in the barn when I bought the place."

Cat felt sick. She didn't want to believe it, but this was the truck. There couldn't be two of them exactly alike. Not with that old café sticker on the back of the driver's side mirror. Not with the metal added to the wooden stock rack.

She stepped around the truck to look at the left-hand side. The dent was there, along with the spot where the paint had been scraped off, leaving the telltale white paint from the vehicle her husband had been driving. No wonder the truck hadn't been found after the accident. It had been in Dylan's barn.

This was the truck that had killed her husband.

"It's so old. It doesn't even look like it would run," she said, wondering what it was she wanted him to tell her— anything that could stop her thinking the worst.

"Surprisingly it still runs like a top."

"When was the last time you took it out for a drive?" she asked, her voice breaking. She could feel Dylan's intent gaze on her. He was standing so close that she could also feel the heat radiating off his body.

"I didn't know you had an interest in old farm trucks," he said, studying her. "It's been months since I even started it up."

Bile rose in her throat. She started to step away. "Cat?" Dylan reached for her arm to stop her. She let him since she felt as if she might crumble to her knees, her body felt so weak.

For months since she took the job, she'd been unconsciously looking for a truck just like it. But she hadn't seen one, not like this one. She'd thought she would never see the truck that hit her husband, that killed him, that left her pregnant and a widow.

Her gaze came up to Dylan's. "This is the truck that hit and killed my husband six months ago."

He stared at her, shock turning his handsome face into a pale mask of disbelief. "You said he was killed in a car wreck but—" He shook his head. "You can't think that I—" He let go of her to take a step back. "Cat, I swear I've never taken the truck off the ranch."

She felt tears burn her eyes. This is what she'd wanted to hear, wanted desperately to believe. She'd trusted this man. Trusted him with her body, her baby, her heart. "Then who?"

Dylan looked lost as he shook his head. "I don't know. The key was in it when I discovered it in the barn. I never took it out. Someone could have stolen it, I guess, and..."

Cat shook her head, fear crushing her chest. "They wouldn't have brought it back. They couldn't have unless they knew the code to get back in the gate."

He looked sick. "When was your husband—" She told him the date and he let out a relieved breath. "I didn't come out to the ranch until three weeks after that. I remember the date. It was my birthday. Cat, I can prove I wasn't in Montana."

She stared at him still stunned and upset. "If it wasn't you, then..." She met his gaze and held it. "Didn't you say your wife was out here six months ago getting the house ready?"

He nodded slowly. "But why would Ginny take the truck out? What possible reason would she have?"

Cat looked at the truck with its huge wooden stock rack on the back. "Maybe she had to haul something." Like a body. Or furniture. Or load of machine parts she was taking to Canada to sell before bringing back drugs. Cat had no idea. "I'm going to have to get forensics to check out the bed of the truck as well as the cab, Dylan."

"Make the call. We need to know who was driving that truck not just last night but six months ago." As she started to pull out her phone, he stepped to her, pulling her into his arms and holding her. "I'm so sorry, Cat. So very sorry."

She nodded into his shoulder, thinking again of life's curves.

LEAVING THE TRUCK and the information with DCI, Dylan insisted on taking her to lunch. "I know you're not hungry, but maybe your daughter is."

She'd smiled at that. "I'm sorry I suspected you yet again," she said as they drove to a café.

He shrugged. "How could you not? All of this seems to have landed on my doorstep. No coincidence there. I'm tangled up in this every way but loose. My deceased wife, her friends, my brother." He shook his head as he parked. "I still can't fathom Ginny driving that truck the night your husband was killed. I married her, lived with her a short time. I realize now that she was a liar and probably a cheater, but to be so cold-blooded as to crash into your husband's car and not stop to help."

"I suppose it would depend on why she was driving the truck to begin with," Cat said after they'd gotten out and were walking toward the front door of the café. "I doubt she wanted anyone to know what she was doing out that night in the truck so close to the Canadian border. I'm just glad that Taylor was able to make a call for help or I wouldn't have gotten to say goodbye to him."

"Or learn about the truck that hit him," Dylan said as he opened the door, and they stepped inside.

Once seated, he said, "I'm so sorry. If I'd never married Ginny—"

She reached over and put a hand on his and shook her head. "This isn't your fault. No one can control fate."

He turned his hand over to take hers. "So true."

She looked lost in thought for a moment before she said, "Are you sure Ginny was out here alone?"

Frowning, he said, "You think Rowena or one of the others was with her?"

"I was thinking more like your brother."

He stared at her in surprise, realizing that he'd never questioned how long Ginny and Beau had been…what? Conspiring or just simply having an affair behind his back? The waitress approached, took their orders and left before he dared speak or, worse, cuss.

"You think he was driving the truck that night?"

Cat seemed to wince. "No, I hadn't been thinking that, but if he was out here with her and they were hooked up in this scheme…"

"Scheming," he repeated. "Why not? He could have been driving. I'll see if I can find out if he was in the states during that time." He had no idea how long Ginny and his brother had been, as Cat put it, scheming. Or even if they had been. He made the call, quick and to the point, and disconnected.

"I'm sorry," she said as if it was a foregone conclusion

that his brother had been in the states six months ago. He still held out hope that he was wrong.

"You have no reason to be sorry. I never cared what their story was." He laughed scornfully. "Probably because whatever it was would only make me feel worse."

"That's why I hate bringing it all back up."

"The investigation is bringing it back up. Rowena, Athena's death, her missing baby…" His gaze softened as he looked at her. "I've been hiding out here in Montana from the truth, but it's going to come anyway. It's time I faced it."

His cell rang and he quickly picked up. He listened for a few moments. He could feel her watching him, trying to see by his expression how bad it was. He wished he could hide his feelings better. He used to be good at it. He didn't want to be anymore. "Thank you. I appreciate this." He disconnected and looked at her.

"Beau was in the states. Want to bet he was in Montana?"

CAT ATE AS much of her salad as she could, the two of them having fallen silent as if both were lost in their own thoughts. "This doesn't mean Beau was driving the truck," she said after a while. "Nor does it mean he was on the wrong side of this. I'd like to take a look inside his lake house."

"No problem," he said after paying for their lunch and leading her outside to his pickup. "Want to pick up your SUV or go in the truck?"

"Let's take your truck."

They climbed in before he asked, "Anything special you're looking for?"

"Just a thought," she said. "Let's say Beau was trying

to help Ginny get out rather than joining her. Let's say they weren't alone out here. Ginny didn't get the list from you. Maybe she wasn't the one to get it at all. Maybe she took it from Rowena, flew out here and met Beau asking for his help."

"That's a whole lot of supposition," he commented as he drove toward Flathead Lake.

"Then Ginny and Beau were killed in the bombing, but they didn't have the list with them." He nodded. "We know Rowena came out here looking for something. What if Beau and Ginny left it in his lake house so you would find it and take it to the right people."

"That really is a long shot," Dylan said, but she could tell he wanted to believe it. He wanted to believe in his brother—and maybe that there might have been something good in his deceased wife. "Then who was driving the truck not just last night but six months ago?"

She shrugged. "We have a lot of suspects. I'd put Rowena at the top of the list, but I doubt she can drive a stick."

"Something tells me you can, Sheriff," he said grinning over at her.

"I'm a Montana girl. I can put my own worm on a hook, catch and gut a fish and fry it up for dinner."

He laughed. "My kind of woman." His look sent a bolt of heat right to her center. She felt her face flush as she thought of him between her legs. "So not Rowena," Dylan said.

"Let's not forget Sharese and her brother Luca."

"Or that Rowena visited Sharese in Libby before we were run off the road," he added.

"Just curious," Cat asked. "Did Ginny know how to drive a stick shift?"

DYLAN HAD NO IDEA. He couldn't believe how little he'd known about the woman he'd married. He also realized, as he pulled up to Beau's lake house, that Cat still thought Ginny might have been driving the truck six months ago.

The house felt colder than it had the last time they were there. He thought about how he'd brought Cat here wanting her desperately. That feeling hadn't gone away; he had a feeling it never would. There was something about her, her strength and yet her compassion that had him falling for her.

He reminded himself that he'd fallen this quickly for Ginny and look where that had left him.

"Did you know your brother was buying this place?" she asked as he snapped on the lights.

"Not until he'd already purchased it and invited me out."

They split up and began to search the house. It wasn't large, but it was nice. As he moved through it, seeing some of his brother's things, he hoped Cat was right and that his brother hadn't gone to the dark side.

But for the life of him, he couldn't imagine where his brother would have left the list. It made no sense that Beau was involved at all—unless he added in Ginny. Was Beau in love with her? Or was it a business deal? It would have been just like his brother to want to save the femme fatale in distress.

When he finished his part of the search, he found Cat back in the living room.

"If your brother got his hands on the document and realized what it was, why wouldn't he have just handed it over to you?"

Dylan shook his head. "We'd been at odds for a while before his death. I didn't like the way he was living. He

didn't think I was doing such a great job of my life either."
He shrugged. "Brothers, they disagree."

"But he was at your wedding."

"Apparently busy with Athena," Dylan said with a curse.

"Did he like Ginny?" she asked.

Dylan had to consider that. "He was wary. I got the impression he thought I jumped into it too quickly."

Cat nodded and looked around the room. "Did you spend any time here in this house with him?"

"I did when he first bought it." He saw that she'd walked to a shelf full of board games.

"Did you play any of these?"

He had to think. "Monopoly. Beau loved to make his own money, refusing to touch his inheritance. So he especially liked to take every penny I had in the game."

"I think we should take a look at the game," Cat said. "We've looked everywhere else." She reached for it but was too short to take it off the shelf. Dylan stepped over to her, pulled down the game from the top shelf and took it over to the table.

"Is that where he normally kept the game?" she asked as she joined him.

He frowned. "I don't think I ever paid any attention." He lifted the lid and looked down at it, remembering their last game. He and Beau had fought tooth and nail, Dylan not about to let him win. "He always wanted the top hat," he said picking up the piece and turning it in his fingers.

"And you?" Cat asked sitting down before digging into the game box.

"I usually had the dog. Better than the wheelbarrow or the iron."

She chuckled at that. "I like the car." She picked up one

stack of money and thumbed through it, then another, putting them aside.

Dylan took out the land titles and the Chance and Get Out of Jail Free cards. Nothing. He was ready to give up when Cat lifted the cardboard bottom up. He heard the sound she made. Her gaze shot to him as she moved the cardboard aside and he saw the envelope taped to the floor of the game box.

Chapter Eighteen

The sound of a boat motor grew louder. Dylan grabbed the envelope and started to open it when he realized the outboard motor had stopped. He quickly glanced out the window to see a boat pull in at Beau's dock. Two figures, one male, one female, were climbing out. The female secured the boat, the male had already started toward them.

"Let's go," he said putting the envelope into his jacket pocket and reaching for Cat. They hurried out the back door and into his pickup. He was backing out when he saw the male come around the corner of the house. He hit the gas as he whipped the pickup around and took off, losing sight of the man as they sped off.

"Did you recognize the man?" Cat asked.

"No, you?"

"Luca Harmon," Cat said as Dylan drove while watching his rearview mirror to see if they were followed. "Sharese's brother. I found a high school photo of him."

"I know what Fuller said about not destroying the document—if that's what's in this envelope, but I don't like having it in my possession." He glanced at her.

"Because it puts me in danger too," she said. "I am trained for this, you know."

"I know," he said and looked over at her again. "But I can't bear the thought of something happening to you and your baby."

He pulled out his phone to make the call. When the man answered, he said without preamble, "Fuller, I have it. How do I get it to you?" He listened to the directions the man gave him. "I'm on my way. I just have one stop to make."

"You trust Fuller?" Cat asked after he'd disconnected.

"I don't trust anyone." He looked over at her. "But you."

As DYLAN STARTED out of the wrecking yard, following Cat's patrol SUV, his cell rang. "Ike," he said, hoping his friend had some good news. "There seems to be a problem with the DNA found at the scene of the bombing. They can't find a match and some of the DNA has been misplaced."

"What does that mean? I was told that my brother and wife were in that car." He realized that while he'd seen Ginny get into the car, he'd never seen the driver. It was only later that he learned it had been Beau behind the wheel. "Are you telling me it wasn't my brother?"

"I'm telling you that they are running the DNA again. It was probably just a mix-up at the lab and that will be the end of it. I thought this would relieve your mind."

Dylan only wished it had. He found himself questioning everything. "Has anyone else that we know died recently?"

"You're asking about Allen Zimmerman."

"I am. If someone had a list of names and was coming after us…"

"It doesn't appear so," Ike said.

"I'm wondering who leaked the list." Dylan couldn't believe he was saying this.

"Not our own boss," his friend said. "I'll see what I can find out."

"Thanks." He hated to think he might be right. He had trusted Zimmerman with his life numerous times. But he also knew that people changed, circumstances changed.

He took out the envelope they'd found in the Monopoly game and opened it as he drove. Inside was a very slim thumb drive and a note in his brother's handwriting:

Be careful who you give this to.

That's all it said.

He put it back and followed Cat to Fortune Creek. Once he saw her safely into her office, he thought about going by the ranch to put the drive into his computer to see if the list was actually on it. But going near the ranch right now felt too dangerous. Only one person knew where he was going at this moment. Officer Fuller.

That thought made him suddenly uneasy.

Be careful who you give this to.

Dylan swore. He didn't know who to trust. But at least Cat should be safe back at her office. He told himself that this would all be over soon. But would they find his nephew?

He'd done his best not to think about the missing baby. It hurt too much to think that Beau had left something so precious, and Dylan might never get to see his nephew, let alone hold him.

He had to end this, but was giving the thumb drive to Fuller the right move?

He checked his rearview mirror to make sure he hadn't picked up a tail. Earlier he'd worried that he and Cat might be followed from the wrecking yard. They hadn't. It was hard to follow anyone on these narrow highways with so little traffic—unless you didn't mind being seen, he thought, remembering his big truck trying to force Cat off the road.

DYLAN HAD INSISTED on following Cat back to Fortune Creek. He now sat behind the wheel of his pickup parked in front of the sheriff's office determined to make sure she was safely inside. She waved as she pushed open the door and Helen looked up, pursed her lips and went back to her knitting.

Cat turned to see Dylan drive away, her heart in her throat. She hoped he was doing the right thing giving the information to Fuller.

"Any messages?" Cat asked.

"On your desk."

"Any chance the baby has been found?"

Helen looked up, her needles still going. "Probably would have mentioned that right away if he had been."

Maybe, Cat thought, not so sure about that. "And I would have appreciated it." She saw that Helen was now making something small out of pink yarn.

Turning away, she headed for her office. Dylan had the document. Once he handed it over and word was released that the list had been found and was back in safe keeping, this still wouldn't be over. It wouldn't be finished until Athena's and Beau's infant son was found.

In her office, Cat dropped into her chair. Her daughter had been kicking all day, especially when she'd recognized the truck that had hit Taylor. The statute of limitations on hit-and-run in Montana was three years. Whoever was driving that truck that night six months ago could still be arrested and convicted. Was it the same person who'd tried to run her off the road last night?

She went through her messages. Most were updates on the case. It had been Athena's blood in the passenger side seat of Patty Cooper's car. The baby had also been in the car. But there was no update on where Patty or the baby were now.

Same with Rowena. She too was missing.

Cat assumed Dylan would tell Fuller about Luca Harmon coming to the lake house as they were leaving with another individual, probably his sister Sharese.

According to the message from the DCI lab, DNA was taken from the truck windshield and steering wheel. No word on a match yet. There was a BOLO out on Rowena and Patty, but neither had been found. And Athena's baby was still missing. There had been numerous sightings of a woman with a baby, but none of them had turned up Patty Cooper and the missing baby boy.

Cat filed the messages, followed up on a few other things, cleaned her desk and noticed the time. The day was almost over. Helen was already packing up her things to go home and let dispatch in Eureka take over.

"You look tired," Helen said, appearing at Cat's office door. "You should go upstairs and get some rest."

Surprised at Helen's concern, Cat opened her mouth, but nothing came out. Before she could respond, the older woman turned and left, locking the front door behind her. She found herself smiling. That was the nicest Helen had been to her since she'd started this job. She was winning the woman over.

It was a small victory, but Cat would take it. She picked up her belongings and turned out the light as she headed for the back door and the stairs that would take her up to her apartment.

Her thoughts circled back to Dylan Walker, as they had since the day she'd met him. She'd let down her guard with him in a way that shocked her. She more than liked him, and she felt that he liked her as well. But they both had so much baggage. She cupped her protruding baby bump. Not to mention, the timing was definitely off. The last thing she wanted was Dylan to feel guilty for what had happened to Taylor and think he could make it right by… by what? Being with her?

What had happened the other day at the lake house, the way she'd surrendered to the passion, made her wonder. He'd done it for her pleasure, her satisfaction, she told herself as she climbed the stairs to her apartment. What about his own? He'd said another time, but another time hadn't presented itself. Because he thought their lovemaking had been a mistake?

Opening the apartment door, she reached in and flicked on the light. For a second, she was blinded by the sudden brightness. For a second, she didn't see the shape standing silhouetted against the front window. For a second, she didn't recognize the woman from the photographs she'd seen of her.

She did a double take, her voice cracking with both her fright and her shock as she said, "I thought you were dead."

Chapter Nineteen

Dylan called his friend Ike again. "I have some classified very sensitive data. I honestly don't know who to give it to. Can you find out what you can about a man named Brian Fuller. He spelled both names. He introduced himself as an officer with the regional CIA agency with a photo ID badge that would get him into the CIA office building. But my question is, can I trust him?"

"I'm going to have to get back to you."

Disconnecting, Dylan pulled off the main road and drove back into the hills to a spot where he could see the road behind him. It was empty. He waited, wondering how long before Fuller called. What he was really wondering was how anxious Fuller was to get his hands on this data. Too anxious might make Dylan suspicious.

The sun dipped behind the mountains, casting the landscape in shadow as clouds gathered and the temperature dropped. Spring in Montana, he thought. It was the ficklest of seasons, teasing with warm sunny days only to turn into winter in the snap of your fingers. He thought of his nephew and hoped he was someplace warm and safe. His thoughts turned to Cat only moments before she called.

"Hey, I was just thinking about you," he said without

preamble when he picked up. Silence. He felt the hairs rise on the back of his neck, the cab of the pickup suddenly colder than just moments before. "Cat?" The word came out on a breath as his chest tightened and his heart began to pound harder.

"And I was hoping you were thinking about me," said his wife.

He gripped the phone. Some kind of DNA mix-up, wasn't that what Ike had said. He'd thought it had to do with Beau's DNA from the bombing. He thought of those few seconds when the car with his wife had been out of his sight. Enough seconds that she'd gotten out of the car before it blew? And what? Someone else had climbed in?

"Ginny?" He sounded calmer than he felt. His mind raced. This was no trick. It was definitely Ginny, and she was definitely calling from Cat's cell phone. "What's going on?"

Her laugh chilled him to his bones. "I was just visiting with your... Cat." She laughed again. "Really, Dylan?"

"Catherine Jameson is the acting sheriff there in Fortune Creek, Ginny."

"Yes, I'm aware of that. I'm also aware of your...relationship with the very pregnant acting sheriff. Not yours."

"I wish, but no. Didn't meet her until recently when she came out to the ranch suspecting me of murder. But you wouldn't know anything about that, right? Because you've been playing dead."

"You sound bitter. I had really hoped that you had found happiness out here in the sticks and were getting over me."

"Let me talk to Cat."

"She's busy."

He ground his teeth. His hand gripped the phone so hard it ached. "Ginny, I was hoping that it would turn out that you were one of the good ones, double-crossing your bad friends to do the right thing and that's what had gotten you killed."

"You never understood me, Dylan."

"But I'm definitely beginning to."

"Good, since we should meet. I'll bring your little sheriff along for the ride. Come to the ranch, oh and, lover...? Be sure to bring the thumb drive. Make sure it is just you, no feds; otherwise, it would be awful if anything happened to your... Cat."

With that, she disconnected. Dylan swore. Ginny was alive. Why wasn't he more surprised? Because the woman was a liar, a spy, a killer since she'd let some other woman dic to cover her tracks. Some relative of hers since the DNA had been a close-enough match that it hadn't been caught the first time around?

He took a breath, let it out and tried to calm down. He couldn't underestimate what Ginny might do, especially to Cat. Rowena must have told her about him and the acting sheriff. He'd only managed to put Cat in more danger, but now he had to play this carefully, he told himself, as he started his pickup and drove toward the ranch.

He made only one call. "Ike, Ginny is alive and has taken the acting sheriff from Fortune Creek, who is seven months pregnant. I'm headed to the ranch. Let the FBI know—but tell them not to move in until I give them a signal."

"A signal."

"They'll know if they are close to the ranch," he said.

"Good luck."

IT DIDN'T TAKE a lot of persuading to get Cat into the van that pulled up behind the sheriff's department. She recognized the driver from earlier today when he'd come racing up in a boat. Luca Harmon drove while Cat rode in the back with his sister Sharese. Cat recognized her from her Montana driver's license photo. Like Cat, Sharese didn't look happy to be there, especially with Ginny holding a gun on them both.

"So how did it work?" Cat asked Ginny. "You got in the car but didn't go far before you got out and someone else got in before the car blew up? Or did Dylan just think he saw you get into the car? Someone in the same dress, about the same height, same hairdo?"

Ginny mugged a face. "What does it matter? I'm alive and here."

"Anyone we know?" Sharese asked, sarcastically. "Or just someone you chose off the street to die in your place?" Ginny ignored her.

"But where did Beau Walker fit in?" Cat asked.

This got a smile out of Ginny. "He was very helpful."

"And apparently paid a high price for it," the sheriff said. "Unless he got out of the car too."

Ginny shook her head. "Some people have to die for the cause."

"Just not you," Sharese said, seeming not bothered as the gun moved to point more in her direction than Cat's.

"When's your baby due?" Ginny asked.

"Six weeks or so," she answered, thinking it was probably obvious anyway. "What about Rowena? I'm assuming like Athena, she's dispensable," Cat said. "What about Athena's baby though?"

Ginny shook her head and called up front to Luca. "Are we about there yet? I'm really getting tired of being interrogated back here."

"Rowena is a foot soldier," Sharese said. "She just isn't smart enough to know what happens to the foot soldiers when they are no longer needed. Like Athena."

"Athena turned on us," Ginny snapped. "She knew the price of betrayal."

"Did her baby know that price too?" Cat asked and grimaced, her hand going to her stomach. She saw Ginny's eyes widen just as she'd hoped.

"Where is the baby?" Sharese asked. "If I find out you killed—"

Dylan's not-so-dead wife gave her cohort a warning look. "We aren't monsters. We're no different from people in this country. We just have our own beliefs and see the world order differently."

Cat kept pretending to have contractions. She could see Ginny's worried look since another baby wasn't part of her plan. "Were you driving the truck that night six months ago when you killed my husband or was Luca?"

The question caught Ginny completely off guard. It was the first time Cat had seen the gun in her hand waver. Not that she was about to try to disarm Ginny in this van. They were on their way to the ranch. All she could hope was that she would get a chance once there.

"I don't know what—"

"Sure you do," Cat continued, holding her hand over her stomach and wincing. "You'd taken that big old farm truck out of the barn and driven up to the border probably carrying some form of contraband when you hit a white car my husband was driving on his way home from a fishing trip. He lived long enough to give a description of the truck—just not the driver."

"That was him?" Luca asked, turning from the driver's seat. "I told you to slow down."

"Shut up," Ginny snapped at him, her gaze locked with Cat's.

"So it was you," Cat said. "Once I saw the truck I had a feeling you were driving it that night."

"She's known for her reckless behavior," Sharese said. "Always just looking out for number one."

"You really should shut up too, Sharese," Ginny ground out from between clenched teeth even as her gaze remained locked with Cat's. "That was your husband?" She motioned her head toward Cat's baby bump.

Cat spoke as if in physical pain. "I never got to tell him I was pregnant."

Ginny looked uncomfortable and concerned now. "I always wanted a baby."

"That's not what Dylan says," Cat said.

She shrugged. "There's a lot Dylan doesn't know about me, but it seems he knows you fairly well and in such a short time. He apparently didn't learn anything about falling in love too quickly with me."

"It wasn't love with you," Sharese said. "It was the package you presented with that whole body of yours and the lies you told him. He didn't see the ugly self-centered rotten insides of you."

The tension in the van kicked up a few more notches. Cat half expected Ginny to shoot the woman.

"I do what I do for the cause," Ginny snapped.

Sharese scoffed. "You don't care about the cause. You jumped on board because it gave you an excuse to hurt people in the name of some ideal that I doubt you even understand."

"Enough," Luca called back to his sister as the van slowed and he made the turn into the ranch.

The air felt heavy and dark as they bumped along the road to the gate. Cat wondered if Dylan was already here. He'd said that he'd changed the code. Even Rowena shouldn't have been able to get in.

But as they approached the gate, Cat saw that it was standing open. The sight gave her little hope of how this was going to end.

DYLAN STOOD ON the deck of his cottage waiting. Ginny had Cat. He could feel the thumb drive in his jeans' pocket. His phone was in his other pocket, ready to send in the troops.

His weapon was tucked into the back of his jeans, covered by his shirt. But it wasn't the only one on him. He feared if it came down to gunplay, they would all lose. But at the same time, he knew he'd do whatever he had to so Cat and her unborn baby left here alive.

In the distance he saw a van come roaring out of the trees headed for him. He fisted his hands at his sides for a moment, then tried to relax. He had no idea how many people were in the van or what Ginny would do once she had the thumb drive. Three of her associates were dead— probably killed by friendly fire.

Did she plan on getting rid of everyone who knew about the thumb drive? That led him to believe that she didn't plan to turn it over to either the US or Russia. She must have put it up for auction, betraying not just her native country and her adopted country, but those comrades she'd pulled into her scheme.

The van stopped just feet from the deck. Still, he waited. Ginny was in control—at least for the moment.

The side door on the van rolled open loudly a few moments before Ginny stepped out. If she was scared, she didn't look it. She didn't look all that much different from the last time he'd seen her. Except now she wore canvas pants, a T-shirt and combat boots and held a gun in her hand.

She smiled at him for an instant before she pulled Cat out of the van, using her as a shield. He saw the gun leveled at the acting sheriff's back.

For a moment, no one moved, then the driver of the van killed the engine and climbed out. Luca Harmon. Ginny said something to whoever was still in the van and a moment later a woman he recognized from the salon photo stepped out. Sharese Harmon.

Everyone seemed to be waiting for Ginny's orders.

"You know what I'm here for," his not-so-deceased wife said. "Give it to me or I will kill your… Cat."

"That was cute the first time, Ginny, but now it's getting a little stale. I want to know where my nephew is."

She eyed him, seeming surprised that he didn't look scared or worried or even anxious. She glanced around as if realizing she might have walked into a trap. The spring day had turned into a cloudy, cold evening with the sky spitting ice crystals that hung in the twilight. Any moment it would start to snow.

"Why don't we take this inside where it's warmer?" he said and started to turn toward the cottage. Out of the corner of his eye he saw Sharese and her brother start toward the deck steps and stop abruptly as Ginny spoke.

"This isn't that kind of visit," she barked. "Give me what I came here for and then we'll leave."

"You won't be leaving with Cat."

Ginny chuckled at that.

"I'm still waiting. Where is my nephew?" he demanded.

She shook her head. "I don't know why you're stalling

but it's making me nervous. I hope I don't pull the trigger accidently and kill your girlfriend. The thumb drive, Dylan. *Now!*"

Chapter Twenty

Cat wondered if Dylan believed Ginny was going to let any of them go once she had the drive. Cat didn't think so, but she also didn't want to take the chance that the woman might shoot them all if she didn't get what she wanted.

As far as Cat could tell, Luca wasn't armed. Sharese either. But the hairdresser was feisty enough that she could have a weapon on her. Cat would assume that Ginny would have checked before, when Sharese and her brother had picked her up in the van and then dropped her off at the sheriff's office apartment.

Clearly Ginny didn't trust anyone, even her own cohorts. Cat met Dylan's gaze and held it. She hoped she was reading it correctly as she winked, then suddenly grabbed her stomach, let out a cry of pain and bent over as if having a major contraction. The sound of a gunshot echoed around her, terrifying her that Ginny had pulled the trigger on the gun that had been pressed to her back. She realized that the woman was wounded as Ginny grabbed her by the hair and began to pull her toward the open van door, using Cat as a shield.

But the sheriff made herself into dead weight, slumping forward and slowing their progress. Ginny was yelling for Luca and Sharese to help her. Out of the corner of her eye, Cat saw Dylan launch himself off the deck at Ginny.

What she hadn't seen was Luca. He came flying toward them, intercepting Dylan. Sharese rushed to get behind the wheel of the van and now started it up.

Ginny almost had the two of them to the van door. Cat knew that she couldn't let Ginny force her back into the van. She and her baby were as good as dead if she did. She kicked back at the woman, bringing her boots down on Ginny's ankle. She heard her cry out in pain and jerk hard on the handful of Cat's hair in her fist, forcing her toward the gaping door of the van.

DYLAN DOVE OFF the deck. There was no way he was going to let Ginny take Cat. He almost had his hands on Ginny when Luca charged him from the side, driving them both to the ground. They grappled on the ground, Luca clearly trained for combat. Dylan hadn't had to use his training in a long while. He wished he could say the same for Luca as they fought.

At the same time, he tried to keep an eye on Cat and Ginny. He saw her stomp on Ginny's ankle, then hit her hard in the side with an elbow. Heard the cry of pain she made as Cat swung around going for the gun. He fought harder, terrified for Cat and her baby as he watched the sheriff try to wrestle the gun away from Ginny.

Cat shoved Ginny hard, slamming her into the side of the van, both still fighting for the gun. Ginny still had a death grip on the weapon. She had height and weight against Cat, but the sheriff was holding her own.

As he and Luca fought, Dylan heard Sharese rev the van's engine. She was yelling for Luca to get in when the gun Cat and Ginny had been fighting over went off. A few seconds later, the van lurched and died, rolling slowly backward. The horn began to honk as Sharese slumped over the wheel.

Luca cried out and struck Dylan, catching him in the jaw and knocking him backward before racing to his sister. Dylan righted himself and launched himself at Ginny. She'd been momentarily distracted as she and Cat were forced back from the moving vehicle.

He quickly wrestled the gun away and turned the weapon on her. "Move and I will shoot you."

Ginny stumbled back, blue eyes glittering with malice as he pulled Cat to him. He could see that she was breathing hard but didn't seem the worse for wear. Still he asked, "Are you all right?"

"Fine," Ginny snapped.

"I was talking to Cat."

"Fine," Cat said, but he saw her hand go to her stomach as if she was worried about her baby.

CAT COULD HEAR the worry in Dylan's voice, see it in his expression as the FBI came charging out of the trees. It took little time after that to take Luca and Ginny into custody.

By then, she was in Dylan's arms, the baby between them, both with a hand on her stomach. She waited to feel her daughter kick. Time seemed to stretch out forever before she felt her daughter moving again. Tears welled in her eyes as she nodded. She was all right. Her baby was all right.

But Dylan insisted a helicopter be ordered to take Cat to the hospital to make sure she was all right. He led her over to the deck, insisted she sit as they both gave their statements to one of the agents. His concern comforted her. There was no doubt in her mind that Ginny would have killed them all.

Both Ginny and Luca were now in cuffs in the back of a large SUV as the agents searched for anyone else who might have been involved. Still no sign of Rowena or Patty or the baby. The coroner had been called for Sharese. Agents had had to pull Luca away from his deceased sister. Even now, he was still beside himself, head down, silently sobbing.

Dylan asked to speak to Ginny and Luca before they were taken away. He stood at the open window looking in at Ginny and Luca. Cat heard most of the conversation, her heart breaking for him. "I used to think you were beautiful," he said to his wife. "I no longer do. There is something so cold and cruel in you, so soulless. I don't understand how you could have hurt so many people. Please, Ginny, at least tell me where I can find my nephew."

Ginny stared at him for a moment before smiling. "You'll never have him. He's ours now."

He shook his head. Cat could see that he was fighting the urge to choke the truth out of the woman. Cat felt the same way. It shocked her the animosity she felt. It made her question her time as acting sheriff.

Luca's head came up, his eyes puffy from crying, his face blotchy. "Patty has your nephew," he said between sobs.

"Shut up!" Ginny snapped. "If you say another word—"

Luca spat out the words. *"You killed my sister."*

"It was an accident, you fool."

Luca shook his head. "My sister and I didn't want any of this and you knew it. You dragged us into this." He turned to one of the FBI agents right outside the vehicle. "I'll tell you everything."

"Where can I find Patty?" Dylan asked and Luca gave him an address.

One of the FBI agents said, "We're on it."

"What about Rowena?" Dylan asked Luca, who only shook his head before he said, "Gone."

"Dead?"

Luca shrugged and looked at Ginny. "Probably."

Agents were headed for the address Luca had given them. Cat breathed a sigh of relief, smiling as Dylan put his arm around her and they headed to the chopper now setting down some distance away.

His look said that he'd found out what he could, now all he cared about was making sure Cat and her baby were all right.

After the FBI had arrived, everything had been a blur of activity. Cat told herself that her daughter was fine as they climbed into the chopper. Her baby was kicking maybe more than usual, but other than that...

Feeling exhausted, she closed her eyes as Dylan took her hand and squeezed it gently as if to say everything was going to be all right. She tried to think positive thoughts. Dylan told her that the FBI was going to pick up Patty Cooper Harper and his nephew at the address Luca had given them.

She thought of JP. The coroner had come over to her before he'd left with Sharese's body. He'd said he wanted to be sure she was all right, then given her a thumbs-up before leaving. She was beginning to think of him as a grandfather figure, cranky and yet cool in that he knew interesting stuff. Maybe she was injured, she thought, given the trail her mind had taken.

As much as Cat wanted to tell herself it was over, she knew she couldn't until the doctor told her that her baby was fine. Until Dylan had his nephew in his arms. She couldn't believe the way her boring job had turned out, as she and Dylan were strapped in and the chopper rose up above the trees headed for the hospital in Kalispell.

Once there, Dylan didn't leave her side until the doctor assured her that her daughter was fine. By then, it was morning. "But no more cops and robbers," he said. "Take it easy these last few weeks."

Cat smiled, nodding in relief. She would take it easy, she told herself as Dylan called the chopper to take her back to the ranch.

"He's going to pick us up out back. Ready?"

She hugged her stomach, feeling her daughter trying to get comfortable in the small space. They were both anxious for the infant to come bursting out into the world. Cat couldn't wait to meet her.

When she looked over at Dylan he was watching her, a frown on his face.

"I'm fine," she tried to reassure him.

"I know."

"That's not what's bothering you," she said. "Did they find Patty and the baby?"

He shook his head. "When they got to the address, she'd already left. They found lots of baby clothing and supplies. Apparently Patty is taking good care of him. They'll find her. They have to. The last person who saw them said that she had the baby and was so loving toward him that they'd thought she must be the mother."

"The feds will find him," she said, touching Dylan's arm. She'd been so relieved that her daughter was all right that she'd just assumed the call had been from the FBI and they'd found Patty and the baby.

Nothing was over for Dylan. His deceased wife had

come back and was now headed for jail, but he still didn't know the part his brother Beau had played in all this. Of course, it wasn't over for him and wouldn't be until he had his nephew.

THE CHOPPER LANDED in the same spot it had earlier at the ranch. The van Sharese had been killed in was gone and so was any evidence of what had happened there last night.

Still Dylan felt a chill as he and Cat disembarked and headed for his pickup parked in front of the cottage. Nothing looked amiss, yet he found himself searching for movement, his senses all on alert. He saw that there was a light on in the big house upstairs. Rowena must have left it on.

Cat must have followed his glance because she picked up on his unease. She slowed and moved closer to him. The spring breeze had a bite to it he recognized. Snow. He breathed in the cold, almost welcoming it. They were almost to his pickup when he heard a baby cry.

The startling sound made him freeze, Cat next to him. "I want you to get into my pickup and leave," he whispered as he fished out his truck keys and handed them to her.

She took the keys, but said, "I'm not leaving you."

"Cat," he said impatiently. "Think of your baby."

"I'm thinking of mine and yours." They heard the sound again and both looked toward the cottage. Cat started moving toward the deck. Neither was armed. The feds had taken Dylan's weapons as well as Cat's.

He touched her arm. "Let me get my gun out of the pickup." He moved swiftly to the truck. It was unlocked. He reached in, felt under the seat and knew at once that the gun was gone. No reason to check the glove box. There wouldn't be a small one in there either.

Closing the pickup door, he stepped back and noticed

the odd way the truck was sitting. A glance under it solved that mystery. His right front tire was flat. He no longer thought Cat could get away. They were on their own here.

Cat seemed to notice his expression and looked again to the cottage where the baby had begun to cry louder. He knew there was no stopping her. She moved in that direction again, Dylan at her heels. She reached the door and opened it, but he insisted on going in first, determined to protect her to the end.

Once inside, he stopped to listen. It was dark except for a faint light toward the back of the cottage. He waited for his eyes to adjust. The crying was coming from a bedroom at the back. Seeing no motion, he stepped into the kitchen, drew out a knife from the rack, then followed the sound, afraid of what he would find. Cat was right behind him— after taking a small cast-iron skillet from where it hung next to the stove. It would have been comical, the two of them moving down the hall, if it hadn't been so serious.

The bedroom door was open, light spilling out along with the sound of the crying baby. Reaching the doorway, Dylan hesitated. He told himself it could be a recording to lure them down here. He thought he was right when the crying stopped.

He peered around the edge of the doorway and quickly jerked back, shocked at what he saw.

CAT HAD NO idea what Dylan had seen, but whatever it was had spooked him.

"You can come in," said a weak female voice from inside the bedroom. "I won't hurt you."

Something about the voice sent a chill through Cat. She pushed past Dylan into the doorway and stopped dead. The woman sitting in the chair by the window holding the baby looked like a ghost. Her skin was deathly pale, and a large bump protruded from her forehead. Both her eyes were blackened, her nose sat at an odd angle, and smears of dried blood covered her cracked upper lip.

Cat felt shock ricochet through her. She glanced at the baby, fearing it too had been injured. It didn't appear the infant was hurt, even as he began to cry again. Patty Cooper Harper looked nothing like her photo, but Cat knew it was her. She edged to the woman's chair, setting the small cast-iron skillet aside.

"May I hold him?" she asked, her voice cracking. For a moment she didn't think the woman would release him. The baby was wrapped in a small blanket that was stained with blood.

Patty looked down at the baby, a painful smile on her face as she slowly held him out to Cat.

The instant he was in her arms, Cat moved to the bed and laid him down so she could open the blanket and make sure it wasn't his blood. Her heart was pounding with fear. They finally had the missing baby. *Please don't let him be injured.*

Dylan snapped on the overhead light as she peeled back the blanket and inspected the infant. He appeared unharmed. He looked up at her then began to cry again. "I need a couple of towels," Cat said, trying to keep her voice calm.

Dylan produced several large ones. She placed the baby in one, then wrapped him up in a second one, before she began to rock him. The infant quieted in a few moments.

"Has he been fed?" she asked Patty, who nodded.

"I took care of him," she said quietly. Her eyes looked dark, hollow.

"Who hurt you?" Cat asked as Dylan went to the woman. Patty didn't answer, her eyes on Dylan.

"She's going to come back and kill us all." Tears formed in the woman's eyes and ran unheeded down her cheeks. "The baby too. I tried to fight her off but she…" Patty seemed unable to finish.

"How badly are you hurt?"

"Too bad." She looked to Cat holding the baby, rocking him in her arms. "Don't let her hurt him." Her eyes seemed to widen as if she'd heard the same thing Cat had. Someone had just opened the front door. Patty began to cry silently with sobs that racked her body.

DYLAN HAD HEARD the cottage door open as well. He looked at Cat, a silent message passing between them as she held the baby closer. He hid the knife up the sleeve of his shirt and moved to the door. There was so much he needed to say to her, desperately wanted to say. He just hoped he got the chance.

He could hear someone in the kitchen moving around. Stealthily, he closed the bedroom door and crept down the hallway, unsure who or what he would find. When he'd first bought the house, the Realtor had warned him about bears making themselves at home if he left a window or door unlocked.

But he knew it wasn't a black bear in his kitchen. As he reached the kitchen opening, he started to glance in when he heard Rowena's annoying voice.

"No reason to be sneaking around," she said as she turned from the sink where she'd been washing her hands. She dried them on her bloody pants. He caught the smell of smoke on her as one hand went into her pocket and came back out with one of his guns. She didn't point it at him. Instead, she held it at her side, almost daring him to make a move.

"Can't wait to hear what you've been up to," he said, not bothering to hide his disgust for the woman.

"Just finishing up here at the ranch," she said. "Make a girl a drink?"

His first instinct was to tell her to go to hell, but he curbed it and moved cautiously toward the living room. At the bar, he called back to her, "There's no ice in the bucket."

"I'll rough it this one time and go without," she said.

He didn't think she would shoot him before she had the drink as he slipped the knife from his sleeve and hid it next to the ice bucket. He worried that she was too smart and too well trained to let him get close enough to use the knife anyway. She had his guns from the pickup. He'd bet she'd also searched the house for more. She knew she had the upper hand and that he and Cat and the baby and Patty were now at her mercy.

"It's over, Rowena," he said as he mixed up the gin and tonic she liked. "Ginny and Luca are in jail. Sharese is dead."

"No loss there," the woman said, suddenly closer than he'd realized. He could barely smell her perfume under the stench of smoke. She just wasn't close enough to keep her from shooting him before he could disarm her or stop her with the knife.

He could hear in her voice how she was enjoying being one of the few left standing. Was she now in charge? It would appear so. The power had already gone to her head. This is probably what she'd always wanted. He thought about her relationship with Ginny. Rowena must have been jealous as hell, resenting his wife, wanting what she had.

Did that include him? He thought Cat might have been right about hoping to seduce him. Like that was ever going to happen, he thought.

He took his time finishing her drink with a slice of lime from the small container. Rowena would have preferred a fresh cut wedge, but then again, he doubted she would have wanted him using a knife.

Catching a glow through the nearby window, he looked in the direction of the big house on the side of the hill. It wasn't caused by the small light upstairs he'd seen earlier. This light was much brighter and appeared to be growing brighter by the moment. He realized what it was and let out a small laugh as he turned slowly to hand her the drink.

"You burned down my house?" he asked laughing. "The house I hated and refused to live in?"

"It was a symbolic gesture," she said, sounding angry. "Put the drink down there." She pointed to a side table. He did as she asked and moved again to the bar where there was at least one weapon at his disposal.

As she took the drink in her free hand and stepped back out of his range of attack, he noticed how tired she looked. "You look exhausted. Burning down houses isn't as easy as you thought, huh?"

Her gaze locked with his as she took a sip of the drink, and he saw fury in those blue eyes. He noticed that the gun was no longer at her side. It was now pointed at his heart.

"Mind if I make myself a drink?" he asked, already turning back to the bar and the knife. "I didn't expect you to come back here, figured you got whatever you'd come here for and were long gone."

"You know that's not true," she said with a chuckle. "You made sure I didn't get what I came here for." Again he heard something in her voice, a need for revenge against the woman she'd called her best friend—and that woman's husband.

"Can't imagine why you'd come back, especially just to burn down my house," he said as he poured a drink and considered both the knife and the heavy silver ice bucket partially filled with melted ice.

"Ginny thought she was so smart marrying you," Rowena said. "She was fulfilling her mission and then she was free—as long as she came through with the goods— the names of the US undercover operatives in the Soviet Union who'd been responsible for the deflection of the country's famous ballet star Giselle."

"This is about a ballet dancer?" Dylan demanded, half turning to look back at her. He'd never understand Russian politics.

"She was our leader's favorite," Rowena said.

"Of course," he mocked. "So, what went wrong?"

"Ginny." Her gaze hardened. "She started falling in love with you and wanted out."

He turned back to his drink. This wasn't what he wanted to hear. He'd faced the woman only hours ago. That hadn't been love in her eyes. "I don't believe you."

"She couldn't go to you, so she got your brother to help her. She was going to sell us out for you."

He shook his head, his hands fisting at his sides. "She got my brother killed."

"He knew what he was getting into," Rowena said flippantly.

He finished making his drink and picked up the glass, squeezing so hard he feared it would break. Every cell of him wanted to stop this woman, finish this and get Cat and his nephew to safety.

But Rowena wanted him to try to get the jump on her.

He could feel her waiting, sipping her drink, probably even smiling to herself. He knew she could shoot him before he could spin around. He took a sip of his drink and carefully put it down. As he did, he took hold of the edge of the ice bucket telling himself that if he flung it at her before he attacked, he might stand a chance.

"I hope I'm not interrupting anything," Cat said from behind them.

He froze, his hand loosening on the ice bucket as he slowly, carefully turned to see her standing a few yards behind Rowena. She was holding the baby wrapped in the towels he'd gotten for her, her expression fierce. She'd never looked more beautiful, he thought with a jolt that rocketed through him.

In those seconds, Rowena spun around, leading with the gun. Dylan's heart leapt to this throat as he rushed her. He expected to hear the sound of a gunshot. Instead, he heard a surprised cry from Rowena. Past her, he saw that Cat had thrown the baby at her. Rowena had dropped her drink and raised her arms either to protect herself or the baby—only to see the towels uncoiling as they flew through the air revealing nothing inside.

Taking advantage of Rowena's surprise, Dylan grabbed her from behind and twisted the gun from her fingers. She fought, screaming and crying as he took her to the floor.

"Ginny made me do it," she cried. "I had no choice. It was all her idea. She told me to find the thumb drive, then make you pay."

"It doesn't matter, Rowena," Dylan told her. "It's over. We know that the only reason you came out here in the first place was to find the missing document. You failed."

"That wasn't the only reason." Her gaze was pleading.

"I was as pretty as Ginny, smarter, and I had money. I still have money."

He shook his head as he heard what she was asking. "I'm sorry, but you're not my type."

Rowena jerked angrily under him. "And she is?" she demanded, motioning her head toward Cat.

"She is," he said nodding.

"You are so going to pay," Rowena spat out, the words hard and cold. "Your brother double-crossed us and look what happened to him. Now it's your turn."

"Beau paid with his life, Rowena. Wasn't that enough?"

She shook her head angrily as her gaze shot to Cat. "I wish you'd died the other night on the road. You're the one who should have crashed into the trees!" Her gaze swung back to Dylan. "I knew how to get to you. Take out your girlfriend."

"You were driving the truck?" he demanded through clenched teeth.

"Not me. I can't drive a stick shift," Rowena said. "Patty. But she failed and I got stuck babysitting that brat of Athena's. You should be thanking me. If Ginny had gotten her hands on that baby…"

At the sound of the baby crying down the hall, Cat hurried to retrieve him. When she returned, he saw from her expression that Patty was also gone. She cuddled the infant to her, the crying stopping as the sound of sirens filled the air.

"Patty's gone," Cat said to Rowena. "Everyone is either in jail or dead."

Rowena snorted. "You're the ones who killed Patty, the two of you, running her off the road. When she hit that tree, the steering wheel crushed something inside her. She hasn't been the same since. I'm surprised she survived this long."

"Why didn't you get her to a doctor?" Cat cried, only to have Rowena give her an impatient look.

"Why do you think?"

"Well, it's over now," Dylan said.

Rowena glared at him. "You think this is over? It will never be over. There's more of us, lots more of us."

"And more of us," Cat said. "You're fighting a losing battle."

As Dylan let the federal officers take Rowena away, he reached for Cat, drawing her to him. After a moment, she said, "Would you like to hold your nephew?"

He felt his eyes burn with hot tears. Beau's son. He'd feared that he would never get to see him—let alone hold him. His throat constricted as he nodded, and she put the infant in his arms. He was almost afraid he would break down when he looked into the infant's tiny precious face.

What was he going to do with a baby? But then he did look. He felt a jolt. Baby Doe was the spitting image of Beau when he was a baby. He felt his heart fill and he knew. They were both going to be all right. Wasn't this what he'd always wanted, a family? He just hadn't dreamed of becoming a family like this. But he could do this, he could raise this baby on his own. It was what his brother would have wanted. It was also what he suspected Athena had wanted when she'd tried to reach him.

He glanced up at Cat and smiled through his tears. She too was crying. Peering down again at the beautiful baby in his arms, he whispered, "You're safe now. We're going to be just fine, you and me. You'll see."

Chapter Twenty-One

A strange quiet filled the days after the last of the arrests, Cat thought. It was spring in Montana, the sunny afternoons causing everything around Fortune Creek to turn green. The air smelled of new growth as grass emerged and trees sprouted leaves. The sky even seemed bigger and bluer with each day.

Cat had returned to the office and Helen. Dylan had done what he could for his nephew, who'd been sent by the court into foster care until the paperwork was completed and he could petition for guardianship and eventually adoption.

Then he'd been forced to go back to Washington, DC, to iron out things in the investigation. Cat knew that he personally wanted to give the list to someone he trusted. She wondered where the list of operatives had come from. She assumed that someone had gotten it to Ginny in the first place. She hoped Beau hadn't been in a position that he had access to the list and had foolishly been the one to give it to her, believing she was on the side of good.

But at some point, Beau had learned the truth and hidden the thumb drive in the game he and Dylan liked to play with a note to be careful who he trusted. That told her

Beau was trying to do the right thing and that was what had gotten him killed.

She wanted Beau's name cleared not just for Dylan but for his son. The man she'd come to care for had enough betrayal in his life. Dylan didn't need more. He called every night. She knew he was excited to get back to the ranch. He was anxious to finally have his nephew under his roof. Cat couldn't be happier for him, knowing he was going to make a great father. That was what he would eventually become, not an uncle, but a father after the adoption.

She knew how anxious he was for that. She certainly could understand the feeling. She knew nothing about becoming a mother. But like Dylan, she was excited and ready for whatever it brought. Her daughter seemed to be anxious to make her exit. Cat felt as if she might burst with the life growing inside her.

Meanwhile, she had her own case to finalize. She spent a few days writing up her report. Cat was glad when they got word from Sheriff Parker that he and his bride Molly were returning to town. Molly was anxious to start her store in one of the old empty buildings in town, Cat heard. She hadn't spoken with the sheriff, nor had she met him. He'd already taken off on his honeymoon when she'd been assigned the job. After everything that had happened, he'd decided it was time to bring his wife home.

Cat had been looking forward to meeting this legend in Fortune Creek almost as much as Helen was looking forward to his return. They had both been waiting expectantly when he and Molly walked into the office.

Helen had let out a shriek and dropped her knitting to race over to him. For a moment, Cat thought she was going to throw her arms around the man. But Helen stopped short and said, "Nice to have you back, Sheriff." Then her gaze had taken in Molly, the pretty, dark-haired woman by his side. "You too," Helen said with less warmth.

Molly smiled and said, "Good to see you again, Helen."

By then the sheriff had spotted Cat in his office. "Sheriff," she said, seeing why he was so popular. He was handsome and had a great smile. She awkwardly stood.

"Heard you had your share of trouble, Sheriff."

She couldn't help smiling. "Nothing Helen and I couldn't handle."

He grinned at that. "I can well imagine." He motioned her back into her chair. "I'm just stopping by since I'm not officially back for another few days. Just wanted to introduce myself to the famous Sheriff Cat Jameson."

"Acting Sheriff Cat Jameson," she said, touched by his kind words. "And I believe you mean infamous."

He shook his head. "My hat's off to you," he said as he touched the brim of his Stetson. "It's a pleasure to meet you." He stepped toward her, extending his hand. "Congratulations, Sheriff," he said, his grip strong and warm. "For a job well done."

Cat chuckled. "Thanks, but it's nice to have you back."

She heard Molly telling Helen about the house Brandt was having built for them. Apparently, they wouldn't be staying in the tiny apartment upstairs.

"In the meantime, we'll be staying at the hotel," Brandt told Cat. "You're welcome to stay upstairs as long as you like."

"I'm not sure of my plans," she said, her hands going to her evermore protruding belly. "Except for the birth of my daughter. That is the only plan I have at the moment."

As he returned his attention to Molly, he introduced his wife to Cat, then talk turned to Fortune Creek and how nothing ever happened there, followed by laughter.

With that, the two of them said goodbye. Cat and Helen watched them leave, both looking after him with a little or a lot of awe. Cat felt relief to have him back since she'd been getting more uncomfortable with her pregnancy the past few days. Her daughter just seemed hell-bent to get out into the world.

THINGS IN THE Fortunate Creek Sheriff's Office soon returned to normal. Helen had moved on and was now knitting a huge throw in winter colors.

"It's a present for a friend," Helen said, as if Cat had asked. "Going to take me a while so I thought I'd start it now."

Cat realized she was going to miss the office, miss Fortune Creek. She'd told the sheriff the truth. She hadn't let herself think beyond the birth of her daughter. After that, she'd decide what she wanted to do, where she wanted them to live, what came next. Life had thrown her too many curveballs to make plans too far into the future. If she'd learned anything, it was that.

But Fortune Creek had warmed to her—and she to it. Ash had started coming across the street from the hotel a couple of times a week to bring her lunch courtesy of the local café. He'd bring a couple of lunch specials and they'd sit in her cramped office visiting.

Cat had looked forward to those visits to break up her day. Ash told her about the ventriloquist who'd been murdered in his hotel before her time as sheriff. Since then he'd been trying to learn how to throw his voice, he told her. He'd practice at night, he said, but hadn't gotten it down yet.

It was strange, Cat thought. More people in town said hello to her and Helen was almost downright chatty on occasion. She realized that she felt more at home here in Fortune Creek. She'd been contacted with several job offers. But she was determined not to make any plans until after her daughter was born.

Cat spent the last few days as acting sheriff going through baby names online, trying to find the perfect one. She was thankful that the office gone back to being a place where nothing ever happened.

Until her water broke.

DYLAN COULDN'T WAIT to get back to the ranch—and Cat. They'd left things up in the air with him needing to go out to DC at the bequest of the prosecutor and Cat needing to tie up the loose ends of her case back in Fortune Creek.

He'd finally gotten the answers he'd desperately needed about his former boss, Allen Zimmerman.

"Turns out that his wife had been sick with cancer for several years," Ike told him. "I guess they didn't want anyone to know. But it drained them financially. Turns out also that Allen was deep in debt and about to lose his house just before his wife died. I guess he was desperate, and someone found out and took advantage."

Dylan wished his old boss had come to him. He would have gladly helped him out. But he suspected Allen had too much pride, so he'd sold out the men under him and his country. "Was it suicide?"

Ike nodded. "I think it was. He finally realized what he'd done. But not before he'd contacted your brother Beau."

Feeling a start, Dylan said, "Why would he do that?"

"It was originally thought that Beau was in on it, acting as an intermediary between the two countries. We now believe that he had tried to get Beau to get the list back."

"Why wouldn't he come to me?" Dylan demanded.

"Probably because you were married to Ginny Cooper," Ike said simply.

He swore and raked a hand through his hair. "So Beau—"

"Got hold of the thumb drive and left it for you to find because by then he must have known how deep this Russian cell was—or at least suspected as much. You were the only one he could trust."

"Is there any chance Ginny—"

Ike was already shaking his head before Dylan could finish.

"When she didn't get what she wanted, no doubt needed because of the people pulling her strings, she had Beau killed and faked her own death," Ike said.

Ike would never forgive Ginny for what she'd done. Ginny coming back from the dead had come as a shock to them both. Things had gotten ugly and dangerous at the end. He knew they were both lucky just to be alive. Ginny had admitted that she was driving the truck the night Cat's husband was killed. She and Luca had been hauling a load of stolen catalytic converters up to Canada that night. The sale would help finance more of their plans. It had been Ginny who'd left Taylor Jameson to die in his car beside the road.

Dylan was working on forgiving himself for marrying her, buying the place in Montana and leaving the keys in the old truck in the barn so she could drive it the night Taylor Jameson was killed.

Love was definitely blind since all he'd seen was surface beauty. If he had looked a little deeper…

He thought of Cat and how she radiated a warmth and compassion that made him want to be a better man. He ached for her in so many ways. She'd stolen a chunk of his heart from the very first. The more he was around her, the more he lost of his heart. He was totally taken with the woman, having never felt like this before. He couldn't imagine his life without her, and that scared him since he had no idea how she felt about him.

Now flying into Kalispell, it surprised him how much he'd missed the state. Montana had been a place to hide— but only temporarily. He'd never planned to stay there— not with that large house full of the hopes and dreams he'd had with Ginny, a reminder of everything bad that had happened. A part of him had always thought he'd go back to DC.

But that had changed when he met Cat. He realized he had no desire to be anywhere but on the ranch—with her. The big house was gone, thankfully burned to the ground with everything Ginny had put in it. He wondered why she'd bothered to decorate it. Had she hoped they would make a life there—after she finished her mission for her native country?

He thought again of the house, recalling how Ginny had taken the old truck from the barn to make the run to Canada that had killed Cat's husband. She'd never planned to live there. Like everything else, the house had been a means to an end.

Grass would grow on the site and all memory of Ginny and the house would be gone forever, he told himself. He would have to rebuild. He'd thought about the house he would want if his dreams came true. That was up to Cat. He hated to get his hopes up since he knew he was getting ahead of himself even thinking about them living together with their babies and needing more room than the cottage could accommodate.

He still had to ask Cat to marry him. Hell, he hadn't

even asked her out on a date. Also, he still had to get his nephew adopted and the two of them settled in. But he found himself looking forward to the future full of hope.

Dylan couldn't believe the twisted path his life with Ginny had taken and how it ended the way it had. He knew it wasn't his fault all the terrible things Ginny had done, but if he'd never met her... He would have never met Cat, he told himself. He was just thankful that out of all the bad, it had brought Cat and her baby into his life. Soon he would have his brother's son. He'd been thinking about names, since it was time Baby Doe had one. But he wanted to see what Cat thought.

Dylan couldn't wait to bring his brother's and Athena's child home to the ranch. He was so thankful that Beau's name had been cleared. Ginny had used him, threatening the lives of people he cared about to force him to help her. Beau being Beau had thought she was trying to get away from her birth land and the pressure on her from people who wanted to destroy the US.

But in fact, Ginny had been acting as a double agent the whole time, betraying both countries—and his brother.

He tried to push thoughts of the past away as the plane flew toward Kalispell, Montana. He had so many plans, all of them involving Cat. He just hoped she felt the same way about him.

The moment his plane landed, he turned his phone back on and saw that he had a text from a woman named Helen Graves.

Cat is in labor. She's gone to Kalispell to the hospital.

ONCE IN HIS PICKUP, Dylan drove straight to the hospital. He hated the thought of Cat having this baby alone even as he questioned if she would want him there. He hurried into the hospital, went to the desk and asked where the maternity ward was.

"Are you the father?" the nurse asked. He smiled, clearly anxious and trying to come up with an answer that would get him in to see Cat. The nurse took that as a yes. "Glad you made it. Come with me." She headed down the hall and he followed, wincing at the thought of what would happen when the nurse found out the truth. That truth could come quickly, he realized as they reached the room, and both stepped inside.

Cat lay on the bed, clearly in labor. She saw him, her eyes widening as she breathed through a contraction.

"Your husband made it in time," the nurse announced.

Cat looked from the nurse to Dylan. He gave a slight shrug and an embarrassed smile. She nodded and held out her hand and he stepped to her bedside and took it in his. She closed her eyes and breathed for a few moments as the contraction passed before another one started.

"I think we'd better have the doctor to take a look," the nurse said after checking her.

"What can I do?" Dylan asked. She squeezed his hand in answer, so he just held on to her as another contraction began.

A doctor came into the room and moved to the end of the bad. "Sounds like you're just about there," he said. "This is your husband?" Cat didn't answer as she focused on her breathing.

"Dylan," he said, introducing himself to the doctor. "What can I do to help?"

The doctor laughed. "Looks like you're doing it. Your first, huh? Get ready, you're about to become a father."

He swallowed the lump that had risen in his throat and

looked at Cat. Tears burned his eyes, and he squeezed her hand.

Moments later nurses came in and things got hectic. Dylan kept his eyes on Cat, holding onto her, wishing there was more he could do.

Then he heard the baby suddenly begin to cry loudly. The doctor said, "Got yourself a healthy baby girl. Great set of lungs on her too," he added chuckling as the nurse cut the cord, took the baby for a few moments then handed her back wrapped in a blanket.

The baby in his arms, the doctor moved to the opposite side of the bed and laid the baby into her mother's arms. "Congratulations. You have a name for her yet?"

Cat shook her head, tears running down her face as she looked at her daughter. Dylan had to fight his own emotions, a lump so big in his throat that he couldn't speak if he had to. Then Cat looked over at him. "You want to hold her?"

She didn't wait for an answer as she handed over the tiny bundle. He couldn't believe how perfect she was. "She's beautiful," he breathed. "Just like her mama."

CAT WOKE TO find Dylan stretched out asleep on the cot next to her bed. She noted the stubble that darkened his jaw, his wrinkled shirt, his legs that were almost too long for the makeshift bed that had been brought in.

Between them was the bassinet with her beautiful daughter sleeping soundly. She wanted to wake her just to hold her, but didn't, thankful that they'd both gotten some rest. The past few weeks she'd had a terrible time getting comfortable at night. As much as she kept telling herself that she couldn't wait for the baby to be born, she kind of missed having her tucked protectively inside her body. She missed that closeness, feeling her growing, watching her own body changing as the time came.

Now she would have to watch from the sidelines.

"She's going to be just like you."

Cat looked up into Dylan's face. "I didn't know you were awake." He lay on his side staring at her—and her daughter. "Thank you for being here."

"Thank you for allowing me to. I wouldn't have missed it for the world. It was amazing." He held her gaze. "You were amazing. I was already in awe of you, but now…"

She felt her cheeks heat under his gaze. "Women give birth every day."

"You really aren't good at taking compliments," he said, smiling. "I have such respect for all those women, but especially for you." He glanced into the bassinet. "Have you thought about a name yet?"

"Not yet. How was DC?"

Dylan kept looking at her daughter. "I'll tell you all about it later. Your sheriff back?" She nodded. "I filed all the paperwork to get my nephew. Now it's just waiting and reading lots of books about babies and childrearing. I'm terrified."

Cat looked at her sleeping daughter. "Me too. I thought I was ready, but maybe there is never any way to get ready for your first child."

"Especially when you never expected it," he agreed.

"Especially. We both were surprised. At least I had nine months to prepare myself. You're going to do great."

He sat up and she could tell he was going to leave. "You're going to do great too. I heard you're busting out of here. If you need a ride, a place to stay…"

"The sheriff has insisted I remain in the apartment over the office for at least a month before I make any big decisions. He and his wife are building on his ranch outside of town and living at the hotel until the house is finished."

"You think you'll stay in law enforcement?"

"Not sure about law enforcement. I just want to spend time with my daughter for a while before I decide."

Dylan nodded and slipped off the bed to stand. "If you need anything, call me. But I'll be keeping in touch. What about a ride tomorrow?"

"Ash from the hotel insisted on picking us up but thank you. And Dylan, thank you again for being here. Let me know how it goes with your nephew."

"Don't worry, I will. See you soon."

She could tell that there was more he wanted to say. She felt the same way, but right now, it felt too soon, so she let him walk away.

Chapter Twenty-Two

"You have visitors," the nurse said from the hospital room doorway a few hours later.

Helen came through the door first, followed by the sheriff and his wife, Molly, then residents of Fortune Creek, including Ash. They came with flowers, chocolate and cute baby clothes.

But what touched Cat the most was the present from Helen, a knitted pink sweater and booties. She looked up, tears in her eyes. "These are so adorable. Helen, thank you."

The older woman looked embarrassed. "She's going to need something to wear until it warms up. This is also for you." She handed over a large wrapped bundle. It was the blanket she'd been working on those past few weeks before Cat had gone into labor.

Cat held it to her. "It's so soft and warm. Thank you so much."

Helen bobbed her head and said she needed to get back to the office. "Someone should be working," she said in the direction of the sheriff as she left.

Brandt chuckled. "Seems you and Helen got on just fine," he said, sounding surprised.

All Cat could do was smile. "I might have her teach me how to knit."

The sheriff's wife spoke up. "You're braver than me. I get the feeling she thinks I stole Brandt from her." They all laughed, especially Cat since she knew it was true.

Ash brought her the donuts she loved, then sat and visited for a while. Cat thought he really needed to find himself a good woman and told him so.

"Not every woman wants to come live in Fortune Creek in an old haunted hotel."

"Is it really haunted?" Cat asked in surprise.

"That's what they tell me," was all he would say.

Ash gave her and her daughter a ride back to her apartment over the sheriff's office the next day. Cat heard from Dylan. He'd gone to the state capital in Helena to finish the paperwork to get his nephew and buy more baby books.

"It's going to be fine," she told him, chuckling at how nervous he sounded. She'd seen what the man could do under pressure. She had no doubt that he could handle a baby. She'd also felt his love and affection and knew that his nephew was in great hands.

When she arrived at the apartment, there was a beautiful bassinet full of baby things and flowers, all from Dylan with a note that read, *According to the books I've been reading, these are things you're really going to need. D*

Cat smiled and found that he was right. She'd planned to let her daughter sleep with her for a while, unsure how long they would be in the upstairs apartment. Now that they were staying for a while, the bassinet was perfect.

She texted him a thank you.

You were right! I needed all of this! I just hadn't realized it yet. Thank you for such a thoughtful gift.

Time passed quickly as she found herself immersed in all things baby. In the meantime, she really needed to give her daughter a name. She had wanted to wait until the baby was born. Now that her darling little girl was here, she couldn't put it off any longer. The hospital had called again today about the birth certificate.

She finally decided on Lizzie Taylor Jameson, naming him after her mother, Elizabeth, and her daughter's father, Taylor.

Dylan called every evening, filling her in how things were going at the ranch. The ashes and debris from the big house had been carted away. A foundation would soon be laid for the new house.

For hours, they designed this new house, discussing what it should look like, what rooms were needed, what appliances it should have. For Cat it was like building a house online, just a dream of what she'd want if she ever got to design her own house. It was a game to her. She had no idea if Dylan even took her suggestions seriously.

They also talked about the adoption and how it was going. He'd gotten to spend time with his nephew so they also talked babies. He'd been reading baby books. When he learned about something that worked well, he would send the item to her as well as buy one for himself. Her apartment was now filled.

"Do babies really need all this?" she'd asked him, laughing.

"Apparently," he'd said. "Who knew?"

She often fell asleep talking to Dylan about everything from air fryers to unidentified aircraft he'd once seen. She knew his favorite color and he knew hers. He knew what kind of sheets she liked and why. Just as she knew what kind of coffee he preferred and how he was allergic to shellfish.

Often they would be giving a bottle to the babies when he called during his visitations with his nephew. Cat loved the closeness she shared with him.

In the meantime, she marveled at how Fortune Creek felt like home even though she'd been there for such a short time. It had been bumpy at first, trying to fill Sheriff Parker's big boots. But ultimately, she'd held her own.

With spring turning to early summer, she often took her daughter out in her expensive stroller—thank you, Dylan—for a walk around town. Everyone would make a point of coming out to greet them, so she got to know more residents. Sometimes she and her daughter would go to the café for lunch. Her daughter loved all the attention she got.

As she sat on the couch, she looked into the bassinet at Lizzie. It really had been such a thoughtful gift from Dylan, and she hoped she got to tell him so in person soon.

Her cell phone rang and she picked up at once when she saw it was Dylan.

"I'm downstairs. Is this a bad time?" he asked.

"It's a perfect time," she said. "Come on up. It doesn't lock anymore after Ginny let herself in." A few moments later, she opened the apartment door to him.

He handed her a bouquet of daisies. In his other hand was a baby carrier, and she realized she was finally going to meet the baby she'd been so anxious to see.

"The adoption went through!" she cried as she knelt down to pull back the small blanket to see his face.

"Oh, Dylan, he's beautiful. Come in, come in."

She took the flowers and put them in a vase while Dylan freed his nephew from the carrier. "Want to hold him?"

She nodded vigorously, and he placed the baby in her arms. "Oh, look at those bright blue eyes!"

"He and your daughter could be brother and sister," Dylan said as he came to stand next to her, both admiring the little boy. "He's grown so much since the first time I saw him."

Her daughter let out a squawk from her bassinet and they moved over to her.

"Thank you again for this," Cat said of the bassinet. She handed him the baby and picked up her own. "It's perfect."

"Just like your daughter. What did you end up naming her?"

She told him with a laugh. They had both agonized over naming the babies.

"I wanted to run it by you, but I had to give him a name for the adoption papers. Meet Beauregard James Walker, named after his father and, Beau's and my father."

"That is a mouthful," she said with a chuckle.

"That's why his nickname is BJ."

"I like that," she said and presented her daughter. "Meet Lizzie Taylor Jameson. Named after my mother Elizabeth and—"

"And your daughter's father," Dylan said. "I think it's wonderful. She looks like a Lizzie. She looks like you."

They stood awkwardly for a few moments. All the hours they'd spent on the phone, they'd grown closer. But now being together after hardly seeing each other in person, they both felt shy.

"Any chance you're free for dinner?" he asked. "BJ and I are celebrating his six-month birthday out at the ranch tonight. I know it's late notice. I just realized the date."

"I'm having steak and salad. He'll be having formula, but it won't be long before he gets solids. Check out his two teeth," Dylan said like the proud father he was. "He is definitely a good eater. We'd love for the two of you to come."

Cat smiled. "We'd be delighted. Lizzie will be bringing her own bottle, but I'd love steak and salad. What can I bring?"

"Just you and Lizzie." Dylan's gaze met hers and held it. "Look at the two of us," he said smiling.

Epilogue

Cat moved to the porch at the sound of laughter. She couldn't help but smile at what she saw even as her heart raced a little. "Are you sure about this?" she asked her husband a little anxiously.

Dylan laughed and turned to the two children sitting astride the horse next to him. BJ had his arms around his sister who had one hand resting on the saddle horn. Both gave her a toothy grin. Both were dressed in what they called their cowboy outfits. Checked shirts, jeans and cowboy boots and hats.

"I rode my first horse at two," Dylan said.

"We're almost three!" the two children said almost in unison. Since they'd become brother and sister, they often finished each other's sentences. Anyone who didn't know their separate stories would have sworn they were hers and Dylan's biological children. BJ and Lizzie were inseparable, both growing like weeds, both unaware of how they had come into the world. Cat knew they wouldn't be able to protect them from finding out someday, but for now they were just the intricate part of this family she and Dylan had made.

Cat often looked back, wondering how things had turned

out like they had. Dylan had invited her and Lizzie to dinner at the ranch. There were other dates after that, both of them bringing their babies. She often wondered what people thought—not that she cared. She was too happy being with Dylan and BJ. Lizzie and BJ had taken to each other from the start. Instantly babbling together, later crawling after each other and now trying to outdo each other.

On Beau's six-month birthday and the first time he got solids, Dylan asked her to marry him. She remembered his face in the flickering light of his son's single birthday candle, him on his knees putting a beautiful diamond on her finger. She'd said yes.

Their wedding was held at the ranch. Dylan invited a few people from his past, but not many. Same with Cat. All of Fortune Creek had turned out. A barbecue had followed with local beef and pork on a spit. The day ended with them putting their children to bed. It had been perfect.

Since then, life had only gotten better, she realized as her hand went to her protruding belly and the two babies snuggled in there. Another boy and girl. She thought of the way Dylan had been shocked when they'd gotten the news.

"But I'm sterile," he said to the doctor.

"Apparently not," the doctor had said with a laugh. "Why don't we run some tests." They had. Cat was surprised Dylan had taken the news so well. There was a reason Ginny had been taking birth control pills. Dylan wasn't sterile. His results had been doctored to make him think he couldn't have children.

"How did we get so lucky?" he asked as if in awe.

Had it been luck? Or fate? She liked to think it had been love. There was no denying the immediate attraction she'd felt for Dylan. He'd apparently felt the same way. After going through everything they had, the danger had drawn them even closer together.

They seldom talked about the events that had brought them here or what they'd had to go through before becoming a family. Cat had realized that she wasn't going back into law enforcement. She had babies to raise with her husband.

They often joked about what they would tell the kids when asked how their parents met.

"How about this," Dylan had suggested one night as they lay in their king bed in their newly finished house. "Mommy came out to the ranch to arrest me."

Cat had laughed and said, "Daddy saved me from his evil houseguest with a crush on him."

"Not even funny," he'd said as he rolled her over on top of him and kissed her. There had been an agreement between them when it came to having children. "How about we have as many as we can afford," he'd suggested.

"Not a chance," Cat had said, shocked when she'd found out how much her husband was worth. "Let's just see how it goes."

They'd created the twins she now carried that night. Four children had a nice ring to it, but if she knew her husband—and she did—there would be more. BJ and Lizzie were already excited to meet their new siblings. Cat often marveled that Beau's start in life hadn't seemed to affect the sweet, thoughtful and caring child. Dylan said his namesake had been the same way. Cat knew that was probably what had gotten her husband's brother into trouble. Lizzie was a spitfire like her mother.

"You wanted her to be just like me," she reminded Dylan often. He would always laugh and nod and say, "Right, be careful what you wish for."

It had been a grand day when they'd moved into their new home that she and Dylan had designed with children in mind. It was a warm and welcoming place that often saw visitors from Fortune Creek. The sheriff and Dylan had hit it off, talking horses and ranching.

Brandt and Molly had finished their house just in time since Molly was pregnant. The four of them had become close, often having dinner at each other's houses. Both were great with BJ and Lizzie, though Cat often saw fear in their eyes at the thought of having one of their own.

When Molly announced that she was having a girl, Cat had reassured her the child would be nothing like Lizzie with her bright red hair, mass of freckles and stubborn, fiery disposition, all of which seemed to make Dylan love the child even more. Cat felt as if BJ was hers, the baby she'd almost delivered in her office, the Baby Doe who'd gone missing that she'd prayed would be found, the baby that she'd held in her arms even before Dylan had gotten to hold him. BJ was hers, just as Lizzie was Dylan's. He'd been there when she was born. He'd bought her first bassinet. He'd saved her mother's life.

Helen often drove out to the ranch, offering babysitting services. They had finally taken her up on it one Saturday and had gone into Kalispell for dinner. When they returned they hadn't known what to expect.

They found both children were tucked in bed sound asleep and Helen knitting next to the fireplace.

"Any trouble?" Cat asked suspiciously.

"None at all," Helen said.

"Not even from Lizzie?" she'd asked disbelieving. "We've been having a time getting her to stay in her bed at night."

Helen shook her head. "It might be the way you tell her to go to bed."

Cat was afraid to ask.

The older woman smiled. "Maybe it's the tone of my voice, but children seem to listen to me when I speak."

She'd laughed as she'd looked over at Dylan who was grinning. "Thank you so much." But when she offered Helen money, she'd declined.

"It was my pleasure. I enjoyed them. They're very bright children. Like their parents." With that she rose to leave.

"Stay the night," Dylan said, but Helen declined again.

"I know that road like the back of my hand. I'll be fine. I actually enjoy the trip out here."

"Then you'll be back Sunday for dinner," Cat said and Helen smiled.

"I'd like that."

"Ash is coming out with a date," she told her former coworker.

Helen wrinkled her nose. "What a woman from eastern Montana was doing over here is anyone's guess."

Cat knew how Helen felt about outsiders—even ones from the same state. "I've heard she is delightful." Helen huffed at that as she gathered up her things to leave.

"Helen, thank you again," Dylan said and only got a grunt as he walked her to her car, Cat watching them.

"How did you win that woman over?" he asked as he joined her on the porch to watch Helen drive away.

"I have no idea," she said with a laugh and turned to her husband. "How did I win you over?"

"It was that silver star on your tan uniform," he said pulling her into a hug. "How could I not have fallen for you? A woman with more freckles than stars in the sky and eyes bluer than Montana skies."

She chuckled as they stood like that looking out at all the stars over the mountains, both content in a way she doubted either of them had ever known before.

Looking up at the night sky, Cat wondered what Taylor and Beau would have thought of this family she and Dylan had formed. She found herself smiling as the stars twinkled above them, and she nestled deeper into her husband's arms. She felt sure they would have been happy to see how things had ended.

* * * * *

COLD CASE
MURDER MYSTERY

NICOLE HELM

For those who left us too soon.

Chapter One

Brooke Campbell knew she was being followed.

Okay, scratch that. She didn't *know* it. There was no clear, incontrovertible proof. And there were certainly times when she was deep in a case and her paranoia got the best of her.

Maybe she was imagining things. Her current case was deep and disturbing. She'd originally been brought to Sunrise, Wyoming, to study the found human remains of two bodies, but when that assignment had ended with two police officers being held captive in a cave, it had led to the discovery of even *more* remains.

Brooke's latest count was up to twenty different corpses discovered deep in the cave system of a local nature preserve. As a forensic anthropologist, she had excavated and studied many human remains, but never so many in one place.

Brooke loved her work, but some cases were…more affecting. Especially since the police thought they had the perpetrator locked up and… Brooke wasn't so sure.

Still, it was possible the fact that this same silver sedan had been tailing her every day for the past three days was a coincidence.

She really wanted it to be. When she turned into the parking lot of the little diner, a deviation from the past two days, and the car didn't follow, she breathed a sigh of relief.

Her relief lasted only about ten minutes. She was seated in a booth by the window, sipping her coffee and waiting for her food, when out of the corner of her eye, she saw a familiar silver sedan pull into the parking lot across the way.

It parked. No one got out.

She could keep ignoring it. Pretend it wasn't happening. No one had tried to approach her. There'd been no threat of or attempt at violence toward her, so who knew what it might be about. If it *wasn't* a coincidence, then it might not be nefarious. She likely shouldn't worry about it.

But the last thing she wanted to do was to return to her pretty and cozy and *isolated* rental cabin all by herself for the night knowing that someone *might* be following her. Camped out across the street *watching* her.

She could call the police. She knew quite a few Bent County deputies and detectives now, as well as some deputies and the sheriff from the Sunrise—and her rental cabin was technically *in* Sunrise so these would all be reasonable people to reach out to. But...

If she was going to tell them, she would have done it already. And she *hadn't* told them for a number of reasons. But it came back to a simple one.

She wanted to crack this case. She was so close. It would be the biggest of her career—not just because of the unfathomable body count, but for how long the skeletal remains had been hidden.

Brooke had solved a lot of crimes as a forensic anthropologist, but this one would point to more than just the current suspect. It would, hopefully, allow the police to find another murderer. Worst of all, Brooke still hadn't reached the end of remains—which meant there were more bodies to analyze and hopefully identify. Maybe another person could do it, but she didn't *want* that.

Maybe she wasn't the best forensic anthropologist in the world, but she knew she was good, with a unique set of skills. She couldn't risk being taken off the case.

She was afraid any threat to her—real or only perceived—would have her lifted from it. Granted, isolated Wyoming wasn't thick on the ground with forensic anthropologists, but *still*. She had to protect her ability to keep working.

She sat with that feeling for another ten minutes. Excavating it. Because she did have an alternative to telling the police. But she needed to know, for sure, that she wasn't making excuses so she would *have* to take the alternative.

Zeke Daniels. Oh, he'd been such a mistake. She still couldn't believe she was back in his orbit after all this time, but his friends had needed a forensic anthropologist and he knew one of those.

Or had. Very well. Very, *very* well. Back when they'd both been members of a secret group that had first organized to take down a dangerous and powerful biker gang in South Dakota. After they'd succeeded in that mission, they'd taken on others until the entire organization had disbanded about three years ago.

And in between those two things, she had fallen in love with Zeke Daniels and he'd let her think he'd loved her too. Then he'd broken her heart, crushed it into teeny-tiny pieces. Maybe she'd been naïve enough to deserve it, and maybe it hadn't even been *all* his fault.

Brooke scowled into her coffee. No, she didn't *want* to

see Zeke. Maybe she was curious about how he'd fared, but she didn't want to risk getting caught up in *him* again.

So, she supposed, that was her answer. She didn't *want* his help but kind of needed it.

She pulled out her cell phone, still watching the car across the road through her peripheral vision. She brought up the email he'd last sent her that had included his phone number in case she "needed anything" while in Sunrise. Brooke typed the number into her phone, doing her best to never fully take her gaze off the car.

It rang once, then a deep voice answered.

"Brooke?"

Did he have her number programmed into his phone? *Wow, Brooke, that means absolutely nothing.* Unfortunately the whole *body* reaction to his voice meant more than she'd like.

"Hi, Zeke."

"Everything all right?"

"Of course...not." She certainly wouldn't be calling him if everything was *all right*, and he knew it, even if her first instinct was always to tell everyone she was fine and everything was just great. Luckily, she no longer cared what Zeke thought of her. She didn't care if he thought her request was needy because she didn't *need* him. Or want him.

The end.

"I think I'm being followed." Best to be quick and to the point.

She squinted out the window, to where the silver sedan still sat. She couldn't make out how many people were in it, but she knew no one had gotten out. The license plate was shrouded in shadow and had never been close enough for her to read the letters or numbers, no matter how she'd tried.

There were a few beats of silence. She didn't rush to fill them like she might have once. She'd learned a thing or two about how to use the skills from her job in her personal life. She'd learned a thing or two about *life* since parting ways with one Zeke Daniels.

"Where are you?" he asked.

"The diner." Only one of those around Sunrise.

"Give me about fifteen."

She didn't know exactly what that meant, but the line went dead and she rolled her eyes. He'd never been a man of many words.

Certainly never the ones she'd wanted to hear.

The waitress served her the food she'd ordered and, even though she didn't feel hungry anymore, Brooke forced herself to eat. It was important to keep up her energy and focus for her job, and not let emotions get in the way.

People following her or not, she was going to keep working on this case. She was going to give the detectives every last piece of information she could so they could get to the bottom of it.

So far, she'd unearthed almost twenty skeletal remains in that cave. *Twenty.* And she didn't think she was done. It was a gruesome thought, and gruesome work but it gave people answers. So the nightmares were worth the outcome if she could provide answers.

Her phone trilled. A text from Zeke.

Get up, pretend you're going to the bathroom, then take back exit. Waiting in my truck.

Well, he hadn't gotten any less demanding in the years since she'd last seen him.

Another text came in.

Leave your coat.

Now she scowled at her phone. Typed her own response.

I like my coat.

Leave it so they think you're coming back.

Hard to argue with *that,* she supposed. But she also needed to pay her bill. She could hardly stiff this small-town diner for her meal. Surreptitiously, under the table, she rummaged through her purse until she found a twenty. She slid it under her plate, making sure her arm would hide what she was doing to anyone who might be watching from outside.

Then she got up and made a big show about asking where the restroom was. The woman pointed to the hallway leading to the restrooms…and no doubt the back exit Zeke had spoken of.

Brooke's job was investigation—*old* investigations at that—so she didn't deal with a lot of danger, but she'd seen her fair share as a member of the North Star team.

And before.

But she didn't think about *before* if she could help it. Too many old ghosts, nightmares and regrets.

She walked past the restroom door, through the kitchen, without paying any mind to the speculative look from a dish washer, and then out the back.

Where a large, shiny black truck was parked as close to the door as allowed, its passenger-side door open. Head high, she did her best to crawl up into the seat without looking foolish. She doubted she'd managed. But she settled in the seat and closed the door behind her.

She didn't want to look at him but supposed she had to. She braced herself for impact, plastered a polite smile on her face and turned to face him as he began to drive.

He had not changed. Which was a real bummer. Because Zeke Daniels was ostensibly the most attractive man she'd ever laid eyes on. Worse, he knew it, if he thought about it at all, which was questionable because she figured his thoughts were likely more serious in nature.

He was the tortured-brooding-loner type. And she had, once upon a time, been the kind of silly girl who'd believed she'd get through to that type. Love them into change.

Luckily, she was older and wiser even if he was not any less hot. All dark wild hair and *gigantic* body that made this humongous truck look tailored for a giant of muscle such as he.

It was very, very unfortunate that she could remember just how his muscles had felt under her hands.

"Stay low," was all he said.

Despite her feelings on *him*, she followed instructions, slumping down in the seat so as they drove out onto the road and passed where the silver sedan was parked no one would see her inside.

"I talked to Ida. She called Sunrise SD, saying the car was scaring away customers. Someone will question the driver."

"Oh." Well, that was all good and smart. Not that she knew who Ida was. But Zeke kept driving. Brooke peered at the passing landscape then at him again. His eyes were focused on the road, his square jaw tense—as always—but his hands on the steering wheel looked relaxed enough.

Large hands that have touched every single inch of you.

She tried to ignore the heat that crept into her cheeks—a mix of embarrassment and remembering.

"Where are we going?" she asked.

"My place. You'll be safe there."

Safe? She doubted that.

ZEKE KNEW HE was making a mistake. It wasn't just because Brooke was Brooke, though that was some of it. Part of the mistake was treating this like a North Star mission when his old group of secret special operatives had disbanded, going into civilian work, and leaving him...

At loose ends.

He'd bought a ranch. He still couldn't quite believe it, but since his sister had acted like it was the greatest level of insanity he'd ever stooped to, he'd pretended it had been his plan all along.

He hadn't decided if he liked it or not yet. There was a lot of work to be done to get it back in working order, and he didn't mind the work. He in fact enjoyed work—the harder, the better.

But the chance to jump back into something dangerous...well, that was like coming home. It was familiar. It made him feel...useful.

That was probably not mentally healthy, but a guy couldn't win them all. Besides, Brooke was in his truck looking...like Brooke. Strawberry-blond hair pulled back all sleek and professional, serious blue eyes that should really be *run-of-the-mill* but somehow weren't. Not with her intelligence and warmth behind them. She still had that peaches-and-cream complexion that showed a blush all too well, and he could not go thinking about *that*.

He turned off the highway and onto the bumpy gravel road that led down to his dilapidated ranch house. The drive needed regrading, but that didn't hold a candle to what needed to be done to the house as a whole. He'd made different parts livable—the living room, the kitchen, his bedroom and one upstairs guest room. A work in progress that he'd never once felt even the least bit ashamed of.

Until now.

"Oh, dear." Brooke was looking at the house with a kind of crestfallen expression that made him want to laugh for some inexplicable reason.

"Not quite the accommodations you're used to?"

"It's not about the accommodations, Zeke," she said, affecting that scolding tone that had, once upon a time, made him grin. "It's the fact it's your chosen one."

"I'm renovating." He pushed the truck into Park in front of the house.

She made a considering—and disbelieving—sound.

But she got out of the truck at the same time he did. She walked toward the house, studying the sagging eaves and the one window, currently held together by duct tape, that needed to be replaced. She hesitated a moment before following him up the rickety stairs—he skipped the splintered one.

He unlocked the door and, even though he wasn't watching her, he *was* observing her. Just as he had been since she'd stepped out of the diner.

She wasn't quite the same as the last time they'd seen each other. That made sense. It had been close to four years ago. She had a different kind of…poise now. A stillness that hadn't been in her when she'd been young and…he didn't like the word *desperate*, but there had been a kind of driving need inside her. To be useful, to help, to never be a nuisance or a problem.

So, naturally, he'd taken all that shaky trust she'd had in him and broken it. He didn't like to think he'd been the cause of any change in her, and maybe he hadn't. She'd had four years out in the real world, maybe it had instilled some wariness in her.

Good. He didn't need another chance at shattering the fragile glass she'd once been made of.

When she stepped inside behind him, she made another little noise. A kind of startled *oh* much more positive than the last one.

The note of surprise to her voice made him smile in spite of himself. Because the outside looked pretty awful, but he'd done a hell of a lot of work on parts of the inside. The living room and kitchen weren't half bad—if the duct-taped window was ignored, which he'd fix any day now.

Really.

"Not living in total squalor," he offered, but his phone rang before he could say anything else. He pulled it out of his pocket and took the call from Ida, the lady who ran the diner and kept him fed more nights than not.

He listened grimly then thanked her before relaying the information she'd shared to Brooke.

"The car was gone when the cops got there. Ida said it took off not long after me, though not in the same direction. Not sure I like that." Had they seen her? Or just gotten antsy because she hadn't come back to the table they no doubt had been watching. "Did you get the plate?"

She shook her head. "They didn't have a front plate. I never could get a look at the back."

Zeke nodded. Probably no back plate either if they really were following her. "The crew you're working with at Bent County should know. Is that the detectives?"

She shook her head. "I don't want the detectives to know."

He frowned at her. Surely she'd learned *something* about

keeping herself safe after years of investigating dead bodies. "You have a death wish?"

"No," she replied evenly. "I think we discovered long ago that was your problem, not mine."

Oh, so true. Sometimes he thought he'd changed in that regard. Gotten too old or watching his siblings settle down or something. The kind of *something* that had prompted him to buy this ranch when he'd never owned a piece of property in his entire life, never even dreamed about it. But then something like this came along and…

Well, he didn't know what he felt.

"I apologize," Brooke said so formally. "We shouldn't discuss…long ago."

The way she talked, all prim and proper, like she'd been raised in a mansion, gone to some fancy Ivy League school. But no. She'd affected that on her own through grit and determination.

He wished he didn't know it.

"You called me because you're worried. Clearly, I was a last resort."

"Yes, because I don't want the detectives to know. I need to finish this case. It's… I need to. If they're worried about threats to me, I'll either get replaced or they'll worry more about new threats than the very important information I'm *this* close to uncovering."

"I thought they knew who killed those people. What more important information could there be?"

She hesitated, because clearly she knew more about the case than he did and she probably shouldn't be sharing details with just anyone.

But he wasn't *just* anyone.

"If you want me to keep you safe, Brooke, I have to know what I'm keeping you safe from."

Chapter Two

Brooke knew Zeke wasn't *wrong*. You had to know what a threat was to be able to neutralize it, but she just didn't know for sure if it was a real threat. It skirted a very careful line to let a civilian in on a case.

Especially since she hadn't shared her theories with the detectives yet.

Of course, Zeke was hardly a *civilian*. She didn't know how to classify a man who'd been in the army, been a North Star operative taking down gang members and who knew what else, but "civilian" didn't cover it even if he was no longer affiliated with either of those things.

"Brooke. You came to me for a reason, and you knew I'd need to know."

"I didn't think that far ahead, to be honest. I just knew I didn't want to be alone in my rental tonight." Did that sound like an invitation? It was decidedly *not*, and she almost opened her mouth to say so, but reason won out.

He knew what she meant. She didn't need to embarrass herself on top of it.

"Okay, well, think that far ahead now. Explain to me what you're afraid of. You can trust me."

When it came to *personal* matters, she wouldn't trust

Zeke Daniels as far as she could throw him. But when it came to this sort of thing? Investigations and danger and searches for the truth?

She could trust him implicitly. It was why she'd called him. Why she'd come here, despite wanting to keep as far away from Zeke as she'd been doing the past month of being in Sunrise. He was right, she *had* to explain it to him.

And still… "Can I have something to drink? Some water, maybe?"

He frowned at the diversion but motioned her to follow him and led her into a pretty little kitchen. The furniture was bachelor terrible, but the cupboards were nice—clearly new and part of his renovation—as were the appliances. And a huge window dominated the wall over the sink and looked out over a beautiful mountain view.

She stood a moment, just taking it in. It needed some lace curtains to flutter in the breeze when the window was open, but other than that, it was absolutely, stunningly, perfect. A cozy kitchen with an awe-inspiring view.

That reminded her this ranch, this house he was renovating, was everything he'd once said he'd never want. Bitterness threatened to rise up, and this wasn't the place for that. Their "back then" didn't matter to the present. She *refused* to be bitter over something long gone. Her own mistake for thinking she could change a man like Zeke.

She took the glass of water he handed her and then took a seat at the small kitchen table when he gestured at the chair. He sat across from her—which might as well be right next to her as small as the table was. As big as *he* was.

Well, at least he hadn't filled this house with a wife and children. That might have actually sent her over the edge. Not that she knew for *sure* there wasn't a wife wandering about, but no signs of a woman or children so—

Put the past aside, Brooke.

She sucked in a breath, carefully let it out. "I've been excavating the bones in the cave in the preserve for weeks now, right?" she said, focusing on work, because that was what she did best. Slowly, carefully, methodically pick apart the tiniest thing to create a picture, an answer.

He nodded. He had that intense investigator look on. Paying attention to every word. Filing it away. Like she'd reversed time and landed them back at North Star.

"There's...a lot. A lot of remains. A lot of *victims*, essentially," she continued. "I know that rumor has made its way around Bent County, and it's true. It was clearly some kind of...mass burial. Except, not all done at the same time. Bodies over the course of years."

"So Jen Rogers killed more than just the Hudson parents?"

Here was where it got tricky. Jen Rogers was the current suspect and had confessed to the murders of the first two people Brooke had excavated and identified. Because she'd been living in the cave for a portion of the past few years, the assumption was the other victims had been killed and buried by her hand as well.

But Brooke had a different theory. A more complicated one. "Jen Rogers is forty-six years old. Some of the bones I've found...based on what I've tested, what I've observed... I think they've been there for closer to fifty years."

Zeke absorbed that information. Jumped to the conclusion immediately. "There's another murderer? An older murderer?"

"It's one possibility. It could also be innocuous. Fifty years is a long time. I haven't been able to study all the bodies, determine causes of death. These could be...accidents or have other reasonable explanations behind them." She tried to tell herself that, but she understood too well what she'd found.

"If it was innocuous, you wouldn't be being followed."

"We don't know for sure that I am, or that it connects." But she was gratified that it was his immediate conclusion as well. Even if she felt honor-bound to argue with him.

An investigator had to look at *every* angle. That, he should know, considering he'd been one in his own right. More than the "shooting the bad guys, running into danger" kind and less of the "sending highly scientific reports to law enforcement agencies" kind.

He clearly didn't agree with her that there might be multiple possible answers here, but it was true. In *her* investigations, she had to weigh every possibility, and there was always the possibility that these older bodies were a coincidence. Something innocent from a long ago time.

"Why haven't you told the detectives?" Zeke asked.

"I'm waiting on test results to ensure my observations are correct, or at least more plausible than not. I can't work on supposition, and neither can the detectives. We need facts. I should have answers in the next few weeks and then…maybe."

He stood, that old energy she remembered—and shouldn't—pumping off him. He'd always been this way. *Vibrant.* It had thrilled her back before it had flattened her. So she'd rebuilt her life around the old tenants that had gotten her into adulthood. Peace, calm, the careful unearthing of teeny-tiny facts that lead to bigger pictures.

Never being too big of a burden. Never hoping for too much from anyone. She was an island, and she had to remember that. She had to remember that no matter what *he* was, she was Brooke Campbell.

"Where do these tests get run?" he demanded.

She didn't like being *interrogated*, but she supposed she only had herself to blame since she'd been the one to contact him. And she knew him. Maybe he'd changed in four years—hence the ranch and the settling down. She'd certainly changed herself. But right now he seemed very much like the Zeke she'd known. No use not answering his demanding questions.

"The state crime lab in Cheyenne."

"That means what you send them passes through a lot of hands."

"It's a murder investigation. Of course it does. I doubt anyone has drawn the conclusions I've drawn yet. But they will if someone's looking to connect things. The detectives will, once they have all the facts."

Zeke paced the kitchen in front of that beautiful window view. A beautiful view in it of himself. Like a predator, sleek and smooth and…

Dangerous, if you recall. But aside from breaking her heart there at the end, he'd always been kind and gentle and—

Don't start that again. She looked down at her hands.

"But if someone knows what's in that cave, they might have cause to follow you. Have cause to see if *you* put what *they* know together."

"Those are all *ifs*."

"Don't be naïve, Brooke."

A sharp order that landed with the pain it had four years ago. For a second, she could only stare at him and wonder if she'd wandered into some kind of time slip because it had landed with so much of that old pain she thought she'd gotten over.

But she didn't have time to deal with that as she heard a door slam open and a woman's voice call out his name.

He muttered an oath under his breath. "Prepare yourself for the onslaught."

IT MIGHT HAVE been funny, the look on Brooke's face as Carlyle whirled through his house, if he didn't think Carlyle had the ability to see right through him when it came to Brooke Campbell.

Too many old ghosts still haunted him when it came to her, and it was not a comfortable realization to find that he liked the look of her at his kitchen table. He had not *once* allowed himself to think of her when he'd bought this ranch, started on renovations.

And now she was just *here,* like that's exactly who he'd been thinking about, and he knew he'd never be able to erase *that*.

His sister stormed into the kitchen—not because something was wrong, no doubt, but because she was just a storm herself.

"What are you doing here?" he demanded.

"Hi to you too," Carlyle replied, already studying Brooke. "You're that forensic person, right?"

Brooke smiled, but Zeke recognized it as the prim, professional one she trotted out when she was uncomfortable.

He didn't like the knowledge he remembered all her different smiles either.

"Brooke Campbell." She held out a hand for Carlyle to shake.

Carlyle slid a glance at him then shook Brooke's hand. "You knew each other back when he was being Mister Super Secret Spy?"

"Yes."

This was followed by a beat of silence where Carlyle studied Brooke and then him.

"And about as talkative on the matter as you are," Carlyle grumbled.

Even now, with North Star disbanded, it was second nature for him to just not talk about it. North Star had been a *secret* group, and maybe it wasn't so much now, but he still didn't just hand out details.

He'd spent years disbanding a dangerous and vicious gang, another year unraveling other terrifying missions. He'd leapt into danger time and time again, and his sister didn't need the details on that.

Ever.

"Because there's nothing to talk about," Zeke said gruffly. "Brooke, this is my sister. Carlyle."

He couldn't really remember if he'd ever mentioned Car to Brooke back then. North Star had meant keeping family ties close to the vest. It had meant not letting on that you had a real life outside those secret walls. But Zeke had too many memories of telling Brooke way more than he should have.

Brooke smiled politely at Carlyle. "It's nice to meet you. I've heard…things about you."

Carlyle laughed, loud and brash. "I just bet. Well, I need to talk to Zeke for a sec." She studied the woman then turned her gaze on Zeke. "Come to dinner tonight."

He scowled. "I don't want to go to a Hudson dinner." Carlyle and their oldest brother Walker had entangled themselves in the Hudson family, the Hudson Ranch. Walker marrying and procreating with Mary Hudson— Daniels now. Carlyle hooking up with Cash Hudson.

All sorts of domestic bliss Zeke preferred to keep his distance from.

"I didn't ask if you *wanted* to. I told you to come."

"I'm busy." He looked pointedly at Brooke. "Someone's following her."

"Did you go to the cops?" Carlyle asked Brooke.

She shook her head. "It's…complicated."

"Ah, well, maybe *she* should stay with the Hudsons then. It's got better security than this place. You can both come for dinner and stay."

The denial was immediately on the tip of his tongue. It wasn't a *smart* denial, but there and knee-jerk all the same.

Brooke spoke before he could find the right words to get Carlyle to back off.

"I know what I mean to the Hudsons," Brooke said.

Her voice was cool and calm, but Zeke hated that hint of vulnerability he could see in her eyes. Because she'd always been the girl who didn't quite fit in. Things he never should have let her tell him about herself.

"I don't think I'd be welcome," Brooke said as if it didn't bother her, but Zeke would lay money on the fact it did.

"You gave them answers," Carlyle said with about as much gentleness as his sister gave anyone. "I know you'd be welcome."

"I examined the skeletal remains of their parents. I'm sure they're grateful for the positive ID. Sheriff Hudson has told me as much, but…no one wants to be reminded of that, and my presence *would* be a reminder. Even if they were kind enough to not want it to be."

Carlyle was silent a moment then shook her head. "I'm sorry, you're way too sweet and calm and, like, smart-sounding to stay with this Neanderthal."

It was clearly an attempt to lighten the mood and he knew Brooke was good at that. Going along with the attempts people wanted.

"I don't doubt it. Luckily, I'm not staying with him. I'm just…seeking his counsel on how to proceed."

Zeke's scowl settled deeper. Like hell she wasn't staying with him when she was in *clear* danger. "Yeah, and that *counsel* is going to keep me busy tonight. I'll come up to the ranch some other night." He started ushering Carlyle out of the kitchen, into the living room, *almost* to the front door.

"You messed her up, didn't you?" she asked.

"Goodbye, Car." Before he could effectively usher his sister out of his house, she stopped him with a very simple sentence.

"I think Cash and I are going to get married."

It shouldn't be any kind of shock and yet… "Huh?"

"He asked me to. And I said yes. So, barring end-of-the-world-type stuff brought on by the Daniels clan settling down, I guess it'll happen." She opened the front door herself, stepped out onto the rickety porch. "Anyway, that's what we were going to announce at dinner."

"I'm not settling down." That was perhaps not how he should respond to the news his baby sister was getting married. To a guy he happened to like. But Zeke was who he was.

Carlyle gestured at his house. The one he'd *bought*. He did not allow himself to include Brooke in her gesture. "Sure you're not. Remind me the last time you stayed in one place for more than three months, let alone a year, and—oh, yeah—*bought land*."

"It doesn't mean I'm…" He shook his head. "Congrats, Car. I'm glad. Cash'll keep you in line." He'd only said that to piss her off, because they were who *they* were.

Yet she didn't fume. She didn't even laugh. She studied him with those careful eyes. She didn't trot that out too often, especially now that she wasn't keeping secrets from him and their other brother.

"It doesn't hurt, you know."

"What doesn't?"

"Building something you decide to keep forever."

Since he didn't want to touch *that* with a ten-foot pole, he offered his own version of emotional honesty that would ideally get her running. "They're lucky to have you, Car."

Just as he'd predicted, his sister turned away. "Maybe we're all lucky," she muttered and then strode for her truck where one of her ever-present dogs sat in the passenger side.

She didn't go to the driver's side. She opened the dog's door and shooed it out, then gave it an order to stay.

"I don't need a dog," Zeke said, not quite sure what she was up to as she made her way to the driver's side of the truck.

But she didn't even look at him. She got in her truck, closed the door and leaned out the open window as she backed away.

Carlyle pointed to the house. "She might."

Chapter Three

Brooke was still in the kitchen. She didn't know what to do with the fact she'd just met a member of Zeke's family.

She'd *known* he had siblings. He'd never named them, and hadn't spoken *much* about them, but every once in a while he'd let it slip that he had a brother—older—and a sister—younger. And Brooke had foolishly filed every little detail away and *still* remembered them, apparently.

Now she'd *met* the sister. Carlyle. A pretty, wild thing who didn't look too much like Zeke. Nor did she act like Zeke, who was all still gruffness. Even when she'd seen behind that steely guard of his, there hadn't been a lot of... untamed in Zeke Daniels.

Well...except possibly in one place that it would really not do her to think about at the moment.

She heard a strange noise and looked up to see a large dog trotting inside, Zeke behind it. But she didn't look at Zeke, because the dog came right up to her and pressed its enormous head against her leg, pushing his head under her hand.

Demanding to be petted.

Charmed, and almost immediately in love, Brooke did

just that. Slid her hand down its silky head. "Well, hello. What's your name?"

"Consider him your loaner guard dog."

Brooke blinked at Zeke. She'd figured this was his dog. "What?"

"Carlyle and her... Well, you've met Cash Hudson. They train dogs together. She left this one for you."

"My rental doesn't allow pets."

"Guess you'll have to stay here then."

She sighed, trying not to let the frustration win. She had to be reasonable. "Zeke, I'm not staying here."

"You were scared. You called me because you're scared."

"Yes, but..." What was the *but*? She didn't know. She just...had made a mistake, clearly. Letting fear and instinct lead her to the wrong decision. Because she should have known, even with the past firmly in the past, he would take over. He would be high-handed and too...*him*.

"So, it's me and the dog protecting you and you stay here, or we tell the detectives. Your job or your pride. I'll let you pick."

Had he always been so unreasonable?

Yes.

She kept petting the dog in an effort to keep herself calm. It didn't work. "I'm not your responsibility, and in fact, when I was even a little bit of your responsibility, you didn't handle that very well."

His expression didn't change. Because he was expressionless. Blank. Yes, she remembered that quite well—especially at the end.

"No, I didn't."

That admission felt...heavy. Shifted too many things inside her, made her heart pick up a little. Especially the way he just *looked* at her, those serious, intent dark eyes.

Four years and the way it had ended should have dulled whatever impact those eyes could have.

But they didn't. She felt too warm and could remember all too well the way…

No, Brooke, you are not letting yourself remember that.

"How about this? We'll sit down. Eat a little dinner. You make a list of people who might have some inclination of where you're leaning with your findings. Then I'll work on finding out if any of them have a silver sedan that matches the one following you."

"And what will I do while you work on that?"

"Whatever you need to. You have your computer in that giant purse, right?"

She wrinkled her nose and held it a little closer. "Yes."

"So, work. That's what you'd be doing back at your rental, isn't it?"

She hated that he knew that about her. Even if it was just an educated guess.

"Sit. Make a list." He rummaged through a drawer and then handed her a pen and a pad of paper. "I'll put together something for us to eat."

He used to do that. He wasn't as good a cook as she was, but he was adept enough in the kitchen. He'd always been closed-lipped about his background, but as they'd gotten closer, things had slipped out.

Abusive father. Moved a lot. Mother murdered. She didn't know at exactly what age he'd been when that had happened, but she knew he'd been a teenager and had only been kept on the straight and narrow—ish—by his older brother. Then Zeke had enlisted the moment he'd been able. He'd done a stint in the army for a few years before he'd moved over to North Star.

Did he remember the things about *her* past that she'd

told him? Things she'd never told anyone outside of the people who'd known against her will.

It all made her feel tired and sad, so she sat at his kitchen table and focused on petting the dog. "What's his name?"

"*Her* name. Viola."

She smiled at the dog's warm brown eyes. "Viola. Named after a pretty flower, and you're a pretty thing, aren't you?" she cooed at the dog. Then worked on her list while Zeke did the domestic work of throwing together a meal.

He put a bowl of pasta in front of her after a while and then plopped a plastic canister of Parmesan cheese next to her. "And before you say it, I know the fresh stuff is better, but this keeps longer so it wins for a single guy."

Their gazes caught across the table.

He'd just made it clear he remembered her pasta cheese preferences, all these years later. And her foolish heart fluttered at the thought. Just as bad, he'd also made it clear he was single. Like that was *relevant*, when it was decidedly not.

She looked down at the list she'd made. Slid it over the table to him. "It's short."

"Then it'll be quick and easy."

He looked over it then crossed off the first person on the list. "I know Hart doesn't have a silver sedan."

Detective Thomas Hart was the lead detective on the case, along with his partner, Laurel Delaney-Carson. Brooke liked them both, and knew they weren't the ones behind whoever was following her, but she didn't say that. She let Zeke draw his own conclusions.

"In the morning, I'll take you to your car. You can do everything you normally do in a day. I'll just be…watching. See if we can find that sedan, get a plate, an ID on the driver."

She frowned at that. "What are you going to do? Pull them over?"

"No. We'll play it by ear."

She rolled her eyes. *We*, her butt. Much as she hated to admit it though, she felt more at ease here than she had at the diner or her rental. She could have all sorts of issues with Zeke's heavy-handed overbearing *male* nonsense, and her reaction to Zeke as a *man* she'd once known intimately, but she knew he'd keep her safe. Regardless of how he felt about her. Or how she felt about him.

She sighed and then, when they were done eating, she cleaned up. An old habit from living in the same North Star places. Because those who cooked, didn't clean and vice versa.

"I'll show you your room," he said once they were finished.

An awkward silence settled over them. She nodded, grabbed her tote bag and followed him up stairs that had clearly been recently fixed. The hallway was a bit of a disaster, but he led her to a pretty room. Sparse, certainly. It could do with some…softer touches, but the bed looked big and comfortable, and the window gave the same view as the one down in the kitchen.

"Just one night," she said firmly. Because she was determined. *Determined*. She could butt heads with him and win. She would. And she could do it on her own. After they figured out the silver sedan.

She turned to face him in the doorway, ignored the way his gaze still hit her bloodstream like heat and want. But she did not want him.

She would not.

"Good night, Zeke."

"Night, Brooke," he returned. But he didn't move to walk away.

So she closed the door carefully in his face. Because she was *not* going down that old road ever again.

If she knew even in her head it sounded like she was protesting way too much, she ignored it.

ZEKE TOOK THE dog out for one last bathroom run once he was sure Brooke was settled in her room. He didn't worry that she'd run—that wasn't Brooke. What he did worry about was…everything else.

Someone being after her.

Her being in his house looking the same as she had four years ago when he'd realized he'd needed to purposefully end things before he accidentally hurt her was…

Well, it messed with his head was what it did. Because he didn't like people in his space. Didn't even like Walker and Mary coming over with their baby. Or Carlyle and Cash coming over with Izzy, Cash's thirteen-year-old. Or, the worst, *all* of them coming over and acting like a big happy family.

It felt too much like some old dream of a future he'd never really believed in. Functional relationships and people who were good parents to their kids. Family. Walker and Carlyle had somehow found themselves those sitcom happy endings—not without some pain and danger along the way—but they'd gotten it all the same.

Zeke didn't really know what was worse. Thinking he didn't get to have it, or thinking he was lucky to be part of it regardless of his romantic status.

But he did know what was worse in *this* moment. Brooke

in his house, and the feeling she was what had always been missing. Her smile and blue eyes and floral scent.

When *that* was ridiculous. Maybe he'd loved her way back then, not that he'd have ever admitted it to himself or to her in the moment. Sure, maybe looking back now, he could admit it.

But he'd loved his plans, his revenge, his danger more. *And now you don't have any of those things.*

Yeah, it didn't do to think about that at all. He should think about her case. Her safety.

It seemed whoever was behind those bones didn't like anyone snooping around in them. That meant *anyone* could be following her. Her sending things off to a lab in Cheyenne had left a lot of things open for leaks, for coming back to hurt her.

She needed her own lab. She couldn't trust the bureaucracy of government officials. Hell, that was the whole reason North Star existed.

Had existed. He didn't know how many years it would take him to accept that they were really done. Retired. He'd had enough of his own personal danger since then not to dwell much on it.

Until the past few months.

Now he had a new purpose. Because maybe Brooke Campbell couldn't ever mean anything to him, but he wasn't about to let anything happen to her.

He watched the dog frolic in the yard under a moonlit sky. After a while, he pulled his phone out of his pocket. He dialed an old number.

"Zeke, if you're calling to drag me into another dangerous mission, count me out. We've got a new foster kid, and Shay somehow corralled me into keeping *chickens*."

Zeke smiled in spite of himself here alone in the dark.

"Nothing dangerous. Nothing that requires your time," he said to his old boss. It was hard to imagine the tough and certain Granger MacMillan, once the head of North Star—the secretive group that had eradicated the Sons of the Badlands gang from everywhere they'd had power—cavorting with chickens and a bunch of foster kids out on his ranch in Montana, with his equally tough and perhaps even scarier wife.

But that's what the end of North Star had given Granger and Shay. Love and family. Just like Zeke's siblings had found.

He didn't like to dwell on it.

"Well, I know you didn't call to have a heart-to-heart," Granger replied.

Zeke snorted. "No. Just a question. What would I need to set up a makeshift forensic lab on my property?"

Granger was quiet for a minute before making a contemplative noise. "I can send you some things. Might take a few days, but I've still got all the old connections."

"That'd be great. Thanks."

"Say hi to Brooke for me," Granger said then laughed. Far too hard. Far too long.

Zeke clicked End on his phone.

But Granger's laughter seemed to echo in his head for a long time after.

Chapter Four

Brooke had slept, and when she woke up blinking at a bright sunny morning outside the window, with that gorgeous view right *there*, she didn't quite know how to get her bearings.

She sat up, scratched her hands through her tangled hair and blew out a breath.

It was perfectly normal to sleep well when you knew you were safe, and she hadn't felt safe in quite some time.

And it wasn't silly or foolish to feel safe in Zeke's house. He was a former soldier, a former North Star agent, and while things hadn't exactly ended well between them, it wasn't because he'd been a *bad* guy. He'd been, and was, in fact, incredibly honorable. And he'd been upfront and honest about all he couldn't give her.

She could be hurt about that and still know that she was in perfectly good hands when it came to him helping to keep her safe from a potential threat.

So, no reason to sit here in this nice bed, brooding over the fact her ex-boyfriend made her feel safe and how much she liked his house.

She sucked in another slow breath. Let it out. She went through the rest of her slow-breathing morning ritual. She even managed a few yoga poses in the small room while the sun gilded the mountains outside.

Sunrise, Wyoming, and the surrounding Bent County was a pretty place to be even if the work that had brought her here was gruesome. It was a *grounding* kind of pretty and awe-inspiring, really. Man's capacity for evil could be soul-crushing. The world's capacity for beauty and miracles was the only antidote she'd ever found for that.

She hadn't brought anything to Zeke's house besides her work bag, so she had to get dressed in her clothes from yesterday. She used her fingers as a comb and tried to tame her wild bedhead back into the clip that had luckily been in her bag.

Once satisfied, she left her room, only to be greeted by the dog from yesterday, lying there in the hall.

"Good morning," she murmured to Viola, who thumped her tail and looked up at Brooke adoringly. As much as she dreaded facing Zeke, the dog's greeting made her smile. "Come on then," she said, gesturing for the dog to follow her downstairs.

She could hear the faint noise of movement in the kitchen, and the smell of coffee hit her once she made it to the bottom of the stairs. She paused a second, did a little more deep breathing while Viola waited at her feet with a seemingly quizzical look on her doggie face.

Brooke put on a polite smile, aimed it at the dog, and was determined she'd aim it at Zeke too. But when she stepped to the threshold of the kitchen, he stood at the stove, cooking eggs in a skillet.

He wore a T-shirt that was old, faded. And perfectly outlined the impressive structure of his *very* muscular body that had not lost any of its strength even though his operative days were over. Almost as bad, he wore loose sweats low on his hips and his feet were bare.

Like every ridiculous domestic fantasy she'd ever had about him all those years ago. Futures and forevers and *family*, when she'd always known those things were not in the cards for her. It was hardly his fault she'd fooled herself into thinking they could be.

Had she made a noise? An embarrassing kind of hum or sigh, or both? Probably.

He glanced over to her and he didn't *quite* smirk, but there was a knowing kind of glint to his eyes that just…

She could *not* do this. She had to go back to her rental tonight. No matter what he said, no matter what happened. She would not survive being in his orbit without embarrassing herself all over again. He was just *too much*. And it didn't matter if that was unfair, because it just was.

She'd stood on her own two feet for most of her life. She'd learned, time and time again, it was the only thing to do. Keep to herself. Rely on herself. And only herself.

"Made some breakfast," he offered. He nodded toward the table. "Have a seat."

She might have argued that she didn't need to be fed and that she didn't have any plans to listen to his orders, but in this moment of jittery heart and some very unwanted *lust*, she decided it best not to speak and to just do as she was told.

So Brooke sat at the table as Viola arranged herself at her feet and Zeke put a plate and mug in front of her. She stared at the contents and did not pay any mind that it was filled with things she liked. Everyone liked toast with butter. Everyone liked scrambled eggs with cheese. And it was hardly any great leap to put the exact right amount of cream in her coffee when she knew he took it the same way. He hadn't *remembered* what she liked.

This was all a coincidence.

But then he slid into the other seat at the table, and his eggs didn't have cheese and his toast had jelly on it.

Her inhale was shaky at best, but she studied her eggs rather than look to see if he was looking at her. The bottom line was, it didn't matter what he thought or felt about her. What he might remember or not. She knew it wasn't that he'd hated her or been disgusted by her or anything. They'd had a very serious relationship for a handful of wonderful months four years ago. It had come to an end because they hadn't wanted the same things out of life.

Maybe it had crushed her, but it wasn't...horrible. He wasn't horrible and she wasn't horrible and...

She really had to get off this roller coaster she'd created. She shoved a bite of eggs into her mouth and they ate in silence for a few minutes. Uncomfortable silence to *her*, but she'd learned that what she felt didn't always translate to Zeke.

"So, what's the plan for today?" she asked, frustrated she had to clear her throat to speak.

"I'll take you to your car after you eat. From there, you can go about your day however you like. I'll be keeping an eye out and doing some investigating of my own."

She finished her toast, pondered how much she was going to allow. Because she should allow *someone* to watch out for her. Better safe than sorry, she kept telling herself.

The problem was, Zeke was a different kind of danger. Maybe she *should* tell the detectives everything and then she wouldn't have to worry about her reaction to him.

But she thought about being taken off this case. Thought

about how many times she'd let things beyond her control rule her life.

She had to be stronger than her feelings.

"And how will you be doing that?" she asked, trying to focus on the task at hand, which was *not* her reaction to Zeke.

"Chasing down this silver sedan, for starters. Don't worry, I'll stay out of your hair. Then we'll meet for dinner at the diner. Compare stories, go from there."

This would not be the first time they'd done that. Him watching out for her. Them comparing stories. That's what had led to their relationship in the first place. She'd been his North Star assignment when one of her investigations into some remains had led to threats against her.

But North Star didn't exist anymore. And neither did they.

"This isn't a North Star mission, Zeke."

He didn't say anything for a long, humming moment. A moment in which he looked almost…lost. That was ridiculous, of course. She wasn't sure Zeke Daniels had been *lost* a second in all his life.

Yet, without North Star… She shook away the thought. How he was faring without his favorite coping mechanism was *none* of her business, and she could not let her mind—or worse, her heart—go back to a place where she believed it was.

"Well, I have to get to the caves," she said, pushing back from the table. "We should get going."

ZEKE HADN'T SAID anything else. He'd simply gotten ready, walked with her and Viola to his truck, and then driven into Sunrise to the diner and her car.

If what she said echoed around in his head like an earworm, it wasn't the first time. Lots of people had pointed out to him that he wasn't an operative anymore, that North Star didn't exist, that everything he'd busted his ass for was just *gone*.

All because *some* people had wanted to start "lives." Why were spouses and babies the be-all and end-all for people? He much preferred living his life on the edge of danger. Solving problems. Uncovering mysteries and stopping bad people from doing terrible things.

The same speech he'd been giving himself for years was getting old, even in the quiet of his own mind.

He pulled his truck into the tiny parking lot of the diner. The morning crowd was dwindling—old ranchers got out and back home early, he'd learned—but a few cars still remained in the lot besides Brooke's. Not a silver sedan among them.

He studied the surroundings, brooding over the situation. Too vague, not enough details, just Brooke's feeling that someone was following her.

But one thing he knew about Brooke was that she didn't jump to conclusions, particularly when it came to her own safety. She was under the impression she could fade into the background if she wanted, that no one paid her much mind.

He snuck a glance at her. She appeared serene, but he saw the way she clutched her hands together in her lap. How stiff and straight her posture was. How *carefully* she breathed.

If he thought too much about it, he'd be reminded of how *haunted* he'd been by not waking up beside her after he'd broken things off. How every morning of not hearing those weird deep breathing things she did had sent him into the strangest kind of pain he'd ever experienced. So confusing and all-encompassing that he'd thrown himself into the most dangerous missions he could a few days later.

Over and over again, until North Star was done. Then he'd thrown himself into finding his mother's murderer—which had been complicated and dangerous enough that Brooke had been easy to keep—mostly—off his mind.

Four years was a long time. He'd figured it was long enough for all *this* not to matter.

Well, he'd been wrong before and would likely be wrong again. Didn't matter. He had to figure out how to *deal*. And, above all else, keep her safe.

She got out of the truck and Viola hopped out after her. Brooke turned, concern on her face as she held the passenger door open. "Zeke, I can't take her around with me. Not to work. Not to my rental."

He wished she could, but understood. Besides, Brooke wasn't staying in that rental tonight no matter what she thought. And if she insisted on staying there against all reason, he and Viola would just camp out right outside. "It's okay. I'll keep her with me."

Brooke looked at him slightly askance, like he was full of it, but she didn't mount an argument. She closed the door and he got out on his side. She was already striding for her car, telling the dog in low tones that she'd have to stay behind.

She reached for her driver's-side door.

"Wait," he ordered. *Not a North Star mission, remember?* He scowled. Maybe it wasn't, and maybe it shouldn't be, but he was still going to do what it took to keep her safe.

He inspected her car, ignoring the imperious way she watched him, and when he found it, was rattled at how close he had been to missing it. But at the last second, he felt the ridge of something that shouldn't be there, right under the back door.

Carefully, without damaging the small disk, he removed the piece. He held it up. Studied it in the light. "Tracker." He took a page out of her book and blew out a slow breath, trying to think through the bright, violent haze of fury. Someone was *tracking* her.

He should have seen that coming. He should have known skeletal remains, even if the supposed perpetrator was behind bars, would bring nothing but trouble.

He'd made the call to bring her in. *He'd* made the decision to be hands off and let the Bent County Sheriff's Department handle it from there.

And *he'd* put her in danger by doing so.

It *burned*.

He looked at her, hoping the leaping fury didn't show in his expression. But she didn't look at him. She stared at the tracker in his hand.

"Oh," was all she said. "That's...not good."

She was going to give him an *aneurism*. Not good? Christ. Without a word, he walked over to his truck and fastened the tracker to the bed.

"What are you doing?" Brooke demanded, her voice high-pitched, her expression angry. He didn't know which part made her angry—the tracker's existence or him putting it on his truck.

It didn't matter. One had already happened and she wasn't about to change his mind on the other.

"They want to track something, they can track me."

"Zeke," she said in that soft way that had fooled him into thinking he could have something soft all those years ago.

He'd learned from that. Besides, after all this time, she wasn't worried about *him*. She was just worried in that way she had. She didn't ever want anyone going through any trouble for her. Even when she should.

"I can take care of myself, Brooke."

She nodded. "Yes, you always thought so."

Ouch. He brought a hand to his heart with half a thought to rub the pain there away. But she was watching him intently, so he stood still and motionless.

"Can I go now?" she asked archly.

He gestured her along. "Have at it." But he watched her as she gave Viola a pat and quietly apologized to the *dog* that she wasn't allowed to come with her. Once Brooke was in her car, he whistled and Viola reluctantly padded back over to him.

Brooke drove away, and he didn't bother to hide his scowl. He gave one last scan of the parking lot, the diner, the road. Then got back in his truck, Viola in tow, and set about following her himself.

So no one else did.

Chapter Five

Brooke hated being distracted at work. It was rare she couldn't turn off her thoughts and focus on the task at hand—she'd always been good at losing herself in *something* to avoid her unpleasant reality.

It should have been easy. It wasn't like she was alone in the cave. There was always a deputy or detective stationed with her, so she didn't have to worry about her surroundings or being interrupted. She showed up, set out her tools, and got to work. They handled everything else until it was time for a break or time to quit.

Today, she couldn't seem to turn off the outside. The tracker Zeke had found had shaken her up, and maybe she could have set that aside, but thoughts of the device meant also thoughts of Zeke.

She rolled her eyes. To be unsettled by a *man* as a *threat* was ridiculous and made her ashamed. She needed a new approach. Instead of denial, maybe she needed to try acceptance.

Zeke would be a problem until this was done, and she had a lot of work to do. Apparently, she couldn't just ignore her reaction to him, even for a few hours.

But then, what *was* she supposed to do about him?

She rolled her shoulders and refocused on her current task.

She had battery-powered mobile lights set up carefully around the area she worked on. Luckily, she wasn't bothered by enclosed spaces, because this was tight and dark and damp. Not the best conditions for any kind of anthropology, particularly forensic. It made the work challenging. Just the way she liked it.

She took pictures of the new segment she'd just moved to, documenting everything within an inch of its life. If she was right, and these bones were older—too old to be murders perpetrated by the current suspect—there was absolutely no room for error.

Certainly no room to be distracted by *exes*. Even if he was her one and only ex.

The more she excavated in the cave, the more space to bring in more and better light. And she'd certainly done her fair share of work so far. It was alarming and depressing how much work was left to do. Not because she minded the work, but because someone had used this place as their own personal body dumping grounds. But not just *dumping*. People had been carefully buried in secret here.

Brooke set the camera aside, got some tools to start excavating the next square. She crouched and started to work but noticed something kind of odd next to her foot.

She turned her head, so the lamp on her helmet focused in on it. Not bone. Not cave. It could be animal, but… She leaned in closer. It looked an awful lot like the corner of a book.

She reached out and touched it. Felt like a book too. It was shoved in between two rock formations. She was about to pull it out, but looked down and saw how dirty her gloves were. Not a problem with bones and remains buried deep in the cave floor, but paper…

It clearly hadn't been there long because paper would have a lot more damage if it had been left there for *years*. Maybe it would be some kind of clue to incriminate Jen Rogers.

Or whoever else was killing people and burying them down here.

"Thomas?" She was on a first-name basis with the detectives now that she'd spent so much time with them, and Thomas Hart happened to be her partner today. "Do you have a fresh set of gloves?" Hers were by her equipment and she wanted to retrieve this book as carefully and quickly as possible.

"Sure." He held them out to her and she took them. She switched her gloves. Then, with caution, she pulled the book from the crevice it had been shoved into without tearing anything or dragging it in the wet sediment of the ground more than necessary.

Once freed, she looked at it, opened the cover. "It's… a scrapbook."

Thomas was by her side so fast that Brooke almost bobbled the book. Like the word *scrapbook* had jolted through him.

"Not just any scrapbook," he said, looking down over her shoulder. "I think that's the scrapbook that was stolen from the police department last month when we first discovered the remains on the Brink property."

Last month. She could tell this meant a lot to the detective, but it didn't really mean anything to *her* investigation if it didn't involve the potential for a second murderer… even if she *was* curious.

"I don't have anything to pack up this kind of material carefully, but we need to be very gentle. If it's been down here for a whole month in these kinds of conditions, that isn't good for any of the material in a scrapbook. We should get it out of here and consult an archivist. Someone who would know how best to handle it, if it's as old as it looks, and make sure we're preserving it correctly."

Hart looked at her with a slight frown. "Good point." Then he hesitated. Thomas was usually calm, but she could *feel* the tension the scrapbook brought out in him. It was part of his investigation and he wanted to look at it now rather than later.

"If you put some gloves on, you can take it back to the station right now. I'm fine on my own here for a bit."

He shook his head. "Brooke, I wouldn't leave *anyone* in a mass grave all by themselves, even if studying mass graves *is* your job."

Well, mass graves hadn't been her job before. This was a first. But she could detect the impatience waving off him and didn't like to let other people's uncomfortable feelings to *linger*. She'd learned a long time ago to make certain she wasn't a burden to anyone else. A problem.

Life worked better that way.

"Why don't we break for lunch? You can go back to the station and get that squared away, and I'll grab something to eat and meet you there when I'm done."

He smiled at her. "I appreciate it. Want to leave this all set up? I'll have one of the guys park here while we're gone."

Brooke looked around. She'd had a solid two hours of work, but she was definitely in the middle of things. Still, it would be good to take a break, get her head on straight.

She grabbed a few of the evidence bags and boxes she'd filled. "That'll be fine. I'll send these back to the lab while we're at it." It was still work, and maybe some fresh air would help her refocus.

They worked in a comfortable quiet to turn off the lights and then take what she needed out into the bright light of day. Hart was definitely distracted by the discovery of the scrapbook, and Brooke was well aware the *whole* case wasn't her business. Her business was to uncover the remains, study them, test them, identify and form conclusions about them.

Still…

"This scrapbook… It belonged to Jen Rogers?"

Thomas shook his head as she carefully placed the book in his patrol car. "No. It's kind of a long story. You know Chloe Brink, right?"

Chloe was a police officer, and it had been on her and her brother's property the first skeletal remains had been found. Brooke had met her a few times, since she was involved with the Hudsons. "Yes."

"It was a Brink family scrapbook, discovered by Chloe while we were investigating the first two bodies. She brought it in to us, and then…" He trailed off, as if searching for the right words. "Well, I had it. It was stolen from me when…"

Brooke had been around enough to know the story. Feigning a call for help, Jen Rogers and the women who'd been working with her had knocked Thomas unconscious and then dropped him in the middle of the forest preserve where the cave was located. It was why he still had a faint pink scar from the stitches he'd had to get along the side of his face.

"When they took me…" he finally said, clearly still not over *that*. "It was all a ruse to get their hands on this scrapbook. We never could figure out why. Particularly since Jen was only connected to the Brink family through marriage and it was a Brink family scrapbook. But we'll look through it again with what we know, and we'll consult Chloe and see if we can find some answers. Hopefully implicate Jen even more."

No doubt it would, if it was in the cave. But Brooke couldn't help but wonder if it might connect to what else she was thinking. She'd need a look at the scrapbook though. "If she doesn't have any clear-cut answers, would I be able to take a look through it?"

Thomas raised an eyebrow at her. "Why?"

Brooke shrugged. "I don't know exactly. It's just…it has to connect some way, right? To those remains, if she stole it during the investigation into the Hudson murder. Maybe something would…jump out to me as a connection."

Thomas seemed to give this some thought. "Possibly. I'll run it by Laurel, and Chloe, for that matter."

"Sure," Brooke agreed, fully believing she'd *never* see the inside of that scrapbook. But she couldn't focus on that because a trickle of unease crept up her spine, tightening her shoulders. She looked around the bright daylight as Thomas got in his patrol car.

"You okay?" he asked.

Brooke nodded, forced herself to look away from the scenery and to Hart. "Of course. I'll meet you at the station once I've eaten."

"Sounds good." He closed his door, but she knew he'd wait for her to get into her car and drive out first. He'd follow her to the highway. And then he'd go his own way and she would go hers, because he didn't know someone *might* be following her.

But Zeke did, and she would just have to trust that he would take care of it.

ZEKE APPRECIATED THAT it was Hart with Brooke today. He knew a few of the deputies at Bent County, and for the most part he trusted Bent to do their job, but over the past few months he'd actually become friends with Thomas Hart. He'd do a good job looking after Brooke.

She'd definitely sensed Zeke watching her, though he'd stayed out of sight. He didn't know if that's because her instincts were that good, or because he was losing his touch. He didn't love the thought he was rusty, but he *was* getting older. He'd been out of the following game for a while now, so his skills could have deteriorated.

On top of that, he wasn't sure what to make of their early break for lunch. Brooke had only been in there working for about two hours.

It didn't really matter, he supposed. No matter what she did, he was going to be there.

Zeke followed her throughout the rest of her day, and not once did he see any sign of a silver sedan. Following her *or* him in his truck with the tracker now attached.

He wasn't sure what to do with that. Did they know someone had moved their tracker? Had they given up because she'd stayed with him last night?

Were they better stalkers than he was?

That was a concerning question. Not one he'd let rattle him though. He'd find a way to protect Brooke no matter what. And she clearly needed protecting from something if someone was trying to track her—regardless of the whys.

Track, follow, but not approach. Not threaten. He didn't know why, but that made him far more uncomfortable than a direct threat. He knew what to do with threats—stop them in their tracks.

What did whoever was following her *want* from her if there was no threat? Without motivation, it was going to be harder to get to the bottom of who.

But not impossible, Zeke assured himself as he stood

next to his truck in the Bent County Sheriff's Department parking lot, waiting for Brooke to appear after she'd gone inside with Hart at the end of their afternoon shift at the cave.

He didn't know what her plans were, but he knew that the tracker had to have changed things for her. She had to understand even more fully just how much potential danger she was in.

Viola gave a soft whimper from her spot in the passenger seat, head leaning out the window. Zeke watched as Brooke and Hart walked out of the station, practically shoulder to shoulder. Brooke was smiling, and she said something that had Hart doing the same.

A surprisingly sharp bolt of jealousy landed hard, right at the center of Zeke's chest. He didn't want it, knew he had absolutely no right to it, and still it settled there like an intense, squeezing pain.

Brooke stopped in her tracks when she saw him standing there in between her car and his truck.

Hart's eyebrows rose, but he didn't stop walking, so when Brooke finally moved forward again, she had to walk quickly to catch up to the detective.

"Zeke," Hart greeted. His expression was *way* too close to amused. "Needing a detective?"

"No," Zeke returned. And refused to explain himself, even if Hart *was* a friend. Even if there was no reason to feel…competitive.

Hart gave the dog a pet then turned to Brooke with another *smile*. "See you tomorrow, Brooke."

"Bye, Thomas." Her smile faded as she turned her attention to him. "Zeke, you didn't need to be here."

"And yet here I am."

She sucked in a slow breath, and he *refused* to let her

annoyance with him and her smiles at Thomas stir up his temper.

"No one's been following me today and you removed that tracker, so they can't again. I think it's best if we go back to the way things were before. If I have concerns... I'll let you know." She moved over to where Viola whimpered in the passenger seat and gave her a rubdown, whispering assuring words to the dog.

But Brooke was *wrong*. Someone had been following her today. The fact that it was *him* was neither here nor there. "Did it occur to you that no one's been following you today because you involved me?"

She gave him a cool look. "Do you think your North Star reputation matters to anyone around here?"

He shrugged. "I'm a physically intimidating guy, Brooke. I don't need a reputation to precede me."

She rolled her eyes and he couldn't help but smile. Because a little spot of color showed up on her cheeks. Like she was considering anything *physical* about him. Or maybe that was just wishful thinking.

Didn't matter.

"Besides, trackers are easy and inconspicuous," he continued. "Someone could drop another one at any time."

She stiffened at that. Maybe four years changed a person, but Zeke knew Brooke well enough to know her refusal wasn't some misplaced bravado. It wasn't that she *wasn't* scared or didn't have concerns. She just never wanted to be seen as a burden by anyone. Back then, she'd always been so scared that...whatever support she got was fleeting. That she needed to handle everything on her own or people would simply...kick her to the curb.

It was one of the few things he didn't think she had any self-awareness about. She thought she was being independent, but what she really was, and always had been, was afraid to be a bother.

He understood, too well, where it stemmed from. Not just her awful childhood stuck in the middle of a Sons of the Badlands family, but then as a foster kid getting kicked around the system.

Knowing all that about her made him softer than he should allow himself to be when it came to her safety.

"If you really want to stay at your rental, I can drop Viola off at the Hudsons' and crash on the couch or something. I can even sleep in the truck outside, if that bothers you."

Her face took on a pinched look, but she continued to speak in that careful, detached kind of way. "That's not the kind of alternative I'm looking for. Thank you."

He *almost* smiled at the tacked-on "thank you," but this was too important to be amused by her. "It's the only one you're going to get, Brooke."

Temper flashed in her blue eyes. "I didn't tell you about this just so you'd swoop in and take over."

"Didn't you?"

Her mouth dropped open—not quite outrage. She wasn't mean enough for outrage. Because something like *hurt* tinged in her expression and it made him feel about two inches tall. Enough that he had to fight the urge to reach forward by shoving his hands into his pockets. Enough that he gentled his words.

"Brooke. You're possibly in some kind of danger. There's no point in being stubborn about wanting and taking some protection. It's not offered out of anything other than concern, so you shouldn't feel badly about taking it."

She inhaled. That slow, careful inhale that signaled she was trying so hard to be *reasonable*.

"You're right," she agreed, somewhat surprisingly. She met his gaze with a cool, determined look. "We'll discuss a fee."

He frowned at her, not following. "A fee?"

"Like hiring a bodyguard. I'll pay you a fee."

He could not think of anything she might have said that could be any more insulting. "You're not going to pay me," he growled.

"Why not? You're offering a service, are you not?"

"Brooke."

"Zeke."

Maybe he'd forgotten *some* things about her because he surely didn't remember this stubbornness of hers ever being directed at him. And it poked at an already frayed temper—not because of her, but because of everything confusing and challenging about this situation.

His feelings chief among them.

"I'm going to be there," he told her. Maybe a little *too* firmly, *too* seriously, too *close*. "Until we get to the bottom of this, or until the job is done. And I'm not taking a dime. The end."

She looked up at him, blue eyes flashing and narrowing with her own temper. Close enough he could see the faint scar on her cheekbone that she used to try to hide with makeup. The one he knew her father had given her the night Family Services had finally intervened and she'd been taken away.

She'd told him that one day all those years ago, before he'd been assigned to protect her but after he'd met her. He'd teasingly asked about it, trying to flirt with the pretty woman working for Granger MacMillan. Because as seriously as he'd taken his place at North Star, he hadn't been able to stop thinking about her after that first meeting.

She'd recited the facts like they were rote historical events that didn't concern her, and he'd been...even more fascinated. Because he didn't know how someone so fresh and pretty, so gentle and soft seeming, could have come from as terrible a childhood as he had.

And that was before he'd known hers had been worse.

But this was now. He could tell by the anger in her eyes—because she used to not get angry at him. Just hurt by him. He could tell by the fact she didn't respond to him in any way. At least, any *verbal* way.

She whirled around, started striding to her car, even as Viola whined.

Fine. She could get in that car and drive away, but he would follow. He hadn't been exaggerating when he'd said he was in this until the job was done. She didn't need to like it and he didn't need her permission to keep her safe.

She stopped abruptly. She didn't turn to face him, just stood there with ramrod-straight posture. When she spoke, it was quietly but with enough force he could hear.

"I *have* survived a clear, everyday threat. I grew up surviving that."

"I know." And wished he didn't. Because back then he'd really liked thinking no one could have experienced the childhood trauma he'd had. Abusive dad who'd eventually disappeared. Mother murdered in their apartment. A murder it had taken over a decade of danger and pain and frustration to solve. He'd had his share of sorrow and horrible things.

And she'd been raised by a violent psychopath in some kind of biker cult, and then somehow dealt with the fragile, uneasy life of a teenager in foster care.

But she hadn't let any of her circumstances harden her. Sure, they'd messed her up. They all had scars left from what they'd grown up with—no one who got themselves mixed up with North Star didn't—but she was one of the few he knew who was somehow still...*soft*.

Strong as hell, but penetrable.

Maybe it was wrong, pointless, not his place, or misguided. He didn't care. In this moment, he'd been the one to bring her here. Walker's brother-in-law had needed a forensic anthropologist and Zeke had known one. He'd pulled the strings. *He* was why Brooke was here.

He couldn't and *wouldn't* let anything hit that soft target.

"You shouldn't have had to survive that childhood alone without anyone looking out for you, and you shouldn't do this alone either. Whether you can or not."

He watched her shoulders move. No doubt with those deep breaths she was forever taking. When she turned to face him, the anger in her expression was gone. But the sadness there instead wasn't any better. If anything, it was worse.

"I think the problem with us, Zeke, is we do *everything* better alone."

He wasn't sure why that should land like some kind of slap. He'd always *preferred* working alone, being alone. It was who he was. *Lone wolf,* Carlyle used to throw at him, and he'd taken that as a badge of honor.

But the way Brooke said it made it sound *sad,* and the way she stood there looking alone made him *feel* sad.

That, he wouldn't let himself marinate in. "Not this, Brooke. I'll follow you to your rental. Let's pack up your stuff. Stay with me until we get to the bottom of this. Someone is *tracking* you. You shouldn't be alone. You know that. I know you know that."

She stared at him for the longest time, like searching his face would give her the answer she needed.

But there was only one answer. Even if she didn't like it. Even if *he* didn't like it. She either had to tell the cops or she had to let him help.

"Fine," she agreed, clearly disgusted with the concession. But she'd made it. Still, she looked at him so seriously, spoke so damn seriously. "This isn't the same as last time. It can't be."

Because *last time* had gone too far. Personally. *Last time* had been a mistake. And even now, four years on, that mistake still felt raw. And a little too close to regret.

Because he remembered every second with her. The way she'd felt in his arms. The way she'd tasted. He wanted to pretend he didn't, but being with her was like wiping away all this *past*. So four years felt like nothing and the clawing, yearning need for everything she was existed right inside him.

Like it always had. Like it always would.

But it didn't matter.

Because she wasn't his. Never would be again.

So, he nodded. "I know."

Chapter Six

Brooke was glad to have the time to drive back to her rental cabin in the car by herself. It allowed her the opportunity to breathe, to center herself, and to accept she'd made the right decision.

Sure, it reminded her too much of four years ago when she'd been working on a case for North Star and had come under some threats from the murderer she'd been close to putting behind bars. When the handsome North Star operative had been assigned to her, and their whole *thing* had started.

The serious man who'd smiled like it was just for her. Who'd flirted with her before the danger. And then he'd protected her. She'd fallen in love with him. Quick and easy, so convinced it was meant to be. There'd been a bubble of time where she'd believed that was it. Love would win the day.

Ha. Ha.

She also understood now better than back then that his... protection wasn't about feelings. She'd never considered herself naïve before. She'd had a terrible, eye-opening childhood that had never once had her believing the best in anyone, let alone that *love* was some great magical thing.

But she'd thought Zeke's protection had *meant* something, because of some strange, warped naïveté inside her. Where people didn't help, didn't protect. So the fact he had meant she'd mattered to him.

Now she understood fully. Helping wasn't only intrinsic to who he was. He'd seen the entire North Star mission as one of protection. Of keeping people safe. It hadn't had to be about *her* for him to feel the need to protect. It was just all the things he was made of.

So, he *had* to protect her in this moment, regardless of any feelings he might have had or not had for her. Any old attractions that may or may not still exist between them. It didn't matter. She couldn't let it matter.

It was just…smart to let him step in and help. And protect. Because she didn't know what she was up against. And no matter how she liked to fancy herself a survivor, she'd really only *endured*, not necessarily *survived*. Never fought for herself. Or the people she should have fought for.

So she had to remember Zeke protecting her was just…a job. Even if he wouldn't let her pay him. It was a *job* he was doing. Because she needed help, and he needed to give it.

Brooke repeated that to herself a few times as she parked in front of the rental cabin she'd been so looking forward to staying at. Nestled a little out of town, birdfeeders in the yard and suncatchers in the windows. For almost a month, she'd gotten to live here and pretend it was home while she examined the skeletal remains found on the Brink farm.

If it had been only that, it would have been a nice interlude. But then the remains had been found in the cave. But then she'd felt she was being followed. But *then* she'd been the person to bring Zeke into it.

Her fault. So it was her responsibility to *endure* once again.

Zeke was out of his truck and next to her before she

could even fish her keys out of her purse. He held out his hand, like he was expecting her to just hand over the keys to the cabin. Mr. In Charge. Always.

She opened her mouth to argue with him. To tell him she could take care of it. But what a waste of breath. He wanted to protect. She'd be a lot better off *letting* him, rather than fighting him on it.

Will you be better off or are you just hoping it'll be easier? Survive or endure?

She really wasn't sure about the answer. Everything was so jumbled up and hypothetical. The only thing she knew for sure was that she could not make the same mistakes she'd made four years ago.

Number one, she wouldn't read into him wanting to help. Number two, she would have boundaries. Zeke was the expert when it came to safety, so she'd allow him liberties there. But *only* when it came to safety.

So, she got her key out and ignored his outstretched hand. She walked up to the door, unlocked it herself, then gestured him inside.

He didn't frown exactly, but she could read disapproval in the lines of his face. She ignored it.

"Stay," he said sharply before taking a step inside.

It took Brooke longer than it should have to realize he was talking to the dog. She blinked at Viola then scurried inside to follow Zeke. Because she didn't need to follow anyone's orders if she didn't want to.

It didn't do thinking about if she wanted to or not.

"Anything seem out of place?" he asked, scanning the small living room and tiny kitchen that were immediately visible.

Brooke didn't look at first. There'd been a time when no one would have had to ask her that question. When it would have been the first thing she'd do when she walked into a room. Look for what was out of place, brace herself for whatever might be wrong. Rearrange herself accordingly.

But this wasn't about her childhood in a biker cult. It wasn't even about one of those disaster foster homes. It was just straightforward danger. The kind she got for looking into dead people.

She walked through the cabin, looking for anything that struck her as wrong. Her suitcase was where she'd left it yesterday morning, organized and open. She poked her head into the bathroom. Her toiletries were lined up along the counter just as she'd left them.

"If anyone has been through my things, they were very careful."

Zeke nodded, studying the cabin. He poked at light fixtures, pushed on windows. She didn't ask what he was doing—another lesson she'd learned. She would keep herself…separate from his attempts at keeping her safe.

No teamwork. No North Star to bind them. He was *just* a bodyguard. She was determined to think of him that way. Besides, when it came to her other options—telling the detectives or staying with the Hudsons as Zeke's sister had suggested—surely figuring out how to deal with her ex-boyfriend from four years ago was better than that.

So she packed up her belongings and brought everything out to the front door. She hadn't packed heavy because she didn't have a lot of worldly possessions, even now that she was more financially stable.

Because she was too used to moving, and because her job called for so much travel, she'd convinced herself it was fine not to have a real home base. Fine to be a bit of a nomad and have a small collection of belongings that could be bundled up in less than an hour.

But it always made her far sadder than it should to see her life sorted into a single suitcase and nothing else.

In silence, Zeke hefted the bag—because why would a stubborn, ego-driven man ever let her *help*—and took her things outside. Brooke followed, locking the cabin door behind her. She wouldn't get *rid* of the rental just yet. Maybe it was a waste of money, but it was always good to have a place to disappear to if needed.

She had a bad feeling she was definitely going to need that. An escape hatch, right within reach.

Zeke tossed her bag into the bed of his truck. "Let's leave your car here tonight. It might throw some people off. You've got a routine down, and we want to shake it up in the eyes of anyone who might be following."

Brooke didn't trust herself to speak and not argue, so she just nodded and headed for the truck's passenger side. She'd gotten herself into this mess. She had to take the consequences of her actions in stride. Because maybe it had been four years, but she knew Zeke too well to have thought this would go any other way.

He got in the driver's seat and she hefted herself into the passenger's, but just as she did she caught sight of something out of the corner of her eye. She looked over her shoulder. There was a gravel road out beyond the cabin. Brooke hadn't done any exploring to see where it led, but along with a minor cloud of dust, she saw a flash of silver before it disappeared into the tree line.

Her heart seemed to stop for a moment, and her legs wouldn't keep her up, so she sank into the seat, Viola hopping in behind her. "Did you see—"

"I saw it," Zeke said, his voice detached and very *military*. A little North Star déjà vu. "Get out of the truck. Go back in the cabin and lock the door."

But that would take time, because he wouldn't leave until she was safely tucked away and the car already had too big of a head start. She pulled her truck door closed. "We both know there's no time. Just go."

He slid her one irritated glance then he hit the accelerator.

Brooke held on to Viola as they took off toward where they'd both seen the flash of a silver car.

ZEKE FOCUSED ON driving as fast as he could while also being mindful of the woman clutching the handle of the door for dear life. He didn't want to scare her, but he sure as hell didn't want to miss his chance to get to the bottom of this.

"What do we do if we catch up to him?" Brooke asked, her cool, calm voice a direct opposite to the way she clutched the door and how wide her eyes were. She always had been able to maintain that seemingly calm voice in the face of all sorts of danger.

But he was the one equipped to *deal* with all that danger. She did not have that kind of training. "You'll stay in the truck. I'll handle it."

He ignored her sigh, concentrated on taking a curve in the gravel road without flipping the truck. He saw another flash. They were gaining *some* on the car, and it helped he was in a vehicle that could handle the rough terrain and the stalker was in a sedan that was just as likely to rattle apart as it was to make it over the next gravel hill.

Zeke lost sight of the car as it crested the hill first. And he didn't like that tactical disadvantage. Still, he could hardly let the guy just disappear. Answers were within their reach, and he had to get them.

"Get my gun out of the glove compartment."

Not a sigh this time, just a noise unique to Brooke that he recognized all too well, full of disapproval. Why that made him want to smile in this tense moment was something he was going to have to excavate…some other time.

Still, she did as told, opening the glove compartment and pulling out the gun, not hiding her distaste.

"Can you hold on to it for a minute?" He had to maneuver the truck into a defensive position as he crested the hill. One that would keep Brooke out of the line of potential fire.

And quickly. The minute Zeke took his truck over the hill, the driver of the silver sedan was parked and getting out.

Zeke screeched to a stop on an angle to keep some distance, to keep Brooke not directly in the man's line of sight.

"Stay in the truck." An order for the dog…and the woman.

She didn't mount an argument, just handed over the gun.

He opened his driver's-side door, got out of the truck carefully, using the door as a kind of shield while he held his gun trained on the man—who *appeared* unarmed. Zeke suspected the driver had a firearm on him somewhere. He was way too calm with a gun pointed in his direction not to have some kind of weapon handy.

Unless he had backup. Zeke turned off the safety on his gun and scanned the world around them. He saw one rental cabin in the distance, but otherwise just highway and land. No people. No nothing.

Zeke began to move toward the driver. The guy held his hands up in surrender, though it didn't feel like a particularly scared or submissive move. It appeared far more… *mocking*.

Zeke didn't quite know what to do with this, but he'd been in strange, confusing and dangerous situations before. He'd made an entire adulthood out of it—hell, his entire life had been about getting people, including himself, out of trouble.

With his gun clearly drawn, he continued to inch toward the man. Zeke watched everything and put Brooke and the dog out of his mind. The trick to any difficult situation was to divorce feelings from it and to focus on instincts only.

He'd only ever struggled with that as a North Star agent when Brooke was involved. And she, for some reason, had reminded him of his family. Of Walker out there trying to track down their mother's killer and maybe getting himself killed in the process. Of Carlyle out there chomping at the bit. Of Walker trying to protect her from all the world had to offer.

Brooke had reminded him of what he'd felt for his family, and it had been the first chink in an armor he'd considered impenetrable. It had been the first realization he'd been getting in too deep with her.

And now was quite possibly the worst time *ever* to be thinking about that.

"It seems you've taken a real interest in my friend," Zeke called across the distance. He was close enough to take stock of the man. The guy was tall, big. Definitely wouldn't be easy to take down in a fight. They'd be almost evenly matched, and he had a fighter's kind of stance that spoke of either time in the ring or time in a cell.

Zeke was betting on the latter.

He still didn't see anyone in their surroundings. No backup. Unless he was missing something, but Zeke had to trust his instincts and believe he wasn't. While preparing for *anything*.

"You could say that," the man returned, unbothered. "And you could also say it's none of your damn business."

"You'd be wrong about that."

The guy jerked his chin toward the truck. "Then why is she getting out?"

Zeke knew better than to look, than to be distracted. He really did. He was almost certain he wouldn't have looked back, except he heard the sound of feet hitting gravel.

He wanted to shout at her, but some gut feeling he could still manage to follow caught it in time, so he said nothing at all. Though he did move his body to act as a physical barrier between Brooke's approaching form and the man.

Since she couldn't stay in the damn truck. He wanted to curse. Instead he could only watch her out of the corner of his eye. The dog followed by her side—neither bounding ahead nor lagging behind.

Brooke came to an abrupt stop a few steps behind Zeke.

"Royal?" she said. Her voice didn't seem strong enough to carry, but he noted the way the man by the car stiffened.

Zeke didn't lower the gun but glanced at Brooke, now moving toward the man, clearly without thinking. Zeke grabbed her by the arm with his free hand as she tried to pass him. She looked over at him as if startled to find him still there.

The man crossed his big, tattooed arms over his chest and *smirked* at Zeke. Then his gaze moved to Brooke.

"Heya, Chick."

Chapter Seven

For a moment, it was like being out of time. Like she wasn't a living, breathing, being anymore. Just…mist. Nothing tangible. Because this couldn't be real, so she couldn't be real.

Then Zeke had grabbed her arm, held her in place, and she'd come back together. Her mouth was dry, her hands shook, but she was breathing again. Her heart was pounding in her ears, so loud, she didn't know if Zeke was saying anything to her or not.

Because she was looking at her brother.

Brooke didn't even know why she recognized him. *How* she did. He'd been ten years old the last time she'd seen him. He'd looked so different. Small and vulnerable and decidedly untattooed, though maybe with some of the same belligerence in his expression.

Now he was…a man.

Yet there was something in the eyes. In the way he looked at her. A mix of sibling devotion and massive distrust. Even as a toddler, he'd been a dichotomy. No doubt fighting between all that evil around them and the good Brooke had tried so hard to hold on to. So hard to give him.

She'd *known* it was him in this moment, just from that look alone.

Then he'd called her "Chick," and no one else knew that nickname. Not a soul in the world. It was just theirs. And she hadn't heard it in over a decade. Hadn't *seen* him in over a decade.

Her *brother* was standing there. Right in front of her. Adult. Alive.

It was so easy to forget about everything except that. For a brief, beautiful moment she did. Forgot everything except *relief.*

They'd been separated in foster care, and Brooke had promised to find him. She'd promised. It had taken too long. Even she'd known that. Once she'd finally tracked him down—in jail for work he'd done with Sons of the Badlands, the biker cult their parents had been a part of— she'd started writing him letters. He hadn't responded, and she'd been mostly okay with that. She'd known she'd borne some responsibility for him going down that path. Hard feelings were natural.

She'd hired him a lawyer to make sure he could get out when he'd done his time. He'd never answered one of her letters. Never given her any indication he cared about her, even if he'd used the lawyer. Still, she hadn't heard he was out. She hadn't heard anything.

Now he was following her? Finding her?

There was an initial swing of elation, of love, of hope. But it was quickly soured by the reality of the situation. There was no *good* explanation for her brother to be skulking around following her. If he wanted to see her, he would have known he could contact her. He would have known she would help him with anything. Like she'd tried to do behind the scenes the past few years. He had to know that.

Didn't he?

"Aren't you going to give your baby brother a hug?" he

finally said. She heard the sarcasm dripping from every word, and still she wanted to do just that. Reach out. Hold him. Assure herself he was real.

"Royal..." She started to move forward again, not necessarily to give him a hug. Not necessarily to do anything but to give him a closer look so maybe she could somehow make sense of this.

But Zeke's grip on her arm remained firm. "I don't care if you know him, Brooke," Zeke said on a whisper. "He's been stalking you."

"I can't quite figure this guy out," Royal called from where he still stood a decent distance away. "Not a husband. Not a boyfriend. Just some annoying dude skulking around. What's up with that?"

She kept forgetting Zeke was even there. She just...

She turned to Zeke, placed her free hand over the one holding her arm. "Keep your gun on him all you want, but you need to let me go."

"Brooke." The word was *pained*, not just irritated. She knew he was worried. Confused. But not any more than she was.

"Zeke. It's my brother. Royal."

"The brother you had to..." Zeke didn't say the rest. He knew the whole story of them being separated by foster care. She'd sobbed it out to him one day when they'd been together.

This, of course, did not soften Zeke any to Royal. Because Zeke knew he'd been involved in the Sons and ended up in jail, though she'd never gotten into the nitty-gritty of why. She'd known Zeke would never believe her brother's innocence. No, innocence and being involved in a gang wouldn't make sense to a man like Zeke.

But by some miracle she'd have to think about later,

Zeke actually released her arm. He did not drop the gun from pointing at her brother, but he let her go.

She'd owe him for that alone.

Brooke didn't run to her brother. She knew better than to think this could all be solved by a hug even if her hands itched to grab onto him. To hold on. To assure herself he was alive and well.

But he wasn't a little boy anymore, and she'd failed him. Still, she moved closer. Studying every change. The square jaw, the crooked nose, the tattoos, the scars. So few glimpses of a little boy she'd tried to raise with some semblance of right and wrong. Some inkling of love.

"Royal. What are you *doing* here? How…? Why…?"

He looked at her a long time, his gaze cold. "You told me you'd come get me, Chick. You never did."

"I tried," she said, her voice more rusty than she wanted.

He snorted. Like he didn't believe her. Like she hadn't sent those letters, that lawyer. Like…

"You were in jail, honey. Didn't you get my letters?" She didn't understand how he wouldn't have known it was her. Even though she hadn't been allowed to have contact with him—first because of his sentencing, then because of her involvement with North Star—the letters were supposed to get through. "Who do you think hired that lawyer?"

A small line appeared in his forehead, but his expression was one of distrust. That was…hurtful, when she probably didn't have any right to be hurt.

"That guy…"

Brooke didn't look back at Zeke, though tempted. "Is a friend. And someone who wants to help me. Help me not get *stalked*, Royal."

"I wasn't stalking. I was…" He took a step closer, reached out, but Viola, at Brooke's side, began to growl low in her throat. Royal stopped in his tracks and flicked a glance down at the dog. "Guard dog, huh?"

"Royal." She couldn't be distracted. She had to know. "Why have you been following me?"

Royal glanced at Zeke, still holding that ridiculous gun pointed at her brother. Royal leaned in close, eyes on the dog, waiting for her to growl again.

"Something isn't right," he said, quiet enough Zeke wouldn't be able to hear. "I don't know what it is, but I have a bad feeling it's got to do with Dad." His expression was hard, detached, but she didn't think he was lying. And the mention of their father had a cold ball of dread settling in her gut. "And I was worried enough it had to do with you to come looking."

"You could have told me. You could have…" But no use going down the road of all the things he could have done. She could have done. Sometimes you could only deal with what *was*, not what could have been.

With Zeke and Royal suddenly back in her life, she was really going to have to learn that lesson.

He shook his head. "Best if you don't get mixed up with me, Chick. Unless it's too late." He sighed. "I'm starting to think it's too late."

THE ONLY THING that kept Zeke from rushing closer, from grabbing Brooke and getting her the hell out of there, was the memory of the way she'd cried over the brother she'd thought she'd failed.

He knew too much about the complicated feelings sibling relationships brought out. The way love didn't dim over mistakes and disagreements. Maybe even when it should.

So Zeke watched, his finger still on the trigger of the

gun, ready for anything. He wasn't about to trust the guy just because Brooke shared genetics with him.

Brooke and Royal exchanged a few quiet words Zeke couldn't make out, and then she turned and walked toward him. Zeke searched Brooke's face for a second or two before he reminded himself it was her brother he needed to be paying attention to. That her brother might be a threat.

He wouldn't say she looked happy, but she seemed *awed* to see her brother there. Definitely surprised.

Royal stood by his silver sedan, arms still crossed over his chest, belligerent look still on his face. But he watched Brooke go. There was definitely no awe on his face, but *something* had Zeke carefully lowering his gun.

One of the things all the veterans of North Star had impressed upon him when he'd been young and eager, and they'd had years of missions under their belts, was to trust *all* your instincts. Not just the cynical ones. The ones that wanted to see the bad, the evil in everyone just because some existed in the world.

If you didn't allow for the good and hopeful instincts, you weren't that far removed from the bad you were trying to stop in the world.

When Brooke approached, she tried to smile at him, but it faltered. "He, um, didn't want to see me, but he wanted to make sure I was okay."

Zeke knew he should keep his feelings on that to himself, but… "That doesn't make any sense."

She shook her head. "No. Maybe not. But I gave him the keys to my rental. He can stay there tonight, and I'll stay with you and then maybe I'll… Well, I'll have time to think this over, decide how to move forward. But I'm not being stalked, so there is that."

"You *are* being stalked, Brooke. Just because it's your

brother doesn't mean it's not…" His words fell off because she'd closed her eyes as if in pain.

Because no doubt she didn't need *him* to tell her that her brother might be dangerous. So, best to just…get her out of here. Maybe back at the ranch they could really take stock of the situation, and if they knew where Royal was and he wasn't following Brooke, all the better.

"Okay. Let's head home, huh?"

She hesitated a moment and then nodded. He helped her into the truck and she let him, which was a worry in itself. But Viola wiggled her way into the truck, laying her big head on Brooke's shoulder.

Neither Brooke nor Zeke said a word to one another as he drove them back to his ranch. It was dark now. A bright quarter moon hung in the sky over his house when he pulled up. He thrust the gear into Park, shut off the engine, and got out.

Viola jumped out after him, but Brooke didn't immediately follow. Zeke didn't move forward onto the porch and instead waited for Brooke while Viola ran off into the dark.

Eventually Brooke opened the door and carefully climbed out of the truck, moving like she was injured and afraid to jostle whatever was hurting.

He had to fight the urge to move back to the truck and help her down. Touch her in some reassuring way. She'd had a shock, was still confused, and no doubt hurting, but that had nothing to do with him.

She needed to deal with this on her own.

So, he walked up onto the porch. Viola bounded up from whatever she'd been off doing. Stiffly, Brooke followed. She didn't even lean down to pet Viola when the dog pressed against her.

He unlocked the door, trying not to stare at her to try

to read every little emotion in her eyes. "I've got a frozen pizza I can heat up for us." He pushed the door open and ushered her inside.

She moved in, still acting like a stray breeze might blow her to pieces. "I think I'll just go to sleep."

"Brooke, you haven't had any dinner. You have to eat something."

"I'm not..." Her breathing hitched. "Hungry," she said on a voice that cracked. She shook her head, as if she could shake her tears away, but they began to fall.

He couldn't take it. So many things he could withstand. Pain. Torture. Manipulation. Aggression. You name it.

But her tears undid him.

"Sweetheart." He moved for her, pulled her into his arms. And much like she had all those years ago when she'd told him about her brother, she sobbed into his shoulder.

"He didn't even know I tried. That I was the one who hired the lawyer. Why wouldn't he know that?"

"I don't know," Zeke replied, rubbing her back, holding her close. Trying and failing to put all those old feelings on ice. Because she leaned into him, just like she used to. Like she trusted him. Like she believed he could be the protector she deserved.

It cracked too many things inside him, and even knowing he should push the feelings aside, set her aside, he couldn't. He brushed some hair out of her face because it was sticking to the tears.

She looked up at him. Their gazes held. Hers wet and blue. Too soft, too trusting. Too...much everything. And they just stood in that moment. His heart beating hard, her cheeks turning an alluring shade of pink.

And now was not the time for any of *that*, so he forced himself to speak.

"We'll figure it out though." The words came out rough.

She let out a shaky breath then swallowed and squeezed her eyes shut. She shook her head. "No, I don't think we should." She wriggled away from him.

"Brooke."

She wiped her face, stepped back, and fixed him with a pathetic attempt at a smile. A smile meant to keep him at arm's length. A smile meant to prove nothing was still there.

When there *was*. But this new development had also thrown her for a loop.

"I can't… He's my brother. I messed up. But I also know some part of him blames me for things. I don't think I should go poking around. I think I should let him…have the time and space to decide if he wants to tell me."

Maybe she was right. In a lot of other situations, he'd agree with her. But… "Brooke, he was following you. I don't care what he said, it wasn't just to make sure you're okay. He could have seen that the first day he followed you. It's been what? Three days?"

She hesitated. Only for a second or two, but he saw it all the same. "Well, sure, but—"

"Jesus, Brooke. How long had it been going on before you came to me?"

She shrugged jerkily. "I wasn't sure at first."

At first. So God knew how long her brother had been watching. God knew how long this had been going on and she'd just…let it. "Did being part of North Star teach you anything?"

Her gaze cooled. Even with those tears still on her cheeks, her expression went full ice. "Oh, it taught me plenty."

He reached out for her. "Sweetheart—"

"Stop that," she snapped, sidestepping his arm. "*Sweetheart*. I don't want you to call me that ever again."

That was fair but landed like a blow all the same. "Sorry." Hell, he was botching this six ways to Sunday. Because that's what happened when you did something stupid like *care* about the people involved in dangerous situations. Messed up. Ruined things. Hurt people you didn't mean to hurt.

And still, he didn't know how to keep his distance, because *someone* had to look out for her. When it came to her brother, she had too soft a heart and it was going to get her a lot more hurt than whatever mistakes he might make when it came to her.

She already wasn't taking care of herself, which he tried to use as fodder to piss him off enough to put those walls back up. "You're going to eat something. You don't have to share a table with me, but you're going to eat."

"I'm not your responsibility, Zeke. I know that's what your North Star training told you, but it's wrong. I don't *need* you to worry about me, take care of me, save me."

As if he'd do it if *he* didn't *need* to. As if he'd be standing here with his heart raw and obnoxious if he didn't *need* her to be okay. As if he hadn't spent the past four years keeping tabs on her for that very reason.

That, she didn't know, and it wouldn't do to tell her. "I wish I could feel that way, Brooke."

She closed her eyes and sighed. "I don't want to fight with you. I just…"

"You're going to sit down and eat, and then you're going to get some sleep. We can talk through next steps in the morning." Because she needed those things.

And he needed some space to get a hold of himself so

he could be what she needed. So she would be safe, and when everything was all said and done, go back to whatever life she had out there that didn't involve him.

And rightfully so.

Chapter Eight

In the morning, Brooke left.

Not for good. Just early enough that *hopefully* Zeke wouldn't know what she'd done. Of course, she'd had to take his truck, so it was unlikely she wasn't going to have to explain herself, but she had to do this first.

At the sheriff's department. Maybe Zeke would know she'd done *something*, but she didn't have to tell him exactly what. It was none of his business. Royal was none of his business. No matter how kind he'd been about the whole thing yesterday.

Brooke had never had a *normal* life. Nothing had ever really been easy or routine or settled. The only routine was that unexpected change would inevitably come knocking.

Zeke.

Her brother.

Her *father*.

She still couldn't quite believe what Royal had told her. She should have told Zeke. The guilt was eating her up. Staying in his house, eating his food, and keeping this huge secret.

Yet she would also feel guilty if she told Zeke something Royal didn't want shared.

And at the end of the day, she wasn't sure who the right man to place her loyalty with was. They'd both hurt her in different ways. She'd failed them both in different ways.

Maybe you should just bail.

Tempting. So tempting. Retreat. Isolate. She wanted to. It was the right thing. Everyone was getting too deep and too complicated and too hard.

But she had a job to do. So she didn't choose Zeke or Royal. She'd decided to choose someone who had no *real* connection to her. It was hard to ask for help. It made her feel sick to her stomach. A burden and a bother, when she wanted to handle everything herself.

Nonetheless, she couldn't handle this. So she walked into the sheriff's department and asked for Thomas. She was pretty sure he had an early morning shift to cover her morning cave work, and when the administrative assistant took her through the security measures and then directed her to his office, she let out a slow, steady breath.

This was going to work. This was going to be okay. The police were there to help, and Thomas had been nothing but kind. Besides, she wasn't asking for anything difficult.

His office door was open and he sat at his desk, writing something down on a piece of paper.

"Thomas."

He looked up from his desk, no doubt surprised to see her. He glanced at the clock. "Did I miss a schedule change?" he asked with some concern.

She managed a smile and shook her head. "No. I have a favor to ask you. As a detective. Not related to the cave or the remains."

The concern didn't leave his expression. He pointed to the seat in his office. "Sit."

Brooke didn't let her nerves show. There was nothing to

be nervous about. She was only asking for a favor. *Information*. And once she had it, she could decide what to do about Royal's theories. What to do about Zeke.

Thomas was not the kind of guy to hold it against her, and if it hurt Zeke's feelings that she was asking someone else for help, that was his problem. And if Royal was going to get bent out of shape over her finding the truth... Well.

The only thing that mattered was the truth. The facts. The data from which she could then make an educated choice.

"I don't know what kind of background you guys did into me when I was hired for this case," she began, because she'd been internally practicing this interaction ever since the idea had occurred to her last night.

"Not much. We needed a forensic anthropologist ASAP. I think maybe someone looked into your credentials, but that was all bureaucratic red tape I'm not involved in. So I can't say as I know much."

No doubt because there wasn't much to know. No doubt Zeke had gone through Granger to refer her to Bent County when his friends had needed a forensic anthropologist, which meant Granger had used his *skills* to smooth over anything standing in her way of helping.

Not that she wasn't qualified for the job, or her cases wouldn't speak for themselves. Just that the governmental wheels in place for these things tended to run a little slow, and this had been quick. North Star—or Granger MacMillan—interference quick.

And now *she* had to be quick and get to the point. "My father was a high-ranking member of the Sons of the Badlands." She couldn't believe she was still talking about this all these years later. Almost five years since the Sons had been wiped out.

"That old biker gang?" Thomas responded, eyebrows drawn together as if he couldn't remember. Or couldn't believe it.

She nodded. "Yes. I was under the impression he was in jail. For life. But… I heard a rumor. I just want to know where he's at. What the state of his sentencing is. I thought maybe you would be able to get that information or know someone who would."

Thomas nodded. "Absolutely. Are you worried about your safety?"

She shook her head. "No, nothing like that. Not really. I never really mattered to him. But my brother… I do worry about him. It would just ease my mind to know everything is as it should be."

"Okay. I just need his name and a few other details and I should be able to have some answers to you by the end of the day." He picked up a pen and pulled a pad of paper in front of him. He asked for the normal things. Name. Birth date. What jail she thought he was in.

Brooke recited the information as best she could even though speaking her father's name made her feel…fragile.

Once Thomas was done, he tapped his pen to the pad, studying the information. He was quiet for a long moment before looking up, meeting her gaze. "Did you talk to Zeke about this?"

That surprised her enough to frown at him. "This is none of Zeke's business." She tried not to sound irritated.

"Isn't that his truck you drove up here?"

She wasn't sure how Thomas knew what she'd driven to the station, but she didn't like it. She stood, probably too abruptly. "I don't need you to poke into it. I just need to know the facts. I thought I could trust you to get them and relay them."

He never looked away from her, never let her agitation get to him. He was all cop-calm as he held her angry gaze. "You can," he said seriously.

She almost sagged with relief. It didn't take the stress away but did loosen some of the tight band it had created around her shoulders.

But then, Thomas kept talking about *Zeke*.

"You and I might not be friends, Brooke, but I *am* friends with Zeke. I don't think there's anything worth keeping from him if it's dangerous. For what it's worth, he's a good guy and he can keep you safe, if you're in danger."

"I'm not in danger," she said firmly. Because she *wasn't*. Royal was just… She didn't know, but she wasn't involved with Royal's recent past. "It's ancient history."

"You of all people should know just how dangerous ancient history is."

That felt far too ominous for comfort.

She turned to leave. Because she'd done what she'd come to do, and he was going to help her. She'd asked for help and gotten it, and the world hadn't ended. So there. "I'll see you at the cave later."

Because the job went on. No matter what Royal thought was going on with their father.

ZEKE HAD WOKEN to an empty house and his truck missing. He wasn't sure what took precedence. His anger she'd gone off and done something stupid and dangerous, no matter what it was. Or the fact he hadn't woken up.

What kind of operative was he?

The retired kind?

He pushed that thought out of his head. He assumed Brooke's secret trip was to see her brother, so he'd called

Walker and asked to borrow one of his cars. Carlyle had driven the old junker over, and he owed her one.

That was annoying.

Zeke drove to Brooke's rental cabin, concerned the car might not make it. Walker had to be keeping this clunker for sentimental reasons instead of practical ones. There was no way he'd let Mary drive this thing with the baby. And at the rate they were going, they'd need a minivan soon.

By the time he made it to Brooke's rental, she was already gone. Or, *maybe*, he'd been wrong about where she'd gone. He didn't think so. He knew her. He understood her.

And now it was his turn to have a little conversation with her brother. One *she* didn't get to hear.

Before Zeke had turned off the engine, Royal stood at the door. His arms were crossed over his chest again, but he didn't have a weapon. Zeke considered holstering his, but instead, as a sign of good faith, he left it in the car.

Or maybe, in the back of his mind, he worried what Brooke would think about him showing up armed if it got back to her. Not that he intended to tell her about this, but Royal might.

And that was fine. It was all *fine*. He was just making it clear to this man that whatever he was up to wasn't something Zeke would allow Brooke to be caught in the middle of.

He got out of the car and made his way up to the door of the cabin. He'd left Viola back at the ranch with Carlyle in case Brooke returned in his absence.

"Didn't realize my morning would start with a visit from Brooke's bodyguard."

"You know, speaking as a brother, I'd be pretty happy if someone was looking out for my sister at any point, but especially when someone was sneaking around following her."

"Looking out for her, huh?" Royal replied. "I'm not the only one who's been following her. I saw you at the cave."

That's different, he wanted to say, but knew it would be hard to explain *how* it was different. Because he hadn't told her that was what he'd been doing when he'd followed her around. "Your sister came to me for help. I plan to give it."

"What exactly did Brooke tell you?" Royal asked suspiciously.

"That you told her you've been following her because you wanted to make sure she was okay, which is BS, obviously. Stalking isn't concern."

"That all she tell you?"

Zeke didn't like the idea of there being more, but he had to play it casual. "What else is there?"

Royal shook his head. "Nothing. Look, I don't have anything to do with you and you don't have anything to do with me. Whatever you're trying to do—intimidate me?—it's not going to work. So why don't you just leave me alone?"

"Here's the bottom line. I'm not letting anything happen to her. Whether that's protecting her from you or whatever else, it's not happening. It's best if you know that, straight off."

"What? So I can run away like I'm scared of some…" He looked Zeke up and down. "Rancher?"

Zeke smiled at him. "You should be."

Royal's gaze was more considering than it had been. "You military or something?" he asked.

"Was for a time. Among other things."

Royal nodded as if satisfied with that answer. "That's good, I guess. I happen to think prison offers a better training ground for understanding a criminal enough to stop him, but knowing how to use a gun has its plusses."

"That it does."

Silence settled between them. No doubt Royal was taking Zeke's measure, the same way Zeke was doing to him. But Zeke knew Royal had no concept of who he was. Zeke had heard stories of Royal as a kid, and the ways Brooke felt she'd failed him after they'd been separated in foster care.

He also knew that a childhood like theirs made trouble more common than not. He'd been on the edge of it himself a time or two, but Walker had always pulled him back from the edge. Instilled in him the importance of doing the right thing...for the family.

Where would he have been if they'd all been separated?

He didn't appreciate the wriggle of compassion he felt for Royal. There was no reason to trust him, but that didn't mean he couldn't have a certain level of empathy toward him. It didn't mean he couldn't make the first move. "I've known Brooke a long time," he said, hoping to give some context to why he was here, and what he'd do to keep Brooke safe from anyone.

Even her brother.

Royal shrugged. "I knew her first."

"You knew a girl. I know the woman she is. And I know how it killed her to find out you were in jail, that you never responded to all those letters, and I know she blamed herself for all of it."

"You sure know a lot."

"Damn straight."

"But you know her side. Maybe from my side she *should* blame herself."

Zeke didn't let his hands curl into fists, though they

wanted to. "And maybe she shouldn't. You were both dealt the same shitty hand, and I hate to break it to you, lots of people are. She figured out how to build a real life out of it. You can blame her for that, or you can build your own. But nothing's going to happen to her. I won't let it. So I don't know why you're here, why you've been following her, but it's not going to get past me. You can believe me, or you can run up against me, but Brooke won't be the target."

There was a long, drawn-out pause while Royal studied him and Zeke stood there, letting him.

"You care about her," Royal said after a while, like he wasn't completely sure he believed it. Like it was a question.

"You're damn right." Because what was the point hemming and hawing to her brother? What was the point ignoring it himself? Maybe he hated it. Maybe he wished he didn't. But he did and it wasn't going away. *So.*

"Good. Someone should."

Zeke could only stare at the one person he'd ever seen Brooke cry over, besides his own sorry ass. Multiple times. "Her brother could."

"I could," he agreed. His expression remained grim but wasn't quite so abrasive. "If I thought it was safe. But it's not. And neither is she."

That sounded somehow both like a warning and a threat.

"How so?"

"If she wanted you to know, you'd know."

That was fair, even if it hurt.

"Does *she* know?"

Royal smirked. "You care about her but she's not telling you her secrets?" He tsked. "Maybe you're not quite as important to her as you'd like to think."

"I shouldn't be important to her at all." He shouldn't

have said that out loud. Besides, he'd come here to warn Royal, and now he had. What the guy did with said warning was up to him.

Zeke turned to leave, trying not to concern himself with Brooke's *secrets*. Because she could tell him or not tell him whatever she wanted. It was her life. Her family.

Her safety—that is your responsibility.

"Hey."

Zeke stopped, turned to face Royal, who still stood on the porch.

"Look up what I was in jail for." Then he turned on a heel and disappeared inside, the slam of the cabin door echoing through the quiet morning.

Zeke wasn't sure what kind of parting shot that was, but it was…interesting.

And, surely, Hart could get him Royal's entire rap sheet. So, he hopped in his borrowed car and decided to head for Bent. Maybe he could catch the detective before he headed out to the caves to meet up with Brooke.

He started driving, his thoughts fixing on Royal Campbell and jail, on the fact the brother Brooke hadn't seen in something like fifteen years might know something about her Zeke didn't.

He kept picturing yesterday. When Brooke and Royal had spoken quietly and Zeke hadn't heard what they'd said. He'd chalked it up to sibling stuff.

But what if it was more and she was hiding something big from him?

Before he could give that too much thought, he saw a truck going in the opposite direction on its side of the highway, which was normal.

Except that it was *his* truck.

Chapter Nine

Brooke couldn't imagine getting back to Zeke's ranch before he woke up. She'd have to explain taking his truck, where she'd gone, what she'd been doing.

Or you could tell him to butt out.

She snorted. Yeah, that'd work. Well, she'd just have to lie. As much as she didn't like the idea, telling him she'd been out doing errands wasn't a *full* lie.

She just had to know the facts before she could proceed. And he'd want to proceed with *no* facts. She needed data. He just went on instinct. This was too…big for that. Too personal. Too hers.

This whole morning had been nothing but instinct, and it was already a disaster.

When she turned into the drive of Zeke's ranch, she slowed his truck along the drive because someone was in front of the house. Someone was outside, playing fetch with the dog.

At first, Brooke could make out the shape of what was a woman with dark hair. Something a little too close to hot twisting jealousy poked her right in the chest. That was *ridiculous*. Zeke had made it clear he hadn't been seeing anyone.

Not that it mattered.

Something she could fully assure herself of when she finally got close enough to recognize the woman as Zeke's sister. Maybe she was there to take Viola back? Brooke hadn't left the dog outside this morning. That meant Zeke was awake, but still inside, and…

Now she'd have to explain her disappearance to both of them. *That* was what she got for going on instinct and running out of the house this morning. If she'd really thought it through, planned it out, been *careful,* she wouldn't be in this mess.

Data, examination and the careful drawing of conclusions was always the answer. Go figure, proximity to Zeke once again left her making all the wrong choices.

She parked the truck and got out, forcing herself to smile at Carlyle. "Good morning."

"Hey. I was just in the neighborhood and thought I'd check in on Viola." She gestured at the prancing dog. Brooke frowned though. There was no car, no truck. How had Carlyle gotten here?

"How's she working out for you?" Carlyle asked as Viola eagerly put her head under Brooke's hand in greeting.

"She's great," Brooke replied with feeling. She gave Viola a pat. She did really enjoy having the dog around, not that she could let herself get used to it.

"Good." Carlyle nodded and an awkward silence followed while Carlyle fidgeted. Stepping from side to side, rocking back on her heels, decidedly not leaving or saying anything else.

Until she finally blurted, "I don't know why my brother would call me out here, because he knows I can't keep my mouth shut. What's the deal with you two?"

Brooke blinked. "Deal?"

"Yeah, like it's all tense and weird between you two, or was before. Is it because you two knew each other before? When he was doing his secret spy stuff. That's how he got a forensic whatever you are to come out here so quick when they found..." She paused and wrinkled her nose. "I never know what to call it, considering it was my fiancé's parents."

Right, because the connections here in Sunrise and Bent County were complex and complicated. Luckily, Brooke didn't have to respond to whatever Carlyle was trying to get at because a very old not-in-good-shape car roared up the drive.

Brooke startled, but she noticed Carlyle didn't so much as blink. Brooke might have grabbed for Carlyle, suggested they run, because clearly this was danger come calling, except she quickly realized Zeke was the driver.

Uh-oh.

The car squealed to a stop a little ways behind his truck, and he was out almost before the entire vehicle had stopped. He marched over to them, pointing at Carlyle, and, for a second, Brooke figured that was who he was mad at.

"Leave," he said between clenched teeth to his sister, handing her off the keys he'd had in his hand.

Okay, so maybe he wasn't mad at Carlyle. She didn't know why he was *mad* like this at *her*. She wasn't sure she'd ever seen him *mad* like this. Usually he was a controlled kind of mad. Icy.

This was...not ice.

Carlyle held up her hands in mock surrender and maybe she was trying not to grin, but Brooke didn't think she was trying *that* hard.

"And miss the show?" she asked Zeke.

He made a noise, close to a growl, which had Carlyle

laughing and snatching the keys from him before moving for the old car. She paused next to Brooke though. "Oh, Brooke, he's got it *bad*. I hope you twist the knife."

Brooke wasn't sure she understood Carlyle's meaning, but then again, she wasn't sure Carlyle understood what was really going on here.

And it didn't matter, because now she had to deal with angry Zeke, which didn't seem fair. "I cannot fathom why you're this angry," Brooke said, trying to sound bored and calm. "I just borrowed your truck for a quick errand."

"An errand or a secret?" he demanded.

She wasn't sure how he could see through her so easily, and she might have felt guilty, except *he'd* been somewhere.

"Where were *you?*"

"Well, once I realized my truck was gone, I borrowed one of my brother's cars and drove to your rental, because I figured you were headed out to deal with your brother very purposefully without me."

It hadn't even occurred to her to go talk to Royal until she had more information. Until she had the *facts*.

"You didn't go there at all, did you?" He seemed so hurt by that, when it wasn't like she'd lied to him and told him she had or was going to. That was just some assumption he'd made.

"No," she replied. "I just had an errand to run." She wasn't going to explain herself. She didn't have to. She wasn't in danger anymore. Not from the thing he thought she was anyway. And before she introduced any new possibilities, she had to know...

She had to *know*. So she could protect herself first and, if after that, she needed his help, maybe she'd ask for it.

But she'd have the data first, damn it. No more instincts for her. Those had only led her astray.

And she could ask for his help, she could accept his help, but she could not *depend* on him again. On *anyone* again. Things went best when she only depended on herself.

The man in front of her, case in point. Standing there looking like…like she'd never *seen* him. Because this was a bit like a man…holding on by a thread. When he had always, *always*, been in complete and utter control.

She didn't like it, but it did make her feel sorry for him. It made her want to *soothe*.

"Zeke." She moved forward, not quite sure what she was going to do, just following that need inside her. One she'd just seconds ago been telling herself she wouldn't listen to.

But Zeke shook his head, a nonverbal *stay back*. Because he was getting himself under control or trying to.

"What was your brother in jail for?" he asked quietly and calmly.

The question made little sense in the grand scheme of things. What was he getting at? What could that have to do with anything?

Since she couldn't fathom where he was going with this, she hedged. Because she knew if she tried to defend Royal, it would only make him look more guilty. "A few different charges."

"List them, Brooke."

She didn't have to. She *didn't*. But she just…couldn't stop herself. "Do you remember the child trafficking case in the Sons that North Star was part of stopping? You would have been too new to be on the team that dealt with it, but I think you were with North Star by then."

"South Dakota, right? Shay and Cody Wyatt leading the charge?"

She nodded. She didn't know much about it herself. She just remembered Betty Wagner, North Star's resident doctor and one of Brooke's close friends at North Star, being pretty shaken up by the findings.

"What does that have to do with your brother's jail time, Brooke?"

"Royal was arrested just a little before that. On a murder charge. There was a fight with another Sons's member, and the other man died. The other man who'd been hurting those girls. But the Sons knew how to pick and choose who it got out of legal trouble. How to make sure the ones they saw as traitors saw the inside of a cell."

"You're saying a member of the Sons of the Badlands was arrested and it wasn't fair? The gang member was innocent?"

She hated how ridiculous he made it sound, because her brother *had* been a member of the Sons at that point. She knew how naïve it sounded to believe he was in there to try and stop some of the things they'd seen growing up, yet she couldn't help but hope her brother's motivations had been at least partly honorable.

And if she was wrong…well, so be it.

This was why she hadn't wanted to tell Zeke about it. Because she knew how it sounded. She also knew her brother, or tried to tell herself she did. He could find his own trouble, certainly, but he wasn't a murderer.

She wouldn't let herself believe he was a murderer as long as there was no concrete proof. She knew the case, thanks to her North Star connections at the time. It had been stacked against Royal from the start, with the help of too many people who'd ended up having Sons ties.

"Why do you think Granger agreed to help me with the funds to hire a lawyer?" she asked Zeke instead. Because everyone respected Granger, but some of the younger guys had looked up to him like a father figure.

Just like she had.

"He has a soft spot for you."

Brooke rolled her eyes. Granger had a soft spot for *any* of the people who came into North Star because they had been some kind of victim of the Sons of the Badlands. But he was also a stickler for right and wrong. "Because he knew as well as I did that Royal was in jail for trying to stop something. And I know you won't believe that—"

"Did Granger believe it?"

"Yes. After he looked through the case, he came to believe it." Maybe she'd always wondered if he'd said that just to make her feel better, but she wasn't about to admit that to Zeke.

"Then I believe it."

She let out a long breath, not quite sure how that just took all the wind out of her sails. Never in a million years had she expected it to be that easy, but she should have known. For all of them, Granger MacMillan had been and maybe even still was a kind of hero figure. No one wanted to think about him being wrong.

"I don't know how Royal feels about the charge, the trial, his jail time. I don't know what he'd say if I asked about it. I only know that all the evidence pointed to Royal protecting one of those girls. But the Sons was stronger back then, had more hands in legal pockets. And the legal system was eager to have any of them behind bars—rightfully so. I've always just been grateful the Sons got him arrested rather than kill him."

Brooke shuddered to think about how easily that psychotic cult leader could have just ended Royal's life and that's all she would have ever known. A life cut short.

She'd never know if Royal alive was their father's sad attempt to protect him, or if there was more to it. It didn't matter.

Royal was alive, and now he was here. Talking about the danger she might be in from their father. Talking to Zeke apparently. "Why did you ask me that?"

"He told me to look up why he was in jail."

Brooke didn't understand why her brother would do that, but that was nothing new. The men in her life continued to be obnoxious, ridiculous mysteries.

"Brooke, how am I going to protect you if you run off and never tell me the truth?" he asked, sounding *pained*. Hurt. Not mad at all. Just exasperated, like she was making things hard on him.

That made her feel small, and a bit like running away for good. "I'm not your burden, Zeke." She wouldn't be anyone's burden ever again. "If Royal has been the one following me, I don't need protecting the way I thought I did."

ZEKE WAS GOING about this all wrong. He knew that. He knew how touchy she was about *burdens*, even if she didn't. "You'll never be a burden to me, Brooke." And it was scary just how true that was. "Wanting to protect you is no burden."

"You don't need to," she said, refusing to believe him. Clearly. "Royal is not a threat to me, and it appears there are no other threats at the moment," she returned. As if choosing each word carefully. As if placating a small child who didn't understand complex thoughts.

Zeke didn't groan out loud, though he considered it. But he'd gotten his blazing anger under control. Or close, anyway.

Royal had been the one to say she wasn't safe this morning. Maybe she believed she was safe now, and maybe he should let her believe that, but…something didn't add up. Because she had been *somewhere*.

"Where did you go this morning, Brooke?"

She didn't look away from him. She didn't try to lie—he would have seen through that easily enough. She just shook her head. "It's none of your business."

He nodded, that tenuous grasp on control barely holding on by a thread. She was right. It was none of his business. She didn't want him to keep her safe. She didn't want to be *safe*. Fine.

"It's not some personal insult, Zeke. It's just not about you." She didn't say that with any bite. No imperious looks. She was trying to be reasonable.

"Must be nice," he muttered, because he didn't know how to divorce *her* from anything he was feeling, doing. He didn't know how to look at her and say anything was *not about her*.

She reached out, touched his arm. "Zeke."

He knew she was going to try to soothe or comfort him. And, no. He wasn't letting her do that thing she did. Where she smoothed everything over because she hated people to be upset. Where she tried to make everything okay because she'd been failed by so many adults growing up she thought it was her sworn duty to make sure everyone around her was *okay*. Down to the bones she excavated everywhere she went.

But when she looked up at him with those sympathetic blue eyes, when she touched his arm like she could brush away this conflicting, painful fight inside him, he found he didn't want to be happy. He didn't want to be soothed, and he didn't want her to feel like that was her responsibility.

But he did want something.

Her. And he kept stepping away from that. For her own good and for his. But maybe… There was no good. Only messy pain she couldn't fix with a soothing touch or his name said in soft, compassionate tones.

Maybe there was only breaking down that wall. That's how he'd dealt with this *conflict* inside him last time. Burned it all down. So…

"To hell with it," he muttered. None of his business. Wrong person, wrong time, wrong *everything*, and still he'd spent the past four years haunted by the memory of a woman *he'd* set aside.

Because of *this*. The way she broke down his walls, defenses. Crumbled his control without even trying. He curled his hand around her head and pulled her in, crashing his mouth to hers.

She didn't even have the good sense to stiffen or to push him away. She *melted* to him on some sigh that seemed to say *finally*. Or maybe that was just him.

Finally. Finally. Finally. Four years had been too long without the taste of her, the feel of her, just *her*. And wasn't that what made everything these past few days so difficult? He knew she was in trouble, but all he wanted was *her*.

The kiss was everything it had always been. That wild heat. That sweet comfort. Mixed up in one perfect package that had never made any sense to him. Because she felt like coming home, when he'd never had one of those in the first place. Never wanted one.

She wrapped her arms around his neck and it could have easily been four years ago. When they were together. When he'd been stupid enough to think he could control what was happening. When the idea of a *girlfriend* had been kind of novel, with the potential to be exactly what he wanted.

And nothing he didn't.

Remembering that lack of control she brought out in him had him easing back. He hadn't meant to kiss her. He hadn't meant to get angry. He hadn't *meant* any of this, and she was the only person in his whole life who'd ever mixed him up this way.

She blinked at him, arms still looped around his neck, eyes cloudy with desire and confusion and *hell*. There'd been no point to this, he supposed, but wasn't about to say that.

"It's the same," he said, his voice rough but certain. Because he wouldn't let her deny that like she did with the truth. No talk of burdens, because this had never been a burden.

It had been a wrecking ball.

"It's damn well the same, and I'm tired of pretending like it's not."

With that, he turned and stalked away. Because he couldn't just stand there and keep pretending, and that's what she wanted. To pretend everything was fine, to pretend that kiss didn't mean anything—that *he* didn't mean anything.

And, hell, he was used to that, wasn't he?

Chapter Ten

Brooke stood in the front yard of Zeke's house with Viola prancing around her for a long while, not sure what had just happened. Today. The past few days. Maybe her entire adult life.

Her body was still a riot of heat and want, and her mind whirled with confusion.

The same. Oh, boy, was it. Their chemistry hadn't waned or changed. She wasn't sure she'd really thought it *had*, but the angry way he'd thrown it out there suggested that *he* had. And he wasn't too happy about it.

She almost laughed. Maybe it was wrong, but having a better handle on their situation than he did was somewhat comforting. *She* certainly hadn't initiated any physical contact. *He'd* been the one to comfort her when she'd cried over Royal. *He'd* been the one to grab her and kiss her.

Brooke blew out a long breath. She couldn't ruminate on a kiss when she had work to get to. When she had responsibilities, and her brother, and the threat he thought their father posed. She could not put those aside because she was still hung up on her ex, who just happened to be protecting her because of some strange turn of events.

So, she needed to get ready for work. But before she

could, a Bent County Sheriff's Department cruiser bumped down the gravel drive. She saw Thomas behind the wheel, so she walked over to greet him.

He didn't get out of the car but rolled down his window. "I'm headed out to the Hudson Ranch to talk to Chloe Brink about the scrapbook you found, and I was wondering if you'd come with me. It'll put us a little behind schedule on your excavation, but I think you could help here."

"Oh." The Hudson Ranch. She'd been there once. When Detective Delaney-Carson had informed the Hudson family that they'd positively identified last month's discovered remains as the long-missing parents of the Hudson clan. Brooke had gone along at the detective's request. Since the family was full of police officers and investigators, Laurel had assumed they'd have a lot of questions about the procedures that only the forensic anthropologist on the case could answer.

It had been…awful. Oh, the Hudsons had all handled the news calmly. They'd known it was coming. Still, watching so many people have to sort through their grief, no matter how anticipated, had been…painful. Usually, she was in the background of that part of what she did, not the front lines.

"There were some pictures in the scrapbook that I think are *in* the cave, or near it," Thomas explained. "I'd like your opinion on what we're looking at there. We could arrange a meeting at the station, after your normal hours at the cave, but this is quicker."

And quick was best. Particularly if her theory she hadn't shared with anyone yet was correct. Brooke nodded. "Let me go grab my work bag." She did so without running into Zeke, and that was best too. She doubted he was *unaware* of a police cruiser on his property, so he'd know where she'd gone. Or at least who with.

When she had everything she wanted, she returned to the car and slid into the front seat. Thomas immediately drove back out to the highway.

"I did put some feelers out on your father this morning," he offered. "Got some pretty straightforward answers. He's still in jail. There's no record of him getting out. He's not exactly a model prisoner. Lots of fights, solitary confinement, that sort of thing. I wouldn't anticipate him getting out anytime soon."

It should have been a relief but only left her with a deeper discomfort. Why did Royal think otherwise? Why did it still seem a threat lingered? But that wasn't Thomas's problem, so she wasn't about to lay it on him like it was.

"I really appreciate you looking into that for me," she said.

"Anytime." And he made it sound like nothing, which was kind of him. Like it didn't matter her father was a former Sons member, in jail for too many things to mention.

Further down the road, he pulled under the big archway that would lead them to the main house where most of the Hudson siblings lived and worked—both the ranch and their cold case investigation group, Hudson Sibling Solutions.

During the long winding drive, anxiety settled into her gut like a heavy weight. Thomas stopped in front of the grand ranch house. Brooke hesitated getting out of the car.

"I get that it feels…uncomfortable," Thomas said kindly. "I have to deliver a lot of bad news to people I know, people in my life. And so have the Hudsons. We all know how to divorce the messenger from the message."

Right. She nodded and got out of the car, following

Thomas up the porch and waiting after he knocked on the door.

The woman who answered carried a tiny baby. She greeted them with a politeness and warmth that was antithetical to the situation. She ushered them into a big, cozy living room. Chloe was already there, sitting next to one of the Hudsons Brooke could remember by name. Jack Hudson was the sheriff of Sunrise, and the de facto leader of his siblings. He'd also been shot twice last month in the situation that had led to the discovery of human remains in the cave, causing her to stick around beyond just identifying the remains of his parents.

It wasn't obvious he'd been seriously hurt from just looking at him, but Brooke noted a cane in the corner next to the couch he sat on. And the careful way Chloe sat next to him.

"Chloe. Jack," Thomas greeted. "You remember Brooke Campbell, the forensic anthropologist."

Another woman entered. She didn't look like a Hudson, but a lot of significant others lived on the property, so Brooke assumed she was one of them.

"Brooke, this is Dahlia," Thomas introduced. "She's a librarian, but she has some archivist training. She's helping us keep the integrity of the scrapbook intact, like you suggested."

They exchanged pleasantries then everyone who was still standing sat down around a coffee table where Thomas placed the scrapbook with care. He opened up to a page in the middle. The pages were black, with black-and-white photos pasted in careful rows. He pointed to one such row.

"Doesn't this look like the preserve?" he asked everyone.

Jack and Chloe leaned forward and peered at the picture while Brooke did the same. She felt like an expert of the area around the cave now, but the photo wasn't very clear, and the black and white made it difficult to really determine. The picture could have been any rocky area with mountains in the distance.

Thomas slowly turned the page. "And these."

These pictures had two men in almost all of them. The prints weren't much clearer than the photo of the preserve, but it was obvious the subjects were in some kind of rock enclosure. It could definitely be a cave—but it could be their cave or any others.

"Aren't these pictures too old to use flashes or whatever in a dark cave?" Chloe asked. "Those guys look pretty old-timey."

"Yes, they do, but flash photography is pretty old," Dahlia replied. "Flashes have been around in some form or another for a long time, and there could have been other light sources involved outside the picture. There are photographs of caves over a hundred years old."

"Do you know who the subjects are?" Brooke asked. The surroundings didn't tell them much, but something about the two men drew her attention. She didn't know enough about historical fashion to know what era they were from, but certainly a long time ago.

"Let's see if we can remove the photo from the page. There might be a label on the back. Besides, we'll want to eventually remove all the pictures. The glue and paper used in these old scrapbooks are often harmful to photographs over time." Dahlia rummaged through her supplies, pulled out what resembled dental floss, and then carefully slid it under the upturned corner of the photo. With a sawing motion, she pulled the floss through until the photo detached from the page.

She lifted the photo to the light, looked at the back.

"The writing is faded, but it looks like it says 'F. Brink and L. Rogers.'"

Everyone turned to Chloe, whose father was a Brink and mother was Jen Rogers, the suspected murderer.

Chloe shook her head. "Far as I know, my grandpa Brink's name was George. Never met my mom's father. I always assumed he was dead or a deadbeat. But Rogers certainly explains my mother's connection to the scrapbook."

Brooke studied the picture. She didn't think anyone would assume the background of the black-and-white picture was a cave if they weren't currently dealing with a cave. But she could see what Thomas was talking about.

Certain formations surrounded the people were similar to the area she had just started excavating. Not irrevocable proof of the same cave, but maybe too much of a coincidence to not be.

"I could look into the family histories. See if these are direct ancestors of yours, Chloe. And if they are, it'd help us date the photograph. If you think it might help the case, Detective Hart."

Thomas frowned. "Not sure it'll help, but it can't hurt."

"This book adds to the case against Jen," Jack said. "She was living in that cave. She's the one who took the scrapbook from the police. Now you've found the scrapbook in there and there's a link to the Rogers family. Maybe it doesn't tell us anything new, but it can be used in the case against her."

Thomas nodded in agreement. "But why did she want to steal it then hide it?"

Brooke didn't have any answer for that question, but she kept studying the picture, trying to orient herself. Because caves changed over time, so it wasn't the same as now. But the formations were in the same spots, just different sizes.

And if she was seeing things correctly, and not jumping to conclusions, both men were standing next to each other in a corner of the cave she hadn't yet gotten to but knew made up the edge closest to the center of the cave. She'd purposefully left that spot for last because she'd wanted as much space around the interior studied and opened.

Maybe caves could appear similar, but there were too many coincidences here.

"Do you have a magnifying glass?" she asked absently to no one in particular. Some object at the men's feet looked like…*something.* Maybe if she could make it out, she could be sure one way or another.

Dahlia pulled a magnifying glass out of her supplies and handed it to Brooke. Brooke used it to analyze the lower corner of the bottom photograph. As the magnifying glass settled over the corner, the shape of something that looked like…hair and an ear. But the angle was all wrong. It was straight up and down, like it didn't have a body but had been propped there.

Brooke's heart started beating hard in her chest. She swallowed so her voice would sound calm. She held out the magnifying glass to Hart. "Is that a head?"

No one had been able to agree if the shape was a head. If the strands were hair, if the ear was indeed a human ear. They'd pored over the rest of the photos, searching for anything that might confirm what Brooke thought she saw.

No consensus could be made. Dahlia discussed some photo scanning and editing options to enhance the photos so the Hudsons were going to work on that angle. After all, if the pictures were that old, they might be dealing with a cold case—the Hudson Sibling Solutions specialty.

So, once they'd agreed on how to handle the photographs, Thomas had driven her to the cave. She'd jumped into work immediately, trying to focus on the place in the photograph. It was hard to pinpoint with the changes to the cave over time and from what little she had to go on.

Brooke wanted to dig with wild abandon. To see if she could find a skull right there. But she reminded herself to breathe, to take her time, to fall back on her training.

Finding answers relied on her ability to pay attention to every tiny detail. She couldn't rush just because they'd maybe discovered something.

So, hours went by, of careful, meticulous, slow-moving digging. She couldn't be haphazard. That wasn't her job. Her job was to unearth every last detail. Document them for study.

When she first came across a flash of bone in the cave fill, she nearly cried with relief. Her back muscles screamed, her eyes were gritty, and her hands were cramping. She was both somehow sweating from exertion and shivering from the cold air in the cave.

But she'd found something. So she focused her brainpower on the steps to carefully, correctly unearth whatever it was.

More time passed. She forgot Thomas was even there, and he never suggested they break for lunch, like he usually did. He just waited in silence and out of the way so she wouldn't concern herself with him or breaks.

Slowly, she uncovered what she'd hoped she'd find. A skull. In almost the exact place she might have seen a head in that picture. And just like in the photograph, the skull was buried with the jawbone down, top of the head up.

There'd been some damage to the upper part of the skull. It just had to connect. It had to be the same. Skulls weren't buried like this.

She took a slow breath, reminding herself to remain calm. Reminding herself she was uncovering a mystery, not putting herself in danger.

"Thomas? Can you take some pictures?"

He walked over with his Bent County camera strapped around his neck. He looked at what she'd uncovered. He didn't outwardly react, but she knew he was feeling that same ticking clock she felt.

They were close to some kind of break in the case. So close. And if she could push through everything, they might have one.

"Just take as many photos as you can. I'm going to keep uncovering the skull."

So, that's what she set out to do. If she could remove the skull intact, with photo evidence of how it had been buried... She didn't know, but it was something.

Brooke lost track of anything but unearthing the skull, and once she could remove it from the cave floor and debris, she discovered exactly what she was afraid she might.

There was nothing directly underneath the skull. No bones from the neck or even shoulder that should be within the area she was excavating.

Just like the photograph.

"If that picture included a decapitated head, and this skull is that head, this death occurred before Jen Rogers," Thomas said, his voice devoid of any emotion, though she knew he felt something about that information whether he spoke it aloud or not.

Brooke looked up at Thomas and said what she'd been worried was true for a while.

"I think we're dealing with more than one killer."

Chapter Eleven

Zeke had thrown himself into his project after Brooke had taken off with Hart. He'd thought about figuring out *why* the detective had stopped by to pick her up, but it was none of his business.

Maybe putting together a makeshift lab on his ranch wasn't either, particularly with the stalking threat no longer an issue.

But even if he believed that Royal had done jail time for *maybe* a justified crime, the man was a potential threat. There were still *threats* around Brooke and what she was doing. Zeke couldn't just accept that she wasn't in *some* danger.

And he didn't think she'd accepted that, even if she'd pretended to. Because her things were still in his house. She hadn't told him to jump off a cliff…yet.

Worse, he couldn't even blame her. He owed her an apology, and that burned. He shouldn't have kissed her. He shouldn't have *touched* her. And he could not for the life of him figure out why his usual iron-tight control had deserted him when it came to her.

He studied his work on the makeshift lab. Only some of the equipment Granger had set him up with had been delivered, but the barn was sparkling clean and what he'd managed to get in terms of tables and whatnot had been set up.

He glanced at his watch and ignored the fact it was later than usual and Brooke hadn't returned yet.

He wouldn't read into that. He wouldn't *worry*. Hart knew where she was staying. If something bad had happened, he'd have heard by now.

That became a mantra as evening turned into straight-up nighttime, and he stopped being able to distract himself with work. So he'd ended up sitting on the chair that looked out the front window, waiting for Viola to sound the alarm or headlights to appear.

It was nearing midnight when Viola let out a bark and Zeke saw the Bent County cruiser finally drop her off. He was wound so tight, he couldn't even fully feel relief.

She stepped into the living room, creeping quietly. She looked bedraggled and tired, which was none of his business. None of his concern.

Yet all these things he kept telling himself weren't his business or concern took up residence inside him. And that stupid kiss this morning had illuminated why.

Zeke was not a man who believed in love that didn't come from family and trauma ties. There was nothing romantic about the hell of a world he'd been born into.

But he didn't know what else to call what he'd felt for Brooke all those years ago, and how much those feelings he didn't understand, didn't like, didn't *want*, still existed within him.

Once she closed and locked the door behind her, she turned and crouched to pet an excited Viola. When her gaze lifted, she jumped a little at the sight of him sitting on the chair.

Brooke cleared her throat and straightened. "You didn't have to wait up."

He snorted. Like he would have been able to sleep. "Why'd you work so late?" He'd *promised* himself he wouldn't ask.

She looked at him a little quizzically but took the question in stride as she dropped her bag and then walked over to the couch and sank into it. Viola hopped up next to her. "Break in the case, sort of. Didn't want to stop until I'd gotten something accomplished." She leaned her head on the back of the couch, closing her eyes. "I don't suppose you'd be up to making me dinner?"

The fact she was asking anything of him—kiss or no—was concerning. So was the way she could just completely forget that kiss this morning. Still, he got to his feet. "You must be starving if you're asking me to do something for you."

She gave him the ghost of a smile. "I haven't eaten since… I actually don't remember. We found something, I guess. It felt like nothing and something all at the same time."

"I know how that goes. You relax. I'll fix up something for you to eat." He moved into the kitchen, grateful for something to do when everything was whirling inside of him like some kind of storm. Like this morning. Out of control.

And he couldn't allow that. Certainly couldn't grab her and kiss her again when she was running on fumes. *Or at all*, he told himself sternly.

He could throw a frozen pizza in the oven, but he poked around his pantry instead, frustrated with himself for wanting to fuss over her when he didn't *fuss*. The only place he even acknowledged that impulse was with his family and he'd never had to act on it. Fussing had always been Walker's job.

That was why the best Zeke could come up with was a can of stew and some buttered bread and a couple pieces of cheese. It was hardly the stuff of homemade meals, but it was warm and hearty, and hopefully comforting.

He went to tell her it was ready, but when he stepped into the living room, her head was still resting against the back of the couch, her eyes were closed, her breathing even. Exhausted, clearly.

He wanted to bundle her up in a bed and let her sleep for at least a day. But then she blinked her eyes open, gaze meeting his like a vise around his chest. Squeezing until he popped.

"Food's ready," he managed to roughly rasp. "But you can sleep."

She pushed herself off the couch, looking away from him. "If I let myself go to sleep without eating, I'll regret it. Learned that one the hard way." She walked into the dining room, settled herself at the table, made a contented noise at the view of the food or at Viola settling herself on Brooke's feet.

"Thanks for this. I owe you one."

He nodded with a jerk, so uncomfortable he could hardly stand it. *No one* made him uncomfortable. He didn't let them.

Case in point, he was going to apologize for this morning, because he'd been out of line. He'd been wrong. To be mad at her. To take it out on her. To *kiss* her...even if she'd kissed him back.

He wasn't fazed by his mistakes. He didn't marinate in them. No, sir. He dealt. He'd made a mistake, now he'd apologize for it.

"I'm sorry."

She didn't look at him at first. Her gaze remained on her bowl before she brought a spoonful of stew to her mouth and chewed thoughtfully. "Sorry for what?" she asked after too many beats of silence.

Zeke didn't scowl, though he wanted to. Because she knew *for what*. There was only one thing to be sorry for. Besides, he could tell by the expression on her face she wasn't confused—he knew her too well. She wanted to make him say it.

Well, he wasn't *ashamed*. He was sorry. So... "For kissing you the way that I did. At an inappropriate time and moment."

She seemed to mull that over but said nothing else. That was fine. They didn't need to have a conversation about it. The point was the apology. Not coming to some kind of consensus about what was over and done.

He moved to wash out the pan he'd heated her stew in. He'd tidy up the kitchen and go to bed, like she should. He wasn't going to say another damn thing.

But had she not understood? He'd always thought she had. Wasn't that why she'd scared the hell out of him? She'd seen through him, too easily. And now she was just...sitting there, like his apology or the kiss or *something* didn't mean anything.

She had kissed him back. She had not pushed him away. He'd been the one to end it. So there was *something*, and didn't they both deserve to go over that *something*, so somewhere along the line they could move on and all *this* wouldn't whirl between them?

"Did I ever tell you why I joined North Star?" he demanded. When he *knew* this wasn't the way around what he was feeling. Because he was angry again, this big, huge *thing* inside him taking over. No control. No finesse.

"You wanted to help people like your family," she said, not quite meeting his gaze. "Your cousin was already in North Star and she brought you in after your stint in the army."

He shook his head. Even if he was surprised at how many details she'd retained, it wasn't the real story. Maybe back then he'd told her it was. Maybe he'd even convinced himself it was when he'd been young and in so much denial it should have choked him.

It was hard to look back with a critical eye and know where exactly he'd started to change, mature, evolve. He only knew that, standing in the kitchen of a ranch he'd bought and begun to rebuild, he was different than he had been.

"Yeah, Mallory got me into North Star because our dads were worthless Sons's pawns and I had some military training. But the real reason I joined the army, joined North Star, was because I couldn't *deal*."

Her eyebrows drew together, clearly not understanding what he meant. And he wasn't even sure what he meant. Just all of these...things rambling around inside him, grappling for purchase. He couldn't seem to put them away, any more than the words.

Zeke had never admitted that out loud. Never let himself poke into that old feeling. But here it was, and he didn't know why he thought it a good idea to lay it at her feet, but that's what he was doing.

And he couldn't stop.

"I couldn't hold it together. Every moment since my mother was murdered when I was a teenager, I felt like I was on this edge, ready to explode, because everything mattered too much. Keeping Carlyle safe, figuring out who killed our mother, helping Walker keep us together. It was too much. I couldn't *take* it. But the army? North Star? I could do that, and…well, because they weren't my family. Because they weren't the people I loved. I could set all the feelings aside and do what needed to be done."

When he met her gaze, it was shocked and on his, the piece of cheese in her hand clearly forgotten since she didn't bring it to her mouth. He felt like he'd run a marathon. It was hard to breathe. It was hard to…

Everything was just *hard* because she was sitting at his kitchen table, as pretty as the day he'd met her, even though she was run ragged. And what did it say about him that he was having this conversation with her when she was exhausted and hungry?

But she was in his kitchen, and the past four years had disappeared because she'd never been off his mind. He'd ended things, and he'd been living with a heavy, ignored regret ever since. Keeping it buried underneath *action*—North Star cases, then helping Walker track down their mother's murderer. And for the past few months, he'd had nothing to do except deal with the fact that he was almost thirty years old and likely still had a hell of a lot of life left to live.

With no missions on the horizon. Just all that *life*.

He hadn't wanted to miss her, hadn't wanted to wish she was somehow present when he'd had this realization life existed beyond a death wish.

But he had missed her. The whole time, and now she was here and…in danger. *Danger*.

"So it's like that all over again," he continued, because apparently once he started spouting all this, he couldn't contain the rest. And maybe something could ease if she understood. How hard this was. How much she meant. "This untenable pressure. The thought of anything happening to you is more than I can bear. You matter too much."

She blinked at him once before returning her gaze back to her bowl. "Maybe we shouldn't talk about this," she said quietly.

"That's fine." And he meant it. He wasn't interested in a walk down memory lane. Or he thought he wasn't. But he was the one who'd started all this. He could have let her eat and go to sleep. He could have said he was sorry and left it at that. He was the one pushing.

He didn't *need* to push, not if she didn't want to. This wasn't four years ago. He could give her feelings, her *wants*, the space they needed. Even if they weren't him.

Seemed about the way things usually went anyway.

He finished cleaning the kitchen and then noticed she'd eaten most of her food. She handed him her dishes and he washed them. She dried them in a quiet, easy show of teamwork.

So much about them wasn't easy but working together always had been.

She gave him the dried dishes so he could put them away. Then she turned from him, no doubt to go upstairs and go to sleep. She clearly needed a really good night's sleep. Hopefully she wouldn't wake up at the crack of dawn to sneak out tomorrow morning like she had this morning.

She paused before stepping out of his visibility. When she spoke, it was quiet but so damn sure every word landed like a stab wound. He'd had a few of those, so he knew.

"You didn't love me, Zeke."

He inhaled sharply. "You really don't think I was in love with you?" He stared at the back of her head, at the careful way she held herself. He really hadn't thought she could *hurt* him quite that viscerally. How could she have gone through what they'd been to each other and think that?

"You said you weren't."

That, he *knew* he'd never said. He'd never used the word *love. Ever.* "No, I said I didn't see a future. Because I didn't. A future meant having…hope. It meant caring more about survival than anything else. And you said it yourself back then. I had a death wish. Danger didn't faze me because if I didn't make it out, oh well."

She turned to face him and there was no shock on her face. Those were words she'd said *to* him all those years ago. She'd known, even then, he hadn't valued his life that much. But he wasn't sure he'd ever shared all the *why* behind it with her.

So when she didn't speak, that's what he did. Like this was some kind of confession and the dark feelings he kept locked down had to come out for him to be saved. Absolved.

"I used to think that if I died doing something honorable, my siblings would be proud," he said while she looked at him with heartbreak in her eyes. "It took…maturity, I guess, to realize they'd just blame themselves." He wasn't even sure when that realization had happened. Maybe when he'd been shot in the showdown that had taken down their mother's murderer. The way Carlyle had lost it. The way Walker had babied him afterward.

The way the Hudsons had somehow absorbed them into their world just because Mary had fallen in love with Walker. Or maybe, more importantly, because Walker had fallen head over drooling heels for Mary.

"Well, I'm glad you realized that," she said, her voice sounding strangled.

"Me too." He wasn't sure he had been, until this moment. Glad maybe not for himself, but for the people he cared about.

She nodded carefully, like she was afraid she might shatter if she moved too quickly. "Good night, Zeke."

"Night." And only after she left, the dog padding behind her, did he realize he'd been hoping for a different outcome. Because he could tell himself the old reasons for not wanting her in his life...

But they just weren't true anymore.

BROOKE OPENED HER eyes to sunlight streaming in through the window. It was later than she should have let herself sleep, but her head had hit the pillow last night and she'd been *out*.

No energy to work through everything Zeke had told her. The way he'd looked at her. But it was the first thing on her mind this morning, even groggy and still tired.

You really don't think I was in love with you?

He'd sounded so shocked, and worse, hurt. And maybe he was right. Maybe he'd never told her he hadn't loved her, but he'd never told her he *had*. Then he'd broken it off with her because there'd been no future. Was she really supposed to believe that had been love on his part?

She'd found an entire skull yesterday with no other bones in the immediate vicinity. She needed to get to the police station and process it and send it down to Cheyenne. She needed to check on her lab results for the last set of bones and write up a report for Thomas so he could take the multiple murderer theory to the rest of his investigative team.

She could not lie in this comfortable bed and think about Zeke loving her. Or that kiss yesterday morning that already felt like a month ago.

But for just a *few* more minutes, she let last night's conversation replay in her head. She'd had her own terrible childhood with parents who hadn't cared, and the hell of being separated from Royal and bouncing around foster houses as a teen, but Zeke's story of his mother's murder had always struck her as more sad.

He'd loved his mother and lost her in tragedy. No hope there. She'd only ever loved Royal, and she hadn't really lost him. Maybe their separation had been hard, but she'd always had hope for a future where they were together again.

In fact, at the moment, her brother was another item on her to-do list, because she had to tell him that their father was still in jail, so whatever he thought was happening… wasn't.

Probably.

She shook it away. One step at a time, and work had to come first right now. So she took a shower, got dressed for the day, and typed a to-do list into her phone to help her feel somehow in charge of the overwhelming amount of tasks she had to accomplish.

When she went downstairs, Viola greeted her with a wagging tail and happy yips at the bottom of the stairs. Brooke smelled coffee and bacon. For a moment, she stood and felt a pang.

One she didn't have time to dissect.

When she stepped into the kitchen, Zeke was putting two plates piled high with eggs, bacon and biscuits on the table.

"You don't have to keep cooking for me, Zeke," she said because it settled in her chest like a heavy weight. Why was he doing things for her all the time? "I am capable of feeding myself."

"Sure," he replied easily. "But isn't it nice to have some-one else handle it? You're busy, Brooke. I'm not. I can handle a few chores. Besides, last night wasn't much. I'm not much of a dinner cook, but I can put together a mean breakfast." He gestured to the table. "Sit. Eat."

She looked at the table, hesitating. Because she was afraid she'd…get used to this. Someone taking care of her. Because she'd never once had that.

Except when she was with him.

But she wasn't *with* him. He was just acting as…body-guard. Maybe there'd been some personal conversations. A kiss. That was just…sorting out a past. When she walked off this ranch, it wouldn't be like him breaking up with her all over again.

She couldn't let it be.

"Hart called," Zeke said. "He had court this morning, so couldn't be out at the cave, and Laurel's still out. He said he could send another deputy out with you, but he'd pre-fer from here on out it just be the detectives if you didn't mind taking the morning off from excavating."

She wasn't sure why the detective had shared that in-formation with Zeke rather than leave her a message or text on her own phone, but didn't know if she wanted to dig too deep into anything that involved Zeke at the mo-ment.

So she sat and ate breakfast next to him. She didn't say anything. She really didn't know what to say, and he seemed to be in the same boat. The only sounds in the kitchen were the scraping of forks and the dog occasion-ally huffing at their feet.

They even washed the dishes in silence. But once they

were done and before she could excuse herself, Zeke opened the back door from the kitchen.

"I want to show you something, if you're up for a little walk?"

She hesitated. He wasn't exactly…acting like himself, but she couldn't sort out what that meant. He was more calm than he'd been yesterday, but there was a kind of grimness wrapped into it that she didn't know how to parse.

"Okay."

They both got shoes on and then she followed him out into the sunny late morning. Viola dashed into the yard, then dashed back, over and over again, making Brooke smile as they walked to a building. A barn, she supposed.

Zeke stopped at a normal-size door on the side of the barn, pulled a key out from his pocket, and unlocked it. Then he held the key out to her.

She frowned.

"It's yours," he said, pushing the key into her palm. Then he shoved the door open and gestured her inside.

She stepped into a darkened barn, though it didn't *smell* like a barn. It smelled…clean. And when lights flipped on above her, she realized why. This was no barn to house horses or store crops. It looked like…a lab. Her old lab at North Star, to be precise.

"Is this…?" She stepped forward then stopped herself and looked back at him.

"It's a private lab. To run whatever tests. Granger helped with the supplies, information to make sure everything is up to code, just like you used to have at North Star. So it should be most of what you need, but he can get us anything else. A few things he sent need to arrive yet, but we'll get there."

Brooke felt frozen in place. It was set up perfectly. Not

quite like any of the labs she'd worked with at different police organizations, but that's because they were often multipurpose, underfunded and overcrowded.

Her North Star lab had been different—set up exactly the way she liked—because they hadn't exactly always been working within the law. "I'm not sure anything I do here would hold up in court."

That was a very ungrateful thing to say. When he'd gone to all this trouble. When he'd reached out to Granger. When she could test that skull here *immediately*.

Zeke shrugged and didn't voice any irritation with her response, even though he had every right to. "You don't have to use it. Or you can use it in conjunction with the lab in Cheyenne. Up to you."

Up to her. But that was ridiculous. This whole thing was so damn ridiculous. "Why did you do this?"

"Because I was worried the lab in Cheyenne and the sheer amount of people dealing with your case might have something to do with what was going on with you being followed. So, I got the ball rolling with Granger, and then it just felt like you might as well have some space here to work. You've got a lot of remains to work through."

Didn't she just.

And because her heart seemed too big for her chest, and her eyes were full of tears she wasn't about to let fall, she changed the subject entirely.

"How is Granger?" she asked, inspecting one of the machines. She would have thought he'd gotten rid of all this once North Star had disbanded. She should have known Granger MacMillan might have let North Star the entity go, but he wasn't about to not have the means to help anyone who needed it.

"Looks like him and Shay are swamped in foster kids and farm animals."

Brooke smiled. She hadn't talked to her old North Star bosses in a while. She hated to bother them when they had this new life they were building.

"Do you keep in touch with anyone else?"

"Oh, sure. Here and there. You don't?"

She didn't want to answer that. So many of her old North Star friends she'd retreated from. Because they'd all been starting new lives, and she didn't want to be some old reminder, some old burden. So she'd just…held herself apart. She'd never refused a call, but she hadn't made any. She'd kept to herself.

It was a bit of a surprise Zeke hadn't. Zeke who had provided this… It was really too much. To think about the two people who'd run North Star, who'd taken down the Sons and saved so many people, now married and raising kids and farm animals and just living a normal kind of life… While she was standing here with Zeke.

All she'd ever wanted and known she couldn't have.

That, she just couldn't deal with right now. Old feelings. Mixed-up nostalgia and dreams and delusion.

So she turned to Zeke. The emotional stuff didn't matter, did it? She had a case to solve. And now she had some things she could do right here. Everything else he'd said last night didn't matter, even if deep down she wanted it to.

They'd had their chance. It hadn't worked. She had bigger things to concern herself with right now.

So she smiled at him, and focused on work. "Want to help me smuggle a skull?"

His mouth quirked. "You know me so well."

Chapter Twelve

Zeke waited for Brooke to gather her stuff, and then he drove her into Bent and the sheriff's department. She instructed him not to follow her inside. He was supposed to drive around, get some coffee or something, then come back at one and pick her up.

Her idea, and while he didn't like taking orders from anyone, he found he didn't mind Brooke being in charge. Besides, staying away was easier than trying to explain his presence to the deputies and detectives inside. He would likely raise a few eyebrows and questions that might make it more difficult for Brooke to do what she'd gone there to do.

He was still having a hard time believing she was going to essentially steal remains. Maybe she'd been trained in the North Star way of bending the rules that needed bending, but he'd certainly never seen her bend any rule with ruthless efficiency.

She wanted to be good, always, because the thing about Brooke Campbell was, no matter how she'd grown up, no matter how much time she'd spent in North Star, she was good down to her soul.

Still, she spent her days studying the remains of dead

people. That had really never computed with her personality, either, and yet she did it, and well. Analyzed that gruesome data and put it together in even more grim reports.

Still she managed to be soft and lovely and *her*.

Zeke sighed and tried not to wonder if he'd never seen her again, would he have gone through life in denial of what was missing from it?

He returned to the station a little before the appointed time and just stood outside his truck, watching the comings and goings of a county police force.

He'd considered going to the police academy the past few months. He needed something to do, and he kept resisting the idea of actually trying to ranch. It left a hell of a lot of room for failure.

Police work? He could do that. Well… Following rules and laws had never been in his wheelhouse, even when he'd been in the army. He liked to do things *his* way. But he knew how to deal with people, with clear rules and expectations.

Sort of.

He could have joined the Hudsons like Walker had done. The HSS had invited him to become an investigator. Mostly he'd declined because being around all that family, marriages, babies, *life* made him more itchy than he cared to analyze.

He could have done lots of things. Gone lots of places.

And instead he'd stayed in Sunrise and bought a *ranch*.

It hit him at the oddest times that these past few months had been the calmest of his life and the most uncomfortable and unsettled he'd ever felt. And still, with all that internal upheaval, he hadn't bolted. Because with Walker and Carlyle safe and happy and settling down, it didn't feel right to leave them behind to worry about him.

Luckily he didn't have to consider that any longer because Brooke walked out of the police station, her hands gripping the straps of her backpack. No doubt because she'd succeeded and there was a skull in there. Her grip was all nerves.

But she walked slowly and calmly to him, the sunlight dancing in the reddish strands of her hair. And there was that vise around his chest again, like a full breath would break him to pieces.

Like *she* would.

She got into his truck without looking at him, placing the backpack in the backseat with care.

He got into the driver's seat, trying to focus on the problem at hand over his pointless, roundabout thoughts. She needed to take the remains back to the ranch and work in her lab.

But he had other ideas. "I was thinking we should pick your car up on the way back to my ranch. Keep moving it around. Just to be safe."

"But Royal was the one following me. I mean I'm all for having my car back, but we have that," she said, nodding at her backpack.

Mostly he agreed with her. He'd even tossed the tracker he'd put on his truck the other morning because he was fairly certain Royal had been the one to put it on Brooke's car. He had been the one following her, so nothing else added up.

But…

"I'll just drop you off at your car. *That* can ride with me from the cabin to ranch," he said, jerking his chin toward the backpack. "I'll follow you and make sure we're in eyesight of each other."

She didn't look convinced that this was the best idea, but

she didn't argue, so he drove to the rental cabin. It wasn't that far out of their way, and she should have her vehicle. Even if he didn't like the idea of her having the means to leave without him watching out for her.

Royal had been following her though, and she still might be in danger, but until Zeke figured out what *kind*, leaving her car at the rental just gave Royal the means to cause more trouble.

Zeke pulled up next to her car, not bothering to turn off the engine. She scrambled out of his truck with one last glance at her backpack, then pulled keys out of her purse and headed to the car.

It was fine. She'd lead the way and he'd follow in his truck. What bad could happen? They'd still be together, and they'd head for his ranch.

But before, in that diner parking lot, there'd been a tracker. He was pretty sure it had been Royal, but something in his mind whispered, *What if it's not?*

"Wait." He hopped out of the truck and began to inspect her car just as he had back at the diner days ago. Maybe he was paranoid, but he'd built most of his adult life on following instincts a lot of people called paranoia. Sometimes it was and sometimes…

"Do you smell that?"

Brooke frowned, sniffed the air. "I don't know. Maybe? It just smells like…fertilizer."

And maybe it was, but something buzzed along Zeke's skin. A bad feeling that he'd honed from being in a lot of close calls in his life. He took Brooke's arm and drew her away from the vehicle. "Look, I think—"

The sound of the explosion was small, but still a surprise. Brooke jumped and Zeke tried to shelter her. When he looked back at the car, flames erupted from under the hood. Zeke grabbed Brooke and pulled her behind him, propelling them both back and away from the fire.

It hadn't been anything major. Unlikely to kill anyone, though it could have easily hurt someone near the car. There might be a second explosion if the fire hit the gas tank, so they needed to get some distance from it.

"Did it...overheat?" Brooke asked weakly when it was obvious that's not what had happened.

The door of the cabin burst open and Royal, in his bare feet, ran out holding a fire extinguisher. For a second he stared at the blaze then turned to them.

"You okay, Brooke?"

"Yes," she said firmly, but she was shaking underneath Zeke's hand.

Royal moved forward and put out the fire with quick, efficient movements. Then he shoved his free hand over his short hair. "What the hell was that?"

"We don't know." Zeke surveyed the car, Royal, and Brooke behind him. He sighed, because whatever was going on wasn't over. And it wasn't just about Brooke.

"Get some shoes on, Royal. You're coming with us."

BROOKE WAS STILL SHAKING, but could breathe with more ease when Zeke's ranch came into view. Nothing bad had happened here. They were safe here. Everyone was going to be safe.

She had to believe that. So she'd repeated it over and over inside her head on the drive.

She was surprised Royal hadn't mounted a fight about coming to Zeke's. He'd simply gone inside, gotten shoes and a duffel bag, and returned. Zeke had helped her into the truck and handed her the backpack so she could hold on to it. Royal had climbed in the back.

She was riding in a truck, clutching a skull carefully packaged in a backpack, her brother in the back seat while her ex pulled up to his ranch house. After her car had… exploded. Kind of.

It was a small *explosion*, she kept telling herself. Nothing compared to some of the things she'd seen in North Star. And still, it had shaken her more because it had been *her* car. In front of *her* rental cabin, even if she hadn't been staying there.

She didn't know *why*, but this somehow felt centered on *her*. And worse, it probably wasn't about the skeletal remains at all, because she'd been working on those for over a month now. Nothing had changed this week—not really.

Except Royal's appearance in her life. So maybe it didn't center on her at all. She didn't want to feel this way, but she couldn't help but think it focused on Royal. It had to. Nothing bad had been happening to her or around her until he'd started following her.

When Zeke shoved the truck into Park, they all got out. Viola bounded over, a low growl in her throat as she scurried up to Royal. It was a warning, but also clearly curiosity on the dog's part.

Royal crouched, holding out his hand in supplication to the dog. Viola sniffed, tail stuck straight out, but after a few seconds, it began to wag and the dog let Royal scratch her ears. Royal grinned up at Brooke over the dog. For a moment, they were kids again and she hadn't failed her brother and they weren't in trouble.

"Someone will call that in before nightfall," Zeke said, interrupting her little moment with pesky *facts*. "Someone involved with the rentals will see there's been a fire in that car and will call *someone* about it. Then Bent County is going to know it's your car that got torched, Brooke. If we aren't the ones to call it in, it looks fishy," Zeke said.

"It *is* fishy," Royal muttered irritably as he straightened into a standing position.

"Yeah. Do you want Bent County looking into it?" Zeke asked somewhat pointedly. Like Royal might have a reason to hide. And he might. He probably did. He…

Royal looked over at her. "Did you tell him?"

"Tell me what?" Zeke demanded, his eyebrows drawing together.

But Brooke ignored Zeke. She had to, or she might just… fall apart. And there was too much at stake. She had to get to work on this skull. She had to date it. She had…things to do that weren't *this*.

First, Royal needed to know. "Dad is still in jail," she said to Royal and only to Royal. "Whatever you think he's cooked up isn't true. I had it confirmed yesterday."

Royal frowned, not looking convinced.

"What do you think he's cooked up?" Zeke asked.

"I don't know," Royal said, scowling. "That's the problem."

"And you didn't think that you might mention to me that your father might be the issue here?" Zeke said to her. *Oh* so calmly.

"No, because I confirmed with Thomas that he's still in jail." She lifted her chin, met his calm expression, but saw the anger in his eyes. "So he's *not* the problem." And it just broke whatever last piece of control or something she had within her, because she was just done. With both of them.

"Because you see, Zeke, I've been taking care of myself and my life for the past four years. Without *you*. I appreciate the place to stay. I even appreciate the interference, up to a point, but I won't be made to feel guilty for taking care of myself."

He didn't say anything in response, but there was that old stony expression on his face she remembered all too well. She turned to her brother. "I didn't have any problems with anyone until you started following me. Are you sure this isn't a *you* problem?"

"You think I just lured people here to set your car on fire?" he returned, a lot of belligerence covering up a hurt.

She felt guilty and knew she shouldn't. So she just... let it all out. "I don't know what to think. But I do know I sent you letters, supplied an attorney, did everything I could with the resources I had to find you, to help you, and I never heard a *peep*. And you've waltzed back into my life and suddenly there's danger, and you're giving me attitude. Frankly, I'm sick of both of you. I'm taking my skull and I'm getting some work done."

And that's just what she did. She took the backpack and marched over toward the barn, Viola at her heels. She unlocked the door then carefully knelt down to pet Viola.

"I'm sorry. No dogs allowed in the lab. And I'm about to institute a no men rule too. Maybe you could be my guard dog and keep them out."

With that, she slid inside the barn, keeping Viola out. She hung the backpack up on a hook and then went to the sink to wash her hands. Everything was in working order. Just like her other labs.

She didn't think about Zeke doing that for her. She didn't think about her brother, or her brother and Zeke together. She focused on her *work*.

Because that was the only thing she'd ever been able to depend on. Human remains might be a mystery, but they were a set of data points. Not infuriating, obnoxious, changeable *people*.

Not people who expected you to rely on them, to trust them, to tell them the truth, but didn't extend the same courtesy. Not people you let yourself depend on a *little*, who then disappeared.

Because you're too much of a bother, Brooke. Best keep to yourself.

Since she wanted to cry, she carefully got everything ready, unpacked her skull, then got to work. Right now, her goal was to date the bones as best she could, particularly in relation to the other remains they'd found. So far, they'd uncovered mostly intact bodies. So this was new. It was different. It needed studying.

She didn't know how long she worked. She left her phone off. If Thomas wanted to contact her about the cave…well, he'd have to hunt her down. When the door to the lab opened however many hours later, she saw it was dark out.

She blinked. A whole day in here. She'd gotten a lot done and no one had bothered her. Not even to get her to eat.

Somehow most of the mad she'd had at Zeke was gone. He'd done all this for her, and it wasn't his fault… None of this was about him, but here he was.

"Any progress?" he asked. No bringing up earlier. No being cold to her. Just a genuine question.

So she gave a genuine answer. "Some. I think this skull is fairly old. It's also the only bone we've found that didn't have an intact body with or nearby it. And I can't help but think it matches a picture from that scrapbook Thomas uncovered."

Zeke nodded. "That's good progress, right?"

"It is."

He stood in silence as she cleaned up for the day. She needed something to eat, to stretch out her back. She needed... Oh, she didn't know.

"Brooke, I put this lab together, helped you get that skull, because I thought the stalking might be connected to the case, but now I wonder..."

Probably the same thing she did. "If they're wholly unrelated?"

Zeke nodded. "Royal and I talked, and he agrees. He didn't know anything about what you were doing here. When I explained you had a real human skull in your backpack, I think his opinion of you changed entirely. He was very perplexed."

She wanted to laugh. She really did. But on the other side of her temper was always that awful guilt. And she knew what it stemmed from. You didn't grow up in a gang and then get bounced around to foster homes without developing a certain amount of trauma responses. She didn't want to be a bother, didn't want to hurt anyone in case they might ditch her.

But he already had ditched her, so to speak. And still, she couldn't resist the apology. "I'm sorry I didn't tell you Royal's theory about our father trying to...do something."

"I thought you wouldn't be made to feel guilty about not including me in something that was none of my business?"

This time she did laugh in spite of herself. He recited her words with such dry disdain it was just *funny*. "I tried. But I'm really good at feeling guilty. And the truth is, if you were anyone else, I probably would have told you. I'd probably be more comfortable involving you and asking you for help. But it's...you."

"What about me?" he returned, eyebrows furrowed.

Clearly confused, even if she thought he shouldn't be. "I've helped you lots."

"Yes. You have. In a North Star capacity. But not after. Zeke, I was so desperately in love with you then. I didn't hide that. Surely you know that."

She wouldn't say he looked *uncomfortable* with her saying those things, but he certainly wasn't going to interact with the idea of *love*, even after he'd said all that stuff last night. For whatever reasons, and maybe they were *good* reasons, he didn't want to deal with the idea of love. Then or now.

Still, maybe it was her turn to try to explain herself. Because he wasn't doing it to be cruel. He'd never really been cruel to her. She knew what that was like.

"Those are not just feelings that go away, and it took me a long time to…resituate myself once we broke up, once North Star ended. I don't want to ever have to go through that kind of…upheaval again. I have been bounced around at other people's whims my *entire life*. Finally, I have some…some agency. Some power. I can't just hand it over because maybe something dangerous is going on. I can't lose myself again. I have to stand on my own two feet."

He was silent a moment and then nodded. "Okay."

She blinked once. His easy agreement was the last thing she'd expected. She'd braced for a lecture about protection not being the opposite of agency and so on and so forth. She'd heard something of the like in North Star her entire time there. She narrowed her eyes at him. She did not trust Zeke Daniels's calm acquiescence. "What do you mean 'okay'?"

"I mean okay. That sounds fair and right, and the last thing I want to do is hurt you again. But I also want you to consider that I don't swoop in because… I'm trying to inflict my whims on you. I'm trying to keep you safe, not keep you from standing up for yourself too. In fact, I'd like all four of us to work together to make that happen."

Help was not the enemy. Brooke knew that from an investigative standpoint, but she was still trying to accept it on a personal, adult level. She'd always done everything on her own there. But she couldn't handle whatever this was on her own, and she knew it. So why couldn't she accept help from someone she trusted, even if he'd broken her heart?

Even if, worse, she still had feelings for him and was afraid it would lead her down the same heartbroken path?

Regardless, she had to set those feelings aside and be reasonable. "I'd like that too." She frowned. "But who's the fourth person?"

"Hart. He came by looking for you so you could excavate. I haven't told him everything, and God knows Royal hasn't told us much, but between the four of us… Maybe we can get to the bottom of everything."

Everything. She wasn't sure it was possible, but she supposed now was the time to try.

Chapter Thirteen

They convened in the living room. The afternoon had been…tense at best, but Zeke was hopeful they'd all come to a kind of understanding about the most important thing. Figuring out what was going on so they could keep Brooke safe.

The men in the group made quite a trio. The cop, the con and whatever Zeke was. Some combination of the two, he supposed.

Then there was Brooke. She'd let go of her mad. She always did. Too quickly, in Zeke's estimation, but he couldn't be frustrated with her over it in the current situation. Not when her *I was so desperately in love with you* would echo in his head for the rest of his life.

Both the way she'd said it, so serious and with all that emotion, that hurt *he'd* inflicted just there in her eyes. And then the past tense she'd used. Lov*ed*. Yeah, he found he didn't care for that.

"We dusted your car for prints," Thomas was saying to Brooke. "We're running what we found through our system, but I can't imagine we come back with anything. It was a small very-homemade bomb. Very hard to trace. There was some thought put behind that."

"I think the bigger concern is that we don't know what the hell the point of it was," Zeke pointed out. He'd thrown some frozen pizzas in the oven and they were now eating them over the coffee table in the living room since his kitchen table couldn't hold four people comfortably.

Viola moved from person to person, begging for scraps. It might have been homey. Four friends enjoying a meal.

Instead they were discussing car bombs and murder.

"It wouldn't have really hurt anyone," Royal said. "Not unless someone had the hood open when the bomb went off. Even then, not lethal. Maybe just some burns. So the point had to be to scare, not necessarily to accomplish any injury."

"Scare who, I wonder," Brooke said quietly. Her gaze was on her brother. "Me, because it's my car?"

That, Zeke figured, had been everyone's initial thought.

"Or you, Royal, because you were at the rental?" she questioned.

Royal's expression went even more grim. "Not a soul knows I'm here."

"Did you check *your* car for a tracking device?" Zeke asked. Because even if this somehow connected to Brooke's work, who would just…scare her like that? Without some kind of direct threat, there was no reason to know who or what was behind what was happening. No way to react any way when you didn't know *why* you were being scared.

For a moment, Royal's face registered some surprise. "Well. No." He got to his feet. "I'll go look right now."

Brooke stood. "I'll drive you."

"Brooke."

Zeke tried not to grimace at the fact he and Hart had said her name at the same time.

"He shouldn't go alone," Brooke said, stubbornly to Zeke's mind.

"I'll go with him," Hart said, pushing to his feet to stand next to Royal. "We'll take the cruiser. Check in with where the deputies are at on the investigation while we're there."

Brooke frowned, but she didn't mount an argument. And to Zeke's surprise, neither did Royal. Zeke supposed he'd have to count it as a point in Royal's favor that he was willing to head out with a cop. Another point in his favor was that he'd been willing to consider Zeke's suggestion in the first place.

"I'll drop Royal back here after we're done. If we find a tracker, we'll look at it from a law-enforcement angle this time." Hart eyed them all with a kind of censure. As if they should have come to him in the first place.

"And I'll let Laurel in on everything," he continued. "More eyes until we get a clearer perspective on what this is. But you'll need to get back to the caves tomorrow, Brooke. We've got to determine if we're looking for another murderer there. We have to treat this as two concurrent cases we're working on. Not one or the other."

Zeke could read the guilt all over Brooke's face. No doubt because she had a skull at her lab here on his property and she hadn't told either of the detectives she'd smuggled it out of the station.

Zeke would have to give *her* a point for still not saying anything. He knew it went against her rule-following nature.

Royal and Hart departed and then Brooke and Zeke were left together. She got up and began to clean the remnants of pizza, so Zeke did the same. She didn't say anything. She was quiet and withdrawn and he just…hated it.

"It's totally possible this thing doesn't connect to you,

Brooke," he offered, hoping to get that tenseness out of her shoulders.

"It was still my car they were tracking. And bombed. Maybe Royal is at the heart of it, but I think I connect. And even if I don't, I can't feel okay with my brother being the target. No matter how much trouble he's gotten himself into."

"But if it doesn't have anything to do with you…"

She shook her head, her mouth wobbling just a second before she firmed it, straightened her shoulders, as if going to battle. "He's my brother, Zeke. What am I going to do? Just set it aside and ignore it? Pretend I'm not scared because he's a target and maybe I'm not? I can't. Could you?"

"No." He understood too well the reality of having your sibling in danger. He'd done a lot of things to keep Carlyle safe, and still he'd worried about her every step of the way. Hell, he still worried about her, even knowing she was in a good place over at the Hudson Ranch.

But Brooke worrying, being miserable, tied him into knots. He hated seeing her so damn sad. He reached out and rubbed a hand down her back, some pathetic attempt at comfort.

She didn't pull away. She even leaned into him a little bit.

And he just…had to help somehow.

"Let's see if Granger has a minute to talk. He helped you with Royal's lawyer, right? He's got some insight into Royal's charge and prison time. Maybe he can tug a line on something the cops can't. Make a connection we haven't seen. Granger and Shay are good at that."

Brooke hesitated. "I hate asking them to get reeled back into things they purposefully left behind."

Zeke laughed and gave her shoulders a squeeze before

releasing her, because he needed his distance, or he'd want to… Well.

"They don't mind, Brooke. You know, Granger and Shay and a couple others jumped in to help my family when we finally found my mother's killer." Zeke thought about the gunshot wound he'd received for the trouble. About how close Carlyle and Mary had been to getting hurt. At how beat up Walker had felt after.

But they'd survived, because they'd worked together and because North Star had been there to help. Even after disbanding.

"We'd likely all have ended up dead if they hadn't helped. And I didn't have to beg. They were involving themselves before I even got half the request for help out of my mouth. It's hard to leave all this stuff behind, even when you want to. But even more than that, Brooke, we're all still a family."

"I had no problem leaving North Star danger behind," she said.

A bit stiffly, he noted, and with some of that old primness that might have made him smile if he didn't feel sorry for her. "Yes, the danger. I'm talking about the people, Brooke."

She expressly didn't meet his gaze. And maybe he shouldn't poke. She didn't need him to psychoanalyze her. She'd been *desperately* in love with him and he'd screwed it all up.

But she was here, and maybe he was old enough, mature enough, *finally*, to realize that life didn't present you with many opportunities for something good…so he probably shouldn't be afraid of them.

"And I know you stepped away from all the people too." He'd kept in touch with everyone enough to know only

Granger had been able to touch base with Brooke over the years. "But it wasn't because you wanted to."

"Oh, wasn't it?" she returned with that chin raised in that way she had. But she didn't meet his eyes because she knew he was right.

And he understood, in part, because he'd kept his own family at a certain kind of arm's length for a while there. Thinking if he hid who he was, what he felt, all that untenable *worry* that existed inside him, they'd be better off.

He'd learned the hard way, when they'd fought through a lot of danger to solve their mother's murder, he'd been wrong.

And Brooke was wrong to cut off people who cared about her. He understood why, but that didn't make her less wrong, and she should know it. Sometimes it took someone saying what you knew flat-out to you for you to finally accept it.

"You're always so afraid. That you might ask too much. That you have to walk on all those eggshells your foster families made you walk on. That if you're not perfect, people will turn you away. I suppose I didn't help that any. And I'm sorry. For a lot of things."

She looked at him now, blue eyes wide and startled. "I don't think now is the time to have some kind of postmortem about our relationship, Zeke."

"No, it isn't. But I'm going to take the opportunity anyway. Because it's here. I think you must know I didn't hurt you on purpose, or you wouldn't be here. You wouldn't have called me for help. Or maybe I just hope that. I had my own issues, which isn't an excuse. I'm still sorry."

She stood there, very still, but he knew she was absorbing what he'd said. Taking it in, sorting it through. Her precious data points. And that was fine. He'd said what he'd needed to.

They could focus on the danger at hand now. So he led her to the living room and told her to take a seat on the couch while he grabbed his laptop. Once they settled together, hip to hip, with the computer on the coffee table, Zeke put in the video call to Granger. He was grateful the man answered right away.

Granger's expression registered some surprise, no doubt at seeing both of them on the screen, but then he just smiled. "Well, hello. It's nice to see you two together."

Neither Zeke nor Brooke said anything to that, but Zeke could see in the screen the bland kind of smile Brooke offered at those words. No point in arguing about *together*. But she didn't like it.

"Hey, Granger. We've got a…bit of a situation."

"Of course you do," he returned, mostly with humor. "Lay it on me."

Zeke relayed the information from the stalking to Royal to the car bomb. Brooke explained a little about what she was doing with the remains, and the skull.

She leaned forward, getting closer to the screen. "You helped me get Royal the lawyer, send those letters so they wouldn't be traced back to North Star at all. But he didn't get them, and he didn't know I was the source of the lawyer."

Granger frowned at that. "Not sure how that could have happened. I can go back and look into it. The lawyer. Where the letters would have gone through."

"And more into her father," Zeke added. Because if Royal thought this could involve old members of the Sons, why wouldn't they look into that? North Star might have destroyed a lot of their records, but Granger knew how to get any and all information on any old Sons's activity.

"He's still in jail," Brooke said tightly.

"Yeah, but if Royal thinks it might connect, we need to know... There's something with your family and their ties to the Sons going on here because of Royal. Let's find all the information we can, even if it ends up not connecting to the danger."

"Zeke's right," Granger said. "The more information, the better off you are. I'll see what Shay and I can come up with. We'll get back to you as soon as we can."

"You don't have to—"

"Brooke," Granger cut her off gently. "North Star might not exist anymore, but we're still a family. Always will be."

Zeke took Brooke's hand, squeezed it, tried to get that sentiment through to her. Regardless of...anything. They'd all been connected by something, and it didn't just go away because that something didn't exist anymore.

"We'll be in touch."

They said their goodbyes and Zeke closed the laptop. He looked at Brooke, hoping she'd seem more settled. Relieved or calm or something. Maybe she couldn't believe in all those things *he'd* said, but surely she believed in Granger.

If anything, she looked more upset.

"Brooke."

She jumped up and started pacing. "I just don't know what to do. I feel as powerless as when I was a kid." She made jerky movements with her hands as she moved back and forth, Viola following her path. "Everything is happening *to* me and I just—"

Zeke stood and stopped her by taking her hands in his. He gave them a reassuring squeeze. "Give yourself a break,

Brooke. You've spent the past month studying a cave full of human remains. That's going to weigh on anyone."

"That's my *job*. And I'm good at my job," she said, looking up at him. Her eyes were filled with tears, but they didn't fall.

Maybe that killed him just as much as actual tears would have. He moved a hand over her hair. "Sweetheart." He remembered too late that she didn't want him to call her that anymore. But she didn't snap at him.

She leaned into him.

So he pulled her closer, wrapped his arms around her, hoping he could press some comfort into her. She didn't cry, she didn't speak. She just stood there with her cheek on his chest. And she breathed. In that old way of hers, careful in and out.

He could have stood with her in his arms for eternity. He'd been so afraid of that feeling four years ago. He didn't even know what had changed to make it not so terrifying right now. He still had no real future, no real plans. No way to fold her into his life.

But maybe he'd watched Walker and Carlyle find ways to belong to someone else and that had…opened something inside him.

It hardly mattered because Brooke was pulling away. He'd had his chance and he'd messed it up years ago. No going back and fixing that. He could protect her in the here and now, but he had to stop thinking about love and—

"Oh, to hell with it," she muttered, which sounded more like something he would have said.

But then her mouth was on his. Not wild and angry like the last kiss he'd initiated. Even when she *was* angry, that wasn't Brooke. This was soft, gentle. And, it turned out, everything he wanted. Softness and warmth. A sweetness he'd viewed as a weakness when they'd been together, even when he'd been attracted to it.

Yet here she was. Still so fully Brooke. Strong and smart and doing this incredible job, without hardening herself to anything.

It was a wonder. She was a wonder. And he wanted—

She pushed at his chest then stepped away from him when he released her. She took a few steps back. She inhaled shakily and looked at the front door as if expecting Hart and Royal to burst through at any minute. They wouldn't, but it also wasn't like this was some appropriate time to deal with…whatever was still between them.

Because it was *something*. But danger trumped it all.

"Do you have any ice cream?" she asked, chin up as if daring him to demand they talk this through.

The request made him laugh because he realized that any place he'd lived for any length of time, he'd kept ice cream on hand. Not for himself. He could take it or leave it. But ice cream had always been her favorite, her comfort food.

All these years and, somewhere hidden deep in his psyche, he'd been keeping ice cream in his freezer with her in mind. Wishing for this moment.

"Yeah. Let's have some ice cream."

Chapter Fourteen

Brooke worked very diligently not to think about the fact she'd kissed Zeke. She'd just set it aside. Pretended it hadn't happened.

Because this was like some kind of backsliding. Calling Granger for help. Falling all over again for this man. It was…a past she'd left behind. She couldn't fall back into it just because of some danger.

But it was a really good kiss.

And the fact of the matter was, she could keep pretending. She could convince herself Zeke hadn't thought of her in four years. She could try to tell herself this was just chemistry and it didn't matter.

But he had mint chocolate chip ice cream in his freezer.

She could convince herself she was being self-absorbed but knew Zeke had no great affinity for mint chocolate chip ice cream. It wasn't in there because of him.

That meant it was probably in there because of her. Like the eggs with cheese. Like all the details he seemed to remember so easily.

It's just food, Brooke. Get a grip. She didn't have the time or space to figure out Zeke. Or why the things he'd said about North Star and family and her fears felt like keys unlocking everything she'd kept hidden away for so long.

Or why him holding her felt like home. Kissing him felt like she'd just been on ice for four years, waiting around for this. For him. When she *hadn't* been.

She was relieved when Royal returned, no matter how angry he looked. He was here and she could stop thinking about Zeke and the past and focus on the important danger in their present.

"There was a tracker on my car," he said grimly. "Hart's sending it in to have it tested. See if they can get something out of it. He didn't seem too optimistic though."

Brooke didn't have the words for this development. She expected Zeke to say something, but he didn't. Not even to blame Royal for leading someone straight for her.

Nonetheless, that's what he'd done.

"It's late, guys," Zeke said. "Let's get some sleep. Reconvene in the morning with clear heads and maybe more information from Hart."

Brooke glanced at Zeke, but she couldn't quite read his expression. Except that it was *soft*. And he was being nice to Royal. And that almost made her cry.

"You can take the room next to Brooke's," he continued. "It's not in the best of shape, but there's a mattress in there. I'll rustle up some blankets and a pillow."

"Grab your bag. I'll show you where it is," she said to Royal. She didn't look at Zeke. Not even to thank him. She should have, but she was feeling too soft. And she had to find some way to be strong.

So, she led Royal upstairs, showed him the room next to hers. It indeed wasn't much, and she resisted the urge to offer to swap rooms. She didn't have to be a martyr to him just because of her guilt. When *he* should be feeling guilty, if anyone did.

Besides, Royal didn't complain. He dropped his bag. He

turned to her and studied her face as he crossed his arms over his chest. "Something going on between you two?"

It made her want to laugh, which was a surprising development in this whole confusing night. Like Royal was trying to play overprotective brother when they hadn't seen each other for so long, and never as adults. In her mind, he was still ten. Not this mountain of a tattooed man.

She supposed this was his way of caring, which made her response gentle. And the truth. Mostly.

"Not that it's any of your business, but no. There…was, a long time ago. But not anymore."

Royal made a considering noise, like he didn't buy it, and maybe he shouldn't since she and Zeke kept somehow falling into kissing each other. And she couldn't blame Zeke for that, because she'd initiated the last kiss.

A really, really brain-melting kiss that had only ended because she'd been afraid of where it might lead if she let it. Because it would be so easy to be in love with him again, to lean into all that.

She couldn't imagine surviving the heartbreak a second time. Maybe she was strong enough, but she was tired of the ways life seemed set up to break her. Her brother, case in point.

"Royal. Be upfront with me. What aren't you telling me?"

He paused for a moment, but he didn't look away. "Long story, Chick. And aren't we supposed to get some sleep?" He moved for the door, but she gave him a big-sister glare and he sighed.

"Those foster homes sucked," he said.

That was neither here nor there. But she'd let him start wherever he needed. "That they did."

He looked puzzled. "But you're like…some fancy scientist-type person."

Did he think that was because she'd had a *good* experience? "Getting an education didn't mean I was loved or taken care of, Royal. At a certain point, I was put in a position where failure was not an option." In some ways, she'd been grateful for the strictness of the final foster family she'd had in high school before she'd aged out. Their uncompromising and authoritarian methods had given her the ability to do something with her life. If she hadn't had that, who knows where she would have ended up.

But it had been a hard, cold, four years in that home. Where even the whiff of a B could have gotten her kicked back to a group home.

"I guess I never thought…" Royal trailed off, looking confused, but then he shook his head. "My point is, I hated them all. I never could fit in. I was always itching for a fight. So about the time I turned sixteen and I was back in one of those group homes, I figured I'd just run away and go back to the Sons. The system wasn't too broken up by my absence."

"Royal."

"I didn't go back to like belong or anything. I just thought about us. Growing up there. How bad it was, but how bad the foster shit was. So I figured… What if I went back? I could help kids like us. Be their inside protector. Without all the rules and school and constant interference by people who thought they were giving me charity. It was bad living with the Sons, sure, but not worse than being bounced around, knocked around. At least I had some… status there."

He'd chosen to go back because a system had failed him. It was hard to blame him for that, but… "You could have also chosen to go into law enforcement or social work and helped, Royal."

He snorted. "Yeah, right. *Rules* and me, Chick? We don't get along."

She resisted the urge to roll her eyes. Her brother was telling her what had happened to him, what he'd done. And she wanted to hear it. "So, you went back to Dad?"

"Yeah. I convinced Dad I really wanted back. Wanted to be a part of it. I didn't. I wanted to mess up his plans. I wanted to help kids like us. And the way they treated those girls…" He shook his head. "I just always saw you. So I had to do something. I spent a year doing that, always so afraid Dad saw right through me while I tried to protect those girls. I was always waiting for a real end, but in retrospect, I guess I fooled him."

A real end. Brooke looked at her brother, thought of Zeke. A death wish. The idea that if they died doing something noble, it would somehow make everything all right.

It made her want to cry for them. Maybe *all* of them.

But she could tell Royal all the things she couldn't tell Zeke. Because this was her baby brother and he'd done something noble, even if she wished he'd gone about it in a different way.

"I love you no matter what. I'd have gotten you that lawyer even if you'd been in the wrong. I don't know why it got kept from you that I was behind it, but it doesn't matter. What matters is, I was going to support you no matter what. I always will."

Royal sighed. "Because you think you owe me, Chick. And maybe I let you think that because it's easy, but you don't. We were both kids. Failed by a hell of a lot of people."

Brooke had to carefully inhale then force herself to exhale at his words. She wanted it to be true, but… How could it be? She'd been older. She should have…fought harder. Done something. She didn't know how to explain that to him, and he was talking about the situation at hand anyway. Not their past.

"I don't think it matters how dismantled the Sons is. I disrespected Dad when I tricked him into letting me in then protected those kids. I embarrassed him in that circle. No amount of jail time is going to make him let that go, because it wasn't about the Sons. It was about him and me, and me pulling one over on him. Maybe he's still in jail right now. Maybe he has no ability to reach the outside, but I doubt it. I really doubt it. Men like that don't just stop being sadistic, Brooke."

It wasn't that she disagreed with him. She remembered just how vindictive their father could be. That's how he'd gotten Family Services called on him. How he'd managed to lose his kids no matter how the Sons had tried to wriggle him out of it. Because he'd been determined to make someone else *pay* for their lack of reverence. That had mattered more than any consequence to Jeremiah Campbell.

It was just that she hadn't known her brother as an adult. And he stood there looking and sounding like a *man*. It was disorienting.

"He's the only one who'd know you matter to me, Chick. Someone threatening you to me…it had to be him."

"Or come from him."

"Yeah. Look, leopards don't change their spots. Maybe the Sons is gone. Maybe he's in jail. But it doesn't mean he can't wield a certain group of people against us."

She didn't like it at all, but Royal was right. "Did you tell all this to Thomas?"

"Bits and pieces. Hart seems legit, for a cop, but…"

"I need you to tell him. Everything. Anything. No matter how little. We can't protect you if we don't know what this is. The police can look into Sons's things. They can look into all Dad's prison records. They can really dig into this and keep you safe in the process."

"What about you?"

"It's not about me. You said so yourself."

"No, I said our father is the only one who'd know that to hurt me he only had to get to you. That means *you're* in danger. I don't think he'd be too broken up about hurting you again, Brooke."

She didn't like the way her brother used her real name, though she couldn't pinpoint why. Only that it made this all so much more serious, when she didn't want him worried about *her*. She couldn't be a burden to him when…

Zeke's words from earlier came back to her.

You're always so afraid. That you might ask too much. That you have to walk on all those eggshells your foster families made you walk on. That if you're not perfect, people will turn you away.

Maybe she felt those things, but was it really wrong? Except she'd failed Royal before, and here he was and… It didn't matter. This wasn't about *her*. Even if she got caught in the crosshairs. "Okay, maybe, but—"

"You going to tell your boyfriend?"

She sighed. There was no point explaining, *again*, that Zeke was just… Zeke. Maybe the old feelings were still there, but… There was no ending that wasn't the exact same as four years ago.

Even if Zeke acted like he understood his mistakes. Even if he understood *her*. Even if he'd changed from that angry, edgy, desperate-to-*act* man.

Brooke was the same.

"Here's the deal," Royal said when she didn't answer. "I'll tell the cops everything, if you tell Zeke everything. No point leaving that guy out of it when it's clear he'll protect you."

"I've asked for his help in that department because he's perfectly capable, but—"

"He'd lick your boots, Chick. That's the only reason I'm under this roof, the only reason I haven't messed with him. He's only mixed up in this to save you from it. For whatever reason, that's your deal, but it's true."

That left her feeling too…something. Hopeful, probably. "We really do need to get some sleep."

He nodded. "That's fine. As long as we have a deal."

Brooke blew out a breath. Was there any point arguing? Maybe it was really best that everyone knew everything. "Fine."

"I'll talk to Hart tomorrow."

She nodded and then left him in the room, not sure what else to say. What else to do. Everything felt like such a jumble. One she couldn't list or organize or data point her way through like she had with studying the skull.

Still, she got ready for bed. Crawled into the nicer one than her brother's. She was exhausted and *needed* rest, but her mind whirled.

She thought about Zeke in his bedroom downstairs. Far away from Royal. Far away from the heavy things weighing her down.

He'd always been a safe place to land.

Except that whole time when he broke up with you and left you to pick up the pieces on your own.

But she wasn't that girl anymore, was she?

She could practically hear her old therapist's voice. *Beware self-destructive tendencies brought on by overstress-*

*ing yourself to be perfect in everything and make everyone
around you happy while ignoring your own happiness.*

That's essentially what Zeke had accused her of as well.
Because she did one of two things. Contorted herself for
people or isolated herself from people.

She didn't think she'd done either with Zeke the past
week. Wasn't that funny? And if she were to put her own
happiness in the mix, wouldn't that include a late-night trip
down to Zeke's bedroom? Because she was well versed in
the ways that could make her happy.

Temporarily.

Like ice cream.

The ice cream he'd bought, thinking of her, whether he'd
been conscious of it or not.

ZEKE TOSSED AND TURNED. Even though he'd been the one
to suggest sleep, it felt too much like sitting around waiting
for something to happen. Something to happen to *Brooke*.

He sat up, and the only reason he didn't reach for the
gun on his nightstand was the little flash of something red
he saw in the moonlight.

Brooke.

He pushed into a sitting position as she entered his room,
and then she just stood there, a foot or two away from his
bed.

Meanwhile his heart clattered against his chest like its
own independent being.

"Everything okay?" he asked, his voice rusty.

"Yes," she said calmly. Firmly. "I was just talking to
Royal when we went up, one-on-one, and we made a deal.
He'd tell this all to Thomas, if I told it all to you."

Zeke wasn't sure what to expect "this all" to entail, but

he was more taken off guard by the fact Royal had suggested such a deal. "Why did he want you to tell me?"

"Well, he seems to think you'll protect me."

Zeke didn't think Royal had a particularly high opinion of him, so this was interesting. "He'd be right."

"I know. That *is* why I called you in the first place with this whole mess." She moved closer to his bed and then, to his great surprise, took a seat on the edge of it. Her hip touched his knee. Only a sheet between them.

He knew he couldn't sit there and ruminate on *that*, so he tried to focus on the facts. "So, what is this whole thing you have to tell me?"

She relayed Royal's involvement with the Sons before he'd gone to jail. Royal's relationship with their father and why their dad might make Royal, and thus Brooke, a target. It felt a bit like being back in North Star. Trying to untangle the petty infighting in the Sons. Make sense of where the real issues stemmed from.

And what the real consequences would be from angry men with more weapons than sense, and so much anger and bitterness it had stamped out any empathy they'd been born with.

It was never simple, and almost always involved the outsized egos of awful men.

"It won't be the Sons," Zeke said, trying not to be too aware of the fact he wore nothing but boxers and she was sitting on his bed in a dark room late at night. And it would only take peeling that sheet away for them to be touching.

The desperate, pounding need to touch her would have been distracting if he wasn't such a professional. Or so he told himself.

"They don't have that kind of reach anymore," he continued. "But there are other groups, other ways for a man to wield control from prison. I don't like it. Royal's right. You're *both* in danger and targets, until we figure out exactly where this threat is coming from."

"This isn't what you signed up for."

For a moment, he just stared at her shadow. Did she really not understand? "Brooke. You can't be serious. I signed up for *you*."

She didn't say anything, and he couldn't see her expression in the dim room. When she didn't attempt to speak at all, he set out to reassure her. "You *and* Royal are safe here. We'll make sure of it."

She took one of her long, careful inhales. Let it out slowly. It reminded him too much of a time long gone, when she was just…in his life. In his bed. He'd wake up or fall asleep to her doing her deep breathing, so sure it "centered" her.

Still, she said nothing. Still, she sat on his bed.

Zeke waited for whatever else there was, but she just… never said anything else.

"This…couldn't have waited until morning?" He wasn't about to lie to himself. He was prodding.

"I suppose it could have. But I can't stop my brain from whirling in the same ridiculous circles, and I just couldn't lay there anymore marinating in my own…unsolvable problems. So, I figured I'd tell you."

"Ah." He waited. She didn't leave. Didn't offer anything else. "Well, you've told me."

"Yes," she agreed. And didn't so much as shift a muscle as if considering getting up.

He had a few options. The smart one would be to maintain *his* silence. Wait for her to say whatever she wanted to say, do whatever she wanted to do.

Had he ever been able to maintain *smart* when it came

to her? No. Because even when he'd made what had felt like the right decision at the time to put distance between them years ago, he'd handled it badly. He'd hurt her *badly*.

If he was smart, if he was strong, if he was actually any of the things he prided himself on being, he'd have the control to keep his mouth shut.

But he was nothing he thought he was or wanted to be when it came to her. "Are you trying to tell me you came down here looking for a distraction?"

She made a little noise. Not quite a laugh, but close. "Maybe." She shifted. She touched his chest and flattened her palm over his heart. "Yes, that is what I'm saying. Going to kick me out?"

He circled his fingers around her wrist, pulled her into him. Over him. "I'd be your distraction a million times over, Brooke. No questions asked."

And he spent the night keeping that promise.

Chapter Fifteen

Zeke woke up while it was still dark out, with an empty side of the bed. For a moment, he just stared. The room was dim, but he could make out the rumpled sheets, the indentation in the pillow on that side. A faint floral scent lingering in the air.

He hadn't dreamed it. Probably.

But where had she gone?

He got up, pulled on some clothes, and went in search of her. Not because he needed her to have some sort of postmortem, discuss what this was, what this meant. Just because he had to know she was okay.

At least, that's what he convinced himself of as he moved through the living room, the kitchen. He was about to get really desperate and creep upstairs to see if she'd gone to sleep in her own bed, but he noticed the front door was unlocked.

He'd checked all the locks at least three times last night before she'd come down to his room.

Surely that meant she'd left the house on her own accord. Maybe she'd gone to the barn to work in her lab. But her purse was right there and a quick look through it told him her key to the barn door was still in it.

So, she'd left for some other reason. But *why*? If she'd bolted because…

Well, he'd find her. He didn't care what it took. Maybe she didn't want it or like it, but he was hardly going to let her…

He pushed out the front door and then came to an abrupt halt.

She sat on the rickety porch, in the rocking chair that Carlyle had put there a month back, telling him he'd needed it because he was an old man now. Viola lay at her feet.

Brooke was watching the hint of a sunrise in the east. Or had been, until she'd looked over at him when he'd stormed out.

She raised an eyebrow, clearly at the way he'd burst out the door. "Everything okay?"

"Yeah… I just…" He didn't have the words. Her hair was tangled. She was wearing his hoodie—way too big for her small frame. She had her legs curled up under her and the sunrise seemed to burnish her gold. Ethereal.

He didn't have words for the emotion that swamped him. The *need* clogged in his throat. How much he wanted this. All those things he'd told her he'd never be able to give her four years ago.

And now he couldn't think of a single thing he wanted more.

She sighed heavily. Her gaze moved back to the sunrise, but her words were careful. Deliberate.

"I know what this is, Zeke. I know what last night was. It doesn't have to be all dramatic this go-around. I'm under no…illusions this is going to be something more than what it is."

"Which is?" he returned, not comfortable with the dispassionate way she'd delivered all that.

"A momentary…trip down memory lane." She said it with one of her patented nods, like she could make things true through sheer force of will. "It was a great…interlude. No guilt. No drama. Just…a distraction. Like you said."

"That's *not* what I said."

Her head whipped back to look at him. Clearly an argument was on the tip of her tongue. He didn't let her mount it.

"I asked if that's what you were suggesting. And that's fine. If that's all you want it to be. I can deal." Maybe he'd find some way to deal. Because he supposed he deserved that.

But Zeke Daniels didn't go down without a fight. Why let that change?

"A distraction is not what I'm after though." He didn't know how to do this. How had Walker and Carlyle just… said the things that needed saying to deal with the people they loved? How had they made it all work?

Oh God, was he going to have to ask them?

"What *are* you after, Zeke?" she asked, sounding tired. "Another few months where we're in each other's pockets, pretending to have this…relationship, this domestic thing we never got as kids? Until the danger is gone and reality seeps in and now you don't even have North Star to blame for not being able to have a future. So then what?"

He deserved every single thing she was saying, even if every single word hurt. It's exactly what he'd done back then. But this wasn't back then. "Do you really think I haven't changed?"

She inhaled sharply, though her words remained very, very calm. "Maybe you have, but…" She looked so pained, so confused, so lost. And he had felt all those things. Every moment since the last time he'd seen her. He had convinced himself it didn't matter. It would never matter. He was such a lone wolf.

Yet what had he done? Settled down in the same place as his siblings with some vague idea to start a life. With some…nebulous hope something like Brooke would come along again.

Or maybe, deep down, he'd always just hoped for her.

But on the other side of all that was *her*. What she'd done in their time apart. What she'd thought. And the fact he'd had her trust once and broken it. She shouldn't so easily believe him this go-around. He knew that.

He also knew what it was like to hurt her, and he didn't want to live with that again. That pain had been worse than his fear, his inability to deal with everything he'd felt for her.

And, he supposed, that pain had brought him here. So he tried to find the words to get it across. To make her understand.

"I bought a ranch, Brooke. I put down roots. I sure as hell don't know what to do with them, but they're there."

"Okay," she said, nodding, though he knew her easy agreement wasn't going to go in his favor. She met his gaze with dark blue eyes. Sad, sad eyes. "But they're not *my* roots."

He should leave it at that. He *should*. But he couldn't.

"They could be."

BROOKE DIDN'T KNOW what she was doing. She didn't know what *they* were doing. Why either of them thought now was the time or that this conversation was a good idea. It would only make working together uncomfortable.

And she couldn't blame him because *she* had gone to

his room last night. She'd done that, and on purpose. She had gotten the exact result she'd wanted last night.

She'd woken up…with none of the expected regrets she thought she should feel. It had been too…wonderful to be back in his arms, back in his bed. Relive all the things they could give each other.

It hadn't been a distraction. It had been like coming home. Roots.

They could be yours.

But, without regret, she had to focus on reality. On keeping her feet and expectations grounded. They'd been down this road before. He'd ridden out the chemistry, and she'd let herself believe it was love.

She couldn't make the same stupid mistake again.

Even if he was standing there saying all the right things. All the right things she wished he'd said four years ago.

She hadn't expected this. She didn't know how to weather it. Not with everything else going on.

She pushed herself out of the chair. "I have to get ready. I want to get an early start at the cave. Detective Delaney-Carson is picking me up soon."

He didn't argue with her, didn't push the point of their relationship…whatever it was. He nodded, his dark eyes never leaving her face. "I could drive you down to the cave."

"I know, but I'm going to ask you for an even bigger favor."

He studied her like he couldn't possibly think of one, so he didn't fully believe her. But it was a huge favor for her, and it required trusting him the only way she knew how.

To protect someone she loved.

"Watch Royal for me. I just need to know there's someone here who'll stop him from flying off the handle, given the chance. I think… I think he wants to do the right thing, but I wouldn't put it past him to do the wrong one, thinking it was right."

"I guess I know a little about that."

Her mouth curved in spite of the riot of feelings inside her. Zeke did indeed.

Could she really believe he'd changed? She knew he was different. There was a…stillness to him he hadn't had four years ago. Still tense, still serious, still *very* protective. But not quite so…pumping with unleashed energy. Not so desperate to *act*.

Did that equal change? She wasn't sure she could come to a conclusion on that and believe in it. It required her to be…certain and sure. With everything else going on? How could she be sure of *anything*?

"I'll keep an eye on him," Zeke promised. "And look, we can pretend last night didn't happen. We can do whatever you want, Brooke, and I mean that. Because I care about you. I never stopped thinking about you. I made a mistake, a lot of mistakes."

She didn't know what to say. Maybe nothing. Especially when he kept talking.

"I don't make the same mistakes twice."

He said it like a promise, like a vow. And she wanted to be stronger than the woman who fell for that line, but look at him. All serious. All…perfect. He'd always been just what she wanted.

Remember how hard it was to get over that?

The Zeke of old had never made a promise that didn't have to do with her physical safety. He was right the other day when he'd told her he'd never said he hadn't loved her back then, because he'd never used the word *love*.

And he still wasn't saying it. He was saying a lot of sweet, important things. But not the main one.

"I don't know what I want, Zeke. Except to solve this case. To figure out who's after me or Royal or whatever this is. Maybe after that... I can figure out what we are."

He nodded, his hands shoved deep in his pockets.

She'd expected an argument. Or did she want one? Because an argument would solidify her feelings, but him agreeing with her just left her even more confused.

But she had *work*. Important work. She marched herself inside and got dressed for the day. She grabbed her laptop and took it out to the barn, avoiding everyone. Even the dog.

Holed up in the makeshift lab, Brooke opened the report the lab in Cheyenne had sent her this morning. She read through the report, took notes, lost herself in the work. Putting the data points together.

There was no way some of the bones in the cave didn't precede Jen Rogers. It wasn't Brooke's job to come up with a second suspect. It was just her job to compile and analyze the data.

She put together as much of her own report as she could—this one geared to the detectives with enough laymen's terms they wouldn't be lost by the science. Anything admitted to court would need to be more scientific, but they needed another suspect before they could worry about *court*.

Luckily, Jen Rogers had confessed to the Hudson murders, so there was no way a second suspect got her out of trouble. This just...compounded the trouble.

A knock sounded at the barn door and, a second later, Zeke stuck his head in. "Detective's here to pick you up."

"Oh. Right. I'll be out in just a second." She glanced at

where she was storing the skull. She still hadn't confessed to the detectives she'd taken it, run her own tests.

Now wasn't the time for that anyway. That was for another day. Today was for more excavating. It was for focusing on *one* problem, not the cascade of others.

She greeted Detective Laurel Delaney-Carson with a smile. She'd worked with Thomas more than Laurel the past few weeks, but she'd been more with Laurel the first few, so they were on friendly, comfortable terms.

They chatted about the weather and trivial things before easing into the case.

"I've got a little update on the scrapbook," Laurel offered as she drove. "Dahlia is still doing some digging into the facts behind who the two men were in the picture that might be in the cave, if the label is right and all that, but it looks like the picture was taken in the thirties. Maybe early forties," she said.

Brooke considered the picture. There wasn't a good way to judge the age of the men, at least to Brooke's eye, and no doubt Dahlia would find more information as she researched, but Brooke didn't think those men in the photograph could have been any younger than twenty. That meant, even if that picture was dated into the forties, the youngest either of those men could be now was well over a hundred.

And her preliminary examination of the skull lent itself to her believing it had been *buried* closer to a hundred years ago. That meant…

"If the bones are as old as the picture, we might be looking at a suspect who's long dead." Or worse, a series of murderers who used the same place as their dumping grounds. Purposefully, maybe.

"And spent their life getting away with murder?" Laurel scowled as they drove into the nature preserve. "I don't like that."

"Has anyone questioned Jen Rogers about the scrapbook?"

"We've tried. Last month when she was first arrested, we tried to get her to explain why she would steal it from us. Obviously, she wasn't too keen on letting us in. Unfortunately, with her murder case so open and shut, there's no real leverage on our end to get her to explain now."

Brooke considered keeping her theory to herself. She'd fought so hard in her position, and it required a lot of evidence and not a lot of *theory* on her part. She'd worked with several detectives who'd only wanted the facts. Not her *take*.

But Thomas and Laurel hadn't been like that, and maybe everything the past few days was trying to teach her to stop being so damn self-reliant. To let people in. To *trust*.

She thought of Zeke saying he didn't make the same mistake twice. The way he'd held her when she'd cried. Last night in his bed and…

Good *lord,* now was not the time to be thinking about her personal life. She tried to organize her thoughts on the *case*, but Laurel pulled up to the cave entrance where usually a pair of deputies were stationed.

Not today.

"I don't like that," Laurel said, a frown on her face as she slowed the cruiser to a stop. "Nothing came over the radio about them leaving their post."

She picked up the radio in her car. Brooke didn't follow all the little codes she used, but she got the gist that Laurel was trying to figure out where the deputies had gone and asking a few more to come out. Brooke didn't think the assigned officers were responding.

"We're going to stay right here until we know what's going on," Laurel said. She sounded and appeared calm, but it didn't escape Brooke's notice that her hand now rested on the butt of her weapon as her gaze scanned the world outside her cruiser.

So Brooke looked out into the sunny day as well. Was there another threat out there? Would she ever really be free of them?

Chapter Sixteen

Zeke didn't like feeling like a babysitter, but he'd made a promise to Brooke, so he stuck close to the house and made sure to keep an eye on any and all exits so he would know if Royal tried to bolt. So far, Royal hadn't even ventured outside the house. Zeke wasn't even sure he'd left his room.

With the noonday sun hanging over the ranch, a car pulled up the gravel drive. Zeke had hoped for an early return from Brooke, but it wasn't her. It was Carlyle.

She came to a stop close to the house, hopped out. "Brought more dog food."

He was about to give her a hard time for showing up unannounced, but... Well, maybe they weren't the talk-through-our-problems type of family, but they *could* be. He'd told Brooke he'd changed, so maybe he needed to change in all things. Maybe his sister, who was *engaged*, could offer some...advice.

Little as he liked admitting to her he needed some. But if it was for Brooke, wouldn't he suffer any embarrassment or discomfort?

"Thanks, Car. Hey, listen—"

They both looked over at the front door as it squeaked

open. Royal stood there, making no bones about checking Carlyle out.

"Something Brooke should know about?" Royal called out across the yard.

Zeke supposed there was no reason to be irritated. He should be glad Royal would feel protective at all over Brooke. "I'm pretty sure she's aware my sister comes by from time to time."

"Sister," Royal said, nodding slightly. Then he flashed a grin right at Carlyle. "Hey. Luckily you don't look a *thing* like your brother."

She rolled her eyes. "I don't know who you are, but I don't like you."

"*Brooke's* brother," Zeke supplied.

"Oh." She grimaced. "Maybe I'll reserve judgment. But don't grin at me like that or you'll meet the snapping jaws of my fiancé's rabid dog pack."

Royal rocked back on his heels. He didn't stop grinning, but he gave Carlyle a little salute. "Message received."

"I should hope so," she muttered. She turned to her truck, lowering the gate so Zeke could grab the bag of dog food out of the bed. He hefted it up and over his shoulder.

"You want some breakfast?" he asked his sister.

She eyed him suspiciously. "Already ate. What's up with you?"

"Nothing's *up* with me."

"You've literally spent every second I'm here trying to get rid of me since the day you bought the place, and now you're inviting me for breakfast. Something is up."

He shrugged. "Just wanted to talk."

"Yes, also your favorite thing to do. Us talking is such a common occurrence. How silly of me to be suspicious." She rolled her eyes again.

He scowled at his sister. "Are you going to take this once-in-a-lifetime opportunity to give me advice or what?"

She looked at him then the house. Royal had disappeared back inside, but Viola was racing around the yard excitedly now. "We going to do this while you're hefting a fifty-pound bag of dog food?"

"Walk with me then." She fell into step beside him as he walked toward the house. "You ever screw things up with Cash?" he asked, hoping she wouldn't horrify him with details and make him regret this whole thing.

"Nah, I'm perfect."

Zeke didn't bother to sigh. "He ever screw things up with you?"

"Let me guess. This heart-to-heart has something to do with your little redhead?"

"You're *so* astute." He dropped the bag of dog food inside the back door of the screened-in porch. Then he kept walking, because all this was *his*. Those roots he'd told Brooke he'd made, even if he didn't know what to do with them.

And he still didn't, except that he wanted her here. Tangled in them. With him.

"Look, love's a mess. So you'll screw it up all the time." Carlyle made a kind of *what can you do* hand gesture. "The trick is just figuring out how, and not being afraid to admit that you might be the problem."

"I know I'm the problem," he grumbled, shoving his hands into his pockets.

"You? With your winning personality and ability to verbalize emotion and empathy so well? This is a shock."

"You going to give me a break?"

She grinned at him, humor dancing in her eyes. "Nah."

"Cool. Maybe I'll talk to Walker."

That earned him an even bigger eye roll. "We're not like Walker."

"We're not?"

"No. Walker is a…what would you call it? Caretaker. He's mush on the inside. Always has been, no matter how tough he tried to be on the outside."

That was fair and true. Zeke had always considered Walker the best of them, personality-wise. Not perfect or anything, just…more whole, he supposed. He didn't know why he was surprised to hear Carlyle say the same. "And what are we?"

"Less mush. More razor blade. Can't expose that vulnerable underbelly, right?"

Zeke shrugged even though he supposed that was the crux of it all. Those soft feelings he'd spent his whole life hiding—with razor blades, he reckoned—to protect himself from everything out there.

"And that's what you gotta do with love. Show the vulnerabilities. There's no getting around it. Sucks, but that's life."

"I already sort of messed things up with her once. A while back."

"Ah," she said, as if that explained everything. "So, it's not just current you that's the problem. It's past you. And past you was kind of a dick."

He scowled at her, but she shrugged. "Hey, the *kind of* was me trying to be nice."

Zeke didn't bother to respond to that. It wasn't *untrue*, though he wasn't sure it was *fair* of feral Carlyle to call him out on it.

"Not much experience in the mending-a-broken-heart thing," she continued. "But I guess it's the same as anything else, except with more patience. You love someone, you be there for them, and you tell them. You can't make them get it through their thick skulls. That's gotta be on them."

Tell them. Zeke grimaced. He'd always felt like *love* was a kind of bad word. The sort of thing that had messed his mother up so much she'd gotten herself mixed up with two useless criminals—who'd worked together to end her life.

Zeke *loved* Brooke, because he didn't have another word for the feeling, but saying it felt like…well, he guessed what Carlyle had said. Exposing a soft, vulnerable underbelly when he'd spent his life putting armor around it.

"It's not a magic word, I guess. But if it's real, if you mean it, it feels pretty damn close. And it can heal a lot of broken things. Not all of them, but a lot of them."

They'd come full circle around the house and back to her truck, and she'd been very real, very honest, very her. Somewhere along the instability, fear and danger of their childhood, she'd turned into this stable, adjusted *woman*. He'd always known Walker had that kind of thing in him, but to see Carlyle step into her own, and still be herself, was a confidence boost.

He reached out, took her left hand and jiggled the finger that had a ring on it. An *engagement* ring. So incongruous to everything he thought they'd have. "You really going to do the whole *Mrs.* thing?"

"Don't forget stepmom thing. We'll have a high schooler next year."

When in so many ways Carlyle was still a teenager to him, even if she was in her midtwenties now. But here she was saying things like *We'll have.*

"Izzy's a good kid," he offered, because he liked Cash's daughter. And more, he knew Carlyle loved the girl.

"The best," Carlyle replied brightly.

"And I guess Cash is all right."

She grinned at him. "Didn't need the stamp of approval, but I like it anyway." She moved forward then, after a pause, wrapped him in a hug. "You're a good guy, Zeke. Don't forget it. And don't be afraid to grovel." She pulled back, slapped his arm. "I like what little I've seen of her."

She opened her truck door. This grown woman with a settled, full life that made her happy. And she'd done that mostly on her own.

"Proud of you, Car."

She hesitated only a moment before she climbed the rest of the way into her driver's seat. "Then make me proud of you, Zeke," she returned before closing the door and driving away.

Zeke blew out a breath. Now he just had to figure out *how*.

Love.

Hell of a thing.

THE TWO DEPUTIES who'd originally been assigned to guard the crime scene had returned, and Laurel was talking with them. She didn't look happy, but Brooke just sat in the car pretending to work on her laptop.

What she was really doing was watching the interaction. The deputies looked chagrined. Laurel was *pissed*.

Brooke studied their surroundings from her seat. The preserve was so big, the cave a vast system below it. It gave her a shiver to think about, to remember the day she'd come out of the cave feeling like she was being watched.

But that had likely just been Royal. There was no one out there. There was no threat to her...well, that had to do with her work anyway.

Laurel stalked back to the cruiser and got into the driver's seat rather than gesture for Brooke to get out.

"They claim it was only a few minutes. One of them had to use the restroom, the other heard something and went to check it out. But I don't like the idea of you going in there when the entrance was left unguarded, even if it was brief. If we're dealing with a second suspect…" Laurel hesitated, shaking her head. "There's just no way to make a clean sweep of the cave and make sure no one went in. It's too big. The other entrances and exits are far away, and you'd have a hell of a time making it from one to another, but… It's too risky."

Brooke nodded. But, man, she wanted to get some work done today. "I'd like to point out that this second suspect was killing before Jen Rogers, Laurel. I don't have the data to back this up, so everything I'm saying is supposition, but if those pictures in the scrapbook connect, we really are talking about a suspect who would have to be dead by now."

Laurel took a few minutes, clearly thinking it over. "Jen Rogers lived in that cave for years. Undetected. Who knows what pieces we're still missing. That cave system is huge. I don't like unnecessary risks, Brooke."

"But if the cave system is too big that we can never be fully sure it's clear of people, how will I ever finish my work?"

Laurel scowled even deeper. "I know you're right, but I don't like this." She tapped her fingers on the steering wheel. "Okay, we'll go in. But we'll bring in more deputies. At least three plus me."

"That's a lot of manpower."

"This is our biggest case right now. Well-justified manpower. We can borrow from Sunrise and Hardy if we need to."

Brooke waited patiently while Laurel got more men situated. They did a sweep of the cave as best they could, and then finally Brooke was allowed to go in and set up. By the time she was ready enough to get to work, it was nearing lunchtime.

She could be annoyed about that later. Right now, she had to get to work. Not for the skull this time, but for the square she'd designated. Maybe she wanted to search for a body that would match the skull, but that wasn't how the job worked. She had to follow the standards set out by her profession, by her studies. If she looked for something specific, she might miss something just as, if not more, important.

So, she got to work in the meticulous fashion she'd learned, carefully moving through sediment, on the lookout for more remains.

After a while, as she moved from one section to another, Brooke caught a glint of something out of the corner of her eye. She turned toward it. In the same exact spot the scrapbook had been wedged, there was a tiny silver item. Brooke leaned closer to inspect it. A…thimble? But not a working thimble. No, like a piece from…a board game.

She reached out then thought better of it. Because someone had put it there purposefully. Just like the scrapbook, but only *since* the scrapbook. Because she would have seen this before today if it had been there before.

Someone had been in and out of these caves just as much as she had been.

Or maybe someone had been in and just never out. Laurel had said Jen Rogers had lived in here for *years*. Maybe the police had done their best to search for anyone else, but no one could guarantee there was no one else here. Deep inside.

Brooke sucked in a breath. "Laurel? Can you come over here?"

The detective was quick to move to her side. Brooke pointed to the game piece. "This is exactly where I found the scrapbook. And it was not here then or since."

Laurel's expression was grim. She didn't say anything but photographed the area before pulling on gloves and picking up the item and putting it in an evidence bag.

"Can we get tests run on it right now?" Brooke asked.

"It's so small. I'm not sure we'll get a print off of it. Brooke, I don't like this. I think we should get out of here."

It felt like such a waste. To just get started and then to pack everything up again, but this was concerning. So, she agreed. "I have to pack up though. Especially if someone is in and out, I want to make sure I'm not leaving anything behind. And we're photographing everything."

They all got to work, the other deputies helping Brooke by carting out the packed-up tools while Laurel photographed everything.

"Do you think someone is trying to send some kind of…message?" Brooke asked as she turned off one of her lights, folded it up and handed it to a deputy.

"With board games?" Laurel returned.

"I don't know. But someone put that scrapbook there— and it couldn't have been there that long before I found it or there'd be more damage to it. The thimble is new since two days ago."

"Maybe it's just a sign that someone else is in here. You grab that light and I'll grab this one and we'll be done."

They didn't turn off the lights or dismantle them, just carried them toward the narrow pathway that led back outside.

Brooke heard a strange rumble and then the clatter of pebbles falling, scattering. It almost sounded like some kind of earthquake, but the ground didn't move even as rocks fell from above. "That's...not good."

"No. It's—" But she didn't finish her sentence. Instead, Laurel shoved her back, hard. It didn't take long for Brooke to figure out why, even as she stumbled onto her butt and let out a yelp of pain.

A big boulder fell right at her feet. More rocks were falling, pelting her in the head. It was some kind of...cave-in.

There had been a survey of the safety of the cave before she'd been cleared to excavate. Every report had determined it was stable and perfectly safe to work in.

Were they wrong, or had something...caused this?

Well, it didn't really matter, did it? The rocks were piling up. Laurel was shouting directions at her deputies, but Brooke was afraid to follow as huge pieces of rock rained down between her and Laurel.

She scooted farther back into the cave. Maybe it was the wrong move, but the rocks stopped pelting her here. Her head throbbed from where one had really gotten her good.

But she couldn't go deeper into the cave. She had to get *out*. She reached up, touched the throbbing spot on her head. Her hand came away sticky. That wasn't good.

Brooke pushed to her feet, grabbing the light she'd lost a grip on. She shone it in front of her.

A wall of rocks. There were a few spots at the top that were maybe holes she could get to or through, but she'd have to climb up something to reach them. She'd have to try to move the rocks, but would that cause more of a cave-in?

Panic was crawling up her throat, but not at being caved-in. No. This was worse.

So much worse.

There were sounds coming from behind her. Like footsteps. Splashing in the pools of water. *Squelch, tap. Squelch, tap.*

Fear seized her, but she forced herself to look over her shoulder.

A small, bent-over man was making his way toward her—illuminated by an actual torch he carried as well as the light of hers that still functioned.

"Well, hello." His smile showed off rotted teeth, his beard was long and matted. His eyes were wild, even if he spoke in a calm, singsongy voice. "Welcome to my home."

Chapter Seventeen

"What are we going to do? Just sit around and talk about the damn Sons all day?" Royal demanded irritably while Zeke sat calmly—if he did say so himself—at a table trying to compile Royal's information on his old gang involvement. On who, besides their father, might see Brooke as a viable way to hurt Royal.

"What would you rather do?" Zeke replied. "Let Brooke continue to be a target because of you?"

Royal scowled and crossed his arms over his chest. But he didn't mount another argument or complaint. Though he did mount an accusation. "You sure know a lot about how the Sons works."

"North Star ring any bells?"

Royal frowned then studied Zeke with some renewed interest. "That group that took them down. Vigilante stuff."

Zeke shrugged. "I wouldn't call it that. I'd call it a group of people with military and law-enforcement training who didn't have to get caught up in government red tape in order to launch a campaign to eradicate a threat to the safety of thousands of citizens."

Royal rolled his eyes. "Yeah, there's a real difference. You're telling me you were part of that?"

"Till the day they disbanded. Long *after* they eradicated the Sons."

Royal shook his head. "You don't understand. There's no *eradicating* cockroaches."

"Maybe not, but there's certainly cutting off all their sources of power so all they are is little annoying pests running around. Easily squashed by any errant boot."

Royal didn't have an argument for that and before Zeke could press again for more details about their father's role in the Sons, they both turned toward the telltale rumble of tires on gravel.

Zeke looked out the window to see Carlyle's truck. He wasn't sure why she'd returned so soon, but maybe she'd forgotten something. "Be right back."

He got up and went outside.

Royal followed him. "Your sister's hot," he offered as Carlyle hopped out of the truck.

"I don't even have to threaten you to shut your mouth, because even if her fiancé could take you, even if our older brother would beat him to it, Carlyle would take you out in a heartbeat." But any humor Zeke had for the situation died at the look on Carlyle's face as she jogged over to them.

"There was some kind of cave-in while Brooke was working," she said with no preamble. "Chloe got a call to come in for backup. I'm obviously not supposed to tell you that, but I was there when it happened and I thought you would want to know."

Zeke was halfway to his truck before she'd even finished speaking. *Cave-in*? What the hell did that mean? How could that happen? More importantly, how could he help?

"I'm coming with," Royal said, leveraging himself into the passenger side of the truck just as Zeke climbed into the driver's seat.

"Me too," Carlyle said.

Zeke opened his mouth to argue with his sister then shook his head. What was one more person? Particularly someone sneaky and on his side. Because he knew as well as anyone that he, Royal and Carlyle had no business being down at that cave.

But they were damn well going to be.

He began driving for the preserve, the word *cave-in* rattling around in his mind. "Anyone else stuck in there with her? The detective or the deputies?"

"I don't have all the details. Chloe didn't want to tell me. Probably for this reason right here," Carlyle said, gesturing at the three of them hurtling down the highway.

It curdled in his gut like acid that Brooke might be alone. That she might be hurt.

Or worse.

He refused to take that thought onboard. He'd tear every rock out of the way with his bare hands if he had to.

"I'm sure the park rangers or naturalists know what to do. They're like cave experts or whatever," Carlyle offered, though Zeke knew her well enough to know she was saying this for his benefit and not that she trusted anyone to be an expert on anything. "I'm sure they've dealt with cave-ins before. They must be a natural occurrence."

"We don't know that it *was* a natural occurrence," Zeke returned, keeping his grip tight on the steering wheel as he sped down the highway. "She's investigating mass murder. She's been a target thanks to her brother over here."

Carlyle didn't have anything to say to that, and if Royal had a reaction, Zeke was too focused on the road to notice it.

"Remember when we were looking for Jack and Chloe?" Carlyle said, leaning between the front seats. She pointed at the road ahead. Last month he and Carlyle had helped the Hudsons search for their missing brother.

"Yeah, I remember."

"They found Hart on the west side by the highway, right? After that woman knocked him out and dumped him. I remember there was a little access road for state employees on the map we looked at. I think it's coming up on the left."

Zeke nodded and, once he saw it, took the turn probably a little too hard. There was a No Trespassing sign posted, and a half-gate that was easy enough to off-road around.

"We have to be careful about how we approach, or we're going to get kicked out," Carlyle warned him. "They'll be set up at the cave entrance. We can't go there directly. At least, not all of us. They won't let us help. That, I know."

"I'd like to see them try to kick me out," Royal grumbled darkly.

"Noble and all, but they'll be wasting precious time and resources focused on you when we want them all focused on Brooke," Carlyle said, doing a much better job than Zeke was of staying calm. "There's a map at that trailhead we were at, do you remember?" she asked Zeke. "It had the whole cave system mapped out. With different entrances."

"I also recall the warning that trying to make your way through the cave system has resulted in death." But he followed the service road to the main road and, instead of heading straight to the cave entrance, took a turn that would lead them to the trailhead Carlyle was referencing.

He parked the truck, but left it running, and they all got out to look at the big board with the cave system map. They peered at it.

"Four natural entrances, and that's just what they put on the map," Royal said. "I did some exploring on the west one, to see if I could meet up with her inside and out of sight, but I didn't get very far."

"Scared of the dark?" Carlyle asked with a smirk.

"No doubt they've got cops at all these entrances now," Zeke said, ignoring them both. He'd poked around the east entrance when he'd been watching Brooke. Funny— or not—how he and Royal had essentially been following her in the same way.

Zeke studied the map. The south entrance was a possibility. It would take considerable time and skill to make it from the back of the cave to the front of the cave where Brooke was situated, so why would the rescue start there when there were closer places to get to her from?

"We're going to try this one." He pointed to the map. Right under the dire warning about exploring the cave on your own without any equipment. How dangerous it was. How easy to get lost.

"Let's go," Royal said.

He glanced at Carlyle, who shrugged. "Some backup wouldn't hurt, but I'm all for it."

"Text Walker. He can round up whatever Hudsons won't cause a fuss." Zeke pulled out his own phone. He didn't have much service, but hopefully enough to get a message off to Granger.

You know of anyone in the area? Brooke needs help at the cave.

He didn't bother to send any other details. Granger knew where they were and where Brooke was working. If he knew any former operatives—from his North Star days, or DEA days, or whatever and however Granger knew and collected people—who weren't too far away, he'd send them to help.

"All right," Zeke said, shoving his phone back in his pocket. "Sooner we get started, the better."

Carlyle patted her hip. "I'm armed. What about you two?"

Royal hesitated then lifted his shirt to reveal a holster with a gun in it. Zeke sighed, walked back to the truck, unlocked his glove compartment and got his gun out.

"Let's go."

BROOKE PRESSED HER back to the rocks that had trapped her inside. Some of the smaller ones gave a little and cascaded down to her feet, but most held firm. A wall she couldn't scale to get out of here.

The old man stood all the way across this particular "room" in the cave. There was a narrow hallway behind him that she'd planned to explore once she'd completely excavated this "room."

Maybe she was glad now that she hadn't. Because she did not think this man had happened upon one of the other natural, inhospitable entrances and all the signage warning against going too deep in the cave system.

No, he didn't look like he'd seen the outside of this cave in a long time. And that gave her the feeling that he might have had something to do with the sheer amount of bones buried inside.

"You've been doing a lot of digging in my front yard, young lady. I can't say as I appreciate it. I've worked very hard to landscape." Then he cackled like he'd told a joke.

"Do you live down here?" she asked, trying to sound calm.

"I don't just *live* down here, I *thrive* down here." He

spread his arms wide. "Do you know how many people wander into these caves—purposefully and not—and make themselves easy pickings to the god of the cave?"

Brooke had been part of North Star. She had training. She knew how to deal with a threat. She knew how to protect herself. She would not let herself panic. She would engage with this man while her brain whirled for a way out. "The god of the cave?"

He smiled again. "Me."

Okay, so she was dealing with...actual psychosis. She wasn't sure if that was better or worse than a murderer with a sound mind. If he really thought he was the god of the cave, how could she predict anything he did?

She had to fall back on that North Star training. She'd mainly been in the lab. A scientist, not an operative, but she'd still had to be trained on how to deal with danger. And she'd lived in Zeke's pocket while he'd been protecting her.

Granted, from a with-it criminal who'd just wanted to silence her or to stop her from finding the evidence the case needed. Not someone who was just...unhinged. And perhaps a serial killer.

That meant it was probably in her best interest to remain calm, to play along. "What should I call you?" She half expected him to give her some ridiculous godlike name, but the one he gave her was a shock.

"Leon Rogers."

Rogers, like Jen, clearly, but also like that photograph Dahlia had pulled out of the scrapbook. The writing on the back had said *L. Rogers*. But Brooke didn't think he could be the man in the photograph. He was *old*, but not *that* old, unless their dating was wrong.

She wondered though...was this a family affair? From

the Rogers in the picture, to Jen Rogers. With this man as a link in between? One Leon Rogers to another? The family business of murder and hiding out in caves?

"I don't suppose you have any relation to Jen Rogers?" she asked, trying to keep everything light and conversational. No doubt the deputies would be working to get her out of this cave. She only had to keep herself safe and sound until they did.

She hoped.

"Oh, Jen. My disappointment." Leon shook his head. "She never understood the history. Never respected our fate, or godliness." He put his palms together, pointed his finger up to the cave ceiling. "She only ever focused on her anger. Death isn't anger. It's freedom. You see, we're just freedom fighters down here. She never understood. She used it, tainted this, and she never understood."

"That's…too bad," Brooke said, trying to sound sympathetic even as fear slithered through her.

She had dealt with a lot of terrifying situations in her life, and perhaps this wasn't the most dangerous, but being trapped in a cave with a man who thought murder was freedom was certainly the most bizarre and left her feeling the most out of her element.

She *could* survive this, she knew, but she didn't have the first idea as to *how*. Yet.

"Have you…dealt with a cave-in like this before?" she asked, trying to sound bright and unaffected by the way he stared at her. The way all of this was so deeply and horribly unsettling.

She knew other entrances existed. The marked ones in the preserve, then other ones not usually big enough for people. Just wildlife.

Did he use any of those, or did he really just live in here?

With all these bones. In all this darkness? But he had fire. He'd survived. Surely he had some outside life. *Surely.*

He clucked his tongue. "The cave doesn't treat me that way. I am its god."

"Ah." What was there to say to that?

"*I* did that."

Brooke blinked. "You…caused the cave-in?"

"Of course. It's been so long since I've had a good one. I'm getting too old and feeble. But you're stuck now. I just needed you stuck. You don't carry a gun like they do."

Brooke swallowed and balled her hands into fists so her shakes weren't visible, she hoped. "A gun isn't the only weapon a person has."

There were her tools, for starters, if she could get to them. He hadn't gotten that far inside the room yet. She could get there and grab one before he could stop her, probably, considering how old he was.

But if she ran for one now, she'd be too close to him. She definitely didn't want to be too close to him. Maybe he was old, maybe she could overpower him, but he seemed so calm. Like he had some kind of secret.

"The cave brought you to me," he said, moving closer. "You are its offering. Why don't you sit and accept your fate?"

Okay, this was getting worse. But he *was* old and feeble. And she didn't see any weapon yet. So why would she accept *any* fate? She was young and strong and capable. She could fight her way out of this, no matter how ill-suited she was to fighting.

Or so she thought. He dropped his torch and the flame went out with a sizzle.

Then he pulled out a gun.

Chapter Eighteen

Zeke didn't like how long it was taking to walk to the back of the cave. The map had made it look like a short distance, but this was taking too long. Or maybe he was too impatient, thinking of Brooke sitting in that cave alone. Possibly trapped—on purpose.

His training told him to turn off all thoughts of Brooke. Bank those emotions and deal with reality. He didn't know if it was age, years out of North Star, or the depth of his feelings for Brooke, but he just couldn't manage it. His pace kept picking up.

Luckily, they hadn't encountered anyone yet. Not random hikers or campers and, more importantly, no law enforcement. That led Zeke to believe rescue efforts were focused on the front side of the cave.

So theirs would focus on the back.

"Do you think Chloe will let you know if they get her out of there?"

"Yeah, she'll probably send me a text, but I don't know if I'll get it with the patchy service," Carlyle replied.

Well, then he'd try to convince himself Brooke was fine and they just hadn't gotten the message. He'd slow his pace. Be careful and tactical.

"They ever teach you stealth in the Sons?" Zeke grumbled since Royal seemed bound and determined to rush ahead even worse than him, being loud enough that anyone might know they're coming.

"I wasn't *in* the Sons," Royal returned. "I was *infiltrating* the Sons and lived to tell the tale. I've got plenty of stealth."

"Maybe use it," Carlyle muttered, her eyes moving around the trees that surrounded them.

Zeke didn't mind their bickering. It kind of reminded him of being back in North Star. There was a certain level of…levity you had to maintain when dealing with such serious situations. It was like falling back into old familiar patterns. But not…going back in time. More a nostalgic feeling.

Something he was grateful to have in his past. Not necessarily something he wanted to go back to. And that was…new.

But he didn't have time to think about that, to consider what it really meant, because a little prickle started at the base of his neck and he heard something…off in the trees around them.

Zeke held up a hand. Something or someone was out there. Rescue personnel headed for the back cave entrance? Or a threat—to them or to Brooke? He had never heard of any cave-ins at this cave, and if Jen Rogers had lived there for years, undetected like they'd claimed, he doubted any cave-in was *natural*.

Both Royal and Carlyle stopped on a dime, everyone holding up their guns and surveying the area. Carlyle, knowing the drill, moved back-to-back with Zeke.

Royal caught on quick and moved so they stood in a defensive position, facing out, backs protected.

Zeke heard it again. The crack of a twig. Could be an animal but…

A man stepped out from behind a few trees. He wore jeans and a hoodie and hiking boots. He didn't appear to be carrying a weapon, but he grinned. Right at Royal.

"Long time no see."

He didn't carry a gun, and now had three trained on him, but was far too cheerful to not have a trick up his sleeve.

"Vince," Royal returned, acting as relaxed and belligerent as he had when Zeke had first met him, even with a gun pointed at the new arrival. "Fancy meeting you in Wyoming. Didn't think you ever climbed out of the sludge in South Dakota."

"You've recruited some friends, Royal." The man shook his head. "Too bad for them."

Another former member of the Sons. Clearly. No doubt part of the threat against Brooke, thanks to Royal. Had he caused the cave-in? Was this really *all* about Royal and the Sons? It didn't add up, but Zeke wouldn't put anything past a bunch of embittered criminals.

"You'd be surprised who it'll be too bad for," Carlyle returned, always running her mouth.

"So would you, babe." The man took his gaze from Carlyle to Royal. "You made a lot of enemies that day." As if that was the cue, three other men—all with guns—stepped out from around the cave entrance they'd been heading for. "Time to pay up."

"You guys don't have an independent thought of your own. Always have to be following some vindictive leader. What do you think my father is going to do for you while he's locked up?" Royal demanded.

"I don't think that's any of your business, traitor."

"There's nothing to betray," Royal responded with an

impressive amount of calm Zeke had to give him credit for. "Y'all were held together by a psychopath, and he's dead. Everything else is blown to hell. Why don't you just go live your lives? Why concern yourself with old pointless business?"

For a moment, the ringleader simply blinked, like that had never occurred to him. Then he scoffed. "We're our own group now. Stronger than anything Wyatt ever did. Loyal to Jeremiah Campbell."

Zeke laughed. Couldn't help himself. Ace Wyatt had been a psychopath, albeit a brilliant one. He'd wielded his brand of sadism and cunning to form a powerful gang for *decades*. Whatever these four were involved in, it was nothing like the Sons.

"I've never even *heard* of Jeremiah Campbell," Zeke offered. "And I've personally taken down more Sons members than some low-level lackey like you have probably ever met."

This ticked off all four of the men, based on their expressions, but the three with guns didn't start shooting. So they stood in a ridiculous standoff here in the middle of a nature preserve.

"You'll see," the unarmed guy offered with a sneer.

"Yeah, I bet," Royal said. "So, what? You're just going to have a shootout here? And then what? Disappear?"

"Disappearing is our specialty."

"Imagine this guy thinking he has a specialty," Carlyle said, pretending she was making a throwaway comment to Zeke and Royal rather than addressing the guy specifically.

"You know cops are crawling all over this preserve, right? One shot fired and you'll be done for in no time," Royal said.

"No Sons to wriggle you out of jail time now, is there?"

Zeke added. "Your 'better' group got a passel of lawyers and paid-off cops lined up? Because that was Ace Wyatt's real specialty, as I recall."

"Don't you know about this cave?" Vince said, jerking a thumb behind him where the back entrance to the cave was not too far away. "People who disappear here don't come out, and hey, if you and your friends here were looking for your sister, why wouldn't you get turned around and just...*poof*." He made a little hand gesture to go with the sound effect.

"Guess you better start shooting then," Carlyle said. "See who winds up on top." She dramatically flicked the safety off her gun.

Hell. She never did have any patience. So Zeke followed suit, wondering how he was going to keep all three of them from getting shot.

BROOKE STAYED FROZEN. Leon just stood there, gun pointed at her, though his arm was starting to shake. She didn't know how to get out of this. He blocked the only exit she knew of—with a gun.

She *could* knock him over, and he very well *could* miss shooting her since he was hardly holding the weapon steady. But was it worth the chance? Shot by accident was the same as on purpose when all was said and done.

But there was a slight discrepancy here. "You don't kill your victims with a gun." She hadn't gone through all the remains in this cave, but aside from the ones Jen had confessed to, no remains had showed any evidence of a gunshot wound.

He raised his eyebrows then gave a nod like she was quite right. "You've been studying my prizes. So, how do I do it then?"

Brooke pressed her palms to the cold, wet rock behind her. She used that as a kind of centering. She was still alive. There was still hope. Just keep him talking until she got out. People knew she was in here. They were working to get her out. Not just people. *Police officers.* With guns of their own.

"With the age of the remains I've dated and studied, my guess would be starvation or terminal dehydration is your preferred method."

Again he nodded, like a professor proud of a student for getting a difficult question *partially* right. "Sometimes we found them that way. An offering from the cave. And sometimes Father and I worked as a team." He smiled fondly. "My father was a good partner. He understood the god. The offering. My daughter…" He shook his head and the smile died. "I went through a dark period when she was my partner. It's better alone again."

"That section over there." Brooke pointed to the second quadrant. The one she'd just begun to study. "I haven't gotten very far, but I've found more broken bones than this quadrant."

"Mmm." Leon studied her but didn't offer anything else.

"So, you were more violent with those victims?" Brooke prompted.

"Stop calling them that." His mouth turned into a scowl, his nostrils flared. Anger seeped into his expression. "Not victims. Offerings. Prizes. For me. God of the cave." The scowl curved back up into a psychotic grin that turned her blood to ice. "Violent, maybe. But broken bones don't kill, do they?"

"They can."

"But did they? That's the question."

"I haven't studied that portion enough to know," she

hedged. "It takes time. To study. To excavate. To discern." She glanced at the wall behind her. She didn't hear anything coming from the other side. Had more deputies been trapped? Hurt? Was it worse on the other side?

Brooke looked back at Leon. He pointed to her bag that still sat next to the quadrant she'd been working on. "Take your tools. Tell me."

She didn't want to do anything that he told her, but if she got her tools, she had a weapon. Maybe it wasn't a *gun*, but it was something. She moved forward, keeping a careful eye on him so she knew she was always out of reach. She did her best to keep that gun from pointing directly at her as she gathered her bag of tools. She moved over to the quadrant she'd only just begun.

There could have been a lot of reasons the bones in this sector were more broken over here. It could have meant a violent means of death or something more environmental. She wasn't far enough in her excavation and research to know for sure.

If she dragged this out, took her time, surely someone would be able to get to her by then. No matter what things looked like on the other side of that pile of rocks, too many people knew where she was. People who would save her. The police. Zeke. Her brother. She wasn't going to wither away here.

As long as she survived whatever Leon was up to. So she turned her attention back to the ground beneath her. She had to excavate. Slowly. Much more slowly than even she usually went. Time was her best weapon. She'd have to use it.

Brooke got to work, trying to block out Leon's existence, or why she was doing this. Just fooling herself into thinking it was any other workday. Uncover a bone here, another bone. Carefully. She didn't take pictures like she usually did, but Laurel had been the one with the camera and, well, anyone could forgive her for not attempting that in her current circumstances.

After a while, she became aware of his hot breath on her neck. She tried to breathe through the wave of nausea that swamped her. Tried not to let her hands shake. She didn't remove any of the bones, just uncovered them as they were laid out. Legs to hips to rib cage to…

"What do you think?" he asked just as she uncovered the neck.

Brooke swallowed so her voice would sound calm and clear. So she didn't shudder at the nearness of him.

"I'd need to run tests. I'd need my lab. I can't tell just by looking." Of course she had enough experience to make an educated guess. Broken neck.

Was that what he wanted her to say? But she forgot everything when something wet and sticky touched *her* neck, like a tongue, and on a shriek, she jumped up. Half-way through the knee-jerk reaction, she chose to use it to her advantage. She flung her head back as she came up, the top of her skull crashing into his chin, his frail body stumbling backward. The gun he'd been holding landed on the ground with a dull thud.

Brooke made a dive for the gun, not allowing herself to think about anything else, but she crashed into him trying to do the same. Something he did caused one of the lights to topple over, making a popping sound as it went dark.

He cackled with delight as they both got a grip on the gun at the same time. She ripped it out of his weak grasp, but he must have known she would. Or maybe everything was just against her—because the last light toppled over.

And they were plunged into utter darkness.

Brooke didn't panic…at first. She got to her feet, curled her hand around the weapon and adjusted it until she had it in a shooting position. She tried to feel around for the safety, but she didn't know what kind of gun it was and couldn't find it.

Maybe he didn't have it on. She curled her finger around the trigger, and then tried to decide what to do.

From far too close, a gurgling cackle echoed around her.

And she couldn't see where to go. Or where to shoot.

Chapter Nineteen

Brooke forced herself to breathe. Terror and panic clawed through her. She was frozen in place—which wasn't so bad when surrounded by nothing but a deep, black nothingness.

But she had a weapon. She had a gun. She didn't know if it was loaded or even capable of shooting, but it was something to hold on to.

Once she'd calmed herself enough that she could hear over the roaring beat of panic inside her body, she heard the sound of shuffling. Of rattling breathing. She was still, but Leon was moving around.

Was he trying to find her? Did he have some sort of ability to see in all this black? Wouldn't he stumble and fall in the dips and holes and cave growth? Or was he just so used to it, none of that mattered?

She took in her surroundings again. Surely it wasn't *totally* dark. There'd been an opening not too far away, right? The cave-in couldn't have completely covered the entrance. If she could find that, she could orient herself.

She squinted. Was that a tiny pinpoint of light? Or was she hallucinating? Could that possibly be the caved-in entrance? If it was, then directly behind her would take her deeper into the cave and potentially to another entrance.

Did she dare risk it? Without a light?

Well, standing still and waiting to be saved hadn't gotten her anywhere. She didn't even *hear* people trying to save her. Why not *do* something for once?

Carefully, she turned, making sure she did a complete one-eighty from the pinpoint of light. She paused, listening for Leon. He sounded…far away? Maybe? Or was that just wishful thinking?

You have a gun. You're stronger. No matter what, you can survive this. You are a survivor. Maybe she'd endured more than survived, but she wasn't about to *endure* her death. No way.

She used that as a mantra to keep her thoughts from spiraling to worst-case scenarios. She moved forward one step, carefully feeling the ground with her toe before putting any weight on her foot. It would be a meticulous, long process, but she was used to that kind of thing, wasn't she?

After each step, she paused, listened, tried to ensure Leon wasn't too close. After a while, on one of her pauses, she heard a scratch of something like…the flare of a match being lit. She whirled around, trying to find the light it should make.

She saw just the wink of flame and then it was gone. It had outlined something shadowy, but large. Taller than Leon. Was someone else in this cave with them, or was she losing her mind?

Brooke stopped moving. Held her breath, waiting for something else to happen as her heart pounded.

This time when a light flashed on, it wasn't a match or a torch. It was the beam of a flashlight.

It illuminated the man in front of her—closer than she would have guessed. Bloody and wild-eyed. But Leon didn't have a weapon, even as he smirked his horrible rotted-teeth grin at her.

"I am the god of the cave!" he shouted, raising his hands above his head. Then he sank to his knees. And someone was behind him, jerking his hands back.

A someone she recognized, even if it took a minute to understand what was happening in front of her.

"Granger."

She couldn't believe her eyes. The only man who'd ever been a father figure in her life was tying Leon's hands and then ankles together.

He left him there and walked over to Brooke.

"Are you okay?" he asked, reaching out to take her arm.

She nearly collapsed into him. She didn't even ask how he'd found her. How he'd gotten here. But she knew she was safe now. He'd saved her, and not for the first time.

"Come on, Brooke," he said, pulling her around Leon's laughing body. "Let's get you out of here."

THE GUNSHOT CAME out of nowhere.

Zeke hadn't fired, and the noise wasn't close enough to be Royal or Carlyle's shooting.

Then Royal went down with a jerk and a stumble. Zeke whirled in time with Carlyle, but the shooter didn't even try to hide. He walked through the trees with confident strides, gun held loosely. Zeke could have taken him out, but he had no doubt he'd earn three bullets from behind if he did.

"Hold," Zeke muttered to Carlyle, afraid she'd start shooting and get them both killed. Right now, they were outnumbered and they had to be careful if they were going to get out of this. He edged toward Royal, who was at least moving around. Wherever he'd been hit wasn't a fatal wound. Not yet.

"Never met me, huh?" the gunman said to Zeke. "Maybe North Star hotshots weren't as tough as they thought."

So this was Brooke and Royal's father. Not in jail. If Zeke had to guess, based on the four men surrounding them, Jeremiah Campbell was trying his hand at cobbling together some new offshoot of the Sons. He was hardly the first. In his time with North Star, Zeke had helped take down at least two attempts and had known of at least three other cases.

But what these men had never understood was that any association with the Sons put a mark on their backs. Connection to the Sons no longer meant the power they thought it did. And thanks to Granger, and everyone who'd ever worked at North Star, they never would again.

Zeke had always been proud of his work at North Star, but he hadn't been too thrilled when the group had disbanded. For selfish reasons, he realized now. Because it took this moment to understand all they had done by stopping a powerful group of men who'd hurt untold numbers of people.

Brooke and Royal included.

"Thought you were in jail," Royal said from between clenched teeth, echoing Zeke's thoughts. Blood seeped from Royal's arm, but he was conscious. That was something. And *someone* looking for Brooke had to have heard the gunshot. They'd come searching.

Had to.

"The idea that anyone working those jails knows anything that's going on." Jeremiah laughed. "I'm sure everyone thinks that's exactly where I am, but I've always been smarter than the system."

Zeke laughed. "Ah, yes. That's why you landed in jail in the first place. *Smarts*."

"I have missed going toe to toe with North Star's brainless soldiers."

"And losing? Because we literally had to disband. We'd eradicated the whole Sons network and there was nothing left to do. Because without your psychopath leader, you are literally *nothing*."

"And yet here I am. Outnumbering *you*."

He wasn't wrong about that, but Zeke didn't concern himself with being outnumbered. He'd been there done that a hundred times. His biggest concern right now was that he couldn't take the time he'd like to draw this out. Royal needed medical attention.

So, they had to get this show on the road. He wasn't about to let Brooke's brother bleed out on his watch.

Zeke raised his gun, pointing it directly at Jeremiah. "Guess we're at a crossroads then."

Chapter Twenty

Granger held on to her and led her deeper into the cave. His flashlight helped them not trip over anything, but the dark around the beam of light somehow felt more oppressive as they moved along a cold, wet cave wall.

But he was here, and Brooke had help. She still couldn't get over it. "Why did you come?"

"I was in the area."

She scowled at his back. "Granger."

"It's a long story. We'll get it sorted soon enough. Look, right ahead." He pointed and she saw the little sliver of natural light.

Almost there. She could *cry*. Or just collapse. But she didn't let herself do either. Getting out was only one step. Then they had to deal with the aftermath. Find the police and tell them about Leon, get back into that cave and collect the necessary evidence and so forth.

But, man, all she really wanted was to go home.

And she didn't let herself think too deeply about the fact she didn't *have* a home, but when she thought about one, she pictured Zeke's half-renovated house. Viola. *Him*.

It took longer than she'd expected to get to the entrance, but they finally did. It felt blinding to step out into the sunlight, and she had to squeeze her eyes shut. Granger held tight to her, and she still didn't know how this was possible. This whole weird day.

"You didn't have to come."

He laughed. "Only you would say that to me after I saved your butt, Brooke."

She managed to blink her eyes open and not immediately shut them against the brightness. "It's not that I'm ungrateful."

"You don't want to put me out. I know. I wish you'd get it through your head you're not a burden to us. Any of us." That was not the first time he'd said that to her, but maybe it was the first time she was really taking it on board.

She didn't know what had changed. No, that was a lie. She knew it was Zeke calling her out on not wanting to be a burden. It was Zeke, period. It shouldn't be about him. No matter what he'd done or said, he didn't love her. Not really.

But he'd jumped in to help after all this time. He'd claimed he'd changed, that his roots could be hers, and she didn't feel so afraid with him that she was...well, what Granger had said. Some kind of *burden*.

Something on Granger's phone beeped and he frowned at it. But he smoothed out that frown quickly. He pointed to a trail outside the cave.

"Follow that path and you'll find the rescue team. They've been focused on the west entrance. You can tell them I helped, or say you handled it yourself. I'll back up the story either way."

He even gave her a little nudge in that direction while he moved in the other.

Brooke stared at him in confusion. "Where are you going?"

He paused a second, looked in the opposite direction of

the trail then at his watch. Gauging something, though she couldn't tell what. When he looked at her, his expression was the stern kind of North Star taskmaster she hadn't seen in a while. Because they weren't North Star anymore. "I started looking into Royal, your father, the lawyer, after your and Zeke's call. I don't like what I've found out about your father, Brooke. The ties he might have, and what he might have people doing for him. I'm just going to go make sure everything is good on some of those loose ends."

"That doesn't explain *where* you're going."

"I think I've got a lead on who put that explosive in your car, the tracker in Royal's. I was working on that when we got word of the cave-in. Go find the rescue team, Brooke. Your head's bleeding. I'll handle this."

"Handle *what*?"

He sighed. "Look. There's a little group of guys that have a prison connection to your father. I think they were after you but got…sidetracked when the cave-in happened and they couldn't easily get to you."

"Sidetracked by *what*?"

He looked up at the sky and shook his head. "Fine. Side-tracked by Royal himself. And Zeke. And a woman, I'm assuming that's Zeke's sister."

Brooke immediately turned away from the trail. "I'm going with you."

"Brooke. You've got a rescue squad looking for you, and this is dangerous. You've got a gash on your head. Go get checked out and—"

"You trained me yourself, Granger. Self-defense. How to shoot. If I can help, I should."

"When was the last time you practiced any kind of shooting? I've got a few people coming. No worries, Brooke. I can handle it."

He could. Probably. But she was always letting someone else *handle it*. Hiding in caves with remains that couldn't do anything to her. "I'm not going to leave Royal on his own again. I can't abandon him."

"You never did, Brooke. You were a kid."

She hated that he knew her this well. That, aside from Zeke, Granger and his wife and a few other North Star people were the only ones who did. Because she could fool anyone else.

But not family.

"Maybe you're right, but I'm not doing it now. I can't… always be saved. At some point, I have to be part of the saving."

"He's not alone. We've got this handled."

"He's my brother, Granger."

He sighed heavily. "Why'd I recruit all these stubborn mules?" he muttered. He glanced at his watch. "Gabriel should be here any minute. Reece not far behind. Shay had to stay with the kids, and that was a fight and a half. But I've got Betty on standby at her insistence just in case anything gets hairy. She can patch you up. Come on."

Brooke followed him carefully through the trees, the gun from Leon still in her hand. Gabriel and Reece were former North Star operatives like Zeke. Reece had gotten out himself almost before she'd joined up, so she didn't know him that well. Gabriel had been around a lot during her time and had been there at the end. He'd even married Zeke's cousin, Mallory, who'd gotten Zeke into North Star. Brooke *had* been close to Betty, who was North Star's resident doctor. Since the support staff people had spent a lot of time together, and as Betty and Brooke had both been interested in medical science, it had been a quick and easy friendship.

Though, like with most North Star people, Brooke hadn't kept in good touch, not wanting to bother anyone. Always feeling a little "other" once North Star had disbanded and so many had gone on to start lives and families.

But that was the thing. All these people were married, many with kids. Granger had a wife and a ton of foster kids at home. Reece had a wife and a stepson and, if Brooke recalled correctly, a few more kids since. She didn't know if Gabriel and Mallory had a family, but *still*. Betty had married a sheriff and moved to Montana to help raise his twins, last Brooke knew.

They'd all gotten away from the danger of North Star because of those families, those choices.

"Granger. You don't have to be doing this. I can… I'll handle the stuff with Royal. You all should go home."

"Home," he said, shaking his head. "Home is family, Brooke. And that's what we are. With or without North Star, we're all family. No matter how anybody feels about it. Forever." He gave a glance over her shoulder then pointed through the trees. "Reece is over there. He's watching something. We're going to approach silently, okay? Don't make a sound."

She nodded. She could do that. She might not be good at the whole operative-and-handling-danger thing, but she knew how to follow orders. And she *did* know how to shoot the gun she carried now that she could see it.

She would help. Whatever this was, she was finally going to help Royal. No matter what he'd gotten himself into.

She followed Granger cautiously until Reece's careful hiding spot came into view. He'd created a natural kind of trench with some fallen logs and a rock outcropping. Brooke and Granger joined him behind the barrier.

They all crouched low and spoke in barely-there whispers.

"Five men, four armed. Surrounding Royal, Zeke and an unknown woman." Reece flicked Brooke a look and then one at Granger, who gave a little go-ahead nod.

"Royal's been shot, but he's awake," Reece continued, handing Granger a pair of binoculars. "He's alert. Betty's on standby, not far off. Minute we can, we'll get him to her."

All that fear Brooke had let go once Granger had appeared crept back in. Her brother had been *shot*. He and Zeke and Carlyle were surrounded by *five* people. She didn't dare peek over the barrier. She just had to…deal.

But not alone. Not hiding. Together.

Family.

ZEKE WAS PREPARED to get shot. Hell, he'd survived it a few times, he could do it again. He didn't let himself dwell on the errant thought that here he was in a standoff, finally *not* having a death wish, and he just might get himself killed.

Nah. Not today. He had to make Brooke believe they could make this work. Couldn't check out now. He wasn't going to let this end in any way she might blame herself.

Just then, as if on some cosmic cue, far off but distinct, Zeke heard a whistle. A North Star whistle. Then he saw the glint of something—a gun. And he recognized the hand making a gesture from behind a tree. Walker.

"Cops," Carlyle whispered. "Behind us."

Backup. All different kinds. Zeke grinned.

He aimed his weapon right at Jeremiah Campbell. "Took down too many men like you in my life. Won't faze me to do it again."

Jeremiah must have sensed something because he looked behind him. Walker and Cash stepped out from their hiding places. Both held guns. But before Jeremiah could even react to that, the sounds of heavy footfalls reached them.

"Drop your weapons," Hart shouted, cresting a hill. Gun drawn, with Chloe Brink not far behind. Both in their Bent County uniforms.

"Now," she added.

The man who hadn't had a gun took off running, while two of the gunmen dropped their weapons. Another held on to his and ran. Jeremiah just stood there. Fuming while the North Star contingent quickly stopped the attempted runners.

Reece Montgomery and Gabriel Saunders each took out a gunman, while Cash's brother, Palmer, took out the other.

A convergence of the different facets of his life. All coming together to help. Protect. Save.

Then there was Brooke. She had some crusted blood on her temple but didn't look to be actively bleeding. And she rushed to Royal's side. He wanted to run to her too, but he let her have the moment with her brother while Granger texted Betty to come on down and Hart radioed for an ambulance.

Zeke gave one more glance at Jeremiah. Walker and Cash had guns trained on him while Chloe moved over with a pair of handcuffs. She kept telling him to drop his weapon, but he hadn't yet.

So Zeke walked over.

Jeremiah didn't lift his gun, but he lifted his chin. "You're on my list."

Zeke reached forward and grabbed the gun out of Jeremiah's hand before the man even had a chance to react. North Star training at its finest. He handed it to Chloe. "I'm on everyone you know's list," Zeke returned. "And

I still sleep soundly at night because you all are nothing. Always have been."

Chloe cuffed the man and then jerked him away. More cops were appearing, dragging the now-handcuffed perpetrators back toward the road where, hopefully, cruisers were waiting to take them to the sheriff's office.

Because all of these people had come together to help, to do the right thing, to protect each other. Against a small contingent of people who'd worked together to hurt and harm.

Zeke's childhood had been marked by the inability to save his mother against men like that and, like so many realizations lately, this one hit him out of the blue.

He'd spent most of his adult life trying to make that all right. Solve it, like it was a problem. When all it had ever been was a tragedy. One that he'd had no control over.

Not his fault.

Walker pounded him on the shoulder. "What the hell?"

Zeke shook his head. "Didn't know what we were getting ourselves into. How'd you find us?"

Walker jerked a thumb at Cash.

Carlyle's fiancé shrugged. "Carlyle and I track each other's locations. When she disappeared, I figured she'd gone to see you, but after a while I realized she wouldn't let you hit the cave alone. But when the cops hadn't seen you guys, we checked it to see where she was. Lost service here and there, so couldn't pinpoint an exact location at first, but we got close, then your friend found us."

Zeke scoured the scene. Granger and Gabriel stood just a ways back from where Brooke knelt next to Royal. Betty was with her, clearly working on Royal.

She was okay. *Okay.*

Carlyle sauntered over, wrapped an arm around Cash's

waist but looked up at Zeke. "Just going to stand there staring at her?"

Zeke scowled at his sister. "Giving her a minute with her *injured* brother."

"Give her a *shoulder*, dipshit. They're going to cart him out of here the minute they get a stretcher in. She's going to need support."

When Zeke didn't immediately jump to action, Carlyle made a disgusted sound. "If she walks out on you, you damn well deserve it." Then she gave him a physical push with her free hand.

Zeke grumbled, but he moved over to the scene around Royal. They had him up in a sitting position and Betty had already wrapped a bandage around his arm.

"Nice save," Zeke offered to his old boss.

Granger shrugged. "Only because you two got me started on looking into that lawyer Brooke paid. Led me to Jeremiah, which didn't sit right. Started keeping tabs on a guy who visited the alleged Jeremiah in jail weekly without fail and that led me here."

Two EMTs with a stretcher appeared and gently but firmly moved Brooke out of the way. Zeke reached out and helped her to her feet. Once she looked up at him, she simply fell into him.

He wrapped his arms around her, held her. Up to this point, he'd kept every feeling as much on lockdown as he could, but too many rushed through him now with her in his arms. The kind of relief that threatened to buckle his knees.

"Everything's okay," he told her, holding her close. "Everyone's going to be just fine."

She nodded into his chest. "He'll be okay," she said, and

he knew she was saying it to reassure herself, not because she knew it was true. But it would be true.

They were all going to be okay. He rubbed a hand down her back and promised himself he'd make sure of it.

Chapter Twenty-One

The detectives let Zeke give her a ride to the hospital, but Brooke wasn't allowed to see Royal right away. Instead, she had to let a nurse poke and prod at her head, then bandage her up. Once she was done with that, she had to answer what felt like a zillion questions from Laurel in a meeting room at the hospital. About what happened in the cave.

Brooke really hated recounting it. She would no doubt have nightmares about Leon Rogers for some time. And she still had work to do down there. With three murderers spanning three generations...no telling what unsolved disappearances she might be able to help solve.

"So how does all of that connect to what happened on the outside?" Laurel said, turning her attention to Zeke, who held Brooke's hand under the table they were sitting at.

He hadn't left her side. Hadn't gone more than a few seconds without having one of his hands touching her in some way. It gave her the strength to go on when what she really wanted was to curl up somewhere and sleep forever.

Except when she closed her eyes, she still pictured Leon and shivered.

"I don't actually think there's a connection," Brooke

said before Zeke could. "Two separate issues just happened to merge."

"I agree with that assessment," Zeke said. "The problem people I ran into were connected to her brother, his old life. They wanted to use Brooke as a kind of revenge. I think they were following her, waiting for a chance to get to her. When the cave-in happened and we came to try and help, we just happened to run into them trying to get to her."

Laurel rubbed a hand to her temple. "This is a hell of a case, you guys. That should hold us over for now. I'm sure we'll have more questions as the case—cases—continue, but if you want to go check on your brother, Brooke, we're done here."

They all stood, and Laurel gave her a friendly pat on the back. "Get some rest, Brooke. You did good today."

Brooke managed a smile. "You too, Detective."

They all left the meeting room and Brooke couldn't stop herself from leaning on Zeke. He seemed to be the only thing holding her up. She wanted to be stronger than that, but…

Well, for once, it was nice to be so tired she didn't worry about leaning on someone, didn't worry about being a burden. Because Zeke was here of his own volition, just like everyone else today, helping because they *wanted* to. Because they cared.

"Granger texted me where to go," Zeke said, leading her down one hallway and then into the next. They finally reached one where Brooke saw a familiar face.

Betty moved forward and enveloped her in a hug. "He's just fine," she reassured. "The doctor will run you through all the aftercare you'll have to do, but he's lucky it wasn't more serious."

"Thank you for being there."

Betty pulled back. "Anytime. It's good to see you, Brooke."

"You too." And Brooke meant that, even if she didn't know how to convey it. Not when she was so tired. Achy. Hungry. Someone had tried to get her to eat, but she couldn't stomach the thought.

"You should be able to talk to him now." Betty opened the door to Royal's room. "We'll catch up more when you're done."

Brooke nodded and stepped into Royal's hospital room.

He watched her get close, smiled wryly. "Hey, Chick."

"Hey yourself." She crossed to his bed.

"I'm fine. Really." He pointed to her head with his good arm. "What about that?"

"Just a scratch," she said, touching the bandage. "No concussion. I'm good."

"Best-case scenario all in all, then, huh?"

She couldn't agree with that because she didn't like him hurt, but he was okay. He was alive. This was all…sorted. No more danger. No more… Sons or their father.

But where did that leave them? Her baby brother she didn't know. She wanted to protect him now, but if he was safe, and an adult…

So she just…let herself be a burden to him. Because she loved him, he was her brother, her family. Maybe it wasn't a burden to ask for something. Maybe it was just love.

"I hope you won't disappear on me, Royal. I hope that we can…be each other's family again." She blinked back tears and tried to ignore how horrible it felt to be so… vulnerable. To admit she wanted him around. "You don't have to—"

"Chick."

A tear escaped, but she blinked back the rest. Royal reached out and took her hand in his. "You're the only family I got. And it's not your fault I messed that up. I blamed you all those years because… Well, maybe there's no real reason. I was a dumb kid and it felt like everyone else had it better. Even you. Maybe especially you, because I know you deserved it. And I didn't."

"We didn't deserve any of it, Royal."

"Maybe not all. But I made… I'm not like you, Brooke. I've made some real mistakes. Maybe I didn't deserve all that jail time, but I'm no saint."

"You could reform."

He grimaced then gave a little snort of a laugh. "Reform might be a stretch, but I could probably try out not breaking any laws. And to keep in touch, no matter where we end up."

"It'd be a start."

"It's a promise."

Another tear escaped and she wiped it away. She leaned over. Brushed a kiss across his forehead like she used to do when she was comforting him in the midst of something terrible when they'd been kids lost in a really awful world.

But this wasn't terrible anymore. This was the start of something good. She was determined.

A nurse came in with a kind smile. "We need some privacy to run some tests. Visiting hours are coming to an end tonight anyway. But you can come back tomorrow, of course."

Brooke nodded.

"Go on back to Zeke's, Chick. I'll call you in the morning when they let me out. Promise."

Brooke let out a long, slow breath. She was going to choose to believe that promise. That one, and one for the future. Of her brother back in her life. *Family.* The blood kind.

And all the ones she'd built out there.

She exited Royal's room and Betty was still standing there.

Brooke just wanted to go *home*. But so many people had come to help her. She felt like she had to reach out across that effort, because she'd cut it off.

"Thanks for patching him up, Betty."

"Anytime."

"So, do I get to see pictures of your little ones or do I have to beg?"

Betty didn't hesitate. She pulled out her phone. Scrolled through picture after picture of two adorable toddlers and their handsome father doing all sorts of things—playing in the snow, messily eating spaghetti, just lying on the couch.

An odd ache settled in Brooke's chest. It was lovely and she was so happy for Betty, who was no doubt an exceptional mother.

Every picture was just so homey. All things...well, things Brooke had never had. And now she wanted. She glanced at Zeke, who stood down the hall talking to Granger. They were both serious, but not worried. Not heavy with concern. Likely just going over any last details.

As if Betty could read her thoughts, she nodded toward the two. "You and Zeke again, huh?"

Brooke shouldn't be making any decisions after such a day. She should get some sleep and just...get her head on straight before she dealt with *her and Zeke*. "I... I don't know."

"Yes, you do." Betty patted her on the shoulder.

Zeke happened to look over, offered her a smile.

Well, she supposed she did.

ZEKE'S HOUSE WAS full of North Star people. It had been late by the time they'd gotten done with questioning, and while it wasn't five-star accommodations, it was better than some of their old missions. Besides, it was one night. Everyone would be off again in the morning, back to the lives they'd built.

When Zeke finally got bed assignments sorted, he returned to the kitchen to find Brooke doing dishes of all things. With that bandage on her face and dark circles under her eyes. Because it was late, and she'd been through hell.

"Well, I ran out of beds. You go on and take mine. I'll finish here."

She set the glass she'd been washing aside then looked at him with an expression he couldn't quite read. "That's a terrible pickup line."

He laughed in spite of himself. "I'm going to sleep on the *couch*, Brooke."

She shook her head, walked over to him and wrapped her arms around him, resting her head on his chest. "No, you're not."

He ran a hand over her hair, gave himself a moment to revel in the fact that she was in his arms. "Sweetheart, you need to rest."

"So do you."

He let out a long breath. Yeah, it had been a *day*. He moved his arm around her waist, started leading her toward his bedroom. Everything they had to talk about could wait. There was no rush. Not really. They could sleep in his bed, keep their hands to themselves, and deal with everything tomorrow.

Except so much could have happened today. So much *bad*, so much loss. If they hadn't had help. If they hadn't had each other.

So maybe wasting another second didn't make any sense.

He stopped, turned her to face him in the dim light of

his living room. In a house he'd started renovating, convincing himself it was a just-for-the-hell-of-it project.

But surely it had always been for her.

"I love you, Brooke. I don't want you to go anywhere."

She studied him for the longest time. Long enough to start to make him feel…nervous. Long enough that he wanted to *fidget*.

"You really mean that, don't you?" she finally said.

He tucked a strand of hair behind her ear. "I'd never say it if I didn't. I never will."

Her smile eased every last worry inside him. "I love you too, Zeke."

"So you'll stay?"

She moved to her toes, pressed her mouth to his. "I'll stay," she murmured against his mouth.

And she did.

Forever.

Epilogue

A year later, when they got married in their fully renovated house on their *nearly* working ranch in Sunrise, Wyoming, all their different worlds came together for one perfect night.

Walkers. Hudsons. Daniels. Bent County detectives and North Star operatives. Kids all over the place.

Royal walked Brooke down the aisle, which made her cry. Granger stood up with Zeke, along with his brother, which made her cry harder.

She'd gone from being a lonely teen, desperate not to draw any attention to herself so she didn't get sent away, to a woman who had…so many different places to go, people to lean on. So much *love*.

And as she promised to love Zeke for the rest of her days, and he returned those same vows, she knew that no matter what threatened, they'd always fight it together.

Their whole, huge, cobbled-together family.

* * * * *

COMING SOON!

We really hope you enjoyed reading this book.
If you're looking for more romance
be sure to head to the shops when
new books are available on

Thursday 27th March

To see which titles are coming soon, please visit
millsandboon.co.uk/nextmonth

MILLS & BOON

LET'S TALK

Romance

For exclusive extracts, competitions and special offers, find us online:

- **f** MillsandBoon
- **X** @MillsandBoon
- **⌾** @MillsandBoonUK
- **♪** @MillsandBoonUK

Get in touch on 01413 063 232

FOUR BRAND NEW BOOKS FROM
MILLS & BOON MODERN

The same great stories you love, a stylish new look!

OUT NOW

Eight Modern stories published every month, find them all at:

millsandboon.co.uk